Seek a New Dawn

E. V. Thompson

LITTLE, BROWN AND COMPANY

A *Little, Brown* Book

First published in Great Britain in 2001
by Little, Brown and Company

Copyright © 2001 by E. V. Thompson

The moral right of the author has been asserted.

A CIP catalogue record for this book
is available from the British Library.

HARDBACK ISBN 0 316 85716 5
C FORMAT ISBN 0 316 85717 3

Typeset by Palimpsest Book Production Limited,
Polmont, Stirlingshire
Printed and bound in Great Britain by
Omnia Books Limited, Glasgow

Little, Brown and Company (UK)
Brettenham House
Lancaster Place
London WC2E 7EN

www.littlebrown.co.uk

To the many friends who introduced me to Australia and the splendour of the Adelaide Hills and the Flinders Ranges

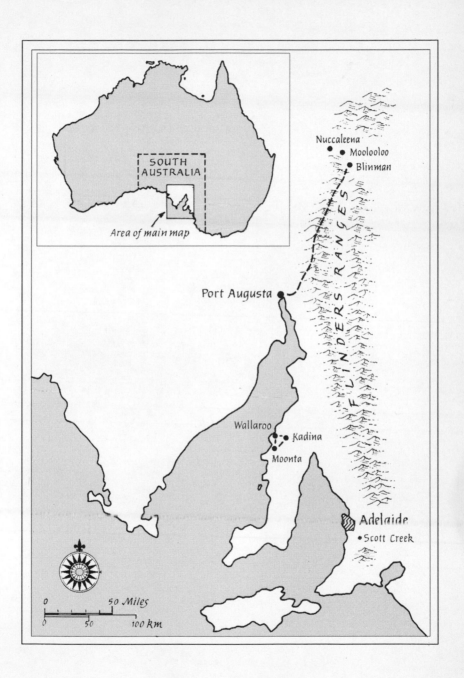

SOUTH
AUSTRALIA

Area of main map

Nuccaleena
Moolooloo
Blinman

FLINDERS RANGES

Port Augusta

Wallaroo
Kadina
Moonta

Adelaide
Scott Creek

0   50 Miles
0   50   100 km

BOOK ONE

1

I

'Emily! Where have you been, girl? Your father has been waiting
for you for almost an hour. You are to go to his study – immediately!'

Emily had entered the vicarage happily humming 'All Things
Bright and Beautiful', only to be confronted by the housekeeper,
Maude Rowe, standing in the hallway, hands on hips, wearing
an expression of stern disapproval.

Her happiness disappearing with the warm sunshine as the
door swung closed behind her, Emily asked wearily, 'What am
I supposed to have done now, Maude?'

'For a start I expect he'll want to know where you've been
since you left church. The service has been over for an hour and
a half but no one's been able to find you anywhere. You're in
trouble and you've no one to blame but yourself. The number
of times you've been told . . .'

'Emily, is that you? Come in here, this minute.'

The voice of Reverend William Boyce reached them from
beyond the partially open door of his study, situated on the far
side of the large hall.

Emily knew there was about to be yet another confrontation

between herself and her strict parson father. As she turned and, with a heavy heart, made her way towards her father's study, she noted that Maude's expression was a combination of smug satisfaction and I-told-you-so righteousness.

Life in the vicarage had not been happy since the death of her mother many years before. The Reverend Arthur Boyce had taken his wife's death very badly, unable to come to terms with his loss.

Emily and her sister Caroline both lived at home, but Caroline was currently away. Twenty-two years of age and older than Emily by two years, she was paying a visit to relatives, near Bristol.

Maude ran the household with the help of house servants. Responsibility for performing charitable duties in Reverend Boyce's parish rested with the two young sisters.

Inside his study, Reverend Arthur Boyce, a tall and gaunt-featured figure, sat stiffly upright behind a desk, facing the door. Light from the window behind him fell upon the fine quality grained leather, stretched to provide a smooth surface for the desk that formed a barrier between him and his errant daughter.

On the desk-top lay sheets of paper covered with evenly spaced lines of impeccably neat handwriting. It was the sermon the reverend had delivered that morning from the pulpit of his St Cleer church.

Arthur Boyce had married late in life and was fifty-three years of age when Emily came along. Now over seventy, his shock of pure white hair and a tired expression were visible manifestations of a man who believed he had experienced more than a fair share of the troubles the Lord sent to try those who served His cause.

Parson Boyce was also inclined to view young people with the unequivocal intolerance of age. Emily deeply resented that she and Caroline were made to bear the brunt of his disapproval – she especially.

While she had been alive and before she took to her bed, their mother had been able to deflect her husband's irritability. Unfortunately, there had been no one to champion the girls for some years now, Maude invariably siding with her employer.

'Where have you been, Emily?' Arthur Boyce put the question to his petite, fair-haired daughter as she stepped through the doorway of the study. 'It was my intention to walk home with you, but you had left the church even before I began my farewells to the congregation. I did not leave the church until late and arrived home in expectation of finding you here, helping Maude to prepare the dinner. However, it seems your plans took no account of duty. I would like to know what they were.'

'I had no plans, Father,' Emily replied, gazing through the window at the lawn beyond, where a blackbird was successfully tugging an elastic-bodied worm free from the tight-packed earth. There was a wooden-armed chair on her side of the desk but she remained standing. She knew better than to sit down without her father's permission.

'Well, girl, where have you been?' he demanded impatiently.

'I went to see some kittens that had been born only yesterday. We all went to see them. All the choir.'

'I presume Samuel Hooper went too?'

'Of course. He's one of the choir. Besides, the kittens were in a barn on his father's farm.'

Arthur Boyce's lips tightened to a thin, pink line of disapproval. 'Emily, how many times do I have to tell you that you and Caroline must keep yourselves aloof from the villagers? Young Samuel is a *miner* and miners are . . . well, let us say that they have "a certain reputation". As my daughters – and nieces of a peer of the realm who is also one of Her Majesty's most trusted ministers – you and Caroline are expected to set an example to others and have morals that are beyond reproach.'

'I wouldn't have thought there was anything immoral in going with others to look at a litter of kittens, Father. Certainly nothing to put Uncle Percy's reputation in danger.'

'Do not be obtuse, Emily. You are well aware of my meaning – and although those with whom you have unfortunately been associating may say "wouldn't" in their speech, I expect you to say "would not". Your poor, dear mother would agree with me, were she still alive.'

It was unfair of her father to bring her mother into the argument and tears suddenly burned Emily's eyes. Nevertheless, she had done nothing of which to be ashamed. She believed her mother, at least, would have agreed with her.

For over an hour Emily argued her case, although she knew from bitter experience there was no hope of persuading her father that he was wrong. Arthur Boyce regularly reminded his children that the Boyces were a family of considerable breeding; his brother a peer of the realm. He himself was a local magistrate and had been educated at Eton college, the most exclusive and prestigious school in England, his fees paid by another relative, knighted for diplomatic services in India.

Reverend Boyce had always insisted on his children remaining aloof from parishioners, even when carrying out the charitable duties expected of them.

Emily, perhaps more than her sister, found her father's narrow-minded bigotry intolerable, which *might* have had something to do with Sam Hooper. Emily was far more attracted to Sam Hooper than she was willing to admit to anyone – including Sam himself.

The outcome of today's argument between father and daughter was never in doubt. Arthur Boyce's strength in debate had been lauded at university. More recently it had been recognised by his bishop with an archdeaconship.

Nevertheless, Emily could be extremely stubborn when she believed right to be on her side and she refused to admit defeat until her father brought the argument to an end with a statement that left her stunned.

'I am deeply saddened that you should choose to defy me on a matter of such importance, Emily. As the youngest of my daughters I feel you have unfortunately been showered with more affection than is good for you. Perhaps there should have been less affection and a little more discipline. Fortunately, your regrettable indiscretion in this particular matter will soon be brought to an end and village gossip silenced once and for all.'

'What do you mean?' demanded Emily. Still angry, she was nevertheless puzzled by his statement. 'If you intend dismissing Sam from the church choir for being a friend to me, tongues will wag even more. It will certainly not prevent me from speaking to him whenever we chance to meet.'

Before the reverend could reply, there came an urgent knocking on the study door and Maude called out to her employer. Arthur Boyce frowned angrily, but before he could tell the housekeeper to go away, she opened the door.

Looking flustered, Maude said, 'Young Donald Rowse has just run here from the village. There's been an accident up at the South Caradon mine. He doesn't know how serious it is, but says they're calling in miners to go and help. He said you'd want to know. I sent Donald off to catch the pony, then get out the trap and harness-up for you.'

The dramatic news brought Emily a respite from her father's displeasure. As the parson of a copper-mining parish it was his duty to attend the scene of a mine accident. There would undoubtedly be a number of Methodist ministers and lay preachers there and competition was keen between Church and Chapel in Cornwall. A Church of England vicar could not be seen to be tardy when such disasters occurred.

Emily knew her father would not forget the matter of Samuel Hooper. He would return to the subject of her innocent indiscretion as soon as an opportunity presented itself. However, right now there were far more important matters to be addressed. Even the smallest mine accident affected a disproportionate number of households in an area where so many families were connected by marriage. In the difficult times currently being experienced in the mining industry, an accident might decide the future of a whole community.

The South Caradon mine was where Sam worked. Because he had been at church that morning Emily knew he would not have been caught up in the accident, but he would be one of those going underground to help in the rescue work. She would be concerned for him until she knew he was safely back on the surface.

II

Riding in the pony-trap, Emily and her father overtook many women and children, all hurrying in the direction of the South Caradon mine. No one yet knew what they would find when they arrived, but few were making the journey for the first time. Such tragedies had always been a part of mining life, but recently they had been occurring with a frightening frequency.

One reason was that the copper mines of Bodmin Moor were going through a lean period. The price of copper had slumped and men were being laid off. Mine 'adventurers' – the share-holders who owned the mines – were not willing to deplete dwindling profits by throwing away money on safety measures for a dying mine.

As a result, Emily had found herself playing an increasing role in such tragedies. When a body was brought to the surface, she would try to provide what comfort she could to the women and children of the dead miner's family. This was a duty she found more harrowing than any other.

Nevertheless, despite her aversion to the task, it was one she performed well, possessing as she did a genuine and natural sympathy for the bereaved.

Not all the women they passed had men working at the South Caradon mine. Nevertheless, their presence at the scene of a tragedy was expected. In return they would receive similar sympathy and support from others should their own menfolk become involved in a mine accident.

As the pony and trap reduced speed to pass through a knot of villagers who were slow to move off the road, Reverend Boyce momentarily forgot his displeasure with his daughter.

Annoyed with the women, he made the observation that if the miners of the South Caradon mine had observed the Sabbath in an appropriate way, such an accident might never have occurred.

Emily's own opinion was that had the adventurers been less concerned with profit-making there would have been no need for Sunday working. However, she kept such thoughts to herself. She did not want to become involved in yet another argument with her bigoted father.

A rapidly growing crowd, comprised mainly of women and children, was gathered around the head of the main mine shaft. Many men from the area had emigrated in recent years, leaving their families behind to cope as best they could. The few men present today were mainly aged or invalids, unable to either work or emigrate.

Bringing the pony to a halt, Reverend Arthur Boyce handed the reins to a young boy from St Cleer before making his way to where the mine captain stood talking to two adventurers, both of whom were local landowners.

Emily hurried to where she could see Rose Holman, the young wife of the Methodist minister, standing among a group of silent, anxious women. These, Emily knew, would be women who had men working underground.

'Is the news bad?'

Emily put the question to Rose in a low voice. Despite their allegiances to different religions, each woman knew and respected the other. Sadly, their mutual respect had grown from just such occasions as this.

'We don't know.'

Pretty and dark haired, Rose had been born and brought up in a moorland mining community. She had witnessed many mine tragedies, even before meeting and marrying her preacher husband.

'There's been a roof fall, but nobody's yet come up to grass to tell us how bad it is. 'Tis fortunate it's happened on a Sunday, I suppose. There are still many men who won't work on a Sunday, even though they might need to tighten their belts a notch or two because of it.'

The two women conversed quietly for a few minutes before Emily hurried to the aid of a distraught and heavily pregnant woman. Her three-year-old daughter had just fallen and grazed an elbow and both knees.

The mother, no older than Emily, was close to tears and seemed unable to cope with the child. Taking charge of the small girl, who parted tearfully and reluctantly with the information that her name was Primrose, Emily brushed off the grazed joints, before tying her own handkerchief around a knee that was dribbling blood.

'There, that's better, isn't it?' When the young child looked at Emily doubtfully, she added, 'You've been such a brave girl that when your knee is better Mummy can wash the handkerchief and you may have it for your very own.'

Primrose gave Emily a fleeting smile before limping away stiff-legged to proudly show off the makeshift bandage to a young friend.

'Thank you kindly, Miss Boyce,' the child's mother said gratefully. 'I'd have tended to her myself, but I'm finding bending down a bit difficult right now. I've only got another two weeks to go – that's if all this don't bring it on quicker.'

The woman looked frightened. Emily was aware her name was Jean Spargo, but she knew very little else about her. 'Is your husband down there?' she asked sympathetically.

Jean Spargo nodded. 'Him and his brother. It's the first

Sunday they've ever worked. We're Methodist, you see. Their father's a lay preacher.'

She spoke apologetically, as though half expecting Emily to walk away because she was not a member of Reverend Boyce's congregation.

When there was no immediate reaction to her disclosure, she added, 'Phillip's pa told him he'd offend the Lord by working on the Sabbath.' Her voice broke as she continued, '"Six days may work be done, but in the seventh is the sabbath of rest, holy to the Lord. Whosoever doeth any work in the sabbath day, he shall surely be put to death." That's what his pa told him. I remember every word, but Phillip wouldn't listen. He told his pa he had a family to provide for and the Lord would understand.' Brokenly, she added, 'I hope he was right.'

'Hush! You must not upset yourself. We don't know what's happened down there, or who – if anyone – has been hurt.'

Even as she spoke there was a stir among those crowding around the head of the shaft. The man-engine had clanked into action. The women pressed forward as the wheel commenced to spin, winding on cable attached to a cage designed to carry men to and from their work below ground.

When the cage came into view and stopped, it disgorged three passengers. Emily realised with a start that one of them was Sam. He was so filthy she had not immediately recognised him.

All three men stood squinting uncomfortably as the light of the early summer afternoon replaced the gloom of the underground mine.

One of the first people Sam saw when his eyes became accustomed to the light was Emily. His expression softened momentarily and he began to walk towards her.

The mine captain was pushing his way through the crowd towards the shaft but Emily noted that her father was still talking to the adventurers. He did not appear to have noticed Sam.

She returned her gaze to the young miner just as he saw Jean Spargo and came to a sudden, uncertain halt. It was immediately apparent to Emily that the two knew each other. Rose Holman knew Sam too and it was she who spoke first.

'What's happening down below, Sam? Has anyone been hurt?'

'I'm afraid so.' He spoke carefully, avoiding the eyes of the pregnant woman. 'There are two dead, but no one else seems to be hurt.'

'Is my Phillip all right?'

It was a direct question and desperately though Sam wished he could avoid giving an answer, he could not.

'I . . . I'm sorry, Jean. He was caught by the roof fall. Him and Wesley . . .' Wesley was Phillip's brother. 'They would have known nothing . . .'

It was doubtful whether the young pregnant woman heard his final sentence. Swaying alarmingly for a moment or two, her head suddenly fell back and she crumpled to the ground.

Emily succeeded in preventing her head from striking the muddy ground, but she could not avoid falling to the ground with her.

The next few minutes were filled with confusion. As Primrose screamed, she, her mother, Rose and Emily were hemmed in by a crowd of concerned women.

While some attempted to revive their cruelly widowed neighbour, others offered loud and contradictory advice on how best this might be achieved.

Holding the thoroughly frightened child to her, Emily struggled free of the crowd – and came face-to-face with her father.

Before he could speak, she said, 'The wife of one of the men who has been killed has fainted. She's heavily pregnant. This is her little girl. I am taking care of her while her mother is revived and helped to her home.'

Arthur Boyce was not an altogether unfeeling man, but he felt uncomfortable surrounded by noisy, grieving women. 'Very well, Emily. Er . . . my pony and trap are at the woman's disposal should it be of help, but I need to be back at St Cleer for the evening service . . .'

The pony and trap were not needed. The women acquired a stretcher upon which Jean Spargo was placed. Then, carried by two men and two women, it was hurried away to her home in a nearby hamlet.

Primrose seemed to have been overlooked in the general commotion. Thoroughly confused by everything happening about her she clung to Emily, sobbing uncontrollably. Holding her close, Emily hurried after those carrying Jean Spargo.

The home of Primrose and her mother was a one-up, one-down terraced house beside the mineral railway line, along which was carried ore from the mines to the small South Cornish port of Looe.

Although small, the house was clean and well-kept and Emily saw sad little domestic traces of the dead miner. One was a home-made pipe rack, fastened to the wall beside the fireplace, containing a variety of clay pipes. Another was a half-completed carved wooden doll lying on a shelf.

Primrose had ceased crying now and wanted to be reunited with her mother, who had been taken upstairs to the only bedroom. However, there was so much coming-and-going in the house that Emily felt obliged to keep the child downstairs with her for the time being.

Suddenly there was the sound of raised voices from the bedroom, followed by a cry of, 'Quick! The baby's coming!', and Rose came hurrying down the stairs to organise a supply of hot water.

Seeing Emily, she said, 'This is no place for an unmarried girl, Emily. You'd best be getting on home.'

'What about Primrose?' The child had become frightened by the increased activity and raised voices. 'She's asking for her mother.'

'It's no place for her either,' declared Rose. 'My sister lives not far away. She has two children of her own. Primrose will be all right with her. I'll send someone round there with her right away.'

From upstairs there came the sound of a woman's voice crying out with pain and Rose said hurriedly, 'Here, give her to me. I'll take her now, before she becomes even more frightened. Jean's baby is pushing hard to come into the world, even though she's not ready for it yet. It won't be easy for her. Come on, Primrose. You get off home right away, Emily. If you stay here listening to what's going on up there you'll be put off for ever from having a family of your own.'

III

Leaving the terraced cottage behind her, Emily chose a path that would take her around the side of the hill that had given its name to the mine. Caradon hill stood guard overlooking Bodmin Moor's southern boundary. It had been the site chosen by King Charles the first to muster his army before he led it to a notable victory against Parliamentarian forces during the Civil War, more than two hundred years before.

The course of the path along which Emily was walking had been trodden by the feet of countless generations of Cornish miners, men who would have witnessed many such tragedies as she had just left behind her.

Eyes cast down, she was wondering what the future held for Jean Spargo and her young daughter. Then, passing a large clump of yellow-flowering gorse, Emily looked up and saw Sam.

He was seated on a large rock of freestone granite scarred by long-dead hard-rock miners. They had practised their rock-drilling skills on it, using a hammer and spade-ended boring tools.

Sam was still as dirty as when he appeared on the surface of the man-engine shaft at the South Caradon mine. He looked weary and despondent.

'Hello, Emily. Is Jean all right?'

'Not really. She's gone into labour, although Rose doesn't think it's her time just yet.'

'Poor Jean.' When Sam shook his head his weariness was more pronounced. Unhappily, he added, 'She's going to have a hard time of it with two young 'uns and no man to take care of her.'

'Do you know her well?' Emily didn't know why she asked this question.

He nodded. 'There was a time when her ma and mine thought we would marry. Then Phillip came along and she had eyes for no one else from then on. They thought the world of each other.'

'Now she has lost Phillip and will have two young children to support. Perhaps she will turn to you once more.'

Sam shook his head. 'We're neither of us the person we were all those years ago. Besides, even if I did feel that way about her, I couldn't bear to spend the rest of my life knowing I was second best to the ghost of a man who had been my best friend.' He gave her a wan smile. 'I was pleased to see you there helping her, though. She needed someone around who could show some commonsense when it was wanted. I hope everything goes well for her with the baby. It's all very, very sad. She and Phillip were so looking forward to the birth. Primrose was too, but, fortunately, she's too small to know very much about what's going on.'

'She's a delightful little girl,' said Emily. Her concern shifting to Sam, she said, 'It must have been horrible for you to be among those who found her father.'

'It was . . . but let's not talk about it any more. I saw Parson Boyce go home alone with the pony and trap and waited here hoping you might take this way home. I've got a special reason for wanting to speak to you.'

As they began to walk along the path together, Sam continued, 'Things have been bad at the South Caradon mine for weeks now. I reckon this accident has put the seal on its fate. Cap'n Rowe told me before I came away just now that the adventurers will probably be shutting the mine down.'

Emily looked at him in concern. 'What will you do?' She was aware that none of the other mines were taking on men. Those mines still working had a hundred men chasing every vacancy.

Sam looked unhappy. 'Pa was talking to me about that only today, Emily, just before the accident happened. In fact, we've spoken about it many times before. We've all known the mine didn't have much life left in it, what with the price of copper being so low. Pa wants me to go to Australia. My Uncle Wilf is there, at a place called Kadina. His letters are full of the marvellous life he has. He says it's a great new country where a man can carve out a good future for himself if he's willing to work hard – and I've never been afraid of hard work.'

'You are not *seriously* considering going all the way to Australia?' Emily was dismayed. Regardless of her father's ban she had been quite determined that she would not stop seeing Sam – and there was much more to her determination than natural stubbornness. If he emigrated to Australia there was little possibility they would ever meet again.

'I have very little choice, Emily.'

'Of course you have! There are other mines. You are a good miner – and a local man. You'll find work.' She spoke with an optimism she knew was ill-founded.

Sam knew it too and he shook his head. 'By the end of the year almost all the Bodmin Moor copper mines will have shut down. There'll be hundreds of men – married men, most of them – chasing every job that's on offer.'

'But . . . you don't need to depend entirely upon mining. Your father has a farm. He can find work for you.'

Despite her resolve not to let Sam realise how much she thought of him, Emily now came close to desperation as the knowledge that he was likely to go out of her life for ever sank in. In truth, he was the only really close friend she had. Being the daughter of a vicar, especially one who was a social snob, was a lonely life in such a poverty-stricken area.

'There's no money to be made from farming in these parts unless miners are making money and buying farm produce. As it is, half the wage-earners have emigrated. The families they've left behind are only half a step ahead of starvation. Pa is a caring man, Emily, he's already giving away more than the farm is making. I'd be just an extra burden for him to bear.'

Emily realised that nothing she could say to Sam was going to make any difference. It seemed his mind was made up. She would need to face up to the fact she was going to lose him.

'When do you think you will be leaving?'

'As soon as a passage can be arranged and that won't be very long. Pa had me do all the paperwork and get references some time ago – just in case. He says ships are leaving from Falmouth and Plymouth every week and Cornish miners and their families are being offered free passages. He's offered to give me enough money to see me started there. I've managed to put a little by too. It should see me all right for a while.'

As he unfolded his plans, Emily realised she was likely to lose him even sooner than she had anticipated. Somewhat bitterly, she said, 'You seem to have everything well worked out and are wasting no time about this.'

'That's Pa, not me. He's been thinking about it for a very long time. I believe he's even discussed it with Parson Boyce.'

Emily suddenly recalled the conversation she was having with her father when the news of the mine tragedy reached the vicarage; her father was smugly asserting that her friendship with Sam would soon be at an end. She wondered now whether the suggestion that Sam should go to Australia might have originated from her father and not from Sam's.

'When did your pa speak to my father about this?'

'I don't know. It must have been mentioned again this morning though, because Pa had a list of sailings Parson Boyce gave him straight after church.'

Emily said nothing to Sam of her belief that her father had

put the idea into Farmer Hooper's head. She remained silent
for much of the remainder of the walk to the village.
Nevertheless, inside she was very, very angry – and extremely
hurt. It was even possible that her father had provided the
money to finance Sam in his new life there.

IV

'I'm going to miss you, Sam. I know the whole choir will, but
I feel I will miss you most of all. You are the only one I am able
to really talk to about things.'

When he made no immediate reply, she added, 'It's not too
late to change your mind, you know?'

Emily and Sam were seated side by side in the porch of St
Cleer's ancient church. Choir practice had ended twenty minutes
before and darkness was lowering over the village, yet neither
Sam nor Emily was in a hurry to go to their respective home.

It was a Friday evening, almost five weeks after the accident
at the South Caradon mine. Sam was to leave for the emigration depot at Plymouth on Sunday, and would be setting sail
for Australia only a day or two later.

'I couldn't change my mind now, Emily. Besides, three more
mines have closed this week. Mining has collapsed in the whole
of Cornwall. It's finished – and this time I'm convinced it's for
good. Miners will be fighting for places on emigrant ships before
long.'

Despite the misery she felt because he was leaving, Emily
knew Sam was right. Things were so bad she had been helping
her father write letters to Church leaders and prominent busi-
nessmen in other parts of the country. Arthur Boyce was calling
for donations to help feed the impoverished families of thousands of out-of-work Cornish miners.

'Why did you come to choir practice tonight, Sam? You won't be singing in church on Sunday – or any other day.'

'I don't really know. I suppose it's because I've got so used to coming here every Friday. Anyway, although I'd said "goodbye" to most of the others, I hadn't been able to see you. I couldn't go off without speaking to you.'

'I would never have forgiven you if you had!' Emily tried to make a joke but failed miserably.

'I'll miss you, especially,' he suddenly blurted out.

'Will you? Will you really?' she seized upon his words eagerly. 'You'll write to me?'

Sam fidgeted uncomfortably. 'My writing's not very good, Emily. I didn't get much schooling.'

This was an understatement of the facts. He could write his name, but little more than that.

Emily should have been aware of this and she was angry with herself for causing him embarrassment. 'But . . . you'll be keeping in touch with your parents somehow. Will you ask whoever writes letters for you to include a message for me, please?'

'If you'd really like me to.'

'I would, Sam. I *really* would.'

'Will Parson Boyce allow you to have a message from me?'

'Why shouldn't he?' she replied sharply.

He shrugged his shoulders, the gesture barely visible in the gathering darkness. 'Pa said the parson had spoken to him about village gossip. It seems he made it very clear he doesn't approve of me.'

'Father disapproves of most people – *me* especially – but when did this conversation take place?'

'I don't know exactly. A few months ago, at least.'

'About the time when your father first suggested you should go to Australia?'

'It might have been . . .' Sam suddenly realised why she was asking the questions. 'You're not suggesting the two things are connected? I'm sure they're not. Pa has said many times that there's nothing in Cornwall for a young man, especially if he works on the mines.'

Emily was less convinced than Sam that her father had nothing to do with his forthcoming exile, but she realised she would probably never learn the truth of it.

'At what time on Sunday are you actually leaving St Cleer?'

'About ten in the morning. Pa's taking me in the light farm-cart as far as Liskeard. I'll be catching a train from there to Plymouth to board the boat.'

'That's very early,' Emily said unhappily. 'I was hoping I might be able to see you before you left.'

'Why don't you come to see me tomorrow?' Sam suggested eagerly. 'Friends and family will be dropping in at the farm all day to have a drink, a bite to eat, and to wish me well. You'd be made very welcome if you could come.'

Emily shook her head, a gesture that was lost in the darkness. 'I couldn't get away. My sister Caroline is returning home tomorrow and Maude has been given the day off to visit her sister. Besides, my father will be home all day. I'm only able to stay talking to you this evening because he is at a diocesan meeting in Bodmin. Even so, I had better go now, or Maude will tell him I was late returning from choir practice and I'll be in trouble once again.'

She rose to her feet and Sam followed suit. As they stood close together in the narrow church porch, he said, 'I'll walk home with you.'

'No!' Emily had not intended to sound quite so vehement and she quickly added, 'The chapel meeting will be turning out about now. Preacher Garland would love to be able to tell Father I had been seen walking in the dark with you.'

Preacher Garland was a lay preacher who had taken it upon himself to crusade against the twin evils of alcohol and a reprehensible lack of morals among the young.

'Then I suppose I'd better say goodbye to you here and now.'

Sam held out his hand to her but Emily could not see it. Beside, she had other plans. Her heart beating alarmingly fast, she said, 'You may kiss me, if you wish.'

His feet shuffled on the stone-paved floor as he moved towards her, then his breath brushed against her cheek as he gave her a glancing kiss.

Emily's experience of kissing had so far been restricted to perfunctory greetings given to her by older family members. Not certain exactly what she had been expecting from Sam, she was yet aware of a feeling of disappointment.

With a boldness that would have horrified her father, she said quietly, 'Is that the best you can do, Sam Hooper? Is that how your Daniel would have kissed Bessie Mitchell?'

The questions were extremely provocative, as Emily well knew. Daniel was Sam's older brother. His passion for Bessie had been the talk of the village, providing a subject for more than one of Preacher Garland's highly critical sermons.

It had come as no surprise to anyone when Bessie became pregnant and the young couple were obliged to marry. They had been married for little more than three years now and had three young children, yet none of the passion had faded from their relationship.

Sam was standing very close to Emily and instead of replying he reached out and pulled her to him.

This time the kiss was all she had anticipated – and more. It seemed to her that every nerve and fibre she possessed was responding to the nearness of his body as she strained against him.

Suddenly, they heard the sound of voices and the spell was broken.

Guiltily, they stood back from each other as the voices drew nearer. Emily's confused emotions untangled themselves and she felt a very real fear. If the voices belonged to her father's churchwardens, coming to the church for some reason, she would be in serious trouble. Not merely for being here alone with Sam, but also for deliberately flouting her father's explicit order that she was not to have anything more to do with him.

Holding her breath, she sensed that Sam was doing the same.

Then the owners of the voices passed by the porch entrance – two miners from a nearby hamlet, taking a shortcut through the churchyard on their way to work on the nightshift at one of Bodmin Moor's few remaining working mines.

Emily and Sam breathed out their relief, yet both were aware it would be impossible to recapture the magic of the moment they had just experienced.

'You'd better be getting home before someone comes looking for you.' Sam spoke the words reluctantly. 'I suppose I should be on my way too, it's going to be a busy day tomorrow.'

'Yes,' Emily agreed, with equal reluctance. Miserably, she added, 'I know I won't be able to see you again, Sam, but take care of yourself and please find some way of letting me know where you are and what you are doing.'

'I'll try,' he promised. 'But let me walk you home . . .'

'No,' she said, more firmly than she felt. 'We've said our good-byes now. We must not risk having villagers see us together and causing more trouble than they have already. Take care, Sam – and God go with you.'

She kissed him once more, but this time it was a brief, almost perfunctory gesture.

Before he could make a move to stop her, she turned and fled into the darkness, taking a path that would lead her to the vicarage.

Left alone, Sam listened to the sound of her running feet until he could hear them no more. Then, feeling very confused and experiencing an increasing sense of frustration and unhappiness, he reluctantly turned his back on the church and made his way home, but he went far more slowly than had Emily.

V

For much of the day before Sam left St Cleer, members of his large family came from miles around, joining with many friends to bid him farewell and wish him a safe journey and success on the far side of the world.

All considered it highly unlikely they would ever meet with him again. The advent of steam had made crossing the oceans of the world less hazardous than in earlier years, but they knew from their experience of the many men who had emigrated from Cornwall during the recent lean years that very few returned to resume life in their native land. Most either sent for their families to join them or regularly remitted money to those they had left behind. Others were never heard from again.

Among those who flocked to the farm were women who had seen loved ones depart never to return, and, ignorant of the vastness of the country to which Sam was voyaging, they pressed letters upon him, urging him to deliver them personally, to places as far apart as Tasmania, Queensland and Kalgoorlie.

They brought presents for him too. Small and simple gifts for the most part. A kerchief, belt, pencil, socks – and a book, for which he gave polite thanks to the donor, even though he could not read it. There was also a hairbrush, a razor – and even a cake, baked for him by a great-aunt. She declared that the farther a man travelled, the more he would appreciate good whole-some home-cooking.

Sam would have been quite content to forego the farewells of both family and friends. Most, after a few solemn words, stood around in small, mildly embarrassed groups, food and drink in hand, talking loudly to each other.

Many of the more distantly related members of the family had not seen him since he was a small child. However, saying farewell to an emigrating relative, no matter how distant, was a duty that could not be shirked. It was as important an occasion as a birth, christening or funeral.

Sam was about to leave Cornwall and all he had ever known, crossing the ocean to make a new life among strangers. It was incumbent upon them to come to his home and offer good wishes.

Their numbers took Sam by surprise and spoiled his own plans. He had been hoping there would be an opportunity to spend a little time at the church, and that Emily might be there. Or that she would see him from the vicarage and find an excuse to sneak away from the house and meet him, if only for a few minutes.

Their parting the previous evening had left him in a very confused state of mind. A strong, unspoken bond between him and Emily had gradually grown up over the months – perhaps years, even – yet he had always been painfully aware of their vastly different stations in life.

For this reason he had thought it impossible there could ever be anything more than friendship between them.

Until last night.

In the church porch, Emily had done what he had never dared contemplate. Her actions had been so unexpected he still found it difficult to believe it had really happened.

Since then she had occupied as much of his thoughts as the forthcoming voyage to Australia and the events of the day would allow. He wondered whether she would ever have behaved in such a manner had his imminent departure not meant their relationship could never go any further.

He dismissed such thoughts. She had made him promise to get news to her of where he was and what he was doing. Why should she do that if nothing was likely to come of it?

Had Emily been anyone else and not the daughter of Parson Boyce, he would have called on her today and asked her how she *really* felt about him.

Had her reply promised a future together he would have deferred his emigration . . .

But this was no more than foolish conjecture. Emily was . . . who she was. Emily Boyce, daughter of the Reverend Arthur Boyce, vicar of St Cleer and niece of Lord Boyce, an important minister in the government of England. He, Sam, was the son of a poor moorland farmer. A miner, unable to read or write . . .

'Hello, Sam.'

A soft voice broke into his thoughts. He turned to see Jean Spargo standing beside him, holding the hand of Primrose.

'Jean! It's very nice of you to come here.' Suddenly remembering, he said, 'I was sorry to hear about the baby . . .'

The child, a boy, had lived for only a few hours.

'I was at Phillip's funeral, but never had an opportunity to speak to you.'

'I saw you, Sam, but was still feeling so ill I didn't want to talk to anyone – but I haven't come to say goodbye.'

'No?' Her statement puzzled him. 'What then?'

'I'm going to Australia too, me and Primrose – and to the same place as you, to Kadina, although I didn't know *you* were going there until last night.'

'But . . . why are *you* going there? I would have thought you would have wanted to stay here, in Cornwall, where you know people.'

'I have no one here in Cornwall, Sam – not now. At least, no one who's close. Besides, everywhere I turn I'm reminded of Phillip. I decided I'd go to Australia to my pa. If you remember, when my ma died at the same time as your aunt, he and your uncle Wilf went off to Australia together. I had letters from him saying how well he's doing and what a wonderful place Australia is. There haven't been any letters just lately, but I'd have heard if anything had happened to him. He always wanted me and Phillip to go out there and join him, but Phillip didn't want to leave Cornwall. Now he's dead there's nothing to keep me here.'

Her news was so unexpected Sam hardly knew what to say. 'It's an incredible coincidence that we should be going to the same place, Jean, but . . . when are *you* leaving?'

'Tomorrow, Sam. We're sailing for Port Adelaide on the *Bonython*, the same as you. I was just talking to your pa about it. He's said that if me and Primrose are here by ten o'clock in the morning he'll take us to Liskeard with you in the cart to catch the train.'

At that moment Primrose pulled away from her mother. She ran to where two children, a year or two older than herself, were being shown one of the kittens that had been the cause of Emily's confrontation with her father some weeks before.

After satisfying herself that Primrose would come to no harm with the other children and the kitten, Jean turned back to Sam once more. 'You don't know what a relief it will be having you close at hand on the ship, Sam. I was dreading the thought of going all that way with Primrose, knowing no one. I'm not sure you'll be as pleased to have *us* travelling with *you*, but I promise I'll not allow Primrose and me to be a burden . . .'

At that moment Primrose let out a scream as the kitten, pulled from one child to another, put out its claws and scratched the little girl.

As Jean hurried to her daughter, Sam watched her go with mixed feelings. It *would* be nice to travel with someone he knew – and he and Jean had been friends for a very long time. However, despite Jean's assurance, he had an uneasy feeling that she and Primrose *would* prove to be an unexpected and not entirely welcome responsibility on the long journey to South Australia.

VI

Jean and Primrose arrived at the Hooper farm more than an hour before Sam and his immediate family were due to leave for Liskeard.

Although Jean protested that she and Primrose were not hungry, they did full justice to the meal placed in front of them by Sam's mother.

In truth, they were unused to eating well. Raising money for the expenses they would incur on a voyage to Australia had not been easy for the young widow. The sale of her household effects and those of her late husband had not fetched as much as she had expected and Phillip's workmates had been able to spare little for the collection made on her behalf.

In the recent uncertain times, she and Primrose had often gone short of food. Being hungry was no new experience for either of them. However, the little money she carried with her would have to last for at least three months – more if they did not immediately locate her father.

But Jean tried not to think of the hardships that lay ahead. She and Primrose were setting off to begin a new life. One devoid of poverty and despair – or so her father had declared in his letters.

Eventually, it was time to set off. Clutching their pitifully scant possessions, mother and daughter settled themselves on the farm wagon, together with Sam, his luggage and members of his family.

Many friends had gathered to wave them on their way, but Sam was deeply disappointed that Emily was not included among their number. He realised it would have been very difficult for her, but he had hoped she might find a way to come and see him off.

Other friends were also absent. Good friends he had known for many years and who had sung with him and Emily in the choir. He tried, unsuccessfully, not to be too hurt by their absence.

Sam's father called for the well-wishers to stand clear. When they obeyed, he shook out the reins and urged the horse into motion.

The wagon creaked away to the cheers of the friends Sam was leaving behind and with a number of excited young children running beside it.

The journey took them through St Cleer village. As they approached the church, Farmer Hooper was forced to bring the wagon to a halt, the road blocked by a group of people – the church choir.

As wagon and horse stopped, the choir started to sing a hymn that began 'For the dear ones parted from us'. Listening to the words, tears stung Sam's eyes, but when the hymn came to an end and the members of the choir gathered around the farm wagon to voice their farewells, he had eyes for only one of their number – and Emily held his gaze.

She was the last person to grasp his hand. Remembering the previous occasion on which they had met, he would have wished for something more demonstrative than a handshake. However, he realised she dared make no show of affection in front of so many witnesses.

As it was, she held his hand for a dangerously long time, at the same time pressing something into it.

'Take care of yourself, Sam, and don't forget to let us know how things are going for you in Australia.'

Closing his hand upon the as-yet-unseen object she had placed there, he said, 'I won't forget, Emily. I won't forget anything.'

His low-spoken words gave Emily more pleasure than he would ever know; at the same time she hoped that none of those hearing them would detect their hidden meaning.

'All right, everybody, stand clear, we have to be on our way,' Farmer Hooper called out to the choir. Moments later horse and wagon were on the move once more.

Sam and the others in the wagon waved furiously until the well-wishers disappeared from view.

Not until now did Sam open his hand to discover he was holding a gold crucifix. It was one Emily had frequently worn on a delicate gold chain about her neck. It had been a present from her late mother.

Sam was aware how much Emily valued the crucifix. It was proof, beyond any doubt, that Emily's feelings for him went far beyond friendship. He wished there was some way he could have thanked her properly for giving him such a valuable and treasured farewell present.

He had thought the gift had gone unnoticed by the others, but Jean caught a glimpse of it when he unclenched his hand. Now she said quietly, 'That's a very nice thing to be given, Sam.'

'It's very generous,' he agreed. 'Far too generous, she shouldn't have done it.'

'Is Emily Boyce your sweetheart?'

The direct question was so unexpected that for a few moments Sam floundered for a reply. Finally, he said, 'She's a friend. A very good friend, that's all. She couldn't be anything else when she's the daughter of the parson, could she?'

He was saved from further questioning because at that moment the wagon came up with a party comprising two women and five children, trudging along the road. Each, including the smallest child, was struggling with a bundle of possessions.

Bringing horse and wagon to a halt, Farmer Hooper called out, 'Are you all going to Liskeard?'

When the women said they were, he invited them to accept a ride on the wagon.

They clambered on board eagerly and a small boy settled himself beside Sam. Hugging a lumpy bundle, the child glanced at Sam uncertainly once or twice before suddenly blurting out, 'I'm going to see my dad.'

'Are you now?' Sam smiled at him. 'And where is he?'

The answer to this simple question seemed beyond the capabilities of the small boy and he looked to one of the girls, perhaps twice his age, for an answer.

'He's in Australia,' she replied. 'Him and our uncle. They're working on a mine. We're going to live with them again. These are our cousins . . .'

She indicated the other children, who were all within a year or two of her own age.

'Why, that's where we're going too,' said Sam. 'Where in Australia are you bound?'

It was the beginning of an excited conversation which soon involved children and adults. The newcomers had walked from North Hill, a village some miles distant, on the edge of Bodmin Moor. They too were sailing from Plymouth, but on a different ship, their destination mines on the eastern side of Australia.

It seemed to Jean that if the present exodus continued there would be no one left in Cornwall in a few years' time.

2

'I wonder what Jean Spargo and Primrose were doing in the wagon with Sam?'

When the Hooper farm wagon passed from view Emily put the question to a choir member as they filed into church to prepare for the Sunday morning service.

'They're off to Australia too,' said the girl to whom she had spoken. 'Jean's father's out there. He's all the family she has now. There's her husband's family, of course, but it's not the same. Mind you, I think she'd have done better to stay here, but it's none of my business and blood's thicker than water, or so they say.'

'I'm surprised Sam never said anything when he came to choir practice,' Emily persisted.

The thought of Sam travelling all the way to Australia in the company of Jean Spargo troubled her. Sam and the young widow had once been close – and Jean was a very attractive woman.

'To tell you the truth, I don't think he knew,' said another of the choir members who had overheard the brief conversation. 'Jean was at the farewell party given at the Hooper farm yesterday. I believe he learned only then. Mind you, I doubt if he'll mind too much, Jean's a fine-looking woman. Any red-blooded man would be happy to spend a few months in her company.'

'Sam will need to watch himself,' another choir member chipped in. 'Jean Spargo's "chapel". If he shows too much of an interest she'll have him standing with her in front of the altar before he knows what's happening.'

The talk moved on from Jean Spargo. Minutes later the choir began to prepare for the service, but for the remainder of that morning Emily found it very difficult to concentrate on spiritual matters.

After the service Emily waited for her father and they walked back to the vicarage together.

Arthur Boyce said very little until they neared the vicarage gate. Then, well out of hearing of members of the congregation walking in a similar direction, he said sternly 'Did I see you talking to Samuel Hooper before the service?'

Emily started guiltily. Her thoughts at that very moment had been of Sam. Defensively, she said, 'Yes, the choir sang a hymn for him, to wish him well on his long journey.'

'Very laudable,' said her father with unashamed insincerity. 'However, it might have been more judicious of you to have allowed the other choir members to say their farewells without you.'

Stopping in her tracks, Emily looked at her father in disbelief. 'Are you saying I must distance myself from the other members of the choir now?'

'Of course not . . . Well, not when they are singing for my services. The choir is much admired by the congregation and I am, of course, delighted that you play such an active part in church activities. However, you need to remain aloof from the others when you are outside the church. After all . . .'

'I know . . .' Emily's bitterness spilled into the open, 'they are not suitable companions for the daughter of the vicar of the parish.'

'Not just because I am the parish priest, Emily, but also because you are the niece of one of Her Majesty's ministers . . .'

As he spoke, Emily silently mouthed the oft-repeated words in time with her father.

'We must remember at all times that we are all of us joint guardians of Uncle Percy's reputation.'

'I doubt whether Uncle Percy's reputation is so fragile that it would be endangered by my singing with a village church choir to bid farewell to a fellow member who was emigrating to Australia,' Emily said scornfully.

'Gossip is an insidious thing, Emily, believe me. It will linger on long after Samuel Hooper has left these shores. I assure you that the reputation of one of my daughters is just as important to me as that of Uncle Percy.'

'Is it?' Emily's anger and frustration suddenly overtook caution. 'Is it really, Father? Is that why you sent John packing when he began to show an interest in Caroline? *He* was not damaging her reputation. Indeed, the villagers thought of the situation as highly romantic. Everyone was delighted for both of them. Everyone but you.'

John Kavanagh had served as a young curate at St Cleer for some eighteen months, during which time he and Caroline had become increasingly fond of one another.

Reverend Boyce had been slow to observe such things for himself, but when a churchwarden made an innocent remark about Caroline and the young curate making 'a handsome couple', Arthur Boyce was quick to act.

There had been a stormy confrontation with the young curate, as a result of which John Kavanagh made a hurried departure. He took up a curacy in Yorkshire, after promising Parson Boyce he would make no attempt to contact Caroline for at least a year.

Caroline had been inconsolable for weeks after the departure of the young curate. Arthur Boyce had forbidden the mention of his name in the vicarage, but Caroline spoke of little else to her sister when their father was absent.

The year-long ban was almost at an end, but it seemed Arthur Boyce's unreasonable ruling had brought the innocent relationship to an end. No word had been received from him since his leaving. Although Emily knew her sister still pined for him, she had not mentioned his name for some months now.

'Is it really our reputation that is of concern to you, Father? Or is it the thought that both Caroline and I might find happiness elsewhere and leave you with only a housekeeper to take care of you in your bitter old age? If so, it is a very short-sighted view – and a selfish one. We could both provide you with grandchildren to bring a great deal of pleasure into your life.'

'How dare you make such an outrageous accusation, Emily! Your welfare, and that of Caroline, has always been my major concern since I lost your dear mother. I cannot even begin to imagine her distress were she alive to hear you speak to me in such a manner. I declare I am quite unable to face you across the dining table. You will go to your room immediately and remain there for the rest of the day.'

Angry that he had once again used a reference to her late mother in an attempt to deflect her, Emily said defiantly, 'Does that mean I am excused choir this evening?'

'It means you will do as I say and go to your room – *now*! If I have any more to say to you today I will say it there. Go!'

Still defiant, Emily entered the vicarage ahead of her father and made her way to her room.

In the kitchen, where she was preparing lunch in the absence of the housekeeper, Caroline heard Emily stomp her way up the stairs to her room and slam the door noisily. Then she heard the quieter sound of the closing of the study door and she knew her father had gone to have his pre-Sunday-lunch sherry.

Caroline realised there must have been words between her father and sister yet again. She guessed correctly it would have had to do with the departure from St Cleer of Sam Hooper. Caroline had hoped the relationship between Emily and their father might improve during her absence on holiday. She now realised it had been too much to hope for. Both possessed strong characters and each was too stubborn to give way to the other.

Caroline felt sorry for Emily. Despite her sister's reticence on the subject, she was aware of her feelings for Sam Hooper – and now he had gone from St Cleer for ever.

In common with Emily – and most of the villagers – Caroline did not doubt that Sam's departure had been engineered by their snobbish and domineering father, just as he had more openly sent John Kavanagh packing.

But John was still in England. Although he had kept his word to her father not to contact her for a year, he had ensured that mutual acquaintances kept her informed of all that was happening in his life.

She firmly believed that when the year's banishment came to an end John would return and provide her with the means of escaping from the unreasonable discipline imposed by the vicar of St Cleer upon his two daughters.

3

I

There was a number of departing emigrants waiting on the platform of Liskeard railway station by the time the train that would take them to Plymouth wheezed to a halt.

Tears mingled with blessings and good wishes as the departing miners and a few dependants struggled to escape from well-wishing friends and relatives and seek a seat on board.

Hanging precariously out of a carriage window, Sam's last memory of Liskeard station was of tearful faces gazing after the departing train and a forest of waving arms still bidding farewell when the train passed from view.

As Sam tugged on a leather strap to close the compartment window, Jean said, 'Now I feel we're *really* on our way.' Hugging Primrose to her, she added, 'Your ma and pa were very nice to us, Sam. I felt as though they were waving Primrose and me on our way too.'

'So they were,' said Sam. 'They know we're all travelling to Australia together and will be sharing whatever adventures happen along the way.'

Jean shivered. It was partly excitement, but there was apprehension too. 'It's an awful long way, Sam. I'm sure that if I'd had longer to think about it – I mean *really* think about it – I'd never have dared to make such a journey. I would probably pull out even now if you weren't travelling with us.'

'You'll be fine, Jean – you and Primrose,' he added hastily, embarrassed by the look she was giving him.

He was quite ready to give Jean all the help she needed on the long journey to Australia. Indeed, it was a great pleasure to have someone he knew so well travelling with him – but he had grown used to her in the role of wife to his friend Phillip. He had liked things that way. Besides, he had some thinking to do – about Emily.

There was a very wide gulf between their stations in life. Such a difference would have remained an insurmountable barrier in Cornwall, but he had been told that such social barriers did not exist in Australia.

If he worked hard and made good there, who knew what might be achieved?

When Sam, Jean and Primrose left the train at Plymouth they were at a loss about where they should go. However, the young boys of the busy seaport had long ago learned to turn the stream of emigrants passing through the city to their advantage. They crowded about the railway station in droves, offering to carry the baggage of the bewildered new arrivals to the migrants' transit depot – for a price.

However, such was the fierce competition for custom that Sam was able to strike a bargain with a young lad who said his name was William, halving the asking price from a shilling and sixpence to ninepence.

The price agreed, their baggage was loaded on a small home-made handcart and they were soon walking through the streets of Plymouth in the company of the cheerful young Plymothian.

After telling them of the 'hundreds' of emigrants he had assisted on their way, William asked their destination. When told they were travelling to the port of Wallaroo, in South

Australia, he commented, 'Then you'll be travelling on the
Bonython. You'll find it's pretty crowded for families on this
voyage.'

'Then it's just as well we're not a family,' Sam corrected him.
'Jean and Primrose will be in the family accommodation. I'm
just a friend and will be in the single men's part of the ship.'

'That's going to be even more crowded,' William said. 'You'll
need to be sure you find a good bunk for the voyage.'

'Do you know the ship?' Jean asked.

''Course I know her,' the boy declared scornfully. 'I knows
all the ships that come in to Plymouth.'

Glancing speculatively at Sam, he added, 'Mind you, I know
the *Bonython* better than most.'

'Oh, and why is that?' Sam was only mildly interested, being
wrapped up in his own thoughts.

'Because the first mate is my uncle and the watchman who
looks after the ship while it's in port is my grandad.'

Sam became more interested. 'If we tell this uncle of yours
that we've met you, will we be given better treatment during
the time we're on board?'

'That depends,' William replied obtusely.

'Depends on what?' Sam asked, aware the boy had a propo-
sition in mind.

'On whether you'd like to put this baggage on board right
away and choose your bunks before any of the others go on
board.'

Sam had heard disconcerting rumours about the conditions
they were likely to encounter on board a migrant ship. All the
reports suggested the great advantage to be gained from
knowing someone on board and becoming a 'privileged'
passenger, but he remained cautious.

'How much is all this likely to cost?'

'Ten shillings. Five for my uncle and half a crown each for
Grandad and me,' the boy said immediately.

Sam shook his head. 'I'm sorry, William, you're far too

expensive for the likes of me. I'm just a poor, out-of-work Cornish miner – and Jean's a widow. We neither of us can afford to hand out such money. I can understand your uncle wanting five shillings, he's an important person, but two-and-six each for you and your grandpa is far too much. I suppose I could manage a shilling each for you, but that's all.'

William realised he had a prospective 'customer', albeit one inclined to haggle. However, he knew his uncle would give him a commission of sixpence for arranging the deal. He eventually agreed a price of seven shillings and sixpence, being five shillings for the mate and two-and-sixpence to be shared between himself and his grandfather.

It was money Sam would rather not have spent at this stage of the voyage, but he believed it would prove to be a worthwhile investment.

Content that he had concluded a profitable deal, William chatted happily to Sam and Jean for the remainder of the walk to the dock area where the *Bonython* was moored alongside a quay in Plymouth's Millbay Dock.

The ship was not yet ready to take on passengers. Until it was, prospective emigrants were being housed in a holding depot a short distance from where the ship, a barque of about eight hundred tons, was moored.

Jean looked at the three-masted wooden barque apprehensively. 'It's a lot smaller than I imagined it would be,' she said tremulously.

'She's bigger than a lot of ships sailing to Australia,' William declared defensively. 'A whole lot faster, too. Some of the ships take four months or more to get there. The *Bonython* can get there in three – more or less.'

Jean was appalled at the thought of her and Primrose spending three months of their life incarcerated in such a small vessel, but she kept such thoughts to herself.

At that moment William's grandfather came across the gangway from the ship to greet them.

When he heard they wished to choose their berths now, and the price they were willing to pay, the old man made a half-hearted attempt to increase his share from the arrangement. Fortunately, as Sam had correctly anticipated, there had been a dearth of emigrants with sufficient money to take advantage of William's offer.

The three prospective emigrants were taken on board to be introduced to the mate, a bluff Cornishman named Henry Hunkin.

After a whispered conversation with William, during the course of which money changed hands, the mate beamed at Sam and Jean and tweaked the cheek of Primrose. After promising to help them in any way possible during the long voyage ahead, he left them in the care of the aged watchman and young William.

While Sam helped William bring their luggage on board, Jean and Primrose were taken below by the watchman to the centre-hold where the families would be accommodated. Returning alone, the old man then preceded Sam down a steep ladder to the rear hold. Divided into two sections, with separate ladders leading to each part, this was where he and the other single men would be accommodated, single women being carried in the hold forward of the families.

Leading Sam to a bunk adjacent to a temporary bulkhead that separated the single men's accommodation from that occupied by families, the watchman said, 'Take the top bunk here, son.' Giving him a lewd wink, he added, 'Your friend and the young girl have the top bunk on the other side. As you can see, there's a gap between the deckhead and the partition. You'll be able to speak to each other through there. The gap's big enough for you to hold hands too if that's what you want, though you won't be able to get up to any mischief. Put what you'll need for the voyage on the bunk to stake your claim. William and I will take the rest of your things down below and make sure they're stowed clear of any bilge water.'

Sam was not entirely happy at trusting, on the recommendation of a Plymouth street urchin, all his worldly possessions to the care of a man he had not met before today and would probably never meet again but the die was cast. Besides, there was already property on some of the other bunks. He slung his bags on to the top bunk beside the bulkhead.

Half an hour later, their bunks reserved and their belongings safely stowed away, Sam, Jean and Primrose walked together towards the huge transit shed. Here they would spend the night after completing emigration formalities.

Jean was complaining of the accommodation on board the *Bonython*. 'It's so *cramped*!' she wailed. 'Primrose and me will be occupying the same bunk for all that time – and it's hardly the size of a single bed!'

'You're only entitled to a space of six feet by eighteen inches,' Sam explained. 'It's a good thing Primrose is no bigger than she is, or you'd have even less room.'

'It's so dark down there too,' Jean said unhappily. 'I don't know how we're going to survive such a long voyage, I really don't.'

'Do you want to return home?' Sam asked her. 'It's not too late. I'll give you the money for your train fare to Liskeard.'

Jean considered his offer for only a few moments. Then, shaking her head, she said, miserably, 'There's nothing for us back on the moor. We'd likely starve if we were to go back there. At least we have the chance of some sort of future in Australia, although I wish I knew more about the country and the place we're going to.'

Sam felt much the same. It was an unknown country, but he said, 'We'll find out soon enough. My uncle says in his letters that with all the mines there are around Kadina, it's easy to imagine you're still in Cornwall – except that the pay's a whole lot better.'

II

The transit shed was a large, overcrowded building, where a couple of overworked men were kept busy checking the documents of would-be emigrants. Their task was to ensure that the departing men, women and children fulfilled conditions laid down by the South Australian immigration authorities.

Some of the prospective emigrants had been in the depot for four or five days. They were complaining that they should now be allowed on board the ship, which had almost completed taking on provisions for the voyage.

Jean did not strictly conform to the stated requirements, having no husband. However, her letters of suitability had been carefully worded to make it appear she would be joining a family already established in South Australia.

This in itself gave Sam a small niggle of concern. If Jean's father was not where Jean expected to find him – and miners had a habit of moving to other mines whenever the mood for a change took them – Sam had an uncomfortable feeling he would need to accept responsibility for her and Primrose for longer than planned.

It was not how he wanted to begin life in Australia.

In truth, he had given little thought to the details of what he would do in the new land. He knew there were mines there but his plans did not extend beyond finding work in the one where his uncle was working. All reports reaching England from South Australia indicated that the mine captains, most of whom were Cornish, were eager to employ miners arriving from the land they themselves had left behind.

By noon the following day, the last of the emigrants had arrived, all formalities were completed and the emigration officer declared they could embark on the *Bonython*.

The announcement was the signal for a frantic exodus from

the transit shed and a dash to the ship in an effort to secure a favourable berth.

Sam and Jean followed more slowly with Primrose. Boarding the ship they stood back from the holds where emigrants scurried back and forth with their belongings.

It was a dull grey day with a light drizzle falling on the docks. The three travellers from Bodmin Moor were glad to take advantage of the shelter of a tarpaulin, rigged on the deck of the *Bonython* to protect the extended cooking area of the upper-deck galley.

This was where food would be prepared and cooked for the three hundred and fifty or so passengers. The ship's cook would be assisted by some of the women emigrants. They would be paid for their work and the *Bonython*'s mate had already promised Jean she would be included in their number.

'There seems to be an awful lot of people travelling on the ship,' Jean said, watching the men, women and children swarming over the *Bonython*.

'There's likely to be more by the time we reach Australia,' Sam said. 'I've seen at least half a dozen women whose time will come before we arrive.'

Remembering her own recent traumatic experience of childbirth, Jean shuddered. 'I should hate to give birth to a baby on board here. It's so cramped and gloomy down below and there's no privacy at all. Heaven only knows what it is going to be like if we run into bad weather.'

'You'll be all right,' Sam said, with more confidence than he felt. 'Treat it as a great adventure. That's what we're going to do, aren't we, Primrose?'

Primrose's response was to cling to her mother's skirt and say tremulously, 'No . . . I want to go home. It *stinks* down there.'

The accommodation for emigrants on board the ship might generously have been described as spartan. The holds of what was essentially a merchantman had been fitted out with bunks, arranged in such a way that the ship could carry the maximum number of passengers in a minimum of space.

It was apparent to Sam that with such cramped accommodation, inadequate sanitary arrangements and no privacy whatsoever, the voyage would not be an enjoyable experience, but he did not pass on such thoughts to Jean.

So much would depend upon the weather, even their eating habits. If the weather proved too bad for cooking to be carried out on the upper deck the emigrants would need to manage as best they could with whatever food they could prepare in the crowded holds.

By the time things had settled down a little, with less movement between deck and hold, the rain had become heavier and was dripping through the canvas awning. Despite her aversion to the accommodation hold, Jean said she would take Primrose below. Sam decided to follow her example.

Climbing down the ladder, Sam made his way to the bunk he had chosen. When he reached it, he was startled to see a fully clothed man lying there, apparently asleep. The belongings Sam had placed on the bunk had been removed and thrown to the deck.

Suddenly angry, Sam took the man by the shoulder and shook him vigorously.

The man reacted like someone waking from a deep sleep. When he turned over to face Sam, the miner caught the strong smell of stale ale on his breath.

'Go away! I'm tired.'

'Then find somewhere else to sleep, this is my bunk. Get up and out of it.'

The man was probably in his early thirties, unshaven and heavily built. Sitting up in the bunk he looked down at Sam through bloodshot eyes.

He saw a young man, almost six feet tall and with the

muscular build of a man who earned his living by physical labour. But so too did he – and Ira Moyle had a reputation as a 'hard' man in the community whence he had come.

'I didn't see any sign that someone else had taken this bunk,' he lied. 'As far as I'm concerned I was the first one here.'

'Is that why my gear has been thrown on the floor?' Sam snapped. 'You're in my bed-space. Get down and find somewhere else, or I'll haul you down.'

Sam was aware that others in the hold were taking a keen interest in the argument, but he was angry and did not care. He had never gone out of his way to look for trouble, but violence was never far away in the community in which he had grown up and he had been involved in more than one fight.

Drink was readily available close to the mines and incoming miners without family or community ties tended to drink sufficient to make them aggressive.

'There are plenty of spare bed-spaces down here—'

'That's right,' Sam broke in upon the man's argument. 'So get down and find one of your own. This is where I'm sleeping.'

At that moment Sam saw Jean peering through the gap between partition and deckhead above the bunk. From her side of the partition she had overheard much of the conversation between Sam and the stranger. She appeared scared.

The older man swung his legs over the side of the bunk, as though about to concede Sam's right to the bunk. Then, instead of lowering himself to the floor, he suddenly lashed out at Sam's head with a heavy, steel-tipped boot.

Had it connected, the fight would have been over before it began, but Sam had seen too many pay-night fights between rival miners to be caught out in such a simple fashion.

A swerve of his body was sufficient to avoid the kick, then he grabbed the man's foot and twisted hard, bringing the other man crashing heavily to the deck at his feet.

As he hit the floor the man screamed in pain as his knee was twisted painfully. Nevertheless, he came up fighting, only to be sent back to the deck by a kick from Sam which caught him between the eyes and left him dazed and confused.

Standing over him, Sam said, 'We can carry on with this argument if it's what you want, but things are going to be hard enough during this voyage without one or both of us coping with injuries as well. What's it to be?'

Ira Moyle rose unsteadily to his feet, seeking support from the tier of bunks closest to him.

'Where I sleep isn't important to me, but there's unfinished business between you and me, son. It'll be settled before we get to where we're going, I promise you that.'

Reaching up to the bunk from which he had so recently been ignominiously ejected, he grabbed the bundle containing his belongings. Limping unsteadily, he made his way between the bunks, nursing a painful leg and heading for the ladder leading to the upper deck. He would seek accommodation in the other half of the divided hold.

His departure was the signal for a series of cat-calls and applause from those who had witnessed the brief altercation.

One of the men sitting on a nearby bunk said, 'You did well there, young 'un, but keep a sharp look-out for Ira Moyle while the two of you are on this ship together. He's not the best of men to cross.'

'Ira Moyle? Is that his name?'

'That's right, you might have heard of him. He's well known in Cornwall and has earned himself a reputation as a hard man among the miners down Camborne way. You've put a dent in his image that he'll neither forgive nor forget.'

'I'm not looking for trouble,' declared Sam, 'but he'll find that Bodmin Moor miners are just as tough as the Camborne men.'

The man who had given Sam the information about the man with whom he had just fought grinned wryly. 'I reckon Ira Moyle has just learned that lesson for himself. No doubt you'll be able to prove it again should the need arise, but be wary of him.

Ira's not a man I'd choose as a friend, but neither would I be happy knowing I had him as an enemy.'

Sam was left with an uneasy feeling that he had not heard the last of Ira Moyle, but there were other things to think of right now. The *Bonython* was preparing to put to sea, setting out on the long voyage to Australia.

4

I

Hardly a day went by in the St Cleer vicarage when Emily did not think of Sam and wonder where he was and what he was doing. She hoped it would not be too long before he was able to send news of his safe arrival in Australia to his family.

However, two months after his departure an event occurred that would have a profound influence upon Emily's life and her aspirations for the future.

She and Caroline spent much of the day in the vicarage kitchen helping to prepare food for a dinner party. It was to celebrate the visit to Cornwall of Lord Percy Boyce, Minister of the Crown and brother to Reverend Arthur Boyce, and extra servants had been engaged for this special occasion.

The guest list included Sheriff John Williams of Caerhays Castle, the Lord Lieutenant, two of Cornwall's Members of Parliament and a number of other notable local gentry.

Emily and Caroline had been up since dawn, supervising an augmented kitchen staff, which included Lord Boyce's own cook, brought to Cornwall by her employer especially for this occasion.

'I don't know what all the fuss is about, I'm sure,' declared the peer's cook, with a scornful sniff. 'I've cooked for ten times the number we're expecting tonight – and with half the kitchen staff.'

It was a comment the Bristolian cook had repeated at least four times during that evening. Standing hardly taller than Emily's shoulder she must have weighed at least fifteen stone. Her ability to organise an incredible variety of dishes ready for pot or oven with a minimum of effort on her part added credence to her words.

'Well, Ada, Caroline and I have tasted your wonderful cooking on our visits to Uncle Percy. We were convinced that nothing short of a whole army of kitchen staff would be required to help you.'

Ada looked sharply at Emily, suspecting she was being mocked.

She saw only Emily's open smile and said, 'Well . . . as Cornish kitchenmaids seem to work at only a quarter the speed of Bristol maids, you were probably wise, but when I'm working I like to have space enough to move around in me kitchen without tripping over them as seem more used to farm work than cooking.'

'You have only to say who you want removed and we will send them off to carry out other duties about the house, won't we, Caroline?'

The older of the two Boyce sisters failed to respond to the question and Emily realised she had not been listening. In truth, she had been preoccupied for weeks. Aware of the reason, Emily felt deeply sorry for her.

The twelve-month ban their father had imposed on John Kavanagh had expired a month before, but there had been no word from the young curate. As the days passed, Caroline became increasingly depressed by his failure to put in an appearance.

Emily had tried to reassure her sister by pointing out that John would have clerical duties to perform that could not be put aside at a moment's notice.

Despite her earlier unshakeable faith that once the ban came to an end, John would immediately return to Cornwall to claim

her, Caroline was now convinced her father had succeeded in his
aim of driving away the man she had hoped one day to marry.

'If you don't keep your mind on what you're doing in the
kitchen you're going to burn something and incur the wrath of
Ada – and I don't doubt she can strike a blow that would fell
a miner.'

Emily spoke jocularly to her sister in a bid to shake her from
her melancholy, speaking quietly so her words would not carry
to the ears of the formidable cook. However, Caroline was not
ready to be prised free of her misery quite so easily.

Caroline was less discreet. 'I really don't care if everything is
burned to a cinder and father's dinner party is a total disaster.'

Her words startled two of the temporary servants and Emily
hurriedly bustled her sister out of the kitchen to the garden.

Once out of hearing, she said, 'What are you thinking of,
Caroline? It was unforgivable to speak like that within hearing
of the servants.'

'I don't care,' Caroline declared defiantly. 'It is how I feel and
I don't care who hears me.'

'You *have* to care. We have a position to uphold in the community . . .'

Even as the words came out, Emily realised what she was
saying and broke off.

'You sound just like Father,' Caroline said accusingly.

'You're right, I do,' agreed Emily. 'But you're not the only
one to feel bitter about the way he's behaved towards us, you
know.'

Emily had never spoken to Caroline about Sam before. She
did so now, voicing for the first time her suspicion that their
father had been instrumental in sending Sam to Australia in
order to avoid any hint of a scandal.

'I wouldn't put it past him,' agreed Caroline. 'He would do
anything to prevent a family scandal, but although you were
friends, losing Sam hasn't broken your heart. I mean, it was not
as though you hoped to *marry* him. That is the difference between

what Father did to you and what he has done to me and John.'

For an unguarded moment Emily thought of revealing to Caroline just how much she cared for Sam, but she stopped herself in time. Caroline despised their father right now, but would share his horror if she confessed to having such feelings for a miner.

'That's not the point, Caroline. He had no right to have Sam sent away just because he did not approve of our friendship.'

'No, of course not. Any more than he had the right to send John away. I will never forgive him. *Never!*'

Despite the smouldering resentment of the two sisters, dinner at the St Cleer vicarage was a grand affair. It was also highly successful. The food was excellent, the drink plentiful and the company in good humour.

Emily had been concerned about Caroline, fearing she might voice some of the resentment she felt and embarrass her father and the guests. However, Caroline had been seated next to the Bishop of Exeter's chaplain, a man of considerable humour, who had happened to be in the area with his wife.

He was successful in temporarily lifting Caroline free of her depression, telling her stories that met with the disapproval of his wife, seated across the table from him. She had heard many of the stories before and when he neared the end of one that was risqué, albeit mildly so, she would cough loudly in a vain attempt to attract his attention and show her disapproval. When he ignored her she would talk embarrassingly loudly in a bid to drown out the punchline. But by so doing she only encouraged her husband to raise his voice further, which meant that far more guests caught the end of his story than would otherwise have been the case.

Nevertheless, the meal was declared a most enjoyable occasion. When it came to an end and the women had remained in the room for a suitable length of time, Emily, as her father's joint hostess with Caroline, announced that the ladies would now withdraw to the drawing room for coffee. The men would remain at the table to enjoy coffee and brandy and discuss current news and events.

As the men pushed back their chairs and rose politely to their feet – some more steadily than others – a maid hurried into the room and crossed to where Reverend Arthur Boyce stood.

'Excuse me, sir, but you have a visitor.'

'A visitor? In the middle of a dinner party?' Arthur Boyce frowned in deep annoyance. Visitors did not come calling in the middle of a formal dinner party. 'Tell whoever it is to come back at a more convenient time.'

'I did tell him you had guests, sir, but he said—'

'I do not care what he said. Tell him to go away,' Reverend Boyce thundered in his best pulpit voice and the words carried far beyond the dining room.

'Yes . . . Yes, sir.'

The maid was clearly unhappy, but she knew better than to argue with her employer. Dropping a quick curtsy, she fled from the room.

The interruption had delayed the departure of the ladies, but they now moved towards the door. As they did so a figure appeared in the doorway.

It was a tall, dark-haired young man wearing clerical garb and carrying a black, wide-brimmed, shallow-crowned hat in his hands.

At sight of him, the blood drained from Caroline's face and she began shaking uncontrollably.

II

'What the devil do you mean by coming here uninvited when I have guests – important guests – and frightening Caroline nigh to death? When I sent you packing I thought we had all seen the last of you.'

Flushed with an almost uncontrollable rage, Arthur Boyce confronted John Kavanagh. Caroline had been taken to her room and was being tended by Maude and a couple of women guests. The remainder of the women had been shepherded to the drawing room by Emily, who was explaining John to those who did not know him.

In the dining room, the effect of the arrival of Reverend Boyce's one-time curate provided an excuse, if one was needed, for a more than usually determined attack on the contents of the brandy decanter. It was currently making its second circuit of the dining table.

'I am deeply sorry, Reverend Boyce, but you knew I *would* come back. The arrangement was that I should go away and make no attempt to communicate with Caroline for a twelve month. I have kept my word. It is now thirteen months since I left St Cleer.'

'All right, so you have kept your word, but, dammit man, could you not have sent a letter instead of barging in to my house in the middle of a party, like some ill-bred young ruffian?'

'Once again, I can only offer my sincere apologies to you and your guests, Reverend Boyce – and especially to poor Caroline. I am very much afraid that in my euphoria at being appointed to my own parish and what it could mean for Caroline and me, everything else was driven from my mind. Besides, I have to be back in Yorkshire tomorrow night in order to officiate at two funerals in my present parish the following day. It left me just enough time to pay a fleeting call upon you—'

'Nothing you have said excuses such behaviour,' snapped Arthur Boyce. 'And what is all this nonsense about your appointment being meaningful to Caroline? I have agreed to nothing. Neither, as far as I am aware, has Caroline.'

'That is my reason for calling here today,' said the younger man. 'As for not informing you I was coming, I could say nothing in case my interview with the patron of my intended parish proved unsuccessful.'

Listening to the young cleric, Lord Boyce felt genuinely sorry for him. In a bid to dissipate some of his brother's anger, he spoke to John for the first time. 'What is the parish to which you are being presented, young man?'

Grateful for his intercession, John Kavanagh said, 'Winterbourne Abbas, in Dorset, sir. My family home is nearby.'

'Winterbourne Abbas, eh?' This from Brigadier Sir Gilbert Ashley, a veteran of the Indian Mutiny who lived in a grand but run-down mansion on the eastern fringe of St Cleer parish. 'My commanding officer in India came from there. Major General Sir Sinclair Rose. A fine soldier. Doubt if he's still alive though, it was a long time ago.'

'He is still very much alive, sir. Not only that, he is now *Lord* Rose. He is my uncle.'

'Is he, by jove? Here, Arthur, allow the boy to sit down and have a drink, at least. It seems he has travelled a damned long way to get here.'

Frowning but less angry than before, Arthur Boyce waved John to a seat. The brigadier poured him a large brandy, taking the opportunity to top up his own glass.

When John had taken the glass, Arthur Boyce said, 'You never mentioned to me that you had an uncle with a peerage.'

'It was given to him very recently,' John explained, grateful for the toning down of the parson's anger. 'He has been performing duties for Her Majesty, in London, for some years.'

'Comptroller of the Royal Household, no less,' said Lord Boyce. 'I know Henry well, please give him my regards when next you see him – and by the sound of it you will be seeing a great deal more of him now you have been appointed as his parson.'

'It's still subject to the bishop's approval, of course,' John replied. 'But I can think of no reason why he should object.'

'He had better not,' Lord Boyce said jovially. 'Her Majesty is

Head of the Church and your uncle is very highly regarded in Court circles. It would be a brave bishop indeed who chose to oppose your appointment without a very good reason.'

'I wholeheartedly agree with his Lordship,' declared the brigadier, who had consumed more than his quite considerable daily intake of brandy. 'But I still do not understand exactly what you are doing here this evening.'

'He was my curate for a while,' Arthur explained. 'We treated him as one of the family.'

This was not quite the truth, but John allowed it to pass unchallenged.

'That doesn't explain why poor Caroline was so upset when she saw him,' persisted the brigadier.

'Why don't we allow this young man to explain it to us,' said Lord Boyce. 'What exactly has brought you back here?'

Instead of giving the assembled men an explanation, John looked at Arthur Boyce before licking his lips and saying, 'I feel I should speak privately with Reverend Boyce before I say any more, sir.'

Lord Boyce smiled and said to his brother, 'This young man has come a long way to speak to you, Arthur. If the purpose of his visit is what I believe it to be I trust you will give him a sympathetic hearing, at least.'

'Thank you for your understanding, Percy. If you gentlemen will excuse me, I will ask John to accompany me to my study. You understand, of course that this situation is not of my making . . .'

Arthur Boyce and John Kavanagh had been absent from the room for about fifteen minutes when Caroline burst into the dining room with two women guests in close attendance.

Looking around the room agitatedly, she demanded, 'Where is he? Where is John? Oh, don't tell me Father has sent him away again.'

She appeared so close to tears that Lord Boyce jumped to his feet and, taking her arm, steered her to the chair he had just vacated at the head of the table.

'The young man is still in the house, my dear. He and your father are having a serious discussion in the study. One in which I have no doubt you figure largely . . . No, my dear, please sit down and be patient. If my reading of the situation is correct, you have shown admirable restraint for more than a year. It is my firm belief that your patience is about to reap its reward. Here, allow me to pour you a small brandy – no, please don't argue. It will do you good.'

Turning to the women who had accompanied Caroline, one of whom was his wife, he said, 'Jennifer, would you inform the ladies in the sitting room that Caroline has recovered and will no doubt be joining them in due course . . . But here is Arthur. You may be able to convey something of even more importance to them.'

Arthur Boyce re-entered the room, accompanied by John. When the younger man saw Caroline, his face lit up with delight and relief. He would have hurried to her, but the St Cleer vicar put a restraining hand on his arm.

'One minute, if you please, John.'

Looking across the room to his daughter, he said, 'John and I have discussed at some length the reason for his most unexpected visit here this evening. We are in agreement on a number of very important matters, but before I make any official announcement it will be necessary for you and he to talk together. You may accompany John to my study. When you have arrived at a decision please come to the sitting room. We will be there with the ladies.'

John and Caroline were absent in the study for some ten minutes. When they entered the sitting room Caroline's cheeks were flushed, but Emily thought she had never seen her sister look so happy.

Their arrival was a signal for all conversation to cease. An uncertain, expectant hush fell upon the room as the young couple paused close to the doorway.

Caroline's hand sought that of the young curate. Taking her hand, John held it very tightly.

'My Lord, ladies and gentlemen,' John spoke confidently, 'I apologise for my unexpected arrival earlier tonight, which caused an unforgivable disruption to your dinner party. However, I trust you will forgive me when I tell you the reason.' He smiled at Caroline before continuing. 'Caroline and I have been parted for more than a year, but this evening I returned to St Cleer to fulfil a promise I made to her before I went away. Soon after my arrival I asked Reverend Boyce for the hand of Caroline in marriage.' Pausing until the burst of applause died away, John continued, 'He was agreeable, but said any decision had to be made by Caroline herself. I have just asked her to be my wife – and she has agreed.'

There was another outburst of applause but, holding up his hand for silence, John said, 'I would just like to add that at this moment I am the happiest man in the whole of Cornwall . . . No, in the whole of Her Majesty's kingdom. I thank you for your understanding.'

The guests of Reverend Arthur Boyce crowded around Caroline and John to congratulate them on their engagement and Emily was the first to hug them both.

Yet, even while she was giving them her congratulations, Emily was aware what this meant for her. She would be the sole daughter living at the vicarage with her elderly father. Full responsibility for him would now rest with her.

He could live for another twenty – or even *thirty* years. By the end of that time she would be fifty years of age. It seemed she was doomed to a life of spinsterhood.

It was not what she had envisaged for herself.

5

I

When the *Bonython* was three days out of Plymouth it ran into a strong north-westerly wind and the ship's movements became alarmingly violent. Emigrants moving about the ship were thrown heavily against bulkhead and bunks, running a very real risk of injury.

The pitching and rolling of the ship was so violent that the captain decided it was far too risky for the women to come on deck and attempt to cook. Not that the majority of those on board could even think of eating. So few could face cooked food that the ship's cook was able to cope single-handed with those who retained an appetite.

It was not long before seasickness struck and conditions below deck deteriorated rapidly.

Sam was as sick as anyone. Doing his best to ignore the overpowering stench of the passenger hold, he sought the solace of his turbulent bunk.

Making a mumbled inquiry through the gap above the partition about the well-being of Jean and Primrose, he was told by a bilious mother that she and her daughter were lying down and waiting for death to put an end to their abject misery.

The bad weather lasted for a full forty-eight hours before, slowly, the wind eased and veered to the north-east.

Now the wind was astern of the *Bonython* conditions on board became far more bearable. All hatches were thrown open to allow in fresh sea air, holds were scrubbed and bedding and soiled clothing fluttered on long washing-lines criss-crossing the upper deck.

The appetites of those on board returned and Jean was kept busy cooking for stomachs that had rebelled against food for two days and nights.

Soon the ship turned on a more southerly course and as it eased slowly down the coast of Portugal the weather became warmer.

However, as the days passed, it was neither the sea nor the weather that became the enemy, but boredom. Games were organised and dozens of fishing lines trailed in the wake of the ship, but as each passing day became a repetition of the day before, tempers became frayed. Quarrels were frequent among the women and there were two fights between the men – both involving Ira Moyle.

'It's this heat, Sam. It's unbearable down below.'

Jean spoke as one of the men involved in the latest fight was helped aft to the cabin occupied by the ship's doctor, although there would be little he could do to treat the man's broken nose.

'You can't blame the weather for the behaviour of men like Moyle,' Sam replied. 'He'd be trouble anywhere.'

Moyle had twice tried to draw Sam into an argument, but he refused to be provoked by the violent miner.

'Isn't he the man you had trouble with on the first day we were on board?' Jean asked.

'That's right – and he hasn't forgotten it. He'll try to get his own back before we reach Australia.'

'If it's the man I think it is, he's spoken to Primrose a couple of times and always says "Hello" very politely to me when we meet on deck.'

Sam was surprised. He was also vaguely uneasy. 'I suppose there *might* be some good in the man, but be careful, Jean, he might be trying to get at me through you.'

That evening another fight broke out among the men on board, but this time Ira Moyle was not involved. The fight was between Cornish miners and a number of Welsh smelters.

On this occasion a knife was wielded and one of the men received a knife wound to his stomach. Although not life-threatening, the wound bled a great deal and women and children in the vicinity were terrified.

This time the ship's mate had the men who had taken part in the brawl escorted to the ship's captain and they returned considerably subdued.

Shortly after this the captain mustered the migrants on deck and warned them that he would tolerate no more fighting on board his ship. If anyone else caused trouble they would be placed in irons until the ship reached Australia, or sent back to England on board the next British warship they encountered. This was not an unrealistic threat; the *Bonython* had passed three Royal Naval vessels since leaving Plymouth and would no doubt meet with more before Australia was reached.

The captain's warning had the desired effect and, soon afterwards, the boredom of life on board was broken by a raucous ceremony to mark the crossing of the equator.

Two days later the *Bonython* was becalmed and the mate had a boat lowered and manned by some of the migrants. They were encouraged to expend their excess energy towing the ship across a calm sea.

Only a week after crossing the equator, the ship experienced the heaviest weather met with since leaving the English Channel.

For eight days the *Bonython* was buffeted by wind and sea. Those on board were kept far too busy maintaining their balance and avoiding injury to think of quarrelling – and soon there was something far more serious to worry about.

The ship began to take in water.

At first it was not thought to be too serious. The pumps were able to cope, even though it meant a great deal more work for the ship's crew. But then it became frighteningly apparent that the pumps were barely holding their own with the incoming water.

The mate called for volunteers among the migrants to help the weary crew to work the pumps. They quickly formed teams, each vying with the others in a bid to pump out more water during their stint on the pumps. Camborne men vied with Bodmin Moor men – and both were determined to outstrip the Welsh.

The ship's carpenters did their best to stem the water entering the ship, but their efforts met with little success. It seemed that shortly before arriving at Plymouth to take on the emigrants, the *Bonython* had run aground on a short voyage to Ireland. Quickly refloated, it was believed at the time that no serious damage had been caused. It now seemed possible that a rock had caused damage to the hull, below the water-line.

Word went around the ship that the captain had decided to head for Cape Town. There were facilities there to careen the ship and effect repairs. It was unusual for an emigrant ship to break its journey in such a manner, but the ship's carpenters needed to work from the outside of the hull.

Unless repairs were effected and very quickly – the captain feared he might lose his ship and the lives of everyone on board.

II

Because the *Bonython* was an emigrant ship the authorities in Cape Town kept it anchored in Table Bay for a frustrating twenty-four hours before they were satisfied there was no contagious illness on board.

The migrants found this a fascinating time. The harbour was situated at the crossroads of two great oceans. Although the opening of the Suez Canal only a few years before had resulted in a reduction in the amount of shipping using Cape Town, it was still a very busy port.

It was also a beautiful one. The town itself was built on flat land about the harbour but houses of the wealthy stretched back to the slopes of the flat-topped mountain that dominated both town and bay.

Named Table Mountain, the plateau-like peak was covered for much of the day by a 'tablecloth' of fluffy white cloud.

During the time the *Bonython* was prevented from berthing alongside the harbour wall, the pumps on board were in constant operation and the captain bombarded the port authorities with angry protests that his ship was likely to founder with great loss of life if they did not allow him to bring it alongside and take immediate steps to stem the leak in the vessel's hull.

Fortunately, once a clean bill of health was given to the ship the port authorities moved quickly. A steam tug came out to tow the barque and it was moored alongside a quay. Here, a team of African workers careened the ship over to one side, supported by ropes and stout timbers.

When this was done the ship's carpenters waited for low tide when, aided by shore-based shipwrights, they hoped to be able to assess and repair the damage to the *Bonython*'s hull.

Due to the uncomfortable but unavoidable angle of the ship and the proximity of the town, with all its attractions, the *Bonython*'s captain felt he had no alternative but to allow his passengers to go ashore and a gangway was put in place to link ship and land.

After almost two months spent on board their never-still 'home' most of the emigrants were eager to set foot on land again. Once there, they staggered about as though drunk, much to the amusement of the harbourside workers.

Watching from the deck of the *Bonython* with Jean beside him, Sam saw Ira Moyle and some of his friends weaving their way towards the town and its many grog-shops.

'I've no doubt some of the men will be staggering just as much when they return to the ship tonight,' he commented. 'Will you be going ashore, Jean?'

'I'm not sure,' she said. 'I'd like to – but only if you're going. But perhaps you'd rather go with the other miners and find a place where you can have a few drinks. I wouldn't blame you if you did. It's not been an easy voyage.'

'I don't have money to waste on drink,' replied Sam, 'but I would like to stretch my legs on dry land for a while. I'm sure Primrose would enjoy it too.'

'Oh, good!' Jean said eagerly. 'I'll just go and clean Primrose up a little. We won't be a few minutes . . .'

Half an hour later Sam, Jean and Primrose were walking towards the town. They too had experienced the nauseous sensation of a lack of balance when they set foot upon land. It had largely worn off now, but Primrose complained that her legs still wanted to 'go for a walk by themselves'.

The trio spent a couple of hours ashore, during which time they bought sweets for Primrose and a number of small items that would help to make life on board a little more bearable.

Using some of the money she had earned by cooking for the other emigrants, Jean purchased some perfumed soap which she hoped might keep some of the odours of shipboard life at bay.

Sam bought a large bag of oranges, which he thought would make a welcome addition to the bland diet available on the ship. He also bought paper, pencils and a book in which to write. During the long voyage he had begun taking writing lessons from Jean. When they reached Australia, he hoped to be proficient enough to pen a letter to his family – with a message for Emily – to inform them of his safe arrival and to surprise them with his newly acquired skill.

Passing through the area close to the harbour there was ample evidence that Sam's fears about the single men travelling on the *Bonython* were fully justified. There seemed to be a party going on in every grog-shop and the uncertain gait of many of the men who made their way from one to another was induced by alcohol and not water.

When they reached the ship they discovered that work had been suspended for the day because the tide was rising. The ropes connecting ship to the shore had been eased to enable the vessel to assume an upright position and make it more comfortable for those on board to sleep. In the morning it would be careened once more for repairs to the hull to continue.

In the meantime, in order to save time when work resumed the following day, some of the great beams that held the ship clear of the harbour wall had been left in place. This meant there was a considerable distance between the *Bonython* and the harbour wall.

The gangway linking the two was narrow and had only a single rope handrail on either side. It was highly dangerous and Sam lifted Primrose and carried her on board rather than run the risk of having her slip and fall in the water.

Sleep was hard to come by that night. Those men who did not return to the ship singing stumbled about in the lamp-lit hold alternately cursing and laughing at their drunken clumsiness.

Eventually, when one of the men in a nearby bunk began noisily retching, Sam decided that sleep would not be possible for a while yet. Rising from his bunk he pulled on his trousers and climbed the ladder to the upper deck.

It was warm up here but a light breeze made it quite pleasant. Standing in the shadow of the cookhouse, Sam took out his pipe, lit it and gazed at the town.

There was an almost full moon climbing in the sky to the north-east and Sam moved towards the guardrail to look at the lights that could be seen twinkling far into the distance on the shore.

'Couldn't you sleep either, Sam?'

He was deep in thought, thinking of Cornwall, of St Cleer – and of Emily – when Jean's voice broke in upon his thoughts and startled him. She had emerged from the hatch that led from the family hold without him noticing.

'No . . . no, it's pretty noisy down below and stifling hot.'

'It's the heat that's been keeping me awake.'

'What about Primrose? Where is she?'

'Walking around Cape Town today tired her out. I left her asleep. The woman in the next bunk is feeding her baby. She said she'd keep an eye on her for me. It isn't often I have a few minutes to myself, Sam.'

'No,' Sam agreed. 'She's a lovely little girl, but having to look after her on your own must be a big responsibility.'

'It might have been worse. Had things turned out differently I would have had two of them to look after on the voyage.'

Remembering the grim day when Jean had lost both husband and baby, Sam's teeth clamped more tightly on the pipe stem, but he said nothing. It was not a day he enjoyed talking about.

'I don't think I could have coped on board with only *one* had it not been for you, Sam.'

Jean was standing close and Sam could smell the perfumed soap she had bought earlier that day. The showers in a wash-room on the harbourside had been allocated to the women for the duration of their stay in Cape Town and she and Primrose had made use of them.

'You'd have managed,' he said. His mouth felt unnaturally dry, his throat tight. Jean was standing very close to him, the perfume of her soap strong. 'Phillip would have been proud of you.'

'He'd be proud of you too, Sam. You've been a true friend and looked after Primrose and me really well. I'm more grateful than I'll ever be able to tell you.'

She reached out a hand to him and he was acutely conscious of the fact that he was not wearing anything above the waist.

Jean was aware of it too. Her hand rested on his arm for a few moments then travelled upwards, to his bare shoulder . . .

Suddenly there was shouting on the harbourside. It was immediately apparent that a fight was in progress. As the shouting grew louder, a whistle was blown and Sam and Jean heard the sound of laughter and running feet.

Jean's hand slipped away from Sam's shoulder and they both looked shorewards. A number of men ran unsteadily along the quay towards the gangway leading to the *Bonython*.

There were lanterns strung along the quayside and by their pale yellow light Sam could see the men but he was unable to make out their faces.

As they approached the gangway one of the men slipped and two of the others began to half-carry, half-drag him towards the boat.

'I'd say some of the men who've been drinking have settled their grudges while they've been ashore,' Sam said.

'Yes.' Jean sounded disapproving. 'It's a pity we can't leave all the troublemakers here.'

The men had reached the gangway now but were having difficulty in helping the almost unconscious man on board.

One of those in the forefront of the group turned to say something to the man behind him. As he did so he lost his balance and clutched at the slack rope-rail for support. The rope sagged alarmingly beneath his weight and before anyone could do anything to save him, he pitched forward, plunging into the water that occupied the large gap between ship and shore.

The accident provoked great merriment from the drunken men, but Sam was aware of the cries of the man in the water. They were coming now from the stern of the *Bonython*, whence the current in the bay had taken him.

Hurrying to where the other men were still crowded around the gangway, Sam called, 'The man in the water – can he swim?'

In the sudden hush that followed his question, one of the men, apparently more sober than the others, replied, 'I doubt it. I grew up with 'im and there was nowhere we could learn to swim on the Wheal Druid.'

Sam ran to the stern of the *Bonython*. The light from the lamps on the quayside was too feeble to illuminate the water, but the sea sparkled silver in the bright moonlight.

He could see no one.

Suddenly and unexpectedly, there was a thrashing of water and an arm and a head broke the surface behind the ship. The man in the water uttered a choking cry of distress as he was swept still farther away.

Without a moment's thought, Sam clambered on to the raised stern of the *Bonython* and dived headfirst into the waters of Table Bay, hearing Jean's scream before he plunged beneath the water.

What the Camborne miner had said was true of most miners. There were few places close to inland mines where a boy could learn to swim. However, Sam, and the boys who lived or worked in the Caradon mining area, were fortunate. Nearby was a deep pool which had formed in an ancient working known as the 'gold diggings'. Generations of moorland boys had learned to swim here, Sam amongst them.

With powerful strokes he reached the spot where he had last seen the desperately struggling man, but he was nowhere to be seen now.

There was a strong current. Sam felt himself being drawn with it – away from the harbour and the *Bonython*. Suddenly there was a sound from nearby and the man he was seeking rose to the surface once more.

His struggles were feebler now but a couple of strokes brought Sam to him and he managed to grab the man's shirt as he went under yet again for what would probably have been the last time.

Hauling him to the surface, Sam said, 'It's all right, I've got you. Just don't struggle and we'll soon have you out of here.'

It was doubtful whether the man heard him. He had certainly stopped struggling and appeared to be unconscious. Sam prayed his condition had not gone beyond that stage.

His main concern now was to get the man out of the water as soon as possible. This was a matter of some urgency, but the *Bonython* was far behind them now as Sam and his deadweight burden were swept out into the bay.

Meanwhile, back on the ship, a panic-stricken Jean had found Henry Hunkin and told him what had happened. The ship's mate took immediate steps to launch one of the *Bonython*'s boats and ordered its crew to search for Sam and the man who had fallen overboard. He also despatched a seaman to inform the harbour authorities and urge them to send out as many boats as could be manned to scour the bay.

None of this was known to Sam and he began to think that both he and the man he was holding were doomed to die. Then he realised the current was carrying them in the direction of a large steamship, which had only recently arrived and was anchored in the bay.

From the number of lights showing on the vessel it was clear that it was a passenger ship.

By kicking out and paddling desperately with his free arm, Sam managed to maintain a course towards the unknown vessel, at the same time shouting as loudly as he could.

Soon he was close enough to observe that his cries had been heard. He could see people running around on the deck, trying to ascertain whence the cries were coming. Even so, he was likely to be carried past the bow of the anchored vessel before help was forthcoming.

Suddenly he was swept against something painfully hard. He grabbed at it instinctively and realised that by sheer good fortune he had bumped against the ship's anchor chain.

Pulling the unconscious man towards him, Sam crooked an arm about the chain. By gripping with his legs too, he was able to hold his burden above water.

Safe for the moment, he redoubled his shouting, able now to tell anyone who was listening exactly where he was.

It seemed to Sam he was clinging to the chain for an age, but he was receiving encouragement from those on board now, as they urged him to hold on, crying out that help was coming.

The current was strong, imposing considerable strain upon Sam's arms and legs. When he was beginning to think he would be able to hold on for only a few more minutes, a boat moved out from the shadow of the ship and edged towards him.

Moments later arms reached out. Taking the rescued man from him they dragged him inside the boat. Next it was Sam's turn. As he was being pulled in to the boat, he gasped, 'He needs a doctor . . . urgently!'

'Don't worry, we've got a good doctor waiting at the gangway. If he can be saved, our doctor's the man to do it.'

A few minutes later Sam and the rescued man were being lifted on to a platform at the foot of the gangway that led up to the ship's deck. Above him a crowd of excited passengers crowded around the guardrail and set up a cheer as Sam was helped on board.

At the top of the gangway one of the ship's crew held a lantern close to the man Sam had saved and who had been carried on deck.

It was now that Sam saw the man's face clearly for the first time and the countenance shocked him. The man he had risked his life to save was Ira Moyle!

III

While the doctor worked swiftly in a desperate attempt to revive Ira Moyle, Sam told the first mate of the steamer, SS *Eastern*

Prince, what had occurred. Around him, a circle of passengers listened in respectful silence.

The first mate said nothing for a few moments, then he spoke gravely, 'You were very, very lucky, son. There is nothing but ocean out there between the *Eastern Prince* and America. If you hadn't bumped against our anchor chain and managed to hold on . . .' He shrugged. 'Not that you'd have suffered for very long, the seas about here are full of sharks. I reckon you are the luckiest man alive right now.'

While the mate was talking, the ship's doctor came upon the scene, unnoticed. It was he who spoke now. 'No, Mr Gordon, it's the *other* man who is the luckiest man alive. This one's a hero. Knowing about those sharks of which you're talking it would take a very brave man to dive into the sea to rescue a drowning man in daytime, let alone take such a risk at night.'

There were murmurs of agreement from the listening passengers, but Sam hardly heard them. He had not given a thought to sharks when he dived in the water, although he knew they were in the area. They had been following the *Bonython* for days before the ship put into Cape Town.

Shaking off the thought of what might have happened, he asked, 'Ira Moyle . . . the man who fell into the water. Is he going to be all right?'

'I think so, although it's more than he deserves. Salt water is a very efficient emetic. It has effectively cleared his stomach of enough alcohol to kill a man not used to it. I'd say that, one way or another, he owes his life to you.'

The passengers crowded around Sam now, congratulating him on his courageous act. A few minutes later the ship was hailed by the coxswain of one of the boats that had put out to search for the two missing men and he was informed that both were on board.

Before the boat came alongside, one of the passengers was able to provide Sam with dry clothing, of a quality finer than any he had ever possessed before.

As he was led to the gangway he asked after Ira Moyle once more and was told the doctor would keep him under observation until morning. Then, if he was well enough, he would be sent back to the *Bonython*.

As Sam was about to descend the gangway, one of the passengers came forward. To general applause, he pressed a small leather satchel into Sam's hands, saying, 'We have had a collection among ourselves to show our admiration for your bravery.'

Before the astonished Sam could stutter out his thanks, the donor of the gift had backed away to be swallowed up in the crowd of applauding well-wishers.

Sam encountered more adulation when he arrived back on board the *Bonython*. Jean was the first to greet him, hugging him warmly and clinging to him when he stepped on board.

She had thought him dead and her tears were of genuine relief. Others reached out to touch him and call out their praises as he crossed the deck.

All Sam wanted to do now was make his way to his bunk space and escape from the fuss that was being made about something he had done instinctively, but he was not to escape so easily.

The captain wished to speak to him and Sam was ushered into his presence by the mate.

Shaking Sam's hand warmly, the captain pressed him to accept a drink of Cape brandy.

Sam was not a drinking man, but he had seen the eager look on the mate's face when the invitation was extended to him too. He decided it would be churlish to refuse.

Waving him to a seat, the captain said, 'The mate has told me what you did, Mr Hooper. I am grateful to you, very grateful indeed. It is my proud boast that in all the years I have commanded the *Bonython* I have never lost a passenger through misadventure – and none from illness during the last two voyages to Australia. Had it not been for your courage and resourcefulness that record would have gone. Do you know the name of the man you rescued?'

Sam nodded. 'Yes, sir. He's Ira Moyle, a miner from Camborne.'

'Is he a friend of yours, Mr Hooper?'

'No.' Sam did not choose to amplify his reply, but the mate did.

'Moyle is a troublemaker. He is one of the men you warned about their future conduct. Probably the ring-leader of all the trouble we've had on board.'

'Was Moyle drunk at the time he fell into the sea?' the captain asked Sam.

Sam remembered what the *Eastern Prince*'s doctor had said. He owed Moyle nothing and could have repeated the medical man's words. Instead, he said, 'I saw him fall and I think it was probably an unfortunate accident. He lost his balance, grabbed for the rope at the side of the gangway, and missed. Had he been able to swim he'd have got out of the water by himself and no one would have known of his accident.'

'But he could *not* swim,' the captain said. 'He was damned lucky that you could – and that you had the guts to go in after him. I hope he realises just how lucky he is. Did he come back on board with you?'

'No,' Sam replied. 'I managed to get him to a steamer, the *Eastern Prince*, anchored out in the bay. The doctor on board said he wanted to keep Moyle there overnight, just to make sure he is all right.'

The captain returned his attention to the mate. 'When Moyle comes back on board I want to see him. He may have been sober, as Mr Hooper seems to think, but he's caused enough trouble since he came on board. I'll warn him that if he so much as sneezes too noisily while he's on my ship, I'll have him clapped in irons for the remainder of the voyage.'

It took three tides for the leak in the hull of the *Bonython* to be repaired and caulked in a manner that satisfied the captain. Once this was done he set sail on the next rising tide – but with fifteen fewer passengers than had set out on the voyage from Plymouth.

Eight Cornish miners, lured by the talk of diamond finds in the Kimberley region, had decided South Africa had more to offer them than the copper mines of Australia. They deserted the ship.

Another seven members of a family from Wales, unable to cope with conditions on board the emigrant ship, had taken advantage of the unexpected landfall and abandoned the *Bonython*, choosing to take their chance in a country about which they knew absolutely nothing.

Although they were now at sea once more, Sam had made no attempt to check on the well-being of Ira Moyle. He had risked his life for the Camborne miner, but his bravery had been very well rewarded.

The purse given to him on board the *Eastern Prince* contained the astonishing sum of ninety-seven pounds – in gold coin. It was as much as Sam might have expected to earn in a good year in the mines of Bodmin Moor.

Added to the money he already carried, it would ensure him a sound start in the new land.

When the ship cleared Table Bay, Jean went to the galley to help in preparing the evening meal, leaving Primrose in Sam's care.

He was playing a string game with her, crouching down and helping her to make interesting patterns on her small fingers, when she suddenly looked up and smiled at someone who had come to stand behind Sam.

Glancing over his shoulder he saw it was Ira Moyle. Standing up slowly, he turned to face the Camborne man.

Ira seemed to be having difficulty in finding words and Sam said, 'I'm glad to see you up and about. It was by no means a certainty when they carried you on board the *Eastern Prince*.'

Finding his voice at last, Ira said, 'The only thing that's certain is that if it hadn't been for you, I'd be a dead man now. There's no one else would have done what you did. I owe you my life, Sam Hooper. I promise you I'll never forget that, not as long as I live.'

He held out his hand and when Sam took it Ira gripped it so hard that Sam felt the Camborne man's gratitude was likely to cost him crushed fingers.

'It's not only the rescuing of me I have to thank you for, either,' Ira continued. 'By telling the captain that I wasn't drunk when I went overboard, you saved me a whole lot of grief.'

'Well, you weren't the worst of 'em,' Sam said, embarrassed by Ira's declaration of gratitude. But there was more to come.

'I'm sorry you and I got off to a bad start when we first came on board. It was entirely my fault. If there's any way I can make it up to you . . . ?'

'Forget it,' Sam said. 'We're both grown men – and Cornishmen, at that. What's past is best forgotten. We're heading for a new life in Australia. Let's look forward to it.'

Still grasping Sam's hand, Ira said, 'You're a good man, Sam Hooper, and I like the company you're keeping on board.'

He nodded his head in the direction of Primrose. Despite intense concentration, she had managed to allow a string 'cradle' to slip from her fingers and now, frowningly, was attempting to untangle it.

'I've noticed you're not travelling as a family. Is the child on her way to join her father?'

Sam shook his head. 'Her father was my best friend. He was killed in a mine accident at the South Caradon mine on Bodmin Moor a couple of months ago. Primrose is on her way to join her grandfather at Kadina, on the Yorke Peninsula, in South Australia.'

Ira Moyle looked duly sympathetic. 'Is that where you're heading too?'

'Yes, I have an uncle there.'

'I'm going to Kadina too,' said the Camborne man. 'I don't know anyone there, but lots of Camborne men are working there. The letters they've sent home talk of there being plenty of work for Cornishmen in the mines in that area.'

'I've heard the same. Let's hope they're right and there's still work to be done. A lot of Cornish miners have gone out there in recent months.'

Ira nodded, but he was looking at Primrose. Suddenly looking up, he asked, 'Do you and the girl's mother have an understanding?'

The question took Sam by surprise. He was about to tell Ira it was none of his business, but something in the other man's expression caused him to change his mind. 'We've known each other since we were small children. Like I said, her husband was my best friend. I'm happy to do what I can to help her on such a long voyage.'

For a few moments Ira mulled over what Sam had said. He seemed uncertain of Sam's reply but instead of pursuing the matter, he asked, 'Would you mind if I played "Cat's Cradle" with Primrose and her string?'

'Of course not, go ahead.'

Ira crouched down beside the small girl and after a few words took the string from her. Untying it, he proceeded to demonstrate more variations of the game than were known to Sam. He made the string patterns skilfully and was able to show Primrose how to copy them, which delighted the young girl.

Watching Ira's patience with Primrose, Sam realised he was seeing a facet of the Camborne miner's character that was not usually shown to the men with whom he associated.

Ira was still entertaining Primrose when Jean came from the ship's galley with a pasty she had cooked for Sam in advance of the main meal.

Seeing Ira crouched down with Primrose, their heads close together, she was horrified and looked to Sam for an explanation.

'He's showing Primrose how to make a cat's cradle,' Sam said. 'And he's a sight better than I am at it.'

Looking up, Ira saw Jean. Standing up hurriedly, he left
Primrose protesting that he had not completed the string pattern
he was weaving on her fingers.

Snatching the cap from his head, he stammered, 'I . . . I'm
Ira Moyle. I . . . was just teaching Primrose a few little tricks
with an old piece of string.'

Aware that this was the man who might so easily have cost
Sam his life, Jean said frostily, 'It seems you have more success
with a piece of string than with a rope, Mr Moyle. Had you
been capable of keeping hold of the gangway rope when you
returned on board at Cape Town, Sam wouldn't have needed
to risk his life for you. It would also have saved everyone
involved a great deal of trouble.'

'That's perfectly true, ma'am. I've just been thanking Mr
Hooper. I realise I owe him my life. It's something I shall never
forget as long as I live.'

Ira's apologetic manner successfully blunted the edge of
Jean's anger. In a less brusque manner she said, 'No matter how
long your life may be, Mr Moyle, you'll owe every single day
of it to Sam.'

Looking to where Primrose squatted, frowning in concentration and frustration at the web of string wrapped around her
fingers, she said, 'You seem to have the knack of entertaining
young children, Mr Moyle. Have you left a family behind in
Cornwall?'

As though she had struck him a physical blow, an expression
of acute pain crossed Ira's face. He said, quietly, 'I had a little 'un,
once. She was about the same age as Primrose when both she and
my wife were carried off by smallpox. That was a couple of years
since. My wife was the daughter of a lay preacher, down by
Camborne, and we were both strong for chapel. When they were
taken away from me I lost my faith. Lost my way too, I reckon.
Perhaps the fact that I was saved when by rights I should've
drowned is God's way of telling me he still has work for me to
do. As the hymn says, "God moves in a mysterious way".'

As though suddenly embarrassed, Ira said, 'That's the first pious thought I've had since I saw my wife and daughter buried. I thank you for giving me that. Perhaps you'll let me speak with Primrose again?'

Ira walked away, leaving Sam and Jean staring after him, momentarily lost for words.

'Well, the world is full of surprises!' Sam said, shaking his head in disbelief. 'Who'd have thought of Ira Moyle as a staunch Methodist? Will you let him have anything more to do with Primrose?'

'Why . . . yes. Yes, of course I will. It sounds as though Ira Moyle has suffered quite enough for one man's lifetime. Perhaps he's right in thinking that God has decided He has need of him again.'

When Jean had returned to the galley, Sam remembered that she too was a Methodist and her late husband's father a lay preacher.

Seating himself on the deck beside Primrose, Sam offered the child a piece of the pasty Jean had cooked for him. Primrose declined it.

Holding up two hands, with the string wound around her fingers, she said, 'I want to do this . . . but you're not as clever as the man. When will he come back?'

6

I

The marriage of Reverend John Kavanagh to Caroline Boyce took place in the St Cleer church of St Clarus at Easter, 1873, seven months after the young couple's dramatic reunion.

John's family travelled from Dorset to Cornwall for the wedding. It caused a great stir in the vicarage when it was learned that Lord Rose was among them and had asked if he and his wife might stay at the vicarage with other members of the family.

Arthur Boyce need not have been concerned about accommodating the peer. Lord Rose was not a difficult man to please. Indeed, he seemed delighted with all that was done for him.

The wedding was a memorable occasion and passed off smoothly. Packed with well-wishers, the church was fragrant with the perfume of a plethora of spring flowers, donated by parishioners.

Outside, even those villagers who worshipped elsewhere were gathered to catch a glimpse of the bride and groom as they left, many calling out messages of goodwill.

It was a wonderful day for everyone. Everyone, that is, except Emily.

Watching her sister, the new Mrs Kavanagh, drive away in a carriage, bound for Liskeard railway station and a journey that was taking her to a married life outside Cornwall, Emily felt very alone, very vulnerable – and hopelessly trapped.

Her feeling of loneliness deepened the next day when family and guests departed from St Cleer. She began gathering about her the threads of a new and more inhibiting way of life that was destined to be her lot for as long as her father lived.

That evening, when Arthur Boyce was attending a meeting of his churchwardens, Emily went upstairs to the bedroom that had been occupied by Caroline since they were both small children.

Standing in the doorway she contemplated the blankets, folded neatly on the bare mattress of a stripped bed, and the dressing table and shelves now devoid of Caroline's personal toiletries and knick-knacks, collected during the childhood and early adult lives of the two sisters.

The only sign of the lately departed occupant was a small vase containing primroses, gathered by Emily and given to Caroline on the eve of her wedding.

Suddenly overcome by the depth of her feelings, Emily burst out crying and fled along the corridor to her own room. Here, flinging herself face down on her bed, she wept as she had not cried since the death of her mother.

During the ensuing weeks, Emily missed her elder sister far more than she could ever have imagined. Not only was there now no one to share the social duties undertaken on behalf of their father, but there was no one with whom she could discuss his constant irritability.

Maude too was becoming increasingly difficult. It seemed to Emily that the housekeeper was intent upon taking advantage of the fact that Emily now had no one else with whom to discuss household matters. The housekeeper began making decisions without consulting her.

Emily was aware that Maude was throwing down a challenge but it was one she was hesitant to do anything about. In
the past, Reverend Arthur Boyce had always sided with the
housekeeper and not with his daughter in any dispute about
household matters. Emily doubted whether he would change
his attitude now.

About a month after Caroline's wedding, Emily was leaving
the outlying home of a sick and elderly parishioner when she
saw Oliver Hooper, Sam's father, on his way back from Liskeard
market, driving a farm wagon. It was the first time they had
met for some months.

It was perfectly natural for the farmer to offer her a ride to
the village and she accepted readily, hoping he might have some
news of Sam.

After inquiring about the health of Oliver Hooper's wife, she
asked if he had heard from Sam, hoping the question sounded
more casual than it really was.

'As a matter of fact we had a letter from him only a week
ago,' the farmer said, adding, with considerable pride, 'written
in his very own hand, it was.'

Taken aback, Emily said, 'I thought Sam couldn't write?'

When Oliver Hooper threw her a look of surprise that she
should know of Sam's lack of learning, she said hastily, 'He
mentioned it once – at choir.'

'That's why we're so proud of him,' declared the farmer. 'That
Jean Spargo started teaching him on the ship to Australia – and
he's kept it up since they arrived, it seems. He's still not a great
writer, mind, but he's learned enough to put a short letter
together for us.'

Emily felt a sharp stab of jealousy at the mention of the pretty
young widow.

'I had forgotten Jean and Primrose were travelling with Sam,'
she lied. 'Are they both well too?'

'I suppose so. He didn't say anything about them, except to
say Jean was learning him to read and write, no more than that.

He doesn't mention young Primrose either, but then, it's his very first letter. I don't doubt it took him a long while to write.'

'Is he settling down in Australia?'

'I expect so. He doesn't say anything about life there, and there's not a mention of his uncle.'

'I wonder if he still thinks of his friends in the choir?' Emily said hopefully. It was always possible there might have been some message for her in the letter, perhaps hidden in an allusion to choir members.

'I'm sure he does,' said Oliver Hooper. 'A great one for the choir was our Sam. He used to enjoy his singing.'

'When you and Mrs Hooper write to him you must tell him you've met me and that I was asking after him. Tell him he's missed by everyone in the choir.'

'I will and it's kind of you to say so – but how about Miss Caroline, or Mrs Kavanagh as I suppose I must call her now? Have you heard from her? I wasn't in church myself to see the wedding, but Mrs Hooper was. She said it was one of the loveliest weddings she'd ever been to. Cried her eyes out, she did. Our Sam would have loved to have sung for that service, I don't doubt.'

For the remainder of the journey to St Cleer the conversation was of Caroline's marriage and of local happenings. Sam's name never entered the conversation again.

Emily knew it would have been very difficult for Sam to have sent a direct message for her in his letter, but she was disappointed that he had not managed to convey even an oblique reference to her. The thought of Jean Spargo being with him also disturbed her.

When she thanked Oliver Hooper for the ride and waved farewell to him she entered the vicarage in a very depressed state of mind.

She would have felt very different had she known that Sam *had* mentioned her in the letter he had sent to his family. Oliver Hooper had been asked to thank Emily for the generous gift she had given to him on his departure. He was to tell her he carried it with him at all times.

During their journey Oliver Hooper had wrestled with his conscience about whether or not to pass on the message to her, but practical considerations prevailed.

Because of the current perilous state of agriculture in general, when harvest time came around Oliver Hooper would need to plead with Parson Boyce in the hope that he would forego some of the tithes due to him.

He could not afford to antagonise the man who held the balance between ruin and survival for the Hooper family.

II

For a while during the summer of 1873 it seemed that mining on Bodmin might make a welcome recovery. The price of copper rose, making it once more a viable commodity. As a result, mines were re-opened and new shafts sunk.

Once again the clatter of steam crushers rent the air over wide areas of Bodmin Moor and families began making tentative plans for the future.

News of a resurgence in the fortunes of copper travelled fast. Out-of-work miners from the traditional tin-mining region centred on Camborne and Redruth flocked to the Caradon area.

Sadly, the euphoria lasted only a few months. As autumn approached, the price of copper plummeted yet again and the mining 'boom' died with the warmth of the summer sun.

Miners were laid off in their thousands and this time the plight of the men and their families was worse than ever before. By coming to Bodmin Moor many had cut their ties with the rest of the county, where they had been born. As a result, they had no family roots on the moor to cushion them against this latest disastrous mining recession.

Miners had the reputation of being proud and independent, but with starving families to support they were forced to swallow their pride and become beggars in a desperate effort to survive. But when their own efforts failed they realised that their wives and children possessed more appeal, and they were sent out to beg in place of their menfolk.

The moorland communities did what they could for the unfortunate newcomers, but their resources were limited. Finally, some of the miners – remarkably few in view of their desperation – took to stealing in order to survive.

One day, when Reverend Boyce had ridden off to attend a meeting in Bodmin, Rose Holman came to the St Cleer vicarage and related a harrowing tale to Emily.

A copper miner from the Caradon mine had left for Australia the previous year, leaving behind his wife and two sons, aged nine and seven. Nothing had since been heard from him.

Desperately short of money and unable to pay even the nominal rent asked for the cottage they occupied, the family had been evicted. For weeks they had made their home in a ditch, with only a rough latticework of sticks and grass to serve as a roof against the elements.

One day the woman fainted from a lack of food. Frantic with worry, the two young boys raided a nearby farmyard and stole half a dozen eggs, which they intended to cook for their starving mother. But their luck was out. They were caught by the farmer and promptly handed over to the local constable.

'They're coming up in Liskeard magistrates' court tomorrow,' Rose explained. 'I shall be in court to see what happens to them, but they really need someone to stand up and speak on their behalf. I'd do it myself but, as you know, most of the magistrates are either parsons, like your father, or else prominent members of the Church of England. If I were to do it I'd probably make matters worse. I thought, with Reverend Boyce being a Justice of the Peace you might speak to him on behalf of the boys. They're only children, Emily, two *good* boys, I promise you.'

When Emily hesitated, Rose added, 'It really is a deserving case – but before you make up your mind let me take you to meet Margaret Minns, the boys' mother.'

'All right, but you mustn't raise your hopes too high, Rose. I will not be able to raise the matter with my father. He never discusses his magisterial duties with me – and he would not dream of trying to influence a case being heard by another magistrate.'

When Rose appeared crestfallen, Emily asked, 'Where is the boys' mother now?'

'Staying with the wife of another out-of-work miner, a woman hardly better off than Margaret, but she does at least have a roof over her head. Others have donated what food they can spare in a bid to put some strength into Margaret before tomorrow's court hearing. She's determined to be in court when her boys are brought before the magistrate. To be honest with you, the way she is at the moment she'll probably drop dead along the way.'

Making up her mind, Emily said, 'Call back here in about half an hour. I'll come with you to see her and bring some food with me.'

As Emily walked through the house to the kitchen, she met with the tight-lipped and disapproving housekeeper and realised Maude had overheard the conversation. Emily was uncomfortably aware that her father would be informed the wife of the Methodist minister had called at the vicarage – and he would be given a highly biased reason for her visit.

It would undoubtedly cause another argument, but Emily decided she did not care.

Still in her twenties, Margaret Minns must once have been a

very attractive woman. Sadly, years of hardship and uncertainty, culminating in the harrowing events of recent months, had taken their toll. She looked frail, tired, and old beyond her years.

Despite this, when Emily and Rose entered the room where she was lying, Margaret made an attempt to sit up to greet them.

When Emily protested that she must lie still and rest, Margaret Minns said feebly, 'I've been lying down for far too long, Miss Boyce. I need to find strength enough to get to court for my boys in the morning. It won't come back to me if I spend my time lying abed.'

Struggling to a position that was half lying and half resting against the brass bedhead, she looked eagerly at Emily. 'Rose says you're going to help get Tom and Albert set free tomorrow?'

'I'm afraid it isn't quite as simple as that,' said Emily. 'The magistrate will make up his own mind about what to do with them.'

She looked accusingly at Rose. It was unfair of her to build up this woman's hopes in such a fashion.

'Margaret was asleep when I came back from speaking to you,' Rose said apologetically, 'I haven't spoken to her since.'

Margaret looked from Emily to Rose and back again, her expression registering dismay. 'But . . . you *can* help them? Your father . . . the parson . . . he's a magistrate.'

'He will not be trying your two boys, Margaret. Even if he were, I doubt if I would be able to influence the outcome of the case in their favour.'

'Oh! I thought . . .' Tears suddenly welled up in the young mother's eyes and overflowed, to run unheeded down her cheeks. Alternately clutching and releasing the bedcover, she said brokenly, 'They're good boys, Miss Boyce, especially Albert. He's only nine, but he's tried hard to behave like a man since his pa's been gone. He only did what he did because he couldn't bear to see me so ill and weak. It's all my fault.

What can be done for them, Miss Boyce? I really don't know what I'll do if they take the boys away from me. I love them both so much!'

'Now, now, Margaret, don't upset yourself any more. The boys won't be taken away from you.' Rose tried to reassure the weak and ill woman.

'Of course they won't,' said Emily, with more conviction than she felt. One of the area magistrates, Sir Richard Jane, had recently committed brothers, aged five and seven, to prison for an offence of fouling the water in a well!

Hopefully, he would not be trying the case of Albert and Thomas Minns and at this moment Margaret Minns urgently needed reassurance. Despite having grave misgivings about the wisdom of becoming involved, Emily said, 'I will go to court tomorrow morning and speak on their behalf, Margaret. In the meantime, you must not worry.'

The two women left Margaret Minns still crying, but with at least a glimmer of hope for her two young sons.

Outside the bedroom, Emily asked, 'Who was the farmer who handed Margaret's two boys over to the police?'

'Farmer Norris, of Tor Farm, over by Tremar.'

'Oh!' Emily's hopes sank. She knew Farmer Jacob Norris. He was an irascible bachelor farmer who had fallen out with his neighbours on many occasions over the years. Now a virtual recluse, he claimed he owed allegiance to no religious denomination.

The two Minns boys could not have chosen a more intransigent farmer from whom to steal.

'I doubt very much whether I will be able to persuade him to drop charges against the boys, but I will go to the farm and speak with him.'

III

Tor Farm was neither the most readily accessible nor the best kept of moorland habitations. The approach was by way of a rough track that had once been regularly surfaced using granite waste from a moorland quarry. That had been before Jacob Norris inherited the farm from his father at the age of twenty-three, almost fifty years before. Little maintainance had been carried out to the track since that time.

As Emily neared the farm she was forced to hoist the long skirt she wore clear of her ankles. Picking her way carefully through the mud, she tried to avoid the most obvious potholes.

Sited in a natural hollow, cleverly sheltered from the prevailing westerly wind, the farmhouse was no better maintained than the track. As Emily drew nearer she looked down upon a thatched roof in sore need of repair; a garden choked with brambles, and paths that were barely discernible beneath a variegated carpet of weeds.

When prolonged knocking at the farmhouse door brought no response, Emily searched the outhouses for Jacob Norris.

She eventually located him cleaning out a chicken house, the same one from which the Minns boys had stolen the eggs.

Norris was wearing filthy moleskin trousers, a collarless shirt and a coat made from the hide of a heifer. Complete with hair, the hide had holes cut in it for the reclusive farmer's arms.

Emily had visited the farmer on previous occasions, usually to check on his well-being when he had not been seen for some time by his farming neighbours. None would check for themselves, having suffered the abuse he invariably directed at them when all proved to be well.

Emily had never fared any better and this visit was no different. She was greeted with the words, 'What you doing 'ere, eh? Them nosey neighbours been minding my business again? Pity they ain't got nothing better to do with their time.'

'My visit has nothing to do with the neighbours, Mr Norris. I've come to speak to you about the two small boys you handed over to the police.'

Detecting a note of sympathy in her voice, Norris said aggressively, 'Small they may have been, but they was big enough to know how to steal my eggs.'

'Stealing anything is wrong, Mr Norris, and the boys have been brought up by their mother to know that. Unfortunately, the family has fallen on hard times – *very* hard times indeed. When the boys' father left to find work in Australia they and their mother were turned out of their home. They have been living outdoors ever since. Food was so scarce the mother starved herself, giving any food she obtained to the boys. As a result she became seriously ill. It was desperation that drove the two children to steal, Mr Norris. They could think of no other way to save the life of their mother.'

'If God had decided it was time for her to die, then so be it. I shouldn't have to remind *you* that it's *His* commandment that says "Thou shalt not steal".'

'But it couldn't have been His will she should die, Mr Norris. What has happened to the boys has brought her the sympathy she was never given before. She has been taken into someone's home. Given such a chance, she will hopefully recover, but the boys are her whole life. Her recovery depends largely upon you, Mr Norris. You seem to have forgotten there are another nine commandments. One of them calls for us to honour our parents and those little boys have certainly honoured their mother. Another commandment says "Thou shalt not kill" and I can tell you that the boys' mother is so desperately ill that if the magistrate deals harshly with her two children it will surely kill her.'

'What the magistrate does is up to him, not me. I was doing no more than any other man would have done,' Jacob Norris insisted defensively. 'What I have every right to do. Protect my own property. Besides, what do you mean by coming here and telling me what I should or shouldn't be doing? For all either of us know, these two have been going around like so many of their kind, thieving from them as has little more than themselves.'

Turning his back on her, the cantankerous farmer said, 'You've wasted enough of my time, now you can go about your business and leave me to tend to mine. Them whose job it is will decide what's to happen to those as can't keep their hands off what rightfully belongs to others. No doubt they'll do no more than pat 'em on the head, tell 'em not to be naughty boys and send 'em back home. Then they'll go straight back to stealing from someone else who's struggling to earn an honest living.'

Emily left the farm disappointed but not surprised at her lack of success. There had been a very brief moment when, as she spoke about the illness of Margaret Minns, she thought she detected a glimmer of sympathy in the expression of the farmer, but she had probably been mistaken. Jacob Norris was not known to be a compassionate man.

Thinking about this, she wondered how the farmer would react if the two young boys *were* let off with a light sentence? There was the chance that, in a fit of pique, he would report her for trying to persuade him to drop charges against them.

It was a serious possibility, yet she allowed herself a wry smile at the thought of her father's outraged reaction were *she* to be the subject of a police investigation and criminal charge!

IV

Despite Margaret Minns' determination to attend the Liskeard magistrates' court in support of her two young sons, she was too weak to stand unaided when she tried to leave her bed.

Nevertheless, she wept and pleaded with Emily and Rose to be allowed to accompany them to Liskeard. Rose was immovably firm. Margaret was unfit to leave the house and needed to remain confined to bed for a few more days.

Emily and Rose travelled to court in Reverend Boyce's pony-trap. In order to borrow the small vehicle Emily had made the excuse to her father that she had shopping to do in the mid-Cornwall market town. Preoccupied with the problem of removing the church bells from the tower for much-needed restoration work, Arthur Boyce gave her trip his distracted approval.

Had shopping really been the purpose of her journey Emily would have left pony and trap with the incumbent at the Liskeard vicarage, as she usually did. Instead, she placed it in the care of the ostler at the Webb's hotel in the town centre, and the two women made their way together to the courtroom.

The court officials recognised Emily immediately and she and Rose were given seats in the front row of the public gallery.

The court was crowded almost to capacity and Jacob Norris was among those present. He was seated, looking down at his feet. Emily was not certain whether or not he had seen her.

When the court was called to order and the magistrate and his clerk entered the room, Emily had a moment of despair. The magistrate *was* Sir Richard Jane, the least compassionate of those authorised to dispense justice in the courts of the area.

Seating himself on his high-backed seat, Sir Richard cast his gaze about the courtroom. He recognised Emily immediately. Although surprised, he acknowledged her presence with a cursory nod of his head. Then, with a similar gesture to his clerk, he signalled for the day's proceedings to commence.

It was soon apparent to Emily that Sir Richard's reputation was fully justified.

The first case involved a young woman who had stolen a neckerchief from a market stall. She pleaded that, having no money, she had stolen it as a birthday present for her desperately ill husband. They had been married for only a few months but he was not expected to live to see the year out.

Commenting that her husband would have been better served with an honest wife rather than a stolen neckerchief, Sir Richard sentenced her to six months' imprisonment.

Unperturbed as she was dragged to the cells screaming and pleading for mercy, he called for the next case to be brought before him.

Two miners were led from the court cells and stood in the dock accused of stealing and killing a sheep on Bodmin Moor. Both men admitted the offence, but claimed to have believed the sheep had no owner. They had killed it to provide meat for more than a dozen hungry families.

Sir Richard informed the prisoners that they were liable to be imprisoned for fourteen years, and pointed out that earlier in his lifetime they would have both been hung for the crime they had committed. He then ordered for them to remain in custody to face trial at the next Assizes.

When the two miners had been taken below it was the turn of Albert and Thomas Minns to be tried.

A murmur of sympathy arose from those in court when the boys were brought up from the cells. Emily's heart, too, went out to them.

Poorly clad and tousle-haired, both boys seemed thoroughly confused and frightened by what was happening to them. Standing side by side in the dock, Tom had to raise himself on tiptoe to peer over the edge. Albert was somewhat taller, but only the top half of his face could be seen as he peered wide-eyed at the impassive magistrate.

The charge was read out that they had feloniously and unlawfully stolen six eggs, the property of Jacob Norris, from a hen house on the farmer's farm. The clerk then asked Tom whether he pleaded 'Guilty' or 'Not guilty' to the charge.

Tom seemed confused but when Sir Richard said impatiently

'Come along, speak up, boy,' his confusion turned to fear and he turned to his brother for support.

'He doesn't know what you mean, sir,' explained Albert.

'Then for goodness' sake tell him,' snapped the magistrate.

'I . . . I'm not sure I know neither,' Albert confessed.

Before Sir Richard could say anything more, the clerk of the court said, more kindly, 'Thomas Minns, I am asking whether or not you took the eggs from the chicken house?'

Over the edge of the dock it was just possible to see Tom shake his head.

'Are you saying you did *not* take them?' asked the surprised clerk.

'No, sir. It was Albert who went into the chicken house. He handed them out to me – but I couldn't hold all of 'em. I dropped two and they broke, so he had to take two more.'

There was a moment of hastily stifled laughter in the court and, looking up at Sir Richard, the clerk said, 'I think we might accept that as a guilty plea, your worship.'

Sir Richard's reply was too low to carry to Emily, but the clerk turned immediately to Albert. 'Is what your brother said true? Did you take the eggs?'

Albert nodded his head vigorously, but the clerk said, 'You must *tell* me, Albert. Yes or no?'

'Yes, sir. I took them.'

'Thank you.'

Turning to the magistrate, the clerk said, 'I will record it as two guilty pleas.'

'Good! May we now have the facts, please?'

A police inspector stood up and presented the facts of the case. They were quite straightforward. Albert and Tom had gone to the farm, taken the eggs and been apprehended by Jacob Norris, who had then handed the boys over to the police.

The brief summary took only a few minutes. When the inspector had concluded he sat down and Sir Richard Jane fixed a stern gaze on the boys in the dock.

'Albert and Thomas Minns, you have heard the case against you, is there anything you wish to say to this court?'

Thomas was as confused as before, but Albert said, 'No, sir.'

It was at this moment that Emily stood up and said, 'If it pleases, your worship, I would like to say something on their behalf.'

Frowning, Sir Richard asked, 'Do you know the two defendants, Miss Boyce?'

'No, Sir Richard, but I have met their mother and I am familiar with their background. I feel it has an important bearing on this case.'

Sir Richard's frown deepened, but he said, 'Very well, you may come forward to the witness box and address the court – but please be brief. I have a very full list to deal with today.'

As Emily made her way to the witness box she was aware of the two young boys peering at her over the top of the dock. Young Tom was clutching the edge of the woodwork, pulling himself up to see the stranger who was going to speak on behalf of him and his brother.

Nervously at first, but with increasing confidence, Emily made an impassioned plea on behalf of the two brothers, pointing out their tender years, the absence of their father, the loss of their home and, latterly, the illness of Margaret Minns.

She referred to the intolerable burden that had been placed upon nine-year-old Albert, forced to take on the responsibility for his mother and younger brother, with no one to turn to for help or to ask advice.

Emily had the rapt and sympathetic attention of every man and woman in the courtroom who heard her speak.

All except one.

Sir Richard Jane listened attentively to what Emily had to say for perhaps two minutes. Then, apparently losing interest, he began studying a document that was lying on the bench in front of him.

Aware of the magistrate's lack of interest in what she was saying, Emily brought her plea to an end. Deeply disappointed, she realised she had achieved nothing.

It was a full half-minute after she had ceased talking before Sir Richard looked up in apparent surprise and said, 'Thank you, Miss Boyce. You waxed most eloquent. Your father would be proud of you. However, I regret you felt it necessary to make such an impassioned plea on behalf of two young scoundrels. By their own admission they chose to steal the property of an honest and hard-working member of our community.'

Emily opened her mouth to speak, but Sir Richard pre-empted her. '*Chose*, I say – and that is exactly what I mean. I have heard nothing in this court today to suggest that Albert and Thomas Minns ever contemplated any other means of solving the problems of their family. Their first thought was to steal. To take what did not belong to them . . .'

Meanwhile, Jacob Norris had listened with great concentration to what Emily had to say. Wrestling with his conscience, he sprang to his feet as Sir Richard dismissed Emily's plea and blurted out, 'Sir Richard, I want to withdraw the charges I laid against the two boys. What they done wasn't right, but neither is punishing 'em for trying to save their sick mother. I want 'em sent back to her. Miss Boyce is right what she said to me yesterday, punishing them is only going to punish their mother more.'

'Mr Norris!' Sir Richard snapped at the farmer. 'You will ask permission before you address this court. As for withdrawing charges . . . it is too late for that. What happens to the two defendants is no longer a matter for your concern. You will sit down and remain silent.'

'But it was *my* eggs they took, not the court's. *I* should be the one to say whether anyone gets in trouble for taking 'em . . .'

'Mr Norris!' Sir Richard's voice thundered out. 'You have been told to remain silent. Another word from you and I will have you detained for contempt of my court. Then you will be able to personally express your sympathy to these two young law-breakers – but I warn you, Mr Norris, *you* will still be there when they are released.'

Emily's hopes of securing the immediate release of the two young boys sank at the magistrate's words. It was apparent he had decided to send Albert and Tom to prison. Nothing she had said in mitigation had made any difference. Sir Richard Jane was living up to his reputation.

When Jacob Norris remained standing, a constable hurried across the courtroom to him. Taking the stubborn farmer by the arm, he led him through the door to the street outside.

When he had gone, Sir Richard brought the case to a swift conclusion.

Looking at the two young boys with a stern expression, he said, 'Albert and Thomas Minns, you have both pleaded guilty to the crime for which you have been brought before me. By so doing you have avoided wasting this court's time. For that I give you due credit. However, thefts by miners and the families of miners have reached alarming proportions. It is my duty to pass sentences upon you that reflect the concern of law-abiding citizens for such unacceptable behaviour. Thomas Minns, you will pay a fine of twenty shillings, or, in default of the same, go to prison for one month. Albert Minns, you are the older of the two and should have set your brother an example. Instead, you were the leader in this dishonest escapade. You will pay a fine of three pounds, or, in default, go to prison for three months.'

Emily's spirits lifted. She had brought with her more than enough money to pay the two fines and have the boys released that morning. For a brief, misguided moment she believed that for all his stern words Sir Richard had shown compassion, knowing she would probably pay the fines.

His next words gave her a rude awakening.

'In addition, as the instigator of this crime, I order you, Albert Minns, to receive six strokes of the birch, to be administered before your release, whether that be from this court today, or from prison on completion of your sentence.'

V

The sentence imposed upon the two young brothers provoked an eruption of outrage from the members of the public inside the Liskeard courtroom.

Sir Richard Jane called in vain for silence, his efforts seeming only to increase the anger of those who had witnessed his 'justice'. Eventually, his face purple with anger, he announced that he was suspending proceedings for thirty minutes and called for the court to be cleared.

Most of those who had watched proceedings inside the courtroom were miners. The heartless sentencing of Albert and Thomas Minns unleashed some of the anger, resentment and frustration felt by the out-of-work men.

Their noisy protests continued when they spilled from the court building to the street outside and quickly spread around the town.

Many miners and their families were in the habit of spending their empty days in Liskeard, preferring the bustle and illusion of wealth found in the town to the silent and wind-swept loneliness of the mine-dotted moor. Attracted by the noise of the ejected courtroom crowd they added their own anger to that of their colleagues when word went around of the sentences passed on the two small boys.

Emily, who had remained in the courtroom with Rose until the last of the crowd had gone, now emerged from the building. She was immediately recognised and loud applause broke out. As she walked through the crowd, hands reached out to touch her and there were shouts of approval for her support of the two Minns boys.

Before leaving the court, Emily had spoken to the senior policeman on duty, a man she knew by sight. She asked him who would carry out the birching of Albert.

'That depends whether his fine is paid or whether he goes to prison.'

'I shall pay the fine of both boys right away,' Emily declared firmly.

Ill at ease, the policeman said, 'Then I'm afraid the distasteful task of flogging the boy will fall to me, Miss Boyce.'

'I trust the blows will land lightly. After all, he's only a child and should never have been convicted in the first place.'

'It's a view as is held by many, Miss Boyce. I'll not hurt the boy any more than is necessary, but Sir Richard likes to be present when a flogging is taking place. If he thinks I'm holding back he's as likely as not to order someone else to step in and do the job instead of me.'

'Your understanding of the situation does you credit, officer. Perhaps you can tell me when the boys will be freed, once I have paid their fines?'

'The flogging will take place at the end of this morning's court, Miss Boyce – though with all this trouble, there's no telling when that will be. It certainly won't be before one o'clock.'

'Then I shall pay the fines and return at that time.'

After hurrying away from the angry scene outside the magistrates' court, Emily took Rose to the hotel where the pony was stabled. Here, she ordered tea before speaking of the events of the morning and deploring the punishment meted out by Sir Richard Jane.

Aware that Emily was extremely angry and upset, Rose did her best to be conciliatory. 'I don't think the magistrate had any alternative,' she said. 'After all, the boys did admit to stealing the eggs.'

'I know that, Rose, and he gave them the option of a fine
– which I am happy to have paid – but having heard the
circumstances leading to the theft he should not have added
a whipping to poor Albert's punishment.'

'The crowd thought so too,' said Rose. 'That was what upset
them so much.'

'Sir Richard will never accept any blame for the disturbance,'
Emily said bitterly. 'He will regard it as proof that the miners
are becoming increasingly lawless and hand out even harsher
sentences in the future.'

'Who would your father support – you or Sir Richard?'

Rose's question was unexpected and Emily needed to think
for a moment how best to phrase her reply. 'My father has a
great deal of sympathy for the miners and their families,' she
said eventually, 'but he would never accept hardship as an
excuse for breaking the law.'

'Is he likely to be understanding when he hears you spoke
up in court today on behalf of Albert and Tom?' Rose asked
shrewdly.

Emily shook her head. 'No, but somebody needed to speak
up for them – and pay their fines. Can you imagine what their
life would have been like in a prison?'

'Only too well!' came the grim reply. 'I've met with children
who have been to prison. They're never the same again. But it
wouldn't only have been the boys who suffered. I truly believe
it would have killed Margaret had they gone to gaol.'

'What do you know of Margaret?' Emily asked. 'She was far
too ill for me to form an accurate impression of her but I would
not have thought she came from a mining family.'

'She doesn't. Before Margaret married she was a lady's maid
in the house of the Earl of St Germans. I don't know how she
met up with her husband but she could have done a lot better
for herself. Between you and me, he's always been a bit shift-
less, never remaining at a mine for long, even when work was
available. I doubt whether she or the boys will ever see anything

of him again, although she's fully convinced he'll send for them when he's made some money.' Rose shrugged. 'Hopefully I'll be proven wrong. I've never been a good judge of men. It was lucky for me that William came along when he did, or I'd have probably ended up just like Margaret and the many others around here who are in a similar situation.'

Looking at Emily, she asked, 'Have you heard anything of Sam Hooper since he went away?'

The question took Emily by surprise and she said defensively, 'No. Is there any reason why he should write to me?'

Rose leaned towards Emily and rested a hand on her arm for a moment. 'I'm sorry, Emily, that was unforgivably rude of me. It was just . . . Oh, I don't know. I saw you together once or twice and thought that if things had been different . . . I mean, had you come from similar backgrounds, what a lovely couple you'd have made. He's a very nice young man. I believe that if his pa had given him a chance in life instead of sending him out to work as soon as he was big enough to pick up a shovel, he'd have made something of himself.'

Aware of how easy it was for the most straightforward statement to be distorted by village gossip, Emily said cautiously, 'Sam is missed by the choir. He had a fine voice.'

'I wasn't thinking only of the choir . . . You know he has asked after you in his letters?'

'How do you know that?' Emily demanded, startled by this news. 'When I spoke to Sam's father he said he had received only one letter from Sam and that it contained hardly anything at all. Of course, that was some months ago.'

'He has had at least two letters since then, although one was little more than a note. You were mentioned in all of them. At least, that's what Bessie told me and she has no reason to lie.'

Bessie was the wife of Sam's brother Daniel. Her father was a staunch Methodist and she and Rose knew each other quite well.

Emily was hurt that Sam's father should have lied to her, but Rose's words gave her a warm glow.

Keeping her feelings to herself, she put down her cup and said, 'Come along, let's see if we might have the boys released so we can take them home. Poor Margaret must be desperate for news of them . . .'

VI

Returning to St Cleer in the trap pulled by Reverend Boyce's high-stepping pony, it was Tom and not his older brother who was shedding tears.

On the instruction of Sir Richard Jane, the young boy had been forced to watch as Albert, the brother he revered, received six strokes of the birch at the hands of the burly police officer.

Albert took his punishment manfully, letting out an involuntary gasp of pain only when the first blow landed, but when he was released and Emily saw his pale and drawn face, she could have wept for him.

Margaret Minns had become increasingly anxious as the morning passed with no sign of her two sons. At midday she insisted upon being helped out of bed and into a chair close to a window, from where she could see the lane along which the boys would be coming.

She had a long wait. It was almost three o'clock before she saw a trap pulled by a trotting pony bowling along the lane. Inside were two women – and two small boys.

'It's them!' she cried. 'The boys . . . they've got them free! Help me up . . . please. I want to meet them at the door.'

The woman who occupied the cottage, assisted by her daughter, helped Margaret to the door. They stayed near and would have supported her, but she shook them off and when the boys reached the garden gate she was standing, unsupported, in the doorway.

'Ma!'

Delighted, Tom ran along the garden path and flung himself at his mother, almost knocking her off balance.

Albert came along the path more slowly, but his expression showed that he too was delighted to see his mother on her feet.

With an arm about Tom, she held the other out to Albert, saying, 'You're taking your time, Albert. Come here quickly, so I can hug you too.'

'He can't hurry, Ma,' Tom cried. 'His back hurts. They flogged him – and they made me watch.'

Margaret's jaw sagged and she looked to Albert for confirmation, but it was Rose who replied as she came along the path behind Albert, with Emily by her side.

'Albert has been a very brave boy, Margaret. The constable who had to birch him said as much.'

'But why was he flogged?' In tears now, Margaret said, 'Oh, Albert, come here, my son . . .'

Reaching out, she pulled him to her but he winced and she released him immediately.

'I'm sorry, Albert, it's all my fault . . .'

It was too much for Margaret in her weakened state and she began to cry uncontrollably.

In a bid to comfort her, Albert said, 'It's all right, Ma. It didn't really hurt me . . . well, not *too* much.'

'It could have been a whole lot worse, Margaret,' said Rose. 'Albert was given a three-pound fine, or three months in prison, and Tom a pound, or a month in prison. Miss Boyce paid their fines. She also spoke up for them in court.'

Margaret switched her tear-filled gaze to Emily. 'Thank you. Thank you very, very much. I'll try to repay you one day. They're not really bad boys. If only I'd been more able to cope with things.'

Emily thought she had never seen a woman more broken in spirit and she said sympathetically, 'It's *not* your fault, Margaret. Albert should not have done what he did, but he is young and had no one to turn to for help. Even Jacob Norris realised it. He actually came up to me afterwards and said he was sorry for turning the boys over to the police. An apology from Mr Norris is without precedent. He would not condone what they did and said they deserved to be fined, but he was horrified that the magistrate ordered a young boy to be flogged for trying to help his sick mother. Others agreed with him. They created such a fuss in court over the sentence that the magistrate could not continue. He had to order the court cleared.'

Margaret began crying once more and Emily said hastily, 'We must put this in the past, Margaret. The important thing now is to get you well, find somewhere for you and the boys to live and see if we can obtain work for you.'

'There are thousands of women looking for the same thing,' Margaret said bitterly. 'I'm not in this state because I haven't tried to find work. It just isn't around to be had.'

'We'll see about that,' Emily said determinedly. 'You leave it to me.'

Once outside the cottage, Rose said to Emily, 'I know you were just trying to cheer up Margaret – and there's no one who needs it more – but she's going to be very disappointed if nothing comes of the promise you've made to her.'

'Something *will* come of it,' Emily declared. 'I intend taking the first steps towards a solution to Margaret's problems immediately.'

Despite her assurance to Rose, it was a slightly less self-assured Emily who picked her way through the mud of Jacob Norris's farmyard half an hour later, her skirts raised halfway up the calves of her legs.

The quarrelsome old farmer saw her coming and prepared

himself for the tirade he felt certain she was about to deliver. But Emily's opening words took him by surprise.

'Mr Norris, outside the Liskeard magistrates' court this morning you expressed regret for having Albert and Tom Minns brought before the magistrate. Did you mean that?'

'I don't say things I don't mean. Not like some folks I could name.'

'Good! Then perhaps you would like to make amends for having a nine-year-old flogged and he and his seven-year-old brother branded as thieves for the remainder of their lives?'

'If it's money you're after, you'll need to think again. I feel sorry for 'em, yes, but I've no money to spare for the likes of they.'

'I'm not asking you for money, Mr Norris, but I believe you own that old cottage along the lane. The one I passed on my way here. I looked in through the windows and noticed a piece or two of furniture in there as well.'

'That's right. My ma's brother lived there until he died. That was nigh on ten years ago. It hasn't been touched since then.'

'As it's been empty for so long, why not allow the Minns family to move in? It would give them a roof over their heads, at least.'

'Ah well,' Norris said cautiously, 'folk'd pay good rent for a cottage the likes of that.'

'The Minnses *have* no money, as well you know,' Emily retorted. 'Letting them move into the cottage would be an act of contrition on your part for what happened to the two boys. Nevertheless, Margaret Minns will be happy to carry out some domestic work for you when she is well enough. The boys could help around the farm for a few coppers too. I have no doubt you could manage that without any hardship. On my last visit I watched you straightening up after you had been working in the chicken house. You are not getting any younger, Mr Norris. A little help around the farm would not come amiss.'

'*I'll* be the one to decide whether or not I need help around the place, not you. There'll be no one poking about my house and nosing into my affairs. No, I'll not have it.'

'Do I take it then that you will allow the Minnses to move into your cottage and ask for nothing in return? That would be a *most* charitable act indeed.'

Emily was aware she was forcing the issue and when a long silence ensued, she feared she might have pushed the eccentric farmer too far, too quickly.

To her relief and delight, he growled, 'There's no one gets anything for nothing in this life. If they're going to move into the old cottage rent free I'll expect the boys to help about the farm and not look for any pay. Their mother too, sometimes.'

'Margaret Minns will need to have money coming in in order to feed her family,' Emily said. 'I am hoping to find more suitable work for her, but I have no doubt the boys will be happy to help you in any way they can.'

Emily left Jacob Norris's farm well pleased with herself. The first part of her plan had been more successful than she had dared hope.

The next would not be quite so easy. Of this she was certain.

VII

Reverend Arthur Boyce travelled to Liskeard to carry out his magisterial duties two days after the trial of Albert and Tom Minns. In St Cleer, Emily awaited his return with considerable trepidation. She had not told her father of her own eventful visit to the magistrates' court, afraid of his predictable reaction. Nevertheless, she was aware he would be given details by the court officials – and would be furious at her involvement.

All went very much as she had anticipated – except that it was Sir Richard Jane and not a court official who told Arthur

Boyce of the role played by Emily in the near-riot that had erupted when the two young sons of Margaret Minns were sentenced for theft.

'I am angry beyond words that I should have learned of this matter from Sir Richard and not from my own daughter.'

Arthur Boyce and Emily faced each other across the width of his desk, as they had on so many occasions before. 'Maude told me that Rose Holman had called at the house and spoken to you, but I thought it most probably concerned some simple village matter. To think I even allowed you to use the pony and trap! Had I known I would have forbidden you to leave the house.'

Emily had been dreading this confrontation, but she was ready for it and determined not to allow her father to browbeat her into submission on this occasion.

'I *wanted* you to hear about it from others first. Then I could be certain that you would come to me, hear the *full* story and it could be laid to rest, once and for all.'

Her reply took Arthur Boyce by surprise. He had been expecting her to make excuses for not telling him what had taken place in the Liskeard magistrates' court.

'If what I have heard is true – and I have no reason to doubt the word of Sir Richard Jane – then it is not a matter that may be dismissed quite so easily. According to Sir Richard you must take responsibility for much of the outrageous behaviour that took place because of your decision to defend the actions of the two young thieves in an open court.'

'No, Father,' Emily said determinedly. 'Responsibility for the genuine outburst of anger from those in the public gallery lies with Sir Richard, as it was the direct result of the sentences handed out by him to children aged nine and seven. It was his actions that were disgraceful.'

'Sir Richard was carrying out his magisterial duties,' Arthur Boyce said pompously. 'Punishing law-breakers—'

'*Punishing!* You talk of punishment for a seven-year-old? Not that Sir Richard has ever shown compassion for children, whatever their age. The sentences he metes out to them are certainly not in keeping with the teachings of Our Lord . . . but I hardly need to remind you of His words. Nor do I believe *you* would commit a five-year-old to prison, as Sir Richard has on occasion, or sentence a nine-year-old to a flogging because in sheer desperation he stole a few eggs in order to save the life of his starving mother. I, and others in court, were incensed that Sir Richard chose to add a flogging to an already severe sentence. It is my sincere belief that had you been on the bench you would have tempered justice with mercy.'

'Not knowing all the facts of the case it is impossible to say what *I* would have done – but that is not the issue here.'

'I know. You are angry because I became involved in a case held in the court where you sit as a magistrate.' Emily was determined not to sound apologetic, but neither did she wish to further antagonise her father if it could be avoided. 'I had little choice, Father. Rose Holman came to the house to see me, explained the details of the case, and asked for my assistance. I could not refuse.'

Momentarily forgetting his anger, Arthur Boyce exclaimed, 'The wife of the Methodist minister came here seeking your help? Are you telling me these two boys are from a Methodist family?'

'I don't know, Father. The question of the poor woman's religion has never been raised, but I have good reason to believe she and the boys belong to the Established Church. For this reason alone I could hardly have refused to help and have it said we lacked the compassion of the Methodists.'

Somewhat mollified, but by no means fully satisfied with Emily's explanation, the parson said, 'Nevertheless, did it not occur to you that the sympathy you were to show to those two young thieves might have been misplaced?'

'Of course.' Emily believed she was on firmer ground now.

'That is why I visited their mother before agreeing to help. Sadly, I found the story told to me by Rose was all too true. The mother is a good woman who has come desperately close to death. Before her marriage she was a lady's maid, for the family of the Earl of St Germans.'

As Emily had anticipated, this latter piece of information impressed her father more than anything else that had so far been said in defence of Margaret Minns and her two children.

'What of her husband?' he asked.

'He worked in the mines, but when he was put out of work he went to Australia, promising to send for the family as soon as he was able.'

Arthur Boyce was fully aware of the problems besetting the Cornish mining industry. Nevertheless, his next words were less than sympathetic.

'I cannot understand any man abandoning his family and going off to a strange land without first making adequate provision for those he leaves behind.'

Observing Emily's momentary unguarded expression, he added, 'Oh yes, I know things are bad for miners at the moment, very bad indeed, but there have been good years too. A prudent man would have put money aside when it was available.'

When Emily made no reply, he continued, 'I am extremely disappointed by the manner in which you have conducted yourself over this matter, Emily. You should have consulted me before taking such foolish action. You must have known it would prove a great embarrassment to me – and might well have brought discredit upon more important members of the family. However, I am prepared to accept that, however misguided, your actions were prompted by charitable motives. I will therefore overlook your indiscretion on this occasion – on condition that your work on behalf of the needy is in future conducted along more conventional lines.'

Emily nodded, as though agreeing with her father's condescending statement. 'Thank you, Father, but with so much need in the parish right now I am finding it very difficult to cope with the many demands upon my time. I have decided I need to take on a personal maid, to help me both in and outside the house.'

'A personal maid . . . ?'

Arthur Boyce looked at his daughter with growing disbelief. 'I trust you are not talking of the mother of those two convicted young thieves? Oh no, that would be carrying charity too far!'

'What you really mean is that it would be bringing it too close to home. That is hypocritical, Father.'

Emily braced herself for yet another of their long and acrimonious arguments, but she was determined to stand her ground on this occasion. 'I want a personal maid and Margaret Minns desperately needs employment. What is more, she has all the qualifications for such a post.'

'Are you not forgetting something, Emily? She also has two sons who have both been convicted of theft. I refuse to have them living beneath my roof.'

'Margaret would be a living-out maid.'

'Really? I thought that one of the mitigating facts produced to the court was that the family *has* no home.'

'When the case was heard that was quite true, but Jacob Norris has allowed them to move into the empty cottage on his land.'

'Norris? The man from whom the boys stole the eggs?' Arthur Boyce was well aware of Jacob Norris's anti-social reputation.

'That's right, Father. When he heard of the family's circumstances he tried to withdraw the charges he had laid against the boys. Sir Richard refused to allow it.'

'By the time the case reached court it was too late for Jacob Norris to change his mind,' said her father, less belligerently. 'But I am amazed that he, of all people, should even have tried – and then to give the family a home too . . .'

'Indeed, but it is an act of charity that should be used as a yardstick for us all, should it not?'

Arthur Boyce realised belatedly that he had walked into the

trap so neatly set by his daughter and there was no escape. The Wesleyans would make much of the fact that Jacob Norris had been shown to be more charitable than the vicar of the parish. He had no doubt that if Emily, his own daughter, did not get her way, it *would* become known that he had refused to employ the mother of the two boys.

'Do you have any proof that this woman *was* a maid in the St Germans household?'

'Rose Holman told me she was. I would not doubt her word.'

'The word of a third party, however credible, is not sufficient in such matters,' Arthur Boyce snapped. 'A satisfactory reference will be required. If one is forthcoming, Maude will interview the woman to ascertain whether or not she is suitable for the post.'

'No, Father, Maude will *not* interview her. If Margaret is to be employed here as *my* personal maid it will be because *I* think she is suitable. *I* will employ her and decide on her duties within the household.'

Emily knew that if Maude became involved Margaret Minns would not be taken on.

For a moment it seemed Arthur Boyce would insist upon Maude's right to interview Margaret. Instead, he shrugged in the manner of a weary man. 'Very well, but if she proves unsatisfactory in any way the responsibility will lie with you. I will leave it to you to inform Maude. You will also ensure that this woman conforms to the routine of the household.'

Slumping down in his chair, Arthur Boyce waved Emily from his presence. For the first time Emily could remember, she actually felt sorry for him. She wanted to go to him, give him a hug and say 'Thank you'.

'Go now, Emily, before I change my mind.'

Emily turned and left the study. As she closed the door behind her she realised this was the first time she had ever won a serious argument with her father.

VIII

Margaret Minns began work at the vicarage three weeks after Emily gained the parson's less than enthusiastic consent to employ her.

The miner's wife was still not fully recovered from her months of near-starvation but she was determined her weak state would not prevent her from carrying out her new duties. Emily had provided her with an opportunity to regain respectability and she was determined not to allow it to slip from her grasp.

The first thing she did was to inspect Emily's clothing, re-ironing much of it and sending some back to the laundry-maid, supervising the girl as she worked and explaining how a lady's clothes *should* be treated.

Maude did not take kindly to what she considered to be 'interference' with the household she controlled and she swiftly took Margaret to task.

Margaret Minns was not a hot-headed person and she refused to be drawn into an argument with the resentful housekeeper. However, she stood her ground over this particular issue, with the result that Maude complained to Reverend Boyce that the new maid was 'disrupting the smooth running of the household'.

Arthur Boyce did his best to placate the indignant housekeeper, but he would not agree that Margaret should be dismissed. The reason was that Emily had received a letter from the Countess of St Germans, praising Margaret as the best personal maid she had ever employed and expressing a wish to call in and speak with her when she was next in the vicinity. The St Cleer vicar would never pass up the opportunity to meet with a leading member of the aristocracy. However, his refusal to act did nothing to lessen Maude's animosity towards Emily's maid.

Emily discussed the housekeeper's attitude with Margaret

when they were carrying baskets of newly baked bread to the soup kitchen set up for miners' families in the changing room of one of the recently closed mines.

'You mustn't take anything she says to heart, Margaret. She has been in charge of the household since my mother died and resents anyone else taking decisions she feels should be hers.'

'It doesn't really bother me,' Margaret said easily. 'I'm aware that she's being spiteful because you took me on without consulting her. It's understandable, I suppose. She sees it as undermining her authority. But I'm in work and grateful to you for it. I'll not be upset by the resentment of a woman who's seen marriage pass her by – and with it the chance of a family of her own. Take away the little bit of power she wields over the other servants in the vicarage and she's left with nothing. I have a husband – even though he's the Lord only knows where – and I have the boys. I wouldn't be without them for the world.'

They spoke about the boys and the work they were doing on the farm of Mr Norris until they arrived at the improvised soup kitchen. There they found a frighteningly large queue of women and children waiting for them, together with a few men.

It was the men for whom Emily felt particular sympathy. When soup and bread was being distributed they shuffled forward in abject misery, ashamed of being out of work, seemingly convinced that their present condition was their fault.

The soup kitchen was a non-denominational venture and Rose Holman and a band of helpers had been at the mine for most of the morning. Using coal supplied by the mine owners they had built up a fire and, in a huge cauldron, made up a soup comprising anything edible the women had been able to obtain.

As the hungry families began to eat, Margaret went among them. Remembering how ill she had been herself, she chastised any mother she saw giving away her own food to her children.

Emily worked in the soup kitchen with a growing feeling of anger and frustration; anger that miners and their families should be reduced to such dire straits through no fault of their own, and frustration that there was so little that could be done to find a long-term answer to their problems.

She expressed her thoughts as she, Margaret and Rose made their way back to St Cleer once the soup and bread had all been distributed.

Rose was surprisingly philosophical. 'Mining is a hard way to earn a living. It always has been. A miner spends his working life underground with death lurking at his elbow. Yet if he's forced to spend too much time above ground he's restless to be down below again.'

'That's right,' Margaret agreed. 'And when he's working his family can never settle, no matter how hard they try, or however long he does the job.'

'That's true,' Rose added. 'A mine closure is a mixed blessing for a miner's wife. Part of her will be pleased to have him above ground but, particularly if there are children, she'll be worrying how she's going to feed them. I know my mother used to say as much on many occasions.'

'It's even worse when your husband is forced to go abroad to try to earn a living,' said Margaret, with considerable feeling. 'You're never certain that things *are* going to get better, or whether you're going to need to make a new life for yourself and the children.'

'Don't give up hope,' said Emily. 'With any luck you'll hear from your husband before too long and he'll send you money to pay the fare for you and the boys to go to Australia.'

Pretending not to notice the sceptical glance Rose gave her, Emily continued, 'Once you're together again, with someone to share your problems, you'll feel on top of the world.'

'That's right,' Rose said encouragingly. 'I've heard a great many good things said about life out there.'

'I sometimes think that Charlie probably doesn't want us out there with him.' Margaret spoke with a hint of bitterness that Emily had never heard from her before. 'It's been more than a year now since he went away. I can't help feeling that life must be better for him without the burden of a wife and a couple of children.'

'You mustn't think like that,' Emily tried to reassure her, even as she remembered what Rose had told her about Margaret's husband. 'The mail takes a long time to reach England. He's probably working in some remote place there and even when the mail arrives at a port it needs to be put on board a ship and I believe the voyage sometimes takes three months or more.'

She was trying to cheer up Margaret, but at the same time she remembered that Sam's family had received a number of letters from him during the time he had been in Australia.

She feared that Rose might be correct in her assessment of Charlie Minns.

7

I

The last, long leg of the voyage of the *Bonython* from Plymouth to South Australia passed almost without incident, although the vessel arrived at its destination with two extra passengers. Both girls, they had been born during the last weeks of the voyage.

There had, in fact, been four births on board. However, despite the earlier proud boast of the ship's captain that he had never lost a passenger on his ship, two of the newly born children died when each was less than a day old and they were buried at sea.

Nevertheless, the record of the *Bonython* compared very favourably with those of the other ships engaged in carrying migrants to Australia.

The latter part of the voyage had also seen Ira Moyle spending a great deal of time with Sam, Primrose – and with Jean. He was now included among the men for whom she prepared meals. He never tired of telling her how much better was her cooking than that of the woman who had provided his meals on the earlier part of the voyage.

Jean was pleased to earn the extra few shillings that cooking for Ira brought her and she was always polite towards him, but she rarely extended to him the same warmth that was part of her relationship with Sam.

However, Ira and Primrose were happy in each other's company and Ira would spend hours playing simple games with the child that would have tried the patience of most men. For this Jean was grateful.

It meant she was able to devote more time to taking classes in reading, writing and simple arithmetic and so was able to add a few extra shillings to the money she was putting aside to give herself and Primrose a secure start in the new land.

When the *Bonython* had been at sea for a hundred and five days, word went around that they might expect to sight Australia at any time.

For the remainder of that day the excited passengers crowded the upper deck, each hoping to be the first to glimpse the land that was to be their new home.

The passengers had spent enough time at sea now. All wanted to leave the ship and face the challenge of the new land where they could begin to rebuild their lives.

When dusk fell over an empty ocean and the wind began to pick up, the disappointed migrants slowly dispersed and made their way below deck to their bunks.

There were numerous remarks about the crew causing them to 'get all excited about nothing', but they knew that land could not be too far away.

Sam would have gone below with the others, but the mate struck up a conversation with him. Soon, Sam was the only passenger left on the upper deck. The two men were standing in the lee of the galley, sheltering from the wind, when the mate said to him, 'Well, son, we'll not be enjoying each other's company for very much longer now. How have you enjoyed the voyage?'

'I won't be sorry to get off the *Bonython*,' Sam admitted. 'But that's not saying anything against the ship, in many ways the voyage has been better than I thought it would be. It's just that I want to be back mining again.'

'You won't find a finer ship than the *Bonython*,' the mate said with pride. 'Or a finer skipper than Captain Carver. I couldn't name you more than two other ships that have ever made this voyage without losing a passenger – a passenger who boarded the ship in England, that is. I'm not counting the babies who died. They'd have probably been lost if they'd been born on land – and a ship's no place for a woman to give birth. It's not natural.'

Sam felt unable to argue with the mate's logic. Jean had lost her baby on land. 'I'm sure you're right,' he said. 'Most of the passengers feel the way I do, too, but tonight they're going to their bunks disappointed. We were all expecting to have our first sighting of Australia before the day was out.'

'Then they should have had a little more patience,' declared the mate. 'Take a look for'd, on the starboard side.'

Puzzled, Sam nevertheless did as the mate suggested. At first he could see nothing. Then, far away where the unseen horizon merged with the sky, a pin-point of light winked at him for a brief moment before vanishing once more.

'What is it . . . ? That light . . . ?' he exclaimed excitedly.

'It's the lighthouse at Cape Borda, on Kangaroo Island,' the mate replied. 'That's Australian territory, son. You're almost there.'

II

The mate's statement that the *Bonython* had almost reached its destination proved somewhat optimistic. It was not until early morning of the fourth day after sighting the Cape Borda lighthouse that the rattle of the anchor chain signalled the arrival of the ship off the busy Wallaroo dockside.

It was the nearest port to Kadina and served the copper mines of South Australia's Yorke Peninsula.

There was great excitement on board and on the harbourside too. News of the imminent arrival of the migrant ship from Plymouth had reached the three copper mining towns of Wallaroo, Moonta and Kadina only hours after it had been first sighted beating its way along the coastline, miles to the south.

Of those living in the mining towns, many were Cornish and were awaiting friends and relatives. Hurrying to the port they hired boats and put out to meet the ship in the hope of seeing a familiar face on board.

There would be a great number of reunions that day, most eagerly anticipated, but some that were not.

Those migrants with friends and relatives waiting for them were almost frantic in their efforts to be among the first to go ashore.

As no one was expecting Sam or Jean, they stayed back, waiting for the excitement to die down. As a result they were among the few who spent an extra night on board.

The following morning, Sam rose early and went on deck to enjoy the quiet of the early morning, before others woke and before work began in earnest on the dockside.

Gazing out at what could be seen, it was something of a disappointment. Beyond the ships and warehouses the land was flat with not a hill of note to be seen anywhere.

Even houses were not immediately in evidence, although smoke rose from a sufficient number of chimneys to give some indication of the extent of the port of Wallaroo.

He had just lit his pipe when he was joined by Jean, carrying a still-sleepy Primrose.

'I thought I might find you here,' she said, by way of a greeting.

'It was too hot down below without a sea breeze to cool things

down. I thought I'd come up here to enjoy the peace and quiet
for a while.'

'Primrose and I couldn't sleep either – so we've come up here
to disturb your peace and quiet.'

Sam smiled. 'That's all right, Jean. I don't find you and
Primrose disturbing.'

Giving Sam a strange look, Jean said, 'No, you don't, do you?'

Unsure what his reply should be to this unexpected inter-
pretation of his words, Sam said nothing.

The silence stood between them for some three or four
minutes, before the strangled note from a steam whistle
announced the first very early departure of a steamship from
the busy port.

It served to break their silence and Jean said, 'It doesn't look
to be very exciting out there, Sam.'

'I agree, Jean, but we won't be staying here very long. Once
ashore we'll head inland to Kadina and the mines. We'll feel at
home there, I'm quite sure.'

'What's going to happen when we reach Kadina, Sam? What
will we both do?'

'I'll find work in the mines, hopefully in the big Kadina mine
and you'll find your father. That's what we said we'd do.' They
had spoken of this so many times he could not understand the
reason for her questions now.

'We've travelled all the way from St Cleer together and have
known each for so many years. Where do we go now, Sam –
you and I?'

When he did not reply immediately, Jean asked, 'How do you
see me, Sam? Just as a girl you've grown up with . . . or is there
more to us than that?'

When he still did not reply, she added softly, 'Do you still
see me as the woman who was the wife of your best friend,
Sam? Phillip's dead now and no amount of grieving is going
to bring him back. I'm no longer his wife, Sam – I'm not
anybody's wife. I'm just a very lonely woman who has a young

daughter to care for – and who's desperately afraid of facing a future on her own. Do you understand what I'm trying to say, Sam?'

'I . . . I think so.'

Sam knew very well what she was saying. She was telling him in as obvious a manner as she could, that she was available – if he wanted her.

'Is there anything you want to say to me, Sam?'

He wished he could say the words he knew she wanted to hear. To tell her there was a future for them – together. But he could not. He thought too much of her to be dishonest.

Lamely, he said, 'We're going to enjoy a good life out here, Jean. When you and Primrose find your pa you'll have someone to take care of you. Someone who's family. If he's still working on the Kadina mine we'll all see quite a lot of each other, because that's where I expect to be working. It'll be good to be below grass again, winning ore.'

Jean said nothing for a long while. Then she said, 'I think I'll go below and make certain I've packed all our things.'

Sam was aware Jean was hurt by his response, but he did not know what else he could have said.

'Jean . . .'

She turned back to him expectantly, but he said, 'Let me know when you're ready. I'll bring your things up on deck, ready to put in the boat.'

'There's no need, Sam, Ira said he'll do it for us, if I wanted him to.'

'Oh! Well then . . . I'll see you when we're all ready. The mate says the easiest way to get to Kadina is by the horse-train. I'll find out a bit more about it before we go ashore.'

'All right, Sam. I'll tell Ira what's happening.'

It should have been a relief to him that Jean understood he would not be assuming long-term responsibility for her and Primrose. It *was* a relief, he told himself. Yet he felt he had somehow let them both down.

Trying hard to shake off the feeling, he went below to the single men's hold to complete his own packing and bring his baggage up on deck.

8

I

When Margaret Minns had been working for Emily for only two months, a tragedy occurred that would lead to a dramatic change in both their lives.

It was a Sunday and Emily had been to the morning service in the village church, singing in the choir, as usual. Margaret had unexpectedly attended the service, leaving the boys to put in a morning's work on the Norris farm.

Emily was talking to Margaret while she waited for her father to finish bidding farewell to his congregation.

His duty completed, Parson Boyce made his way to where the two young women stood. Margaret immediately broke off her conversation. Nodding farewell to Emily and her father, she turned to make her way home.

Looking closely at her father, Emily asked anxiously, 'Are you all right, Father? You don't look very well.'

'I confess I do not feel too well, Emily . . .' His reply was breathless and his eyes appeared to find difficulty in focusing on her. 'I . . . I have a pain . . . a dreadful pain . . .'

Suddenly, Arthur Boyce fell to his knees, then pitched forward on to his face.

Emily let out a cry of horror and crouched beside her prostrate father. As she struggled to turn him over she was aware of the sound of running feet along the path. Soon others were helping her and someone was calling for Dr Kittow. He had been in the congregation and was now making his way towards his pony and trap, left in the lane outside the church.

'Parson's still breathing,' said one of the churchwardens who had helped to turn Arthur Boyce on his back.

Emily took some consolation from his words, but her father was quite unconscious, his forehead bleeding where it had struck the ground.

Taking out a handkerchief, she was wiping away the blood when the doctor reached the scene, the small crowd parting to allow him through.

After only a cursory glance at the parson, the doctor took the unconscious man's hand and felt for a pulse. Nodding his head gravely, he spoke to the crowd. 'Some of you men carry him to the vicarage. Two take his shoulders, two more get a firm grip on his cassock and one of you support his head. Quickly now.'

As some of the village men gathered around their parson, Emily asked the doctor, 'What is wrong with him? Has he fainted?'

The doctor shook his head. 'It is rather more serious than that I'm afraid, Miss Emily. It's your father's heart. He has suffered a seizure.'

Wide-eyed and suddenly afraid, Emily asked hesitantly, 'He . . . he's not going to die?'

'I'll know a little more when we have him at the vicarage and I am able to examine him more thoroughly.'

The doctor was being deliberately evasive. The realisation that he thought this necessary frightened Emily more than if he had told her the truth.

At the vicarage, Arthur Boyce was carried upstairs with some difficulty and placed gently upon his bed. Dr Kittow then sent everyone from the room, declaring he would undress his patient, examine him and put on his night attire.

Emily thanked the men who had carried her father home. After promising to keep them informed of her father's condition, she sent them away.

As it was Sunday, the servants had the day off, but Maude was in the house and had come from the kitchen when the party entered the house. Emily repeated the doctor's brief diagnosis to her, adding, 'We should know more when Dr Kittow has completed his examination, Maude.'

'Heaven help us all if anything happens to poor Parson Boyce,' lamented the housekeeper. 'He works himself too hard, as I've told him many times. He has too much on his mind right now, what with all the changes that have gone on in his own house since dear Miss Caroline married and went away. Poor man, he's reached an age where he should have peace and quiet.'

'I'll go and make some tea,' said Margaret, who had come to the vicarage instead of returning to the Norris farm. 'No doubt the doctor would like a cup when he's finished his examination.'

'I'll do that, if you don't mind,' Maude said indignantly. 'I'll not have you taking over the kitchen as well.'

When Maude had gone, Margaret said apologetically, 'I'm sorry, Miss Emily. I should have known better than to suggest I did something in the kitchen when Maude was around.'

'Maude is upset because of what has happened to my father,' Emily replied. 'She has looked after him for very many years. I am quite certain she did not mean to be rude.'

Margaret thought otherwise, but she said nothing. Emily had more to worry about than animosity between two servants.

'Why not go home to the boys?' Emily said. 'You see little enough of them in the week.'

'I'll wait with you until the doctor has examined Parson Boyce. The boys have been working this morning. If I'm not home when they finish, Albert will get something for him and young Tom. He's a good boy that way.'

'You are lucky to have them, Margaret. No matter what happens in your life you have them to support and care for you. That must mean a great deal.'

'Yes, I have them with me – thanks to you. But you mustn't feel *you* have no one to turn to right now – whatever happens. I'll be here – twenty-four hours a day, if need be. The boys will be ready to give you any help they can, too. They both know how much they owe to you.'

Touched by the other woman's declaration of support, Emily said, 'Thank you, Margaret. I appreciate your loyalty. Hopefully, my father will make a full recovery and things will soon return to normal.'

'Of course. I just don't want you thinking there's no one who cares – really cares, that is. Now, Maude seems to be taking her time with that tea. I'll go down to the kitchen and see what's keeping her.'

Margaret had been gone for no more than a couple of minutes when the door to Arthur Boyce's bedroom opened and Dr Kittow came from the room, closing the door quietly behind him.

'My father . . . he is all right?' Emily was alarmed by the doctor's grave expression.

'He is still unconscious, Miss Emily, and likely to remain so for quite some time. He has had a rather serious seizure, I'm afraid.'

'But he *will* recover in time?' Emily suddenly felt more vulnerable than at any time in her life.

'It would please me beyond measure were I able to give you a categorical "yes" to that question, my dear, but it would be less than honest of me. Your father's life is in the hands of one with whom he has a much closer relationship than I.'

Tea was served to Emily and Dr Kittow in the sitting room by a sullen housekeeper. Maude had taken offence when Margaret had come to the kitchen and offered to serve the tea for Maude, since she must be busily engaged in preparing lunch in the absence of the maids.

Muttering darkly about 'them as can only think of their stomachs at such a time as this', Maude told Margaret she had always been able to manage things on a Sunday, '. . . and could do so well enough now.' Placing the tea on a tray, with cups, sugar and milk, Maude brushed past Margaret and bore the tea off to the sitting room.

Emily, used to the housekeeper's moods, realised she was angry and knew it probably had something to do with Margaret, but she had more important matters to worry about right now.

'What course can I expect my father's condition to take, Dr Kittow?'

The doctor was little more forthcoming than before. 'In cases such as this it is very difficult to make an accurate prognosis, Miss Emily. Sometimes a patient will regain consciousness – sometimes not. If your father regains consciousness in the near future his chances of recovery will be higher, but by no means assured. He is seriously ill. I am afraid I will be a frequent visitor to your home in the weeks ahead.'

While Emily was still mulling over his words she heard a click as the door to the sitting room was closed. She realised the doctor's words of warning had been overheard by Maude.

It made little difference to her at the time, but she would recall this moment later.

II

Reverend Arthur Boyce lay in a coma in his room for almost seven weeks, during which time Caroline, summoned by Emily, arrived at the vicarage and stayed for eight days.

While she was there Dr Kittow called daily, occasionally twice a day. Eventually, convinced her father would never regain consciousness and might lie in a coma for weeks, even years, Caroline decided she would return to her Dorset vicarage home. Now four months pregnant, she could not bear to be separated from her husband.

She departed after assuring Emily she would return immediately should their father regain consciousness, or if Emily felt her presence could serve any useful purpose.

Emily was left feeling that Caroline was reluctant to spend one hour longer than was absolutely necessary in the sprawling vicarage.

She did not blame her sister. Caroline now had a husband she adored, a home of her own and was about to start a family. The gloomy old vicarage was a reminder of unhappier times; the place where her mother had died leaving the two sisters to be brought up by a despotic father and an implacable housekeeper.

Even now, with Reverend Arthur Boyce lying so gravely ill, Maude seemed more concerned with maintaining her status in the household than in trying to make Emily's burden lighter. She and Margaret had another of their frequent arguments, this time about the carelessness of the laundry-maid, who had torn one of Emily's dresses in the wash and failed to say anything about it.

Margaret discovered the tear when she set out Emily's clothes one morning. She wasted no time in taking the maid to task, first for her carelessness and, secondly, for not reporting the matter in order that the dress might be mended immediately.

Maude overheard the admonition and angrily confronted Margaret, declaring that the manner in which the servants carried out their duties was *her* responsibility and not that of a 'jumped-up miner's wife' who was incapable of controlling her own two thieving children!

Hiding the anger she felt at the housekeeper's words,

Margaret calmly suggested that if the laundry-maid was the responsibility of the housekeeper, Maude should take steps to ensure she took adequate care of Emily's clothes.

Maude's angry tirade in response to Margaret's carefully controlled criticism brought Emily hurrying from an upstairs room.

'Maude! What on earth is going on? How dare you shout in such a manner? Control yourself immediately!'

'Don't you tell me to control myself, Miss Emily!' Maude's anger had gone beyond the bounds of reason. 'You may have taken on this hussy, but *you're* not my employer.'

'My father is lying seriously ill upstairs, Maude. Until he is well enough to take charge of his affairs once more I *am* your employer and I have no intention of standing here arguing with you. Kindly show some respect for my father.'

'Respect, you say? I'm the one who should be calling for respect around here. Haven't I looked after your father for all these years – your mother too when she was ill? Yes, and you and your sister when you were left without anyone else? I've sacrificed any chance of a family of my own for you all – and what thanks do I get for it? My authority is undermined and I'm left with no say about who is put to work in the house. I'm not prepared to stay under such conditions, Miss Emily. If you're going to be in charge of the house I shall leave. Your ways are not my ways.'

'It would be very inconsiderate of you to leave just now, Maude, as you are fully aware. Besides, it would be foolish to make such a decision in a spirit of anger. Sleep on it. If you wish, we will talk more about it tomorrow.'

Believing her threat to leave had seriously alarmed Emily, Maude said, 'It's become quite obvious that me and your so-called "personal maid" are never going to see eye to eye, so, as I see it, either she goes or I do. It's as simple as that. The choice is yours.'

Margaret was standing to one side of Maude and Emily could

see her stricken face. Margaret believed that, called upon to make such a decision, Emily would not allow the housekeeper to leave.

'This is foolish, Maude. I refuse to accept such an ultimatum made, as it is, in the heat of the moment. We will talk about it again tomorrow.'

'There's nothing foolish about it, Miss Emily. If the parson recovers I shall be happy to return to take care of him. If he doesn't . . . ? Well, he told me a long time ago that I'll be remembered in his will. I suggest you think about *that*, Miss Emily. If you want me to stay then *she'll* have to go.' And with a maliciously triumphant glance at Margaret, Maude turned and left, heading for her own room.

Margaret was desperately unhappy. 'I . . . I'll leave, Miss Emily. I don't want to cause you any more trouble – but I'd like to be given time to find somewhere else. I don't want me and the boys going back to the way of life we had before.'

'There is no question of you going, Margaret, so we'll hear no more of it. I doubt if Maude will leave, either, once she has had time to think about it in a rational manner.'

It would be extremely inconvenient were Maude to leave right now, but Emily was aware this was a confrontation she could not afford to lose. If Maude stayed – on her own terms – Emily would lose all credibility with the other servants. She was not prepared to allow such a situation to arise.

III

Early the following morning the tension in the Boyce household was almost tangible. Aware of the confrontation that had taken place between Emily and Maude, there was much speculation among the servants about which of the two women would emerge as the victor. The balance of opinion was tilted in favour of the housekeeper, but Emily had her champions.

When Margaret arrived for work earlier than usual, she found servants who had previously ignored her eager to seek her opinion on the imminent show-down between Emily and the housekeeper who had ruled Parson Boyce's household for so many years.

'I don't think Miss Emily will dare let her leave,' declared a maid who had been employed at the vicarage for almost as many years as the housekeeper. 'She's been here for so long the household couldn't manage without her.'

'That's absolute nonsense,' Margaret said heatedly. 'No one is indispensable. True, there would need to be changes, but I don't doubt that most would be for the better.'

'Especially for Miss Emily,' said a more recently employed maid. 'From what I hear, Maude has made her life a misery ever since she was a small girl.'

'That's the truth!' said a longer-serving maid. 'There have been times when I could have wept for Miss Emily. If I was her, I'd jump at the chance of getting rid of Maude.'

'Well, we're none of us Miss Emily,' Margaret said firmly. 'And I suggest you mind what you're saying. Maude has had all night to think about her situation. If she's got any sense she'll stay on and try to put things right between them. She'll not find another household prepared to put up with her ways.'

As the morning wore on without Maude putting in an appearance it became evident the housekeeper was not prepared to contemplate a compromise with the daughter of her employer.

Emily herself went about her daily business aware of the air of expectancy prevailing among the servants, but she said nothing. She felt all that needed saying had been said. The next move was up to the housekeeper.

It was eleven thirty that morning before a tight-faced house-keeper came downstairs and knocked at the door of the study

of Parson Boyce, where Emily was going through the household accounts.

Maude was dressed for outdoors in a long black dress, black
coat, shoes and hat, and a pair of black gloves. It seemed to
Emily that the housekeeper had already decided her father was
not going to recover and had gone into premature mourning.

Wasting no time with any form of greeting, Maude said, 'I
see you're going through the accounts. You'll no doubt be able
to work out what I'm owed. I'll take it with me, if you don't
mind.'

'I have it all ready for you, Maude . . . here.'

Emily opened a desk drawer, took out some banknotes and
coins and handed them to the black-clad woman, saying, 'You
will find it correct. Unfortunately, in view of the suddenness of
your decision to leave I feel unable to offer you a reference.'

'I don't need a reference – or anything else from *you*, Miss
Emily. If the parson recovers he'll want me back here. If he
doesn't then I won't ever need to work again.'

'His generosity towards you doesn't surprise me, Maude. He
always thought a great deal of you. Your decision to leave now,
when he probably needs you more than ever before, will come
as a great disappointment to him.'

'If he recovers I'll explain my reasons to him. He'll understand.'

'Try explaining them to me, Maude, so *I* can understand. I
know you don't like me very much and never have, but for my
father's sake you might have tried to put your grievances to
one side for a little while longer.'

'You just don't know how I feel, do you? You and your sister
never have. I thought once upon a time that *he* did, but I was
fooling myself. You talk of loyalty, but you don't know what
real loyalty is – or the sacrifice it calls for. Well, I'll tell you.
Many years ago I met a man who wanted to marry me. A
shopkeeper, he was, who'd have given me a good life. Then
your mother's health began to fail and the parson begged me

to stay on and help him bring up you and your sister. Said you all needed me. That *he* needed me. I'd never regret staying, was what he said. He led me to believe . . . But never mind what he led me to believe. I did what was asked of me, turned down the shopkeeper and stayed here at the vicarage – and for what?'

Maude gave an unnecessary tug at one of her gloves. 'Well, I *have* lived to regret listening to him. I see women of my age with children and grandchildren of their own to care for them in their old age – and what have *I* to look forward to? I'll tell you, a life with a sister who's a spinster like me, with no one to look after either of us. Oh, we'll both manage on what the parson will leave me, I don't doubt that, but there'll be no one to really care what happens to me.'

Emily felt sympathy for Maude welling up inside her. Then she remembered the times *she* had cried herself to sleep, when a hug from the cold and spiteful housekeeper would have made a huge difference to the loneliness she felt; when even a kind word or a warm glance would have been enough to break the coccoon of despair that had her trapped for so much of her young life.

'The decision is yours to make, Maude. I will not beg you to stay, but for my father's sake . . .'

'You should have thought about all that when you brought that woman into the house against my wishes. It gave me a good idea of what I could expect when you took over the running of the vicarage, as you were bound to, one day. I suppose I should have known, really, seeing as how fond you are of miners and their families.'

'You are being impertinent, Maude. I think you had better leave before you say any more.'

'I'm leaving, but as for being "impertinent", it doesn't really matter any more. I can say what I think – and what I think is that the parson would have been better off if he'd let you run off with that Sam Hooper, instead of having him packed off to

Australia.' Having delivered what she hoped would be a revelation, Maude finished, 'I'll send someone to collect my belongings as soon as I can. They're all packed up in my room.'

With this, the ex-housekeeper to Parson Arthur Boyce swept
out of the study, leaving Emily fighting back tears.

It was not so much that Maude had confirmed what Emily
already believed about Sam's departure from St Cleer, but that
the housekeeper should have nurtured so much hatred and
resentment inside her all these years.

Emily had accepted long ago that Maude did not really like
Caroline and herself, but the depth of her dislike came as a great
shock.

She also wondered how much happier life in the vicarage
might have been had Maude married her shopkeeper and her
father taken on a kindlier housekeeper.

Emily was quite certain of one thing. If, as she sincerely
hoped, her father *did* recover, Maude would never return to
work at the St Cleer vicarage.

IV

Only minutes after Maude's departure from the vicarage,
Margaret entered the study with tea for Emily.

'I thought you might be in need of this. Maude hasn't spoken
to me, of course, but the maids say she was in a vicious mood.'

'They were not exaggerating,' Emily agreed, still shaken up
by the vitriolic confrontation with the ex-housekeeper. 'I never
realised just how much bitterness she harboured towards us all.'

'I fear she isn't entirely normal,' Margaret said sympathetically. 'The other maids are saying so quite openly now. No one
dared say anything against her while she was still employed
here.'

'If only she had told us years ago how she felt,' Emily said unhappily, 'we might have been able to resolve some of her problems and avoid the many years of unhappiness we have all suffered at her hands.'

Margaret could see that Emily had been deeply upset by the ex-housekeeper. She said comfortingly, 'Well, she's gone now. From what the servants have been saying, there's not one of them who's sorry to see the back of her, but it does leave a gap in the household. Will you take over her work?'

'I can't, Margaret. There are still many duties to be carried out around the parish – even more with my father so ill, and I must care for him too. I will need to find another housekeeper – and quickly. Unfortunately, I don't think any of the servants are up to the job, unless . . .' Looking speculatively at Margaret, she asked, 'Do you think *you* could take it on, Margaret?'

'Me . . . ?' Margaret's incredulity was unfeigned. 'I couldn't do it! Well, I *could* but you need someone to live in and I have the boys to think of.'

'That need pose no problems,' Emily declared, her enthusiasm growing as the spur-of-the-moment idea began to take shape. 'The annexe attached to the vicarage is empty. Adam, the gardener, lived there until he married Widow James, who has a house in the village. He moved in with her and her children and the annexe has been empty ever since.'

'What of your father? We're all hoping he'll recover, of course, but, when he does, will he allow us to stay there?'

'That's something I will deal with when the time comes,' Emily assured her. 'If you take on the post of housekeeper it will be permanent, I promise you. What's more, you will be paid a housekeeper's salary. What do you say?'

Margaret gave it some thought, then she said, hesitantly, 'I don't want to sound pessimistic, Miss Emily, but what if Parson Boyce *doesn't* get better? The Church will want to put another vicar in and we will have to move out – you as well.'

'That's quite true, Margaret, and I fully understand your

concern. No doubt the new incumbent will need servants, but if you didn't suit each other . . . well, I will have to find somewhere to live too and will need household staff. Whatever happens, I promise you you will not lose by becoming the housekeeper here.'

Satisfied, Margaret nodded. 'In that case I will be delighted to become your housekeeper, Miss Emily.'

In truth, the offer could not have come at a better time for her. Jacob Norris had lived alone for so long that he was unaccustomed to having others about him. Although at first he seemed pleased to have Margaret clean his house once a week, he was beginning to find fault with her for being *too* tidy. The house of the eccentric farmer had not been properly cleaned for half a lifetime and it seemed he preferred it that way.

With the boys, too, he was a hard taskmaster, expecting them to take on tasks more suited to grown men.

Margaret had decided to put her trust in Emily for whatever the future held in store for them all. It would be more secure than relying upon the whims of Jacob Norris.

When Reverend Arthur Boyce regained consciousness it came as a complete surprise. Dr Kittow, apparently resigned to the belief that his ecclesiastical patient would never regain his faculties, reduced the frequency of his visits to two a week. The last had been only the day before, when he reported that there was no change in his patient's condition.

Emily was in the parson's bedroom, arranging some flowers in a vase that stood on a sideboard. The window was open and from a side lawn came the sound of Albert and Tom's laughter as they played with a ball.

She had her back to the bed and was startled by a barely discernible, hoarse whisper from her father.

'I can hear children playing.'

'Father! Oh, Father, thank the Lord! You have come back to us.'

'Is that Caroline and Emily I can hear in the garden?'

He did not appear to have heard her. Aware that he had not fully regained consciousness, Emily took one of his hands in both of hers and said, tearfully, 'Yes. Yes, Father, it's Caroline and Emily.'

The ghost of a smile crossed Arthur Boyce's face and he said, 'It is a delightful sound, my dear. A truly joyful sound.'

He had not opened his eyes and now he ceased talking and seemed to relax.

Releasing his hand, Emily rushed from the bedroom. In the hallway outside she bumped into Margaret.

'Margaret, my father . . . he just spoke. He heard the boys laughing as they played in the garden and said what a delightful sound it was. He thought it was Caroline and me. I must send someone to Dr Kittow!'

Emily was so excited that before Margaret had time to say that *she* would send someone for the doctor, Emily was running downstairs to tell the good news to the servants and to send someone hurrying to fetch the doctor.

There was a babble of excitement coming from the servants gathered in the hallway when Margaret made her way slowly downstairs.

'Margaret, I have sent Albert to fetch the doctor,' Emily said as soon as she saw her. 'He can run faster than anyone else here. I will give him a shilling as a reward—'

Her excited chatter came to a sudden halt when she saw Margaret's eyes fill with tears. 'Margaret . . . ! What's the matter?'

'I'm sorry, Miss Emily. It was wonderful that your father was able to speak to you one last time, but . . . I just put my head around the door to see if there was anything he wanted. He was lying so still I went in to check him. He's gone, Miss Emily. The parson is dead.'

V

When the funeral service was over and Arthur Boyce had been laid to rest in the St Cleer churchyard, his family gathered in the vicarage study to hear solicitor Benedict Goldsworthy read the vicar's will.

Caroline and her husband were present, as were Lord and Lady Boyce, together with five nieces and nephews and two cousins. It seemed that each would receive a bequest.

Elsewhere in the house were many of Cornwall's churchmen, local gentry – and the Bishop of Exeter. On a visit to the county, he had caused a stir in the community by putting in an appearance at the funeral and delivering a eulogy to the late vicar of St Cleer.

Benedict Goldsworthy was seated behind Arthur Boyce's desk, preparing to read the will he had drawn up on the instructions of his late client. He was the archetypal English country solicitor. He even wore a pair of gold-rimmed pince-nez, perched low enough on his nose to enable him to peer over the rim at the gathered family as he coughed to gain their attention.

When those present fell silent he began to read from the document on the desk in front of him. There was a number of minor bequests to be distributed among the assembled family, but the bulk of his substantial estate was to be shared out equally between Emily and Caroline, making them both wealthy women.

Lord Boyce and a couple of the cousins murmured their approval of the monies inherited by Arthur Boyce's two daughters when, suddenly, there came the sound of raised voices from the direction of the hall. The door was thrown open and Maude entered the room so quickly she stumbled and almost fell.

Behind her Margaret hesitated in the open doorway, an expression of consternation on her face.

'Miss Rowe! What is the meaning of this unseemly interruption? This is a solemn occasion for the reading of your late employer's will. You are the last person I would have expected to show such unforgivable disrespect!' Benedict Goldsworthy fairly bristled with indignation.

'I am here to claim what's rightfully mine. I know I wasn't invited here for the reading of the will, but I don't intend to be cheated out of my rights by her!'

Maude jabbed a finger at Emily and one of the Boyce nieces closest to the ex-housekeeper started back, as though fearing lightning was about to issue forth from Maude's fingertip.

'My dear Miss Rowe, had you possessed any "rights", as you call them, in the will of the late Reverend Boyce, I assure you I would have notified you and requested your presence here today. Now, will you kindly leave, in order that I might conclude what is a purely private affair?'

'Are you telling me Parson Boyce never mentioned me in his will? If you are then I'll call you a liar. I know I'm in there. He came back from Liskeard one day and told me he'd left me money in his will. Enough to see me comfortable for the rest of my days, he said. I can even tell you the date if you like, because I wrote it down at the time. It was not many months before he sent that Sam Hooper off to Australia.'

'I have no doubt your recollection of the date is perfectly accurate,' said the solicitor. 'So, too, is the fact that you are mentioned in the will of the late Reverend Boyce. However, you are *not* a beneficiary.'

'What do you mean?' Maude demanded. 'If I'm in Parson Boyce's will then I'm entitled to what he promised me.'

'No, Miss Rowe,' Benedict Goldsworthy said firmly. 'Am I correct in saying that you left Reverend Boyce's employ prior to his death?'

'She didn't give me no alternative.' Once again the finger was extended in Emily's direction. 'Taking on that miner's woman against my advice—'

'Your reasons for leaving Reverend Boyce's employ do not matter. The terms of the will are perfectly clear. Reverend Boyce did bequeath you a sum of money – a very *generous* sum, but it was conditional upon you being in his employment at the time of his death. I am sorry, you have no entitlement, so I must ask you once again to leave this room. Immediately, if you please, Miss Rowe.'

One of the churchwardens had been standing outside the door and heard what was said. He now stepped inside the study and led the stunned ex-housekeeper outside, closing the door behind him.

'Poor Maude, I could almost feel sorry for her,' Caroline whispered to her sister as the somewhat ruffled Benedict Goldsworthy rearranged the papers and documents he had inadvertently placed in the wrong order during the initial confusion caused by Maude's unexpected dramatic entrance.

'My Christian instincts are to feel the same,' Emily whispered in return, 'but, try as I might, I can find no compassion in me for her. I wish I could, truly I do.'

'Shall we proceed?' Benedict Goldsworthy peered disapprovingly over his pince-nez at the two sisters. 'I must apologise for the interruption. It was most unfortunate and not a little upsetting, but the formalities will take only a few more minutes of your time . . .'

The following evening, when the last of the funeral guests had departed, the house felt strangely quiet. Emily was in her father's study, writing acknowledgements of the many letters of condolence she had received, when there was a soft knock on the door.

'Come in!'

The door opened and Margaret entered the room. In her hand she carried a mug of steaming milk. Placing it on the desk in front of Emily, she said, 'I've put the boys to bed and was heating some milk for myself. I thought I'd bring some for you. It will do you good and help you sleep after the strain of the past few days.'

'Thank you, Margaret, it is very thoughtful of you. Did you heat it in the kitchen?'

'Yes, Miss Emily, I hope you don't mind, but the stove was still hot.'

'Of course I don't mind . . .' Emily paused. She was still looking at Margaret, but appeared to be thinking. 'Look, why don't you fetch your milk and bring it in here? I think we should have a chat about the future.'

It was a despondent housekeeper who went off to do Emily's bidding. Margaret felt that nothing good could come from the forthcoming discussion. She had already spent many sleepless nights thinking about what the future held. Albert too was mature enough to realise they could not remain at the vicarage now Parson Boyce was dead. He had said he hoped they would not return to living in a ditch and risk her becoming seriously ill again.

Despite Emily's earlier promise, Margaret was aware that Caroline had asked her sister to go and live with her. She hoped Emily might be able to find employment for her elsewhere, but it was unlikely to be as either a housekeeper or a lady's maid. Not with two young sons to support – and she was determined never to give them up.

'Sit down, Margaret.'

Emily indicated the chair on which she herself had so rarely been allowed to sit on the occasions when she had been summoned to this room. Aware of Margaret's apprehension, she did not delay.

'I am quite certain you realise the reason I want to talk to you, Margaret. The death of my father means there will be changes – great changes – in all our lives. Not least of them, of course, is that I will shortly need to vacate the vicarage.'

Nodding acknowledgement of her employer's words,

Margaret asked, 'Do you know when that will be?'

'As soon as they appoint another vicar. Probably in some two or three months' time.'

Margaret relaxed a little. At least she and the boys were not in imminent danger of being made homeless. 'Perhaps Mr Norris will let us move back to the cottage. The fact that I'm now well enough to work on the farm might make a difference. There wouldn't be any pay, of course, but it would mean we had a roof over our heads.'

A pained expression crossed Emily's face. 'I would not allow that, Margaret. You and the boys deserve better than that. I have grown very fond of you all during the time you have been living here.'

'What will *you* do?' Margaret asked. 'Will you go and live with Mrs Kavanagh? I know she's asked you to.'

'No,' Emily replied emphatically. 'Caroline is very happily married with a home of her own and expecting her first child. The last thing she really wants is to have another woman about the house. No, Margaret. There's something else I have had in mind for quite some time. It was no more than a forlorn dream while I was taking care of my father, but now . . .'

Leaning back in her chair and looking speculatively at Margaret, she asked, 'Have you heard from your husband since you have been at the vicarage?'

The question took Margaret by surprise but, shaking her head, she replied, 'I've heard nothing from him since he left Cornwall, that's more than a year ago, now.'

'Would you care if you *never* heard from him, or ever saw him again?'

Startled by the question, Margaret replied indignantly, 'Of course I would. He's the boys' father.' Recovering her composure, Margaret's expression softened. 'Besides, he's my husband. Yes, I'd care very much.'

'Good! That's exactly what I hoped you might say, Margaret. Do you care enough to travel to Australia and try to find him?'

Emily's earlier questions had taken Margaret by surprise. This one left her dumbfounded.

Recovering, she asked, 'You mean . . . me and the boys . . . travelling alone?'

'No, Margaret. I am suggesting we all travel together. You as my personal maid and travelling companion – and the boys coming along with us.'

Margaret looked at Emily as though she had suggested they should fly off to the moon together.

Emily smiled. 'I spoke to my uncle and the bishop about it while they were both here. My uncle has a number of friends and acquaintances in Australia and the bishop said the Church was greatly concerned about the danger posed to the morals of young men in the mining camps of South Australia – many of them Cornishmen. He feels there is great scope there for someone who knows and understands the problems of a mining community. Someone like myself. He believes I might be able to help those wives and families who are suffering hardship under the primitive conditions of some of the camps too. He suggests I might help organise social activities to wean the men away from more sinful pursuits.'

'From what I've heard about some of the places out there, that won't be easy,' Margaret said doubtfully.

'Of course it won't,' Emily agreed enthusiastically. 'But just think what a wonderful challenge it poses! I intend taking up that challenge, Margaret. Will you come with me?'

'I'd like a little while to think about it, Miss Emily. I'll talk it over with Albert, he's a very sensible boy for his age.'

Hiding her disappointment that Margaret had not shown more enthusiasm for her proposal, Emily said, 'Of course, you need to give it a great deal of thought, but it would give you an opportunity to look for your husband – and offer the boys a new start in life. Now, I think I'll take this milk off to bed with me. These last few days *have* been something of a strain.'

* * *

As she climbed the stairs a few minutes later, Emily felt excited at the thought of the future she had mapped out for herself.

The excitement was not entirely due to the challenge she knew she would face in the mining communities of Australia.

There was the hope that in Australia she would meet with Sam once more.

BOOK TWO

1

I

The last passengers from the *Bonython* were taken ashore by lighters, together with their belongings. Once on land, the excited but apprehensive immigrants said emotional farewells to those with whom they had shared danger and cramped quarters for more than a quarter of the year, before going their separate ways.

Wallaroo was one of three towns marking the angles of the so-called 'Copper Triangle', the others being Moonta and Kadina. A great many mines of vastly differing sizes existed within this area, all producing copper, and most employing Cornishmen.

Many of those who arrived at Wallaroo on the *Bonython* had friends, relatives, or, at the very least, a contact in one or more of the mines within this 'triangle' of mining activity.

Ira was in possession of the names of a number of Camborne men who might be able to help him to find work. However, for now he was content to go along with Sam – and with Jean.

The remaining migrants from the ship were travelling to their destinations by various means, but Sam, Ira, Jean and Primrose were the only ones to use the horse-drawn train to travel to

Kadina. The fare of a shilling for each passenger might have deterred some of them, especially those with large families, or it could have been the lack of comfort in this mode of transport. The carriages were no more than empty ore trucks returning to the mines, with the addition of logs, sawn in half lengthways, serving as primitive seating.

Primrose thought it fun at first, but the novelty soon wore off.

'When are we going to see Grandad?' she queried for the third time in ten minutes after the small 'train', pulled by three horses in line, had been travelling for an hour.

'It won't be long now,' Ira reassured her, knowing he had to be proved right very soon. The distance between Wallaroo and Kadina was no more than six miles.

Pulling from his pocket the string with which he had kept Primrose amused on board the ship, he said, 'I think I might have a new cradle for you to try. Come and sit by me.'

Jean threw him a grateful smile as Primrose eagerly scrambled from her place beside her mother and went to sit beside him.

Seeing Jean's smile, Sam felt a fleeting twinge of unexpected and unreasonable jealousy. He berated himself silently, knowing that he had been given every opportunity by Jean to take his own relationship with her forward. The fact that he had not done so meant he could hardly complain now that she was looking elsewhere. She was a young woman with her future to consider – and a young daughter to support.

Nevertheless, he had grown accustomed to having her depend upon him. Although such responsibility had sometimes troubled him, there had also been a vague comfort inherent in the unspoken arrangement. Now Jean had shifted her dependency to Ira it left an unexpected gap in Sam's life. He found himself thinking of the home and family he had left behind in Cornwall – and of Emily. He wondered whether she too might find herself a new 'friend'.

He felt in his pocket and his fingers closed about the crucifix she had given to him as he was leaving. Their final moments in the church porch had been proof that her feelings for him went beyond friendship. Such a generous and highly personal present had provided additional proof, if such were needed.

He reminded himself that others had been aware of her feelings for him too – especially her father, and therein lay the barrier to taking their relationship beyond friendship.

Had Emily not been the parson's daughter, had she been, say, the daughter of a farmer, or a miner, Sam had no doubt they could have married and been very happy together.

As it was . . . he fingered the crucifix once more. They could hardly be farther apart than they were at this moment, with little chance they would ever meet again. And yet . . . ?

'You're not saying very much, Sam.'

At the sound of Jean's voice, Ira looked up from his game with Primrose and smiled at each of them in turn, his fingers entwined in a complicated pattern of string.

'Were you thinking of home? Of St Cleer?'

Sam nodded. 'It seems an awfully long way away right now.'

Jean flapped her hand vigorously in front of her face in a vain hope that the action would produce a hint of cool air.

'Do you think it might be raining there? Cool, wet, lovely rain?'

'Most probably,' Sam said shortly.

'Are you disappointed with what you've seen of Australia so far?' she persisted.

'We've hardly seen any of the country yet, although I must admit it's different to what I was expecting. But if there's work to be had here – underground work – then it's where I want to be.' He stood up to look over the edge of the high-sided truck. 'Talking of mines . . . look what I can see, up ahead.'

Both Ira and Jean rose to their feet, Ira holding Primrose with one arm and supporting himself with the other.

'It's a mine!' Jean exclaimed excitedly.

'More than one by the look of it,' Sam said. 'It must be Kadina.'

There was one other passenger in the truck. They had given up trying to talk to him early on the journey because it was evident that he spoke hardly any English. Now, at mention of 'Kadina', he smiled, showing yellowing teeth, and nodded vigorously. 'Is Kadina,' he said. 'Is Kadina.'

II

After Sam and Ira had unloaded the luggage, the two men accompanied Jean and Primrose to the office of the mine captain, close to where the train had been stopped especially for their benefit.

They stood back, not making their own requirements known while Jean inquired after her father from a heavily bearded mine captain with a strong Cornish accent.

'Jeremiah Hodge?'

The captain scratched his head and tried to concentrate. 'As I recall we have seven or eight Hodges at work on the Kadina mine, but I can't recall a Jeremiah. How long ago is it that he came to work here?'

'It was some years ago now,' Jean admitted unhappily. 'Before I married and had Primrose. I suppose it must be at least five, possibly six years, since he left Cornwall to come here.'

'Well, his name should be in one of the employment books . . .' He nodded at the office clerk, who selected a large leather-bound ledger from a shelf above his desk and lifted it down for the captain.

'Here we are, here's a book that begins in eighteen sixty-eight. It should be in here. Let's see . . .' Poring through the book, he suddenly jabbed a finger at the page in front of him. 'Here are the Hodges. Hodge, Brian . . . , Hodge, David . . . ,

Frederick . . . Ah! Here we are, Hodge, Jeremiah. He worked on a pare with a number of other Cornishmen. But he's not working at Kadina now. None of them are. They've been gone for quite some time.'

A 'pare' was a group of miners who worked together as a team.

'Oh!' The mine captain's words brought Jean very close to tears. The reunion she had been so eagerly anticipating was not about to take place after all. 'But . . . I've come all the way from Cornwall to be with him. I've brought Primrose . . .'

She was utterly demoralised and Sam asked, 'Is there any record of where he went after he left Kadina?'

The captain shook his head. He could add little that would be of further help. 'None at all. We don't ask the men where they're going when they leave us. Most wouldn't tell me the truth if I did. If I was asked to *guess*, I'd say he went off to the Northern Territory. That's where most miners went about that time. There was a gold find up there and we lost more than a quarter of the workforce. I've no doubt he was one of them. Whether he's still there – and where *exactly* he went to – is a very different matter. As far as I can recall, the gold strike didn't amount to very much on that occasion.'

Jean was absolutely devastated and Ira moved closer to her, murmuring, 'Don't upset yourself, Jean. We'll find him.'

'Well, if that's all I can do for you . . .' the mine captain began.

'It isn't,' Sam said quickly. 'We've all just arrived from Cornwall. Ira and I are both experienced copper miners and we're looking for work.'

The mine captain shrugged his shoulders. 'I only wish I could be of help to you. Had you arrived here only six months ago I'd have taken you on, there and then, but the way things are right now . . .' He shrugged again. 'The price of copper is falling and we're having to go deeper to find ore. As a miner you'll know that the deeper we need to go, the more it's going to cost to win ore. In fact, we're about to put out a notice telling the men they'll need to take a cut in pay if they want to stay in work. I'm sorry, but we're looking to cut down on the numbers of the men working at Kadina, not taking on more.'

His words stunned the two Cornishmen. They had come to South Australia in the firm belief that this was the promised land for all Cornish miners. To be told there was no work for them was a major calamity!

'But . . . what can we do? We're here because we've been told there would be work waiting for us – and because Jean and I thought we had family here. Now you're telling us there's no more work in South Australia than there was in Cornwall!'

'No. What I'm saying is that there's no work at the Kadina mine – and that Jeremiah Hodge is no longer here either. But you mention having family in the area – would I know them?'

'My uncle, Wilf Hooper. He came to Kadina at the same time as Jean's pa, or thereabouts.'

'Ah, yes, *Captain* Wilf. I have no need to look him up in the ledger. He went north to the Blinman mine, up in the Flinders Ranges, to take a job as underground captain. As far as I know he's still there. They were lucky to get him. Captain Wilf is a good man.'

'The Blinman mine . . . ? Flinders Ranges . . . ? Where are they?' Sam's knowledge of South Australian geography was virtually non-existent and he admitted it to the Kadina mine captain.

'Blinman is probably about three hundred miles north – as the crow flies. The best way to get there is to take a boat to Port Augusta, then pay for a ride on one of the bullock carts. They bring ore to the port and return to Blinman with supplies.'

Sam looked at the Kadina mine captain with an expression of dismay. 'How long is it likely to take to get there?'

'If you wait for the steamer from Wallaroo you can get to Port Augusta within twenty-four hours. From there? Ten, fifteen days . . . maybe twenty. I couldn't tell you exactly, I've never made the trip myself and haven't spoken to anyone who has.'

Sam and Ira exchanged concerned glances. Meanwhile, Jean sat in a chair and stared down at the floor. She looked utterly defeated.

'The steamer's not due in here for a few days – that's if you want to catch it. If not, well, you could always stay around in the hope that things will pick up and you find someone to take you on. It's happened before.'

Sam shook his head. 'We'll most likely move on – but are things likely to be any better at Blinman?'

'Probably. It's a long way from anywhere. Men who go that far out to find work are usually looking to make money in a gold mine, not in copper. Besides, Captain Wilf's your uncle. He'll probably take you on whether or not the mine really needs men. I'd say that's certainly your best bet.'

'What about me?' Jean asked plaintively. 'What can I do? I've got Primrose to think of and was expecting my pa to be here . . .' Her voice broke and she could say no more.

Embarrassed, the mine captain could offer her no words of comfort. He remained silent.

'We'll need to find a place to stay while we think this over,' Sam said to the mine captain. 'Do you know anywhere we could put up for a few days?'

'Well, there's the Miners' Arms Hotel, but that might prove a bit pricey if you're looking to watch your spending. If you don't mind being a bit cramped for space I can recommend you to Widow Pengelly – Florence Pengelly. She's from Cornwall and is always looking to take in boarders to make herself a bit of extra money. She's a fine cook too and will look after you. She lives in Goyder Street. I'll send a man ahead to tell her you're on your way, then give you directions to get there.'

Looking sympathetically at Jean, he added, 'I'll get one of the drivers to take your baggage there in a donkey cart. I'm sorry I haven't been able to be of more help to you, but I wish you luck.'

III

With Primrose riding on Ira's broad shoulders, the dejected new arrivals walked away from the mine, following the directions given to them by the Kadina mine captain.

All were concerned about what the future held for them. Jean, very close to tears, kept shaking her head in disbelief at their misfortune.

Aware of her deep unhappiness, Ira moved closer to her. 'Don't despair, Jean. Everything will turn out all right, you'll see.'

'How *can* it?' Jean demanded fiercely. 'I've brought Primrose all this way in the belief that her grandpa would be here to take care of the two of us, only to find that he's apparently disappeared off the face of the earth and there's no more work here than there was in Cornwall. We're worse off than we were.'

'Don't distress yourself, Jean,' Sam tried to reassure her. 'Ira and I aren't going to desert you. We'll make certain you and Primrose are all right before either of us moves on.'

'That's right,' Ira agreed. 'Whatever happens, we won't leave you and Primrose to fend for yourselves.'

Jean's eyes were brimming with tears as she looked from one to the other gratefully. 'Thank you. Thank you both.'

'Why is Mummy crying?' Primrose asked.

'She's upset because we haven't been able to find your grandad yet,' Sam explained. 'I expect you're unhappy about it, too.'

'Is he dead, like my daddy?'

The question was so unexpected that for a few moments no one could think of a suitable reply. As Jean turned away, no longer able to control her tears, Sam said, 'No, he's not dead, Primrose. He's gone off somewhere to earn lots of money, so that when you *do* meet, he'll be able to buy you lots of nice things. Tell me, what is it you'd most like to have?'

Sam had put the question to her in a bid to change the subject to something that would be less upsetting for Jean, but Primrose's reply had the opposite effect.

'I'd like to have a daddy again, so that Mummy won't cry so much.'

Sam saw Jean's shoulders begin to heave. Reaching her as the first sob broke free, he signalled urgently for Ira to take Primrose on ahead.

Jean had regained control of herself by the time they reached the home of Florence Pengelly. As they were ushered into her home, she told them with great delight that she had been born in the hamlet of Tremar, in Cornwall, a very short distance from St Cleer.

She chatted happily to Sam and, to a lesser extent, Jean, as they discovered mutual acquaintances. However, her delight at having guests in the house who were familiar with her old home did not impair her perception.

After showing Jean and Primrose to their room, she returned to fix Sam and Ira in turn with a stern, thin-lipped gaze.

'That young woman's been crying. Why? I don't want any trouble or goings on while you're in this house. If there's something I ought to know then you'd better tell me now.'

'There's no trouble, Mrs Pengelly,' Sam said. 'It's just that something Primrose said on the way here touched a raw nerve at a time when Jean's feeling particularly low.'

He told the landlady briefly about the death of Jean's husband and the loss of her baby, which had prompted her to leave Cornwall, and of her dismay at not finding her father here, in Kadina.

Florence had been scrutinising Sam's face unnervingly as he related Jean's story. Now, satisfied he was telling her the truth, her expression softened.

'My dear soul!' she exclaimed, with great feeling. 'I know what it's like for a woman to lose her man, but at least the Lord gave us a long and happy life together. To have him taken away like that – and a baby too! 'Tis enough to turn a young woman's mind. Then to come all this way with a young child to be with her father, only to find he's no longer here . . . I'm not given to questioning the actions of the Lord, but He does seem to give some folk greater burdens to carry through life than He does others.'

'Don't worry, Mrs Pengelly,' said Ira. 'We'll see that Jean and Primrose are properly looked after.'

Giving him a searching look, Florence said, 'Will you now? Well, I hope you've told her. There's nothing worse when things are going wrong than the feeling that no one cares. Now, I don't doubt you'll all be wanting something to eat – and you've chosen a good time to arrive. I've a whole batch of pasties almost ready to come out of the oven. They're for the Miners' Arms, but it doesn't matter how many they get. They're pleased to take as many as I care to cook. You won't find a finer pasty anywhere outside of Cornwall – and not many can better them there neither.'

Florence Pengelly was convinced that food was the answer to most of life's problems. Her paying guests were treated to meals they had not dared to even dream about during the months they had spent on board the *Bonython*.

If there was one tiny complaint Sam might have made about their sojourn in the widow's home, it was that they were given no time together to discuss plans for the future. He had hoped they might be able to arrive at a decision during their first evening there, but it was not to be. News of the new arrivals from Cornwall had spread rapidly among the closely knit community of Kadina and there was a steady stream of visitors to the Pengelly house. Many came in the hope that Sam, Ira or Jean might have news of friends and relatives they had left 'back home' in Cornwall.

Although delighted to be able to talk about Cornwall, most

went away disappointed. But a few were given comparatively up-to-date news of those they had left behind them – some as long as twenty years before.

Because of the manner in which Florence had welcomed him and the others into her home, Sam felt that by chatting to her friends he and the others were repaying her in a small way for her generous hospitality. However, when Florence asked Sam the following morning to accompany her to visit a house-bound woman named Polly Luck, who had left St Cleer many years before, he protested. He told her that he and the others needed to have a serious discussion about their future plans, as a matter of some urgency. The monies given to him for his act of bravery at Cape Town meant he would not immediately be pressed for money – and he would take care of Jean where money matters were concerned – but he and Ira both wanted to find work as soon as possible.

'I can understand your concern,' said Florence, 'but you come out with me now and I'll make certain no one disturbs you this evening. One or two matters might very well have resolved themselves by then and you'll have a much better idea of what everyone wants to do.'

'What do you mean by that?' Sam was puzzled by her statement.

'If you *really* don't know then you wouldn't believe me if I was to tell you what I'm thinking,' Florence said. 'Now, if you're ready you can go and fetch Primrose. We'll take her with us. It'll do the child good to get away from her mother for an hour or two and Polly will enjoy meeting her. She has umpteen grandchildren and great-grandchildren, so there'll no doubt be a few toys round to keep Primrose amused.'

Polly Luck turned out to be a garrulous, meandering old woman who certainly knew St Cleer and the families who lived there. She had known Sam's father when he was a small boy, but she kept confusing Sam with others she had known. By the time he, Primrose and Florence left the house, his brain was almost as scrambled as Polly's talk had been.

However, Primrose had been given a doll to which she had formed a particular attachment and she, at least, was extremely happy.

On the way back to Goyder Street, Sam said to Florence, 'When you were talking earlier about things sorting themselves out, were you thinking of Ira and Jean getting together?'

'I was – so it seems the idea doesn't come as so much of a surprise to you as you made it out to be.'

'I've known for some time that Ira is sweet on Jean, but I've never been quite sure how serious it is – and I doubt very much whether Jean looks upon Ira as a potential husband.'

Florence snorted derisively. 'When a woman who's been widowed has a young child to support and there's no other way of doing it, all single men are a potential lifeline. Not that I'm saying that's *all* he is to her. I've seen the way she's looked at him once or twice. They weren't calculating looks. Those two have quite a lot to offer each other.'

Fixing him with a direct look, she continued, 'From what I've gathered it was you and Jean who set out from Cornwall together. How would you feel if the two of them decided they wanted to make a go of things?'

Choosing his words carefully, Sam said, 'Jean and I have known each other since we were both Primrose's age. I was best man to her husband when she married him. If Jean feels she can be just as happy with Ira I'll willingly stand as best man again.' He grimaced. 'Mind you, had you asked me that question after Ira and I had met for the first time you'd have got a very different answer. We both know each other a lot better now. Even so, it will come as a big surprise to me if I learn that Jean feels the same about him as he does about her.'

'If Jean can still surprise someone who's known her all her life there's not much wrong with the girl. At times like this I wish I wasn't prevented by my Methodist upbringing from having a small wager with you.'

When Sam entered the house it was immediately apparent that Florence had read the situation between Jean and Ira far more accurately than he.

They were both in the kitchen, standing as far apart as was possible in such a small space. Jean looked flustered and Ira seemed to be finding it difficult to stand still.

Oblivious to anything but the doll she was carrying, Primrose ran to Jean, holding out the toy given to her by Polly Luck.

'Look what I've got! The lady said her name is Rose. She's got a flower's name, just like me.'

'It's lovely, darling. Very nice indeed. Aren't you a lucky girl?'

Pulling the doll back from her mother, Primrose held it up for Ira's inspection. 'Do you like her too?'

'She's beautiful,' Ira agreed enthusiastically. 'But not as beautiful as you. Here, come and let me give both of you a great big hug.'

As Ira scooped up the small girl and the doll in his arms, Florence gave Sam a triumphant look that said clearly, 'I told you so!'

Intercepting the other woman's glance, Jean blushed and said, 'Me and Ira have had a long talk while you were out . . .'

Aware of what she was about to say, Ira's cheek, pressed against Primrose's face, turned a bright scarlet.

'We spoke of the situation we're all in out here, in South Australia. Ira is particularly concerned about me and Primrose. He wants to take on responsibility for us . . .'

Ira saw the uncertain expression that fleetingly crossed Sam's face. Aware that Jean had not made his intentions as clear as was intended, he said hurriedly, 'I've asked Jean to marry me, Sam – and she's said "yes".'

'I trust there's more to the pair of you getting married than uncertainty about the future,' Florence said before Sam could reply. 'There's nothing more uncertain in life than marriage.'

'We both know that,' Ira replied. 'It's not the only reason we want to marry. I've grown to admire Jean more and more since we first met on the boat. Sam knows that's true. It's taken Jean a bit longer to feel the same way about me, but that's hardly surprising. I wasn't any woman's idea of an ideal husband or father when she first saw me. I'm not proud of the man I was then. But she's given me a reason to put my life back together again. I want to share that life with her – and to be the daddy that Primrose said would be the best present anyone could give her.'

It was the longest speech Sam had ever heard the Camborne miner make and he did not doubt his sincerity.

Neither did Jean. Moving to stand beside Ira, she shyly took his hand. 'Primrose and me are lucky to have found Ira. I'll do my best to be a good wife to him.'

'That sounds far more promising.' Florence's approval was accompanied by a warm smile. 'What do you have to say about it, Sam?'

'I'm very, very happy for everyone concerned,' Sam said, with the utmost sincerity. 'Ira and Jean came to South Australia looking for a new life. They couldn't have got off to a better start than this.'

After kissing Jean warmly, he shook hands with Ira and said, 'Does this mean you and Jean will be going off following a trail of your own now?'

The happy smile left Ira's face for a moment and he said, 'I hope not, Sam. It's not what either Jean or me want. We'd both like it if the three of us and Primrose could stay together. It's just . . . well, when we decide what we're going to do it will be with me and Jean coming along as a married couple, that's all.'

'That's fine with me,' Sam said. 'Let's hope Uncle Wilf can still be found. I believe our best hope of finding work will be with him, at the Blinman mine.'

IV

When Sam made inquiries the following day he learned that the paddle-steamer *Marquess* was not due to make the journey from Wallaroo to Port Augusta for another four days.

During the wait, the newcomers to South Australia were given the benefit of Florence's knowledge of the country and her views on what *she* thought they ought to be doing.

'If you really want to make some money for yourselves you should go up into the Adelaide Hills searching for gold,' she said at breakfast one morning. 'It's there – my William found it. I went with him to a gold diggings when I first came out here to join him. I can tell you that some of those gold camps were rough places. There were no Methodist preachers around then to stop a man – or a woman – from enjoying a drink at the end of a hard day's work, or to celebrate a rich strike. Things are very different on a copper mine. You'll be lucky to be given work in any of 'em if you don't go to chapel at least twice every Sunday and if your "Hallelujah" isn't louder than the next man's. I was brought up a Methodist, but I don't hold with a lot of what they teach these days. They seem to have made up most of it along the way. It certainly isn't what John Wesley intended them to teach. It wasn't the life for my William, neither. We worked hard and played hard. By the time we'd done we'd made enough money to buy this place, where we could put up folk like yourselves and advise them on what they ought to be doing.'

'We're very grateful for your advice, Mrs Pengelly, we really are,' Sam said, 'but I know that Ira wants to have a little money put by so that Jean will be comfortable, come what may, and I'm looking to find my Uncle Wilf, up at Blinman, so it looks as though it's going to be copper for us.'

'You know what's best for you, of course,' Florence said, unconvinced. 'But don't let anyone put you off seeking gold if you think it might be there. Copper may keep you from starving, but it's gold that will make you rich.'

The few days spent in the house of Florence Pengelly proved a welcome period of recuperation for the immigrants from Cornwall. During this time they met with more of Florence's friends who had benefited from gold finds in various parts of Australia.

Sam was impressed by the stories of the wealth that finding gold had brought to these people. However, such success stories were counterbalanced by the stories of failure he heard a couple of days later.

Jean, Ira and Primrose had left the house with Florence to visit the shops to buy a few things that Primrose was likely to need when they reached Blinman. Florence had warned them that Blinman was so remote it might not be possible to buy all the things they might need there.

It had been Sam's intention to remain in the house, but as it was a very hot day he decided to go for a walk in the hope of finding a breeze on the streets of Kadina.

On a street corner, he was accosted by a grizzled old man, who asked Sam to spare a coin or two for 'an old man, down on his luck'.

Recognising the man's dialect as that of a Cornish moorland man, Sam chatted to him for a while before accompanying him to a shanty bar, sited amidst scrubland, beyond the perimeter of the bustling, township that was Kadina.

Here, in a bar constructed of uncut timber and corrugated iron, Sam met others like his grizzled companion. He spent more money than he had intended, buying rounds of 'swanky', the locally brewed beer, while listening to tales of woe. Many of the men here were ex-goldminers, down on their luck, who had returned to the Copper Triangle hoping in vain to find work.

The stories they told were depressingly similar. All had originally come to South Australia from Cornwall to take work in the copper mines that had sprung up on many parts of the country, with varying degrees of success.

In due course, lured by stories of miners who had become rich men overnight, they deserted the copper mines and set off in search of gold.

Some went to the hills just outside Adelaide, South Australia's capital, where gold was being found in varying quantities. Others sought their personal Eldorado farther afield. All had the same story to tell.

For every man who found gold there were hundreds who discovered anew the anguish of the poverty they had known in Cornwall.

Some travelled from claim to claim in the vain hope of changing their luck. Many actually discovered gold, but never in sufficient quantities to halt the downward slide their life was taking.

Most of those here had returned to their original work places in the vicinity of Kadina, only to learn that their places had been taken by younger, more energetic men, deemed by the mine captains to be more dependable than those lured away by the prospect of instant riches.

Now, penniless and without hope, they lived in makeshift hovels in the countryside surrounding what had become for them an uncaring community. Scrounging and begging, and occasionally killing wild – or even domestic animals, they contrived to stay alive.

Sam returned to Florence's house sobered in spirit if not in body. He found the household in a state of high excitement.

Whilst out with the others, Ira had become the township's hero by stopping a runaway horse that was pulling a baker's van in one of Kadina's busiest streets.

'Ira was *marvellous*,' Jean gushed. 'The baker was just stepping down from his van when a dog suddenly rushed at the horse, snapping at its legs. When it took off the baker was knocked down by the cart and lucky not to be run over. There was chaos on the street, with people screaming and running to get out of its way. Then Ira jumped out and caught the horse's bridle. He was dragged for a long way and I thought he might be killed himself, but he managed to bring the horse to a halt without anyone being hurt. You should have been there to see all the people crowding around to congratulate him.'

'Well done, Ira,' said Sam, shaking the other man by the hand. 'I wish I'd been there to see it for myself.'

'I was *frightened*!' Primrose added. 'I *cried*.'

'There would have been tears from a great many people had Ira not had the courage to jump out and stop the horse,' Florence declared. 'He was a hero today.'

'Someone would have been killed for certain,' Jean agreed.

'It was a very brave thing to do, to jump out in front of a horse like that,' Sam said. 'I doubt if I could have done it.'

Ira looked embarrassed. 'That isn't true, Sam. I did nothing that you wouldn't have done had you been there – as we all know. Besides, I grew up with horses. My pa used to break in the ponies used on the mines, and I'd help him. Horses have no fear for me, whatever mood they're in – and this horse wasn't bad, only frightened.'

'It was a bold enough thing to do, whatever Ira says,' declared the Cornish landlady. 'What's more, it didn't go unnoticed. Councillor Mintoff was in the street and saw what happened. He came across to congratulate Ira, wanting to know who he is and where he's staying. He says he intends organising an official presentation to him for his bravery. I'm sure he will. He's trying to win nomination to the state parliament but folk around here are lukewarm about it. If he doesn't get nominated he'll probably have to stay with local politics and there's likely to be too much dirt raked up about him, given time. I don't like Mintoff and wouldn't trust him any farther than I could throw him, but that needn't concern any of you too much. What's certain is that Ira will leave Kadina richer than when he arrived.'

'It's no more than he deserves,' Jean said vehemently. Giving

Sam a sidelong glance, she added, 'I think Primrose and me are very lucky to have two such brave men taking care of us.'

She then needed to explain to Florence how Sam had saved Ira's life when he fell into the sea at Cape Town.

'Well I never.' Florence's admiration now encompassed both men. 'There have been more than one occasion in the goldfields when I've prayed that men like you two would come along to help me out. There were always plenty of the wrong sort who offered, but none who could be depended upon when things got tough. The pair of you are a bit late for me now.'

Turning to Jean, she said, 'Make certain you hang on to at least one of them, my dear, there aren't too many like them around.'

'I will, Florence,' Jean said, smiling warmly at Ira.

'Now, let's all go into the front room,' said Florence. 'I think I might be able to find something that's more suitable than swanky for a small celebration.'

The following day, at a private ceremony to which local officials and the editor of the local newspaper had been invited, Councillor Stefan Mintoff presented Ira with a 'bravery award' of twenty-five pounds, donated, as he pointed out, from his own pocket.

Florence commented, unkindly, that had Ira's deed been witnessed by any other member of the city council, there would have been an official presentation in front of a full council. The absence of such recognition was indicative of Mintoff's unpopularity.

However, aware of none of this, Ira was delighted with the money. He acknowledged it with a stammering modesty that was in marked contrast to the long and highly political speech given by Stefan Mintoff.

Later that evening, when Jean was putting Primrose to bed and Florence was in the kitchen preparing an evening meal for her lodgers, Sam and Ira sat in the 'front room' enjoying the

Cape brandy Florence had first produced as a celebratory drink the previous day.

It had been apparent to Sam for many minutes that Ira wanted to say something to him but could not quite muster the courage to express himself.

Eventually, Sam said to him, 'You're as fidgety as a stoat in a chicken run, Ira. Is there something on your mind?'

'Yes . . . yes, there is, Sam. Jean and me would like to be married before setting off for Blinman, but it will mean staying here for a few more weeks, while we arrange everything and have the banns read.'

'That shouldn't be too much of a problem, Ira. Not now that you've been given the money from this Councillor Mintoff.'

'Are you quite sure, Sam? After all, it will mean that while we're here you too will be spending money instead of earning it.'

'Your marriage to Jean is a lot more important than a couple of weeks' pay, Ira. You go ahead with the arrangements, I'll happily fall in with them.'

V

Jean and Ira's hopes of marrying at Kadina were dashed when a measles epidemic swept through the township. By the end of a week it had claimed the lives of a score of young children. Schools were closed and mothers were afraid of taking their children out on the streets.

After a discussion on the increasing seriousness of the outbreak, Ira and Jean reluctantly decided that for Primrose's sake they must catch the first boat out of Wallaroo, putting off their marriage until they reached Blinman.

After bidding Florence an emotional farewell, they were

fortunate to catch a paddle-steamer that day. It would carry them north on the Spencer Gulf to Port Augusta. Although this was the nearest seaport to Blinman, they still faced an overland journey of a hundred and fifty miles. The mine was situated in the heart of the Flinders Ranges, a spectacular series of mountain ranges which ran parallel to the course their steamer was taking.

Jean was thankful that on this occasion they would be spending only a single night on the boat. She and Primrose had spent enough time afloat to last them a lifetime. She hoped that their arrival at Blinman would mark the end of their travels. Certainly the end of journeys by boat.

In fact, the short voyage on the steamship turned out to be a very enjoyable experience. The accommodation was certainly a great improvement on the vessel that had brought them from England, the men sharing one cabin and Jean and Primrose having another to themselves.

It was a welcome experience too not to be at the mercy of winds and tides. With its great paddle-wheels threshing the water, the steady throb of the engines was reminiscent of the mine-engines that had been an ever-present feature of moorland life in Cornwall during the good years of copper mining, and the men, in particular, found the sound strangely comforting.

They did not have sufficient time on the steamship to become bored. Primrose was the only child on the vessel and during daylight hours the crew delighted in pointing out interesting features on ship and shore to her. In turn, she repeated the information to her doll, embellishing each piece of information with childhood fantasies.

The travellers went to their beds that night happy in the knowledge that when they woke the next morning they would have reached Port Augusta.

Soon after dawn the passengers were awoken by the sound of men calling from the decks of the ship to the shore. At the same time the engines were continually changing speed as the telegraphs rang out a stream of instructions to the sweating men in the engine room.

They had arrived at Port Augusta and the ship was edging towards a berth at a small jetty.

This was a very busy seaport. In addition to copper ore and smelted copper, there was an ever-growing variety of farm produce passing out through the docks. Arriving ships brought in manufactured goods and foodstuffs from all over the world.

The town of Port Augusta spread inland from the docks and in the distance could be seen the dark grey mountain ranges of the Flinders. Somewhere among them, far to the north, nestled the mining community of Blinman.

Finding a bullock cart and driver willing to take the small party to its destination proved to be no problem; there was a number readily available.

A price for the long journey was eventually agreed with Piet van Roos, owner and driver of a bullock team and dray. A South African by birth, he had arrived in Australia almost forty years before. Small and heavily bearded, his skin had the dried-up, leathery texture of a man who had spent a lifetime out of doors.

They had not been travelling for long before the immigrants learned that Piet had been a prospector for much of his life. He informed them that although his labours had not netted him a fortune, he had found gold in sufficient quantity to buy himself a dray and a team of bullocks.

'Is there gold to be found in the Flinders Ranges?' Sam put the question to the teamster as he and the old man plodded along beside the lead animal, following a track that had little more than the ruts of many wagons to mark it out as the main thoroughfare between Port Augusta and the copper mines of the Ranges.

'Gold, silver, copper . . . a man can find whatever he's looking for in the Ranges if he keeps his eyes open when he's walking around. Mind you, most of those who call themselves "prospectors" wouldn't recognise gold if they tripped over it. Would you?'

Sam shook his head. 'Copper and tin, yes. We've never had much gold in Cornwall.'

Spitting to one side of the track with scornful abandon, the old man said, 'How would you know, if you don't know what it looks like?'

It was a good question and one to which Sam had no answer.

There were many such conversations with Piet van Roos during the days and nights they were on the trail. He particularly enjoyed talking of his early days in South Australia, once they were seated about a campfire at night and the contents of the whisky jar he kept on the dray had loosened his tongue.

Piet told them there was much gold to be found in the country, adding that some of the most likely locations were so close to the South Australian capital that the early pioneers had probably 'dug up gold and thrown it away when they were putting in foundations for their fancy houses'.

Piet repeated this statement to Sam the following day when they were once more walking together beside the slow-moving bullock cart. It prompted Sam to ask, 'If there's gold where you say it is, why aren't you out there digging for it instead of driving a bullock cart here, in all this emptiness?'

The old man looked at Sam pityingly. 'If you think it's empty here then you must have bottle-stops instead of eyes in your head. There's more things of interest – far more – than you're ever likely to see in a place like Adelaide. There are too many people there. A man can't live life in his own way when he's surrounded by strangers. Besides, there are some days when my knees don't do what they're made to do. If I was there I'd most likely have folk fussing about me until it drove me out of my mind. When it happens out here I can take my time hitching up the bullocks, then ride on the dray until my knees start working again.'

'What happens if your knees give out one day and you find you *can't* hitch up the bullocks?'

Piet shrugged. 'When that happens I'll know my time has come. I'll die the way I've lived. In a place where I want to be, under God's sky and thinking my own thoughts.'

Sam realised that Piet van Roos was one of life's true 'loners'. A man who derived more pleasure from his own company than from that of others.

Before he could think of a reply, Piet said, 'As for this place being empty – we've had company for two days now.'

'What do you mean by "company"?' Sam asked sharply.

'A "Yura" – an Aborigine. That's the name they're known by, up around Blinman. He's got a woman with him. A child too, I think.'

Sam looked at his companion in disbelief. 'How do you know? I've seen no one.'

'It's like I said, son. You've got bottle-stops instead of eyes. They're out there all right and not far behind us, either.'

Sam looked back apprehensively, not certain of what he might see. He saw nothing.

'If they're really there, why haven't they shown themselves to us?'

'I've seen 'em. You will too when they're good and ready.'

Sam would have pursued the matter, but at that moment Primrose called out, 'Look, there's a kangaroo! It's the closest one's ever come to us.'

They had seen many kangaroos on their journey, but when Sam looked in the direction in which the young girl was pointing, he saw one of the animals no more than twenty paces from the dray, looking at the travellers with fearless interest.

'Well done, girl,' said Piet, hurrying to the seat at the front of the dray. 'You've just found tonight's dinner.'

Taking up a gun from beneath the seat, he put it to his shoulder, took aim at the inquisitive kangaroo, and fired.

As the kangaroo dropped dead, Primrose screamed. The shot

and the small girl's scream frightened the bullocks. For a moment Sam thought they would take off, dragging the heavy dray, its load and passengers with them. However, the steadiness of the older animals in the team quickly calmed the others and they came to a restless halt.

'Come and give me a hand to get the 'roo back to the dray,' Piet called out to Sam and Ira, ignoring Primrose, who was sobbing and clinging to Jean.

The kangaroo was still twitching when Sam reached it, but Piet said it was 'dead enough' and the twitching had ceased by the time it was carried back to the dray.

Jean turned Primrose's head away when the three men and their burden were close enough for her to see the hole in the animal's chest where the bullet had struck it.

Heaved into the back of the wagon and covered with a piece of tarpaulin in order to keep the flies away, the kangaroo was no longer a living thing.

On his way back to the bullocks, Piet paused alongside the dray where Jean sat with Primrose in her arms. The small girl saw him and turned away, burying her face in her mother's dress.

Seemingly oblivious to Primrose's anguish, Piet said, 'The girl's got sharp eyes. Thanks to her we'll eat well tonight.'

With this, he strode to the head of the bullock team and, cracking his whip, shouted the command for them to move off.

That evening, when the party had made camp for the night, Piet roasted the choicest portions of the kangaroo over the campfire. It was now that the Cornish party met up with the first Aborigines they had encountered.

A very small family group, composed of a man, woman and a child perhaps a little older than Primrose, they seemed to materialise from nowhere.

There was not a stitch of clothing among the three of them.

They emerged from the scrub beside the camp so silently that they startled Sam. He jumped to his feet, quickly followed by Ira.

'Sit down,' ordered Piet who had not moved. 'They're hungry and know we have food.'

Without getting up, he said something to the newcomers in a language that was quite unintelligible to the others. The Aboriginal man replied in the same language and Piet waved his hand to where he had discarded the remainder of the kangaroo, telling the others it would not keep in the heat of the outback.

Going to the spot where the unwanted kangaroo meat had been thrown, the Aboriginal man said something to his wife and the meat was gathered up. Without another word the trio then vanished back into the thick scrub – the 'bush' – whence they had come.

'Will they come back again?' Sam asked, when they had gone.

'I doubt it,' Piet replied. 'They wanted food. We've given it to them. Most of 'em are peacable enough, unless they're stirred up. All the same, make certain you sleep with your belongings close by you – and I'll sheet down the stores. There might be others around with scores to settle. If you take my advice you'll buy yourselves guns when we reach Blinman. They'll make you feel more secure.'

When Piet went off to secure the load he was carrying on the dray, Jean asked querulously, 'What sort of country have we come to where we need to carry guns to protect ourselves?'

'Don't let Piet frighten you, Jean,' Sam said. 'He needs a gun because he travels a lot of miles through pretty wild country and, as you've seen, he uses it to get food. This may be a young and unknown country, but we'll none of us need a gun when we reach the mine at Blinman. It'll be just like St Cleer, you'll see.'

Sam's words were meant to be reassuring and to a certain extent they were. However, bedded down beneath the wagon with Primrose that night, Jean found sleep elusive. The slightest sound caused her imagination to run riot. Despite an intense dislike of firearms, she decided that having one beside her during the dark hours of an outback night would have been comforting.

She did not relax until the sun rose above the horizon the next morning and the surrounding country suddenly became less menacing.

VI

Not every night was spent camping out in the open on the journey to Blinman. The travellers would occasionally stop at one of the small pastoral communities which, although struggling for their very existence in the parched outback amidst the Flinders Ranges, made the travellers welcome.

Piet van Roos also knew of several shepherds' huts where the owners, although absent, were agreeable for Piet and his passengers to sleep there, accepting a small amount of non-perishable provisions left behind as payment.

When they vacated one such hut, Jean asked why the shepherd was not living there.

Piet gave her a pitying look. 'You've got a whole lot to learn about this country, missus. This station alone runs sheep on a piece of land about half the size of the place in England you've just come from . . . Cornwall, isn't it?'

When Jean nodded, Piet continued, 'The shepherd might be as far as fifty miles from here right now, staying in another of his huts. He goes wherever there's food and water for his sheep.'

Jean was not fully aware of the dimensions of Cornwall and was unable to comprehend the size of the sheep station, but she was becoming aware of the vastness of the country they were passing through and felt awed by the sheer majesty of the Flinders Ranges.

Eighteen days after leaving Port Augusta, the creaking, dusty bullock dray reached Blinman. As they drew near, the new arrivals were pleasantly surprised by the extent of the township.

Beyond Blinman they could make out a number of buildings and tall, smoking chimneys sited on the side of a hill.

'This is more like it,' Ira said enthusiastically. 'It looks as though someone here is serious about mining!'

As they drew nearer, Sam felt a great feeling of excitement surge up inside him. They could make out the mine in more detail now – and the buildings were familiar. They and the sound of mine-engines reminded him of better days in Cornwall.

'I'll take you right up to the mine office,' Piet said. 'They'll take care of you.'

The last bundle had been set on the ground before a tall, gaunt man appeared in the doorway of the office, shielding his eyes against the glare of the sun. When he saw Sam his eyes opened wide in astonishment.

'Sam! By all that's holy . . . What are you doing here?'

Delighted and not a little relieved to find his uncle, Sam stepped forward and the two men embraced warmly.

'You're the reason I'm here, Uncle Wilf. You praised Australia so much in your letters that when things became bad in the mines on Bodmin Moor, Pa insisted I should come out and join you.'

'How is your pa . . . and your ma and the rest of the family?'

'They're all fine, and they'll be overjoyed that I've found you well too.'

'It's a pity your pa didn't come with you, Sam. There's plenty of room for Cornish farmers as well as Cornish miners out here – and there'll be more as time goes on.'

Their initial enthusiastic greetings over, Wilf Hooper looked questioningly at Jean, Ira and Primrose, and Sam introduced them.

'This is Ira. We came out on the same ship. He's a Camborne man. Like me, he was expecting to find work at Kadina, but they seem to be going through a bad time right now, so he came to Blinman with me.'

Wilf and Ira shook hands and the captain said, 'Well, I'm in charge of the mine right now because Captain Paull has gone to Adelaide for a month or two. If you know mining as well as do the other Camborne men I've got here, I'll be happy to offer you work.'

Beaming with delight, Ira surprised Sam by saying, 'I stood in for the shift captain more than once on the Wheal Mary. You won't find me lagging behind any other Camborne man when it comes to mining.'

'Good!' Captain Wilf now turned to Jean and said, 'You look familiar, are you from St Cleer?'

Replying for her, Sam said, 'This is Jean Spargo, Uncle Wilf – Jean Hodge, as was. She married Phillip Spargo, who I'm sure you remember . . . ?'

The Blinman mine captain inclined his head. 'Now I know why you're familiar. I knew your mother well. You're just like her.'

'Phillip was killed in an accident at the South Caradon,' Sam explained. 'Jean had no one at home, so she's come out here to try and find her pa. She believed him to be working at Kadina, but when we were there they said he'd moved on. Probably to some goldfield, they thought.'

Captain Wilf nodded. 'I know Jeremiah. He was going to come to Blinman with me, then he met up with someone who told him of the gold that was being found way up north. He decided to go there instead. Exactly where he is now I don't know. I've spoken to men who've met up with him in at least three different camps. But what made you come here, Jean? I'm delighted to welcome anyone from St Cleer, of course, especially anyone from the Hodge family, but there's little work to be had in Blinman for a widow with a young child to support.'

'Jean's come here to be with me,' Ira said. 'We had intended marrying in Kadina, but they were suffering a serious measles epidemic. We left in a hurry fearing for the safety of Primrose. We hope to marry as soon as it's possible.'

'Congratulations. We don't have our own minister, but Reverend Maddison is due in Blinman in two weeks' time to perform two marriages. If you're serious about wanting to marry I'll make arrangements for him to marry you too.'

Ira looked eagerly to Jean for confirmation. She gave a barely discernible nod of approval and Ira beamed. 'Yes, Cap'n Hooper, we would like that very much.'

'Good! It'll also be as fine a way as any of introducing you to the folk of Blinman – although I have no doubt many will have sought you out before then. We have a great many Cornish men and women in the township who are always hungry for news from "home". Now, we'll need to find places for you all to live. I know of a nice little cottage for you and Primrose, Jean. Ira can move in with you once you're married. Until then, Ira, you can share a room in my house with Sam. But before we do anything else we'll get you and the little maid settled, Jean. I don't doubt it will be a great relief for you to be in your own place, with a roof over your head, after spending so long travelling. It's a corrugated-iron roof and the cottage is made of timber and clay, but it'll be comfortable enough, if hotter than you've been used to. You'll find many things are a bit strange at first, but I'm sure you'll enjoy Blinman. It's a good place to live. Some of the younger miners tend to get a mite out of hand on settlement night, but there's no harm in any of 'em and we have two police troopers stationed here. They're usually able to nip any trouble in the bud.'

Jean and Ira, along with two other couples, were married a fortnight later in a brief ceremony that brought almost the entire population of Blinman to the primitive chapel building to witness the multiple weddings.

Even some who lived outside the boundaries of the township attended, among them a number of women who lived in tents and makeshift huts and earned their living from prostitution.

They were shunned by the respectable women of the township. Miners, whether married or single, were careful not to catch the eye of any one of the prostitutes and be forced to acknowledge that they knew or were known by her.

Reverend Maddison was aware of their presence in the chapel and preached a sermon that drew heavily upon St Paul's Epistle to the Corinthians, making much of quotations such as 'he that committeth fornication sinneth against his own body . . . know ye not that your body is the temple of the Holy Ghost . . . ?' and '. . . it is better to marry than to burn'.

After the ceremony the three couples were given a reception at the Blinman hotel, the food paid for from mine funds. Drinks were also readily available but, miners being notoriously thirsty, those who wished to consume them were obliged to purchase their own.

The newly married couples wisely left the reception when it showed signs of rowdiness. However, the town's policemen made only three arrests that night; two were for fighting and one for causing damage to a hotel window.

There might have been a fourth and highly embarrassing arrest for drunkenness had not the minister who performed the marriage ceremonies been hastily whisked away when he fell into a drunken stupor.

Unfortunately for Reverend Maddison, he was carried away by a group of young men who possessed a wry sense of humour. They put him to bed in a hut occupied by three of the prostitutes who had attended the wedding ceremony. He would awake in the morning with a piece of card tied about his neck upon which an unusually erudite prostitute had written 'Every harlot was a virgin once – it took a man to make one of the other.'

Celebrations were still going on at the Blinman hotel when Sam made his way back to his uncle's cottage. It was a happy sound, Sam reflected, one that had been absent for too long from the mines he had left behind in Cornwall.

He and Ira had found employment on the Blinman mine with different pares. Each was working on a pitch richer in ore than they were used to. When settlement day came around, they would be paid an amount that reflected the quality and quantity of the ore they had won from the mine.

It was a state of affairs that would make any true miner happy.

Mining was a fickle occupation, subject to great fluctuations in fortunes, but Sam felt that for the first time in years he could look forward with confidence to the immediate future.

2

I

The voyage undertaken by Emily in May 1874 was very different from that experienced by Sam, Jean and their fellow travellers.

Emily, accompanied by Margaret and her two boys, booked passages on the SS *Great Britain*, and the small party occupied first-class cabins.

The *Great Britain* would have dwarfed the *Bonython* had the two ships ever met, and the steamship made the voyage to Australia in less than two-thirds the time taken by the sailing vessel. It was fitted with powerful engines to ensure a good speed would be maintained, and in addition, there were three masts, capable of carrying a fair spread of sail. When the weather was light the vessel could bowl along without the sound of engines to disturb the fare-paying passengers.

There was another difference. Despite the fact that the *Great Britain* carried more than three hundred passengers and a crew of more than a hundred, there was no feeling of overcrowding and steerage passengers were kept out of sight and hearing of the cabin passengers.

The ship carried live sheep, pigs, ducks, geese and chickens to ensure there were always fresh eggs and meat for the first-class passengers to enjoy when they dined.

Because of its huge bulk, the *Great Britain* was less affected by sea conditions than smaller vessels and Margaret and her boys thought that travelling a steamship was a marvellous experience.

The voyage terminated at Melbourne but details of Emily's arrival had been telegraphed ahead of her. When the ship berthed at her destination, a representative of the Church was waiting to escort Emily and her companions to a hotel.

Twenty-four hours later they took passage on another steamship that would carry them to the port of Wallaroo and thence to Kadina.

Emily's work would take in the three towns of the Copper Triangle, Moonta, Kadina and Wallaroo. Having been told she was free to take up residence in any of them she had chosen Kadina.

Emily had made discreet enquiries before setting out from Cornwall and had learned that the mine where she hoped she would find Sam was situated here. It should not be difficult to locate him. Hopefully, Margaret's husband would be found working somewhere in the area too.

Emily had come to South Australia on behalf of the Church of England on an open-ended mission. She was to set up prayer groups and educational centres in the area and involve herself in any activities calculated to improve the spiritual and physical well-being of the miners and their families.

Before she left England, Emily's uncle, Lord Boyce, had arranged for telegraphic messages to be sent on behalf of the British government, requesting that Emily be given every assistance during the long journey and on her arrival. As a result, when the steamer carrying her to Wallaroo called at Port Adelaide, she was greeted by a representative of the Bishop of Adelaide, who invited her to a dinner being held in the South Australian capital that evening.

The following day, back on board the ship, Emily and Margaret were taking the air on the upper deck in the late afternoon when a dapper, moustached man approached the two women.

Giving them a stiff bow, he addressed Emily. 'Good day to you, Miss Boyce. Please forgive me for approaching you in such an informal manner, but I was at the dinner yesterday evening which was graced by your presence. I am Stefan Mintoff, a councillor in the town of Kadina, which I believe is to be your destination. I felt I should introduce myself and offer to assist you in any way while you are there.'

The man had a European accent that Emily could not place.

'That is most kind of you,' she replied. 'I am afraid I do not recall seeing you at the dinner . . .' This was not true; she had seen him sitting farther along the long table at which she had been seated and was aware of the interest he was taking in her.

'I would not, of course, have expected you to notice me, but I doubt whether there was anyone present at the dinner who did not notice *you*, Miss Boyce.'

There was a strange sound from Margaret, who might have been trying to stifle a laugh. Stefan Mintoff glanced briefly at her before returning his attention to Emily.

'I was talking to the Bishop's chaplain, who informed me you are newly arrived from England with the purpose of carrying out welfare work in the copper towns. It is an admirable task you are taking on, Miss Boyce. I am quite certain you will receive the full support of all concerned. I recently allowed an institute building to be erected on land I own, next to my general store. I will ensure that all its facilities are available for your activities. I hope I may be of further service to you during what I trust will be a long and happy stay in Kadina.'

'Thank you, Mr Mintoff.' Emily was genuinely delighted that her mission had got off to such a start. Having the institute building made available to her would make her work very much easier. 'Your offer is most kind. I will certainly bear it in mind.'

Inclining her head to him in farewell, she turned to Margaret. 'Come, Margaret. I feel I would like to rest before we make ready for dinner.'

Emily moved off and Margaret followed. When they were out of earshot, Margaret commented, 'That's as smooth tongued a man as I've come across in a very long time.'

'Really? I thought he was rather charming.'

Margaret looked sharply at Emily but was unable to tell whether or not she was being serious. She felt a moment of concern. There were times when she was aware that Emily's experience with men was limited.

'He was certainly *charming*,' she agreed. 'The trouble is that he knew it. You be careful of him when we get to Kadina.'

The relationship between Margaret and Emily had undergone a change since leaving St Cleer. It was largely at Emily's instigation. She had told Margaret that she was a 'companion' and no longer a lady's maid. They were to be on first-name terms and Margaret was not to use the prefix 'Miss' when she addressed her.

The two women had also become good friends. Emily suddenly smiled at her companion. 'You need not worry, Margaret. I have no doubt I shall have more to think about in Kadina than Stefan Mintoff.'

She did not add that one of the things she *hoped* to have on her mind in Kadina was Sam. The thought of seeing him again excited her more and more as they came closer to the South Australian copper-mining area.

II

The Church in South Australia had a very efficient system of communication. When the vessel on which Emily was travelling docked at Wallaroo, the Reverend Arnold Weeks, acting vicar of Kadina, was at the dockside to welcome her.

He apologised for the absence of the regular incumbent of

the Kadina church, explaining that he was on his way to Adelaide to officiate at the wedding of his daughter.

'He had hoped to see you there,' the apologetic young priest explained. 'However, it would seem that you missed one another. But I will be happy to assist your mission in any way I can.'

'Thank you, Reverend Weeks.' Emily had taken an instant liking to the young vicar. 'Is there a serious moral problem among the miners of the area?'

Arnold Weeks looked embarrassed. 'Not on the larger mines. The mine captains are Methodists. To give them their due, they maintain a strict discipline among their men, who are largely Methodist too.'

'But there are non-Methodist miners working on the mine, surely? I know of church-going miners from my home village who have come here to work.'

Emily was thinking primarily of Sam – indeed, there had been few waking hours in recent days when she had *not* thought of him.

'They might have come to Kadina,' said the young rector. 'But such men probably took work on the smaller mines and would not have stayed long. Most men tend to move on after a while, unless they have close family with them – especially since the mines began cutting down on the number of men they employed.'

Emily felt a sense of dismay. She had not seriously considered the possibility that Sam would not be here. When a mine was working and bringing in profit, miners tended to stay in one place, especially if they had relatives working on the same mine. She had not known that the mines of South Australia were having troubles too.

Then she remembered that she was not the only one anxious to locate a Cornish miner. Turning to Margaret, she said, 'This is my companion, Margaret Minns, and these are her two sons, Albert and Thomas. She is hoping to find her husband, Charlie.

He came out from Cornwall almost two years ago to find work on the mines. She has heard nothing from him since.'

The young vicar looked at Margaret sympathetically. 'It will not be easy to check on him unless he worked on one of the larger mines where they keep records. If he didn't . . .' Arnold Weeks shrugged apologetically. 'Thousands of miners have passed through the Copper Triangle in recent years.'

Margaret was crestfallen. She too had expected it to be comparatively easy to locate her husband once she and the boys arrived in Australia.

'Well, we will do what we came from England to do and find time later to enquire after them, after Charlie Minns . . . and one or two other names I have. In the meantime it is possible that Charlie will hear about our presence and realise that his wife and sons are in Australia.'

The young Kadina vicar had expected Emily to stay in the rectory with him and his wife of two years, but Emily had other ideas. She, Margaret and the boys were guests at the rectory for only two nights. By then Emily had made a tour of the area, met a number of the miners, married and single, and spoken to women who lived in the townships of Kadina, Wallaroo and Moonta. She arrived at the conclusion that nothing could be achieved by someone who lived in the rarefied atmosphere of a Church of England vicarage.

There *were* problems that needed to be tackled in the mining communities of the area and certain needs to be addressed, but in order to succeed in her aims she would need to live among those she sought to influence.

Her decision brought her into contact with Stefan Mintoff once more. Over the years he had bought up cottages vacated by those forced to move out of the area by a change in their circumstances. For the most part, the departing residents had been desperate for money and Mintoff had bought up their houses at ridiculous prices. Now all but one had been rented out by him. Some had been taken by a constantly changing tenancy of anything up to a dozen out-of-work miners. Clubbing together to pay the rent, they took whatever work was available to earn sufficient money.

The unoccupied cottage was in a highly insalubrious section of the township. Although he was anxious to see a high return from his property investments, Stefan Mintoff was horrified when Emily, accompanied by Margaret, arrived at his store and informed him that she wished to rent the cottage. The two women and the boys would like to move in at the earliest opportunity.

'I am sure I can find somewhere more suitable for you, Miss Boyce. Ewing Street, especially that particular end of the street, is not a suitable place for the niece of an English Cabinet Minister. Indeed, I would not recommend it to any lady of breeding.'

Emily looked at him coldly. 'Then perhaps you will tell me how I am to achieve the purpose of my mission to Australia? Perhaps I should sit in the Bishop's study in Adelaide and write notes to explain what has to be done?'

As Stefan Mintoff struggled for a suitable reply, Emily continued, 'When you introduced yourself on the ship, you offered your support for my mission, Mr Mintoff. If you have had second thoughts I shall seek assistance elsewhere.'

'You still have my fullest support, Miss Boyce,' Mintoff said hastily 'I am thinking of your comfort and safety. That particular cottage is in a part of Kadina avoided by respectable women.'

'Then it is where my work is most needed. Will you rent the cottage to me or not?'

Stefan Mintoff made a gesture of resignation. 'If I cannot persuade you to change your mind you may have it rent free, but—'

'No "buts", Mr Mintoff – and I intend paying you a fair rent. Shall we say two-and-sixpence a week?'

'The cottage is yours, Miss Boyce, and I shall donate the rent to assist your work. Now, as you can see, the cottage is furnished – after a fashion. The previous occupants could not take everything with them when they left. If there is anything else you need . . .'

'We will purchase anything else we need, Mr Mintoff,' Emily said firmly. 'I am appreciative of your generosity. Margaret and I will move our things in later today, but first the cottage needs a thorough cleaning. Margaret and I will begin work on it right away.'

After they left the store and had been walking for some time, Margaret said, 'Mr Mintoff is sweet on you, Emily. If you'd asked him he'd have had the whole cottage decorated and refurnished for us.'

'I do not flatter myself he is attracted to *me*, Margaret. Reverend Weeks told me that Mr Mintoff has ambitions of being elected to the state parliament. He quite obviously thinks I have sufficient influence to help him get there.'

'Do you?' Margaret asked.

'I doubt it,' Emily replied honestly. 'I might be able to help his nomination, but the electorate will decide whether or not he is elected – and Arnold Weeks does not seem to think our Mr Mintoff is the most popular man in these parts.'

'Nevertheless, he would seem to be a useful man to know,' said Margaret.

They had arrived at the cottage now. Margaret stopped and looked critically at the front of the home they had just rented. 'Shall we wash those curtains right away, or leave them until we can be sure of having them back up again by nightfall? I don't fancy having the people around here able to look in on us after dark . . .'

III

Because the road on which the cottage was built led nowhere but to open bush country, Emily had thought it would be quiet, at least. Unfortunately, her assumption proved quite erroneous.

There was a large grog shanty somewhere in the bush beyond the town and for some time before darkness fell men could be seen making their way along the road, heading out of town. Their numbers increased after dark when they were often accompanied by women – women with loud, raucous laughter who shouted remarks to groups of men which, while she did not fully understand their meaning, left Emily in no doubt about the class of women to which they belonged.

Soon after Emily and the others had retired to bed there was a loud banging on the door. Emily decided it would be better to ignore whoever it was, but the knocking persisted.

She rose from her bed in time to stop Margaret going to the door. Peeping around the edge of the curtain, the two women were in time to see a roughly dressed man stagger drunkenly along the pathway to the gate and make his way out on to the street.

After discussing the incident with Margaret and telling her firmly that she was not to open the door to anyone after dark, Emily returned to bed, but found sleep difficult to come by.

Much later, in the early hours of the morning, drinkers began to return to the township and they were even noisier than before. Some of the men – and women – were singing. Others were less kindly disposed towards the world at large. There were at least two fights in the street outside the house, one accompanied by the screams of women and much shouting and swearing by both sexes.

Listening to the sounds, Emily grimaced in the darkness of her bedroom. She could hardly say she had not been warned of what she might expect by living in this particular area. Stefan

Mintoff had gone as far as propriety would allow in his warning. However, there was nothing she could do about the disturbances tonight.

Turning over, she tried to ignore the sounds that the thin, corrugated-iron roof could not exclude and, before she knew it, she had fallen asleep.

Talk at breakfast time the next morning was about the noises of the night. The two boys were not unduly concerned; the sounds were not unfamiliar to them. It seemed that before their father had left to come to South Australia the family had lived close to an unlicensed grog-shop where mayhem reigned supreme on settlement nights.

'In that case,' Emily said to the boys, 'it is something we will be able to live with – for a while. I think it might be circumspect to learn a little more about Kadina and our neighbours before I try to change things *too* much. Now, I intend spending this morning visiting the Kadina mine, which I believe is the largest in the vicinity, in order to make some inquiries about your father.'

An hour later Emily and Margaret were standing in the same office visited by Sam almost two years before. They were greeted by the very same mine captain and his clerk. The boys had been left outside to take a look around the mine, which they declared enthusiastically was the largest they had ever seen.

Opening the ledger he had perused on behalf of Jean Spargo, the mine captain ran his finger down the list of 'M's and shook his head. 'I'm sorry, ma'am, it doesn't look as though there's ever been a Minns working at the Kadina mine.'

'Oh!' Margaret could not hide her disappointment. 'I didn't really expect him to still be here, but I thought you might know where he had gone. This is where he was coming to when he left Cornwall.'

'A lot of miners bound for Cornwall have a change of mind about their destination while they're on the ship. They strike up friendships with men who tell them of places where they have friends or relations and where they can earn more money. As a result we never see them once they arrive. You could make inquiries in other mines in the area. They don't all keep records but you might find someone who knows him and can tell you where he's likely to be. Who knows, you might even find him working in one of them.'

'Thank you,' said Emily. 'In the meantime would you post a notice on your board asking for anyone with information about Charlie Minns to get in touch with Margaret or me?'

'Of course, and I'll be happy to do anything else that might be of help.'

The two women had almost reached the door, when Emily stopped and turned back to the mine captain. As though it were an afterthought, she asked, 'There is something else, while I am here. Do you have a Sam Hooper working on your mine? He came from the village of St Cleer, in Cornwall.'

'Hooper is a very common name, both here and in Cornwall, Miss Boyce, but I'll have a look in the ledger. Do you know when he arrived?'

'It would be almost two years ago,' Emily replied, trying to contain her excitement.

The mine captain had begun turning the pages of the ledger when the clerk asked Emily, 'Did this Sam Hooper come to Kadina to join his uncle, Wilf Hooper?'

'He certainly came to Australia to find an uncle,' Emily agreed. 'I do not know the uncle's Christian name.'

'It sounds like the Cornishman who came here with a young widow,' the clerk said to the mine captain. 'You must remember her, she had a pretty little girl with her.'

'Was the little girl named Primrose?' Emily asked the question, her heart beating a little faster. She believed the Kadina mine captain might be able to offer her news of Sam, but was beginning to fear it would not be news she wanted to hear.

'Yes . . . yes it was,' replied the mine captain. 'Her mother was an attractive young woman too, as I recall.'

'Where is he now?' Emily asked. 'I mean, where are they all? Are they still in Kadina?'

The mine captain shook his head. 'Wilf Hooper moved on to the Blinman mine as underground captain some time before his nephew arrived here. Young Hooper went there to find him. As far as I know the young woman and her daughter went with him.'

'Thank you.' It seemed that Sam and Jean Spargo's travels together had not ended when their ship reached Australia. 'This Blinman mine . . . is it near here?'

'No, Miss Boyce,' the mine captain replied. 'It's in bush country hundreds of miles to the north – land far less hospitable than you'll find around Kadina. But Reverend Maddison is the Methodist circuit preacher in that area. His daughter lives in Kadina and he visits her whenever he can. I don't know when he'll next be here, but when he is I'll have a word with him. He may know something of this Sam Hooper. It's worth a try.'

Walking back to the cottage with Margaret, Emily thought of what the mine captain had said. She was not at all certain she should pursue the fortunes of Sam since his arrival in Australia. It was likely to bring her a heartbreak she had not anticipated when she set off from Cornwall with such high hopes for the future.

IV

Although Emily was unhappy that a swift reunion with Sam was not possible, and she was disturbed by what she had heard from the mine captain, she did not allow it to affect the work she had come to Kadina to carry out on behalf of the Church.

While Margaret and the boys tramped around the mines in the vicinity, enquiring after Charlie Minns and making arrangements for the boys to begin lessons at the local school, Emily met many people named on a list prepared for her by Reverend Arnold Weeks – and many who were not.

As a result of her own contacts, Emily had notices placed on the noticeboards of institutes and mines, calling for volunteers to form a choir. She also announced that, in addition to taking a regular Sunday school, she would start a ladies' guild.

Emily felt the latter was important in order to sound out the women of Kadina on the needs of the township. Some of the other problems encountered in the community, she was able to see for herself.

The grog-shop outside the town was still going strong and she suspected that at least two of the cottages situated on Ewing Street were being used as bawdy houses. Both were so close to her cottage that they could not be ignored.

One night, soon after moving in, Emily waited at the unlit window of the cottage's living room in order to confirm her suspicions. From here she had a clear view of one of the suspected brothels, and a rather more restricted view of the other.

She watched for two hours, during which time a number of women entered one of the cottages, accompanied by men. More significantly, during the same time no fewer than a further seventeen men also entered the house, each staying for a period of about half an hour.

This particular problem was close to home and Emily wondered about the best means of tackling it. At the present time there was only one policeman in the town, and she realised that until he received reinforcements he would be unable to take any action about the illegal grog-shop or the bawdy house. Besides, she was also aware that if she called in the police it would alienate the very men and women she was hoping to help.

On her second Sunday in Kadina, with the problem still

unresolved, Emily attended the morning service held in the church in the centre of the township.

From the outside, the church building, with its castellated tower and rough stonework, might have been lifted direct from a Cornish village. Inside, the decor was less ornate than the exterior had promised.

Emily arrived later than she had planned and took a seat towards the rear of the church. After spending a few minutes on her knees in silent prayer, she sat back and glanced at the loosely packed congregation.

Her attention was immediately drawn to a woman seated in the row of pews immediately in front of her. She had the whole row to herself. It was apparent to Emily that other members of the congregation were deliberately avoiding her.

Then, when the woman turned to glance at a couple who were taking their places to one side of her, Emily realised she had seen the woman before. She was one of those who occupied one of the bawdy houses in Ewing Street.

The woman sat on her own throughout the service. When it was time for Communion, Emily saw that other communicants were jostling for position in order that they should not take the Communion cup immediately after the woman.

Because of this, it proved an easy matter for Emily to take up her position beside the woman and smile at her when they rose from the Communion rail.

Later, as the congregation filed from the church, it was equally easy for Emily to take up a position behind the woman as they left the building.

Reverend Arnold Weeks was at the door to bid farewell to the congregation. He would have spoken at some length to Emily, but she had other plans and cut the conversation short.

She hurried after the woman she had sat behind in the church. When she caught up with her, she tried to sound casual. 'Hello, I believe we're both heading in the same direction. We might as well walk together. I am Emily Boyce. I have only recently arrived in Kadina from England.'

'I know who you are, Miss Boyce – and why you're here. I suppose I should be flattered that you've chosen to speak to me.'

Emily was genuinely puzzled. 'I'm sorry, but why should my speaking to you be anything special?'

The other woman gave Emily a quick, quizzical glance before saying, 'Well, you're a relative of a minister of the British government, friend of the Bishop of Adelaide – and of our Councillor Mintoff – and I believe you're here to make life better for everyone? In fact, it seems we lucky people in Kadina are having a visit from a female Jesus Christ.'

It was an outrageous statement to make, but Emily could not resist a smile. She realised too that in spite of the other woman's calling, she possessed both intelligence and an education.

'That's just the sort of blasphemous remark that used to land me in trouble with my father. He was the vicar of St Cleer, in Cornwall. By the way, I do not know your name.'

The woman walking beside Emily glanced at her once more, but with increased interest. 'You *do* know how I earn my living, Miss Boyce? I sell my body to men – lots of men. I'm a prostitute.'

'No one has actually pointed you out to me, but I have both eyes and ears. We live in a noisy district and much of the din centres around your house – and another on the opposite side of the road – but I still do not know your name.'

'It's Ruth. Ruth Askew, from Wales. I'd tell you what *my* father did for a living if I knew who he was. All I can say is that he must be a fairly wealthy man. He kept my mother in as much comfort as anyone else in the Welsh village where I lived, and paid for me to go to school. Unfortunately, he never made himself known to me, not even when my mother died. She took the secret with her to the grave. Today is the anniversary of her death and I always go to church to say a prayer for her – whether I'm made welcome or not.'

There was only the faintest hint of bitterness in her voice and Emily asked, 'Is that why you came to Australia, to . . . to the life you are living now?'

'No, I came here because of a man. He worked in the smelting works close to Swansea. We walked out together for three years and had an understanding. At least, I *believed* we had an understanding. Because I believed, I let him take liberties with me – isn't that the delicate way of putting it, Miss Boyce?'

When Emily did not answer, Ruth Askew continued, 'Like many women before me the inevitable happened. I fell pregnant. Had they known, the women in the village would have said it was "in the blood". No doubt they'd have been right. But I didn't really care. After all, more than half the women in the village I came from became mothers within six months of their wedding. David and I were going steady. We'd get married, or so I thought. I got the shock of my life when I told David of the state I was in. He said he'd got a place on an emigrant ship to Wallaroo. Said he'd been keeping it as a surprise for me. That he'd planned for me to follow on a later boat and we'd marry as soon as I reached Australia. Do you know, I *believed* him. I really did.'

Ruth gave a mirthless laugh. 'I didn't know as much about men then as I do now. If I had I'd have made him marry me right there and then, or taken him before a magistrate. Instead, I let him board the boat to come here without me. The plan was that I'd follow him as soon as I could arrange a passage. There would still have been time for us to marry before the baby was born, even if I went up the aisle waddling like a plump duck.'

The unhappy laugh was repeated. 'Oh yes, I was a very naïve young woman in those days. They wouldn't give me a free passage, so I sold everything my ma had left me to buy a passage on a boat that would get me to Wallaroo about a month before the baby was due.'

Ruth looked at Emily again, but the smile was gone now. 'We had some dreadful weather when we were only a couple of weeks away from Wallaroo. The worst he'd known in all his years at sea, the captain said. We were all being tossed about like feathers in a wind and were certain the ship would founder. I was as sick as a dog. So sick I lost the baby.'

Emily made a sympathetic sound, but Ruth said philosophically, 'It turned out to be for the best, really. When I got to Wallaroo I found David had met a girl on the ship he came out on – a Cornish girl, as it happened. They were married a month after reaching Wallaroo. He'd got her in the family way too, you see.'

'So you turned to the way of life you're leading now,' said Emily.

'There was no "turned to" about it,' Ruth said, with more bitterness than she had shown so far. 'When I left the ship at Wallaroo I was a very sick woman. Because of the *reason* I was sick none of the respectable women on board wanted anything to do with me. Oh, I can't say I blame them, they were starting new lives in a new land. The last thing they wanted was to have to take care of a "fallen woman" – and that's what I was, wasn't I? The only woman who took pity on me was Gladys. She was another Welsh girl nobody wanted to know on board the ship. At least none of the women; the crew and many of the men passengers were more enthusiastic. In fact most of them knew Gladys a great many times on the voyage. She walked down the gangway at Wallaroo with a lot more money than she'd had when she boarded the ship. Well, she was the one who took care of me, both then and later when I learned about David and his new wife.'

A brief bout of coughing interrupted Ruth's story for a few moments. Looking at her, Emily realised she was thinner and more fragile than she appeared at first glance.

'When Gladys came here and bought the house where we're now living it seemed natural I should come with her and help with what she was doing. After all, I owed my life to her – and it wasn't as though I was some innocent young virgin, was it now?'

Instead of replying, Emily put her own question to the other woman. 'Is it what you want to be doing for the rest of your life, Ruth? You are an intelligent woman, you know such a way of life cannot last. Would you take something else if it were offered to you?'

'What do you suggest I should do, Miss Boyce? Go into domestic service, perhaps? Somewhere I'm not known? No, when it's settlement day in the mines I can earn more in twenty-four hours than a servant earns in a whole year!' Giving Emily a sidelong glance, she asked, 'Does that shock you?'

'No,' Emily lied. 'But it does sadden me. I feel you are a woman who has much more to offer the world than the life you are leading here.'

'I've never yet had a man go away dissatisfied,' Ruth retorted.

Aware that Ruth was deliberately trying to shock her, Emily said quietly, 'But they *do* all go away, Ruth.'

'That was hurtful, Miss Boyce.'

'The truth often is, Ruth, but while you are doing what you are, the men who know you will always go away. One day you will have nothing – and no one.'

Ruth shook her head vigorously. 'No! I may or may not have a man, but as soon as I've made enough money I'll leave what I'm doing – and leave Australia too. I'll go back to Wales, to a place where I'm not known, and buy myself a small inn.'

'What if the police move in and arrest you and the others, Ruth? What will you do then?'

'Are you going to go to the police and complain about us? Is that what's going to happen?'

They had reached the street where they both lived and stopped outside the small, unkempt garden in front of Ruth's brothel home.

Emily shook her head. 'I cannot condone what you are doing, Ruth. It is wrong – very wrong. But I do not condemn you. However, you and the others have offended a great many towns-people by your behaviour. Moves to have the police take action against you began long before I arrived.'

While Ruth thought about what had been said, Emily continued, 'I would like to talk to you again, Ruth. I could not help noticing in church that you have a fine voice. Why not come along to one of the choir practices I am organising? You would be a great asset—'

Ruth's laugh was genuine this time. 'Do you really think I could join your choir, Miss Boyce? You would lose all your women members immediately and they would forbid their men to attend. That would leave only the single men – and most of *them* would be frightened away for fear I might acknowledge I knew them already.'

She was still chuckling as she went up the path to the house of ill-repute.

Emily walked the few paces to her own cottage, feeling confused. Ruth was sinning against all that Emily had been brought up to believe was right and moral and was leading a patently sinful life. Yet Emily felt unable to condemn her out of hand. What was more disturbing, she actually *liked* her!

V

The two brothels in Ewing Street were raided four days later by a police sergeant and three constables. They had been sent from Adelaide for this express purpose, at the request of the town's mayor.

The whole operation had been such a well-kept secret that even Kadina's own constable had not been told. It was known that his sympathies lay with the prostitutes; they helped restrict vice and much of the miners' drunkenness to a section of the town where no one of importance lived – until Emily moved in.

Unfortunately, the operation failed because of its very secrecy. Had the township constable been consulted he would have told them that at the time they chose to carry out the raid, the 'ladies of the town' would be at the grog-shop beyond the town limits. Here they received free drinks in recognition of the trade they brought to the unlicensed and makeshift shanty.

As a result of their error of judgement the police were able to arrest only two girls when the brothels were raided. The house where Ruth lived was empty.

However, the raid provoked great anger among the men who were in the habit of frequenting the two establishments and it soon spread to others who were not.

When word of the swoop reached the illicit grog-shop the paying customers hurried back to Kadina, accompanied by the residents of the two brothels.

By the time they reached Ewing Street the police had departed, taking the two prostitutes with them.

From the cottage, Emily and Margaret watched the men and women milling about the nearest of the two houses. Emily thought they resembled a swarm of bees, with everyone hurrying around in an angry mood, achieving nothing.

Then, suddenly and alarmingly, one of the prostitutes pointed in the direction of the cottage occupied by Emily and Margaret, shouting that the new arrivals were responsible for the sudden police interest in the two brothels.

No reason was given by the woman, but none was needed. The angry mob was looking for scapegoats. Believing it had found them it switched its attention to the cottage.

Alarmed, Margaret backed away from the window and appealed to Emily. 'What are we going to do, Emily? They're angry.'

'*We* are going to do nothing. At least, *you* are not. Stay in here and keep away from the windows. I shall go outside and reason with them.'

'You can't reason with a mob like that. They've been drinking!'

'I have no intention of cowering in here while they smash our windows, or whatever else they decide to do.'

'Then I'll come with you—'

As Margaret hurried after her, Emily rounded on her. 'Stay here with the boys. If the house is attacked they will be terrified. Take care of them and leave *me* to deal with the mob outside.'

For Emily to have ventured outside would probably have been quite as foolhardy as Margaret predicted, but by the time she reached the door someone far more qualified to deal with the angry miners had intervened.

Emily heard the raised voice of Ruth Askew shouting at the mob. It seemed she was standing just the other side of the door.

'Have you all gone quite mad?!' The Welsh accent was more pronounced than Emily remembered. 'What do you think you're doing? You, Manny, put down that stone. Put it *down*, I say!'

'You'd protect someone who's had two of your friends arrested?' called a man's voice. 'Whose side are you on, girl?'

'The side of reason,' Ruth retorted. 'I'm as upset as anyone else about the arrest of Annie and Martha, but what's it got to do with Miss Boyce?'

'Everything!' It was a woman's voice this time. 'We've never been raided before. She's a do-gooder who has no right to come and live here, among us. She belongs on the other side of the town.'

There were shouts of agreement, but Ruth ignored them. 'Where she lives is her business, not ours.'

'Not when she stops us earning a living because she doesn't like what we're doing,' called another woman. Once again there was agreement from the mob.

Ruth raised her voice, scornful now. 'Are you really looking for whoever's to blame for having Annie and Martha arrested – or are you just looking for a scapegoat, eh? Someone to have a go at, so you can walk away feeling better, whether what you've done is right or not? Mick heard what the police said when they arrested Martha. What was it, Mick?'

When there was no reply, Ruth continued, 'It seems Mick has gone, but he said he heard the sergeant tell her she was being arrested for keeping a bawdy house . . .'

There were indignant shouts from the crowd, including a woman's voice crying, 'Shame!'

Even in her present precarious situation, this particular word of protest brought a wry smile to Emily's face, but Ruth was still talking.

'That wasn't *all* Mick heard. The sergeant also said they'd had a man keeping watch on the houses for weeks.

'That's right!' Ruth cried triumphantly. 'They'd been keeping watch on our houses for *weeks*. They were watching the house before Miss Boyce moved in. How can she have had anything to do with what's happened tonight, eh? You tell me that.'

There was a great deal of angry murmuring among the mob, many of whom did not *want* to exonerate Emily, but Ruth was quick to follow up the advantage she had gained.

'If some of us girls put our minds to it I think we could come up with the names of one or two *men* who want to get us out of town. Men who were eager enough to make use of us before their wives came to Kadina to join them. Now they want us gone before someone tells on 'em.'

The shouts that greeted this statement were mixed with laughter, but Ruth had not finished with the crowd yet. 'There's another man – and we all know who I'm talking about – a man who thinks he's grown too big for Kadina. Who's grown too big for his boots, in my opinion. He's been a good customer – even though he's always used the back door . . .'

Her words brought a murmur of agreement from the men and shrieks of laughter from some of the women.

'Yes, I see you know who I'm talking about. Now he's going up in the world he wants us out of Kadina. For my money, *he's* the one who brought in the police to close us down. Think about it and you'll realise I'm making good sense.'

There was dissension from some members of the crowd, but Ruth had succeeded in taking the heat out of their anger. As it evaporated, they slowly began moving away.

When Emily opened the front door Ruth was still standing outside.

'Thank you, Ruth, you handled that admirably. Far better than I might have done.'

'*Did* you bring in the police to have us closed down?'

The question was so unexpected it left Emily floundering for a moment. 'You *know* I didn't. The man who overheard what the police sergeant said—'

'I made that up,' Ruth said nonchalantly. '*Did* you complain about us?'

'That's not my way,' Emily replied. 'I would have come to your houses and spoken to you all first – and I fully intended that was what I was going to do.'

'That's what I thought,' said Ruth, satisfied.

At that moment one of the miners on the fringe of the mob, disappointed there had been no action, showed his displeasure by throwing a stone he had been holding. It was meant as no more than an angry gesture of frustration, but it caught Ruth on the side of her face. She staggered backwards with a cry of pain, a hand to her cheek.

'Quick, inside and let me have a look at that.' Emily took Ruth's arm and helped her inside. Slamming the door shut behind them, she led the injured woman to the kitchen where there was a lamp, turned low.

Emily led Ruth to a chair, then she turned up the wick and examined the other woman's injured face. 'It's bleeding rather badly, but I think it probably looks worse than it really is. I'll bathe it for you, then I should be able to see it more clearly.'

At that moment Margaret entered the kitchen and gasped when she saw the blood streaming down the side of Ruth's face.

'Here, let me help.' Producing a basin for Emily, she hurried to a cupboard and brought out a bottle of iodine. Handing it to

Emily, she said, 'This will sting, but it will prevent any infection. At least, it works well on grazed knees.'

As the two women fussed over Ruth, Emily told Margaret of Ruth's part in preventing the mob from attacking the cottage.

'Thank heaven you were there to help us,' Margaret said. 'I was in the bedroom with the boys and the noise the crowd was making was alarming. Young Tom was quite frightened. That reminds me, I came out here to fetch a drink of water for him. Can you manage if I take one to him, Emily?'

When she had left the kitchen, Ruth said to Emily, 'Word has gone around that you're making enquiries about Charlie Minns. Is Margaret his wife?'

'Yes. She and the two boys came out with me expecting to find him straightaway, but I think we are all beginning to lose hope. He came to South Australia long ago but Margaret has heard nothing from him.'

'Charlie Minns *was* here. He stayed in Kadina until the end of last year.'

Startled, Emily demanded, 'You knew him?'

'I knew him well,' Ruth confirmed. 'Too well. He wanted me to go away with him when he left Kadina, but I was having none of it. He'd have had me working all the hours that God made, plus a great many more added on by the Devil – just to keep him in drink and gambling money. *She* doesn't seem too bad a person, Miss Boyce, and I like what little I've seen of the boys when they've been playing in the street; but Charlie Minns is a bad 'un, believe me.'

Upset though she was by Ruth's words, Emily remembered what Rose, wife of the St Cleer Methodist minister, had said about him. The two very different women seemed to be in agreement.

'Margaret and the boys will not give up trying to find him,' she said. 'Do you have any idea where he might be now?'

'I don't know for certain,' Ruth replied. 'When he left Kadina he said he was heading for Burra, well to the south-west of here, but I've heard he left there and went prospecting, up north. The last time I met anyone who'd seen him, he was working in bush country up in the Flinders Ranges . . . somewhere close to Blinman.'

3

I

'How do you feel about a change of scenery for a while, Sam?'

Wilf Hooper put the unexpected question to Sam one evening when uncle and nephew were seated on the porch of the captain's cottage, enjoying an evening drink together.

Almost two years had passed since Sam had arrived at Blinman with Ira and Jean. Recently, Captain Wilf had taken charge of the mine once more, the regular captain journeying to Adelaide to seek medical advice for a heart ailment.

The copper industry was facing yet another of the difficult periods that had become so much a part of the worldwide mining scene. The Blinman mine was still in profit, but had been forced to cut expenditure wherever possible.

Many miners, fearing a repetition of the bad times they had experienced in other mines, had left. Some made for the gold-fields of New South Wales, others intended trying their luck mining silver, lead, or any of the other minerals to be found in Australia. They were willing to go anywhere in order to make use of the unique skills they possessed.

Although the Blinman mine was rich in good quality copper ore, it was proving necessary to go deeper for it and water had become an increasing problem in the deeper levels.

'You're not laying me off?'

Given the present uncertainty in the copper-mining industry, the seemingly frivolous question contained an element of genuine concern.

'Far from it,' Captain Wilf replied. 'I'd like you to take on a task that would normally be carried out by a captain – me, probably.'

'Tell me more.' As Sam spoke he flapped at a fly that seemed determined to share the beer in his tankard.

'There's a mine about twenty miles from here called the Nuccaleena. It started off a few years ago with a lot of promise, but folded shortly before you arrived. We've bought the engine to help with the pumping and I'm sending a team along to dismantle it and bring it back to Blinman. What I'd like you to do is go with them and survey the workings. Let me know if you think it's worth the company buying the mine as an investment for the future, should copper prices pick up once more.'

'You'd trust my judgement on something as important as that?' Sam was both delighted and apprehensive at such a prospect. He was being asked to make a decision that could lose the mining company a great deal of money if his appraisal proved to be wrong.

'Is there any reason why I shouldn't?'

'There are probably a great many reasons.' Sam grinned. 'But none come to mind right now. Thanks, Uncle, I would enjoy a few days away from Blinman. When do I leave?'

'As soon as I can organise enough bullock teams to bring the engine back. Hopefully it'll be within the week. Some of the track to Nuccaleena will have been washed away by last season's rains, so it'll take a couple of days or so for the bullock drays to get there, but you can start putting a few things together – and take a gun. The sheep stations have reported trouble from Aborigines lately.'

'I thought they were fairly friendly in this area,' Sam said, in some surprise. There had been no trouble in the area between the mining communities and native Australians during the time he had been at Blinman.

'They've been quiet until now,' Captain Wilf agreed. 'There *was* trouble some years ago, when members of a northern tribe came down to dig out ochre at Parachilna to use in a tribal ceremony, but that didn't involve the local Aborigines. Something must have happened to seriously stir them up, but until we find out what it is we're not likely to get it sorted out. I'm putting Piet van Roos in charge of the party. He knows the Aborigines better than anyone else I know.'

Sam was not unhappy to be leaving Blinman for a while. He had been working in the mine without a break since his arrival. Jean and Ira were very happy together and Sam was delighted for both of them but, in an occasional irrational moment, usually when the temperature soared to new and breathless heights and he was suffering sleepless nights, he resented their happiness. He felt it should have been his late friend, Phillip, enjoying life with Jean and Primrose.

On such days, Sam also felt deeply the knowledge that the only woman who had ever really meant anything to him was on the other side of the world. Yet, even at such moments, he realised she would have remained beyond his reach had he stayed in St Cleer.

Nevertheless, he was very disappointed that she had found no way of writing to him in response to the messages he had sent to her via the letters he had written home. He had to remind himself, guiltily, that he had been at Blinman for more than a year before sitting down to the laborious task of writing to tell his parents he had not settled at Kadina.

There was a possibility, albeit a remote one, that Emily *had* written to him and that the letter had gone to Kadina.

He felt he would be able to put such thoughts behind him for a while in the unfamiliar surroundings of Nuccaleena.

Sam was not particularly concerned about the trouble currently being experienced with hostile Aborigines. Travelling in company with forty other miners, most of whom were armed, he did not anticipate trouble.

It was a slow journey, the first night being spent at the remote sheep station of Moolooloo. The owners were delighted to have company – even in such great numbers. They killed and roasted two sheep and, in return, enjoyed a share of the beer being carried in considerable quantities by the Blinman miners.

During the course of a very pleasant evening, Sam was astounded to learn that the area grazed by the sheep station was almost the size of Cornwall! It helped him to appreciate once more the vast size of the country to which he had come.

The following morning the bonhomie of the previous evening vanished when it was discovered that more than a hundred in-lamb ewes had been speared to death during the night. The sheep had been in a pen close to the house – given the ferocity of the attack, too close for comfort.

The wagons of the miners had been secured nearby, yet no one had heard a thing.

Deeply distressed, the owners of the sheep station had difficulty coming to terms with the atrocity.

'Why would they do such a thing?' the wife lamented. 'We have always been good friends with them. In bad years we've kept them supplied with water and given them the occasional sheep. In return, they've helped find stock that have broken away from the main flock. Nothing like this has ever happened before.'

'I don't believe these "*yuras*" are from the local tribe,' said Piet van Roos. 'They're from outside the area – and they're telling us something. It's possible the Blinman miners have stirred them up in some way. If only we could catch one of 'em we might be able to find out what it is. In the meantime . . .' He shrugged. 'I suggest you stay on your guard at Moolooloo. We'll do the same.'

* * *

Halfway between the Moolooloo sheep station and Nuccaleena, Sam was walking alongside Piet when the bullock driver said in an undertone, 'Say nothing and don't look round. Just keep walking as though you suspect nothing . . .'

With this mysterious directive, the South African casually walked back along the wagon train, passing an occasional remark with some of the other men.

When he disappeared into the bush no one noticed until, ten minutes later, there was a sudden commotion to the side of one of the rear wagons. Moments later Piet reappeared, the fingers of one hand firmly locked in the short black hair of an Aborigine boy who could have been no more than twelve years of age.

As the two drew near to the South African's own wagon, Sam saw that Piet's arm was bleeding profusely.

'What's happened?' Sam asked, in concern.

'Nothing much,' replied Piet. 'I glimpsed this youngster some way back. He fancies himself as a warrior, but he's got a bit to learn first.'

'By the look of your arm he's not doing too badly,' Sam commented.

'I got careless, that's all,' Piet said. 'He's no more than a boy. The sight of my blood scared him more than it did me.'

Other miners were gathering around now and Sam asked, 'What do you want to do with him?'

'Let him go. I've managed to have a brief chat with him about what's going on. It seems he and his people are looking for someone who has deeply offended them. I've managed to convince him that none of us are involved. When we release him he'll return to his people and tell them what I've said. Hopefully, they'll then leave us alone and go off and look elsewhere for the man they want.'

In an attempt to convince the boy's people that the party meant no harm, the boy was released ten minutes later, carrying presents of food from Piet.

Watching him heading for the security of the surrounding

bush, Sam felt relief. Once the Aborigines knew that the column from Blinman had nothing to do with their grievance, the miners might be able to proceed without risk of further attack.

The young Aborigine had almost reached a patch of dense bush when a shot rang out from the rear of the wagon train, startling the patient bullocks and echoing around the adjacent hills. The boy stumbled, as though he had tripped on a stone, then pitched forward on to his face, dropping the stores he had been carrying.

Sam ran forward to where the boy had fallen, Piet close behind him, but no one else from the mining column joined them.

As he turned the boy over, Sam saw blood trickling from the corner of his mouth. He knew even before he checked that there would be no pulse.

The boy was dead.

Advancing a few steps towards the wagon train, Sam demanded angrily, 'Who fired the shot?'

When no one replied, Sam said angrily, 'I suppose someone is going to return to Blinman and brag that he's a hero for shooting a young boy in the back? Well, for what it's worth, I'm saying right here and now that he's a coward. Someone who wouldn't have had the courage to fire on a twelve-year-old boy armed only with a spear had they met face to face.'

Some of the men looked resentful, others uncomfortable, but still no one spoke.

'Whoever he is, he's more than a coward,' declared Piet. 'He's also a damned fool. That boy told me his people are looking for a particular man who's wronged them – he wouldn't say how. He was going back to tell them the man they are after isn't with us. Once they'd accepted that – and they would have – they'd have gone away and left us alone. Now they won't learn the truth and they have the boy's death to avenge. Someone, probably more than one of us, is going to die because the truth didn't get back to the *yuras*. The blame will rest fairly and squarely with the fool who fired that shot.'

There was still no response from the men with the wagon train. Turning away from them in disgust, Piet said to Sam, 'Come on, boy, let's you and me go and deal with the lad.'

'What do we do?' asked Sam. 'Are we going to bury him?'

Piet shook his head. 'We'll leave that to his people. They have their own customs. I want you to take my rifle and keep your eyes skinned while I find the spear he used when he attacked me. When I've found it we lay the boy out and put the spear alongside him. It shows we respect him as a warrior. He deserves that, at least.'

The spear was quickly found and, their tribute paid to the boy, Sam and Piet walked together back to the wagon train.

'How are we going to inform the police about this?' Sam asked.

'We aren't,' Piet said curtly.

'But—'

'There's no "buts" about it,' Piet said. 'Rightly or wrongly that's the way it is. This is Australia, not some sleepy Cornish village. It's happened. Although it shouldn't have – it has. Now we forget it. All right, boy, we've done our duty, now let's get back to the job we're being paid to do.'

There was one more abortive attack on the wagons along the long and difficult track between Moolooloo and Nuccaleena, but no one was hurt. When shots were fired by the miners, the Aborigines faded away into the bush.

II

Soon after passing a remote and deserted inn, the wagons rounded a low rise and an engine house, complete with engine, came into view. It was built on the lower slopes of a round-topped hill.

Facing the mine, on the far side of a shallow creek, was a small, empty township made up of a haphazard mixture of stone cottages and shacks constructed from wood and corrugated iron.

But it was the engine house that took Sam's breath away. It was *exactly* like a hundred others to be found on Bodmin Moor.

'There's no doubting who built that, is there?' The speaker was another Cornishman named Tim, who had been at the Blinman mine only a few months longer than Sam. Proudly, the miner added, 'I don't doubt it'll still be standing here in a hundred years' time.'

'Not the way it is now,' remarked a practical Welsh engineer. 'We'll need to knock it about a bit to get the engine out. The first thing we'll have off is the roof, so we can lift out the beam.'

'Well, we'll at least have a roof over our heads while the work's being done,' Sam said. 'There are more than enough houses for all of us. What beats me is how anyone found copper here in the first place – then managed to persuade a company to build a township here!'

'It was a good mine in its day.' This from Piet. 'I've taken many a load of high-grade ore from Nuccaleena, but transport costs are high this far out – and there you have the reason why it's not working now.'

'Well, I'll start checking out its prospects in the morning,' Sam said. 'For now let's help the cook prepare something for us before it gets dark.'

The engineers began work on dismantling the Nuccaleena mine-engine the following morning. Normally, bullock drays would have been sent back to Blinman as they were loaded, but given the hostility of the Aborigines, it was decided that they should remain at Nuccaleena until all work at the site was completed and then they would all return together.

On the second day of work the men were assembling for a midday meal when the sound of a shot rang out from farther along the shallow valley.

At first it was thought some of the men had gone out shooting kangaroos, but it was quickly established that everyone in the mining party was present on the mine.

Temporarily abandoning all thoughts of eating, miners hurried away to collect their guns. They were discussing whether or not they should go into the bush to investigate the shot when two figures emerged from the bush farther along the valley. One was a white man, the other an Aborigine woman.

As the two drew nearer, the Blinman miners speculated among themselves about what they were doing out here, so far from civilisation.

The man was carrying a gun and those watching had no doubt he had been responsible for the shot.

When the couple was within hailing distance, Piet called out, 'You're a long way from anywhere, friend.'

The man waited until he was much closer before replying. 'Not far enough, it would seem,' he said ungraciously. 'There's no sense in looking for anything worthwhile in places where others have been before.'

'He's a prospector,' Piet spoke quietly to Sam.

'Isn't it dangerous for him to be out on his own at a time like this?'

Piet shrugged. 'A true prospector lives with danger every minute of the day. He prefers it to people. Most can't stand even their own company, some of the time. But this one isn't a natural loner. If he was he wouldn't have the woman with him.'

The man was closer now and Sam had no need to shout when he asked, 'Was that you who fired the shot we just heard?'

The man nodded and, matter-of-factly, replied, 'A bunch of *yuras* armed with spears came at me. After I shot one the others kept their distance.'

While Sam was left speechless at the casualness with which

the newcomer had spoken of shooting and possibly killing a man, Piet said, 'We've had trouble with 'em too. You'd better come into camp. Stay out there and sooner or later they'll get you.'

Glancing at the Aborigine woman, the prospector looked back at Piet with an unspoken question.

'She'd better come in too,' Piet said reluctantly. 'Find yourselves a hut, there's more than enough to go around.'

The prospector went off without another word, the woman trudging behind him, her glance fixed firmly on the ground. Her companion headed for an empty hut, never once looking behind him to see if she was following.

Watching them, Sam said thoughtfully, 'You know, I can't help feeling I've seen the woman somewhere before.'

Piet smiled. 'You've not seen enough *yura* women at Blinman to know one from another.'

'You could be right,' Sam conceded. 'But it doesn't matter. There's work to be done and the problems we've got at the moment aren't making it any easier. We can do without any more.'

Pointing to the prospector, one of the miners standing nearby said, 'If you really want to avoid trouble you'll send him and his woman packing right now. He's bad news. I worked with him on the Burra mine a while back. He stabbed a man in a fight there and was lucky to get away with a plea of self-defence. Some called it murder and would have taken matters into their own hands if he hadn't left in a hurry.'

'Hopefully he won't be with us for long,' said Sam. 'What's his name?'

'Minns,' came the reply. 'Charlie Minns.'

III

Assessing the future viability of the Nuccaleena mine was not as straightforward as it might have been. Sam's task was made more complicated because a series of heavy storms had swept across the Flinders Ranges, causing the lower levels of the mine to flood badly, making an accurate assessment difficult.

Sam believed there was probably copper here, but the water would need to be pumped out before it could be located – and the pump was being removed.

The upper levels proved almost as impossible to assess. The result of Sam's first cursory survey indicated that the ore had been exhausted, yet Sam was not convinced this was so. He had a gut reaction – a miner's intuition – that the copper lode had been pursued in the wrong direction.

For three days he kept returning to the mine, examining the direction of the worked-out lode before making up his mind about what needed to be done.

Most of the men sent to dismantle and remove the Nuccaleena engine were miners, predominantly Cornish. That evening, Sam discussed his problems with these men and with the engineers.

He wanted four men to help him clear a partially collapsed adit and extend it a little farther than it went at present. He believed this was where the lost copper lode might be found. Whoever had begun the tunnel was going in the right direction, but Sam felt they had given up too soon. Either that, or the man in question had been in the adit when it collapsed.

When the engineer agreed to spare the men there was no shortage of volunteers. For a true miner, any other work smacked of unskilled labour. The Blinman miners would do whatever Sam required of them – just as long as it was underground.

It took a half-day of hard work to clear the roof fall, then Sam directed the men to extend the tunnel at an angle from the course taken by the departed miners.

'Are you sure that's what you want?' A miner who had been employed at Nuccaleena during the time it was producing copper was sceptical. 'Cap'n Morrison always reckoned the lode ran to the west, not the way you're going.'

'Captain Morrison lost the lode and the mine closed,' Sam retorted, by no means as confident as he sounded but determined to follow his instincts. 'We'll go *this* way.'

'Whatever you say,' said the dissenting miner, reluctantly. 'You're cap'n for this trip.'

Sam and his fellow miners worked until sundown without finding what Sam had hoped. As they emerged from the adit, weary and dirty and looking forward to their evening meal, a group of Aborigines broke cover. They had crept undetected through the undergrowth in the valley as far as the small creek that separated mine and township. Now, with shrieks of fury, they ran through the near-empty township, hurling spears at any miners they saw.

It all happened so quickly that the attack was over and the Aborigines were disappearing into the thick bush beyond the camp before the first of the miners was able to reach his rifle and fire a shot after the fleeing warriors.

Behind them, the Aborigines left one miner dead and three others with spear wounds.

As the wounded men were receiving attention, Sam spoke to Piet van Roos. 'That was a determined attack, Piet – and a daring one.'

The older man nodded. Speaking past the short-stemmed pipe clenched firmly between his teeth, he said, 'They're determined, all right. Something has really upset them. Rightly or wrongly, they're blaming us for whatever it is.'

'Could it now have something to do with the boy who was shot?'

Piet shook his head. 'It won't have helped, but they were stirred up before that. I wish I understood what it's about. I'm not even sure these particular *yuras* are from this area. If they're not, something has brought them up here. They won't leave until they've got what it is they're after.'

'You don't think the woman who came in with Minns might know something?'

'She might, but the only way I'm likely to get any of her time is to pay Minns for it and that's against the few principles I have.'

Sam looked at Piet in disbelief. 'You don't mean . . .'

'That Minns is a pimp? That's *exactly* what I mean. Men have been in and out of the hut she shares with Minns every night since they've been here, with Minns at the door taking the money. There's another reason we ought to speak to her. I think you were right about seeing the woman somewhere before, but I can't remember where. Perhaps she's been hanging about Blinman.'

'I don't think so,' Sam said. 'I was thinking about it today while I was working in the mine. I believe she's the woman we met when you brought me and the others to Blinman from Port Augusta.'

Removing the pipe from his mouth, Piet frowned and looked thoughtful. 'That woman had a husband – and a child.'

'I know – but I still think it's her.'

Piet remained thoughtful for a long time before speaking again. 'You might be right, Sam. If so it could be the cause of our troubles. You thought I was being generous towards that *yura* family – and so I was. The husband was a son of an influential tribal elder, as I remember. He was on his way to negotiate for the supply of a special red ochre found only up here, in the Ranges. It's used in one of the *yuras*' most sacred ceremonies. If this woman *is* his wife, then something must have happened to him. I think we'll go and have a word with her – but there'll be no money changing hands!'

* * *

Minns and the woman were not eating with the Blinman miners. Their hut was some little distance away and they were cooking on an outside fire. The skinned carcass of an animal Sam was unable to identify was cooking over the fire, the fat from it dripping down to the hot embers, producing spasmodic spurts of hissing yellow flame.

It was dusk now and Charlie Minns was seated in the shadows beside the doorway, a long-barrelled rifle leaning against the wall of the hut beside him.

Nodding in the direction of the weapon, Piet said, 'If you'd used that just now you might have scared off some of the *yuras* and a man would still be alive.'

'I didn't have the gun to hand when they attacked,' Minns replied. 'Besides, there was no sense drawing attention to ourselves.'

'I can see why you wouldn't want to attract attention from the *yuras*,' agreed Piet. Pointing to the woman, he asked, 'What tribe is she?'

'How should I know?' Minns replied aggressively. 'She's an Aborigine, that's all. Anyway, what's it to you?'

'It could be a matter of life or death for every man at Nuccaleena. The *yuras* who attacked us are going to come back again and again. I want to find out why. Do you mind if I talk to the woman?'

'Yes, I *do* mind.'

Minns stood and when the woman looked at him, Sam read fear in her expression. At a signal from Minns she lifted the meat and the spit and placed it upon a flat stone beside the fire before hurrying inside the hut, turning her head away in order not to meet the eyes of either Sam or Piet van Roos.

'I knew it would be a mistake to come into your camp,' said Minns, still aggressive. 'People just can't mind their own business.'

'That needn't bother you or anyone else who has nothing to

hide. But lives are being lost for a reason none of us can understand.'

'That's nothing to do with me, so you can go now.'

'I will. But I'd like to ask you just one question before we do. What happened to your woman's husband and little girl?'

The question clearly alarmed Minns, but he recovered quickly. 'I don't know what you're talking about – and you're not going to ruin my meal. I'm taking it inside. Picking up the hot carcass from the flat stone, he turned his back upon the two men and entered the hut.'

Calling after him, Piet said, 'I'll be having a chat with the others. If there's another attack on this camp while you're here we'll all be wanting answers.'

As they walked away from the hut, Sam said to his companion, 'You got through to Minns back there. I'm more convinced than ever it's the woman we saw when you brought me, Jean and Ira to Blinman.'

'It is,' Piet agreed. 'More than that, Minns knows why the *yuras* are attacking us, but he's not going to tell and he'll prevent the woman from saying anything – if he can.'

The Aborigines launched another attack on the camp the next morning, shortly before dawn. On this occasion they did not attack the main camp but set fire to the mud and wattle hut which had been occupied the previous evening by Minns and the Aboriginal woman.

At first, the miners feared Minns and the woman were trapped inside. However, as they were attempting to dowse the fire, Minns put in an unexpected appearance.

'Where have you been?' asked Piet. 'We thought you were trapped inside.'

Minns shook his head. 'After what you said last night I feared me and the woman might be a target for the Aborigines, so I changed huts under the cover of darkness. It was just as well, by the look of things.'

'Where's the woman now?' Sam asked.

'Gone,' Minns replied. 'I thought of what van Roos said, you know, about them being after her, so I told her to go. She left during the night.'

There was something about Minns' story that did not ring true to Sam. However, unable to disprove it, he said nothing.

A couple of hours later all thoughts of Minns and his woman went from Sam's mind when he and the men extending the abandoned adit came across the lode for which he had been searching.

It was rich – as rich as any he had seen at Blinman, but Sam realised that in order to work it the mine company would still be faced with the crippling cost of transportation to Port Augusta. Nevertheless, his hunch had proved correct.

Emerging from the tunnel, Sam accepted the congratulations of the Blinmen miners.

Piet said, 'Now you've found what you were looking for and we have the engine loaded on the drays, I reckon we can make a move back to Blinman.'

'You make ready to move,' Sam said. 'I'd like to just check the depth of the water in the main shaft before we go. If prices ever rise enough to make it economical to reopen the Nuccaleena, we'll need to know how much water needs to be taken out to get at the ore that's down deeper – and I'm convinced it's down there too.'

Sam went back in to the mine accompanied by one of the miners who had been helping him. While Sam took another couple of samples from the newly discovered lode his companion attached a large rock to a rope and lowered it down the flooded shaft.

He called to Sam that the depth was some thirty fathoms. After a few minutes' silence, he called again, 'Sam, there's something floating in the water . . . it looks like a body!'

Taking his lamp from the rock shelf, Sam hurried to the flooded main shaft to add the lantern's light to that of his colleague's.

The body – and there could be no doubt about it now – was floating just beneath the surface of the water. It would probably not have been noticed had it not been disturbed by the makeshift plumb-line.

The body was only just within the range of the lantern's light, but by throwing the stone attached to the rope over the body, the two men were able to gradually draw it closer to the edge of the shaft.

When it was nearer they could see the body more clearly. It was an Aborigine, floating face downwards.

'Help me pull it out,' Sam said, when he was able to take a grip on a thin arm.

The two men heaved the body clear of the water and realised even before turning it over that it was that of a woman.

When the body was turned over on its back, Sam was over-whelmed with a feeling of horror. It was Charlie Minns' woman.

IV

When Sam and the miner carried the body of the Aboriginal girl from the mine workings, it was Piet van Roos who voiced the question that was in the mind of every man who crowded round.

'Where's Minns?'

'I saw him going into his hut about ten minutes ago,' one of the younger miners replied. 'He's probably still there.'

'Go and fetch him,' Piet said grimly. 'We need some answers from him.'

A number of the miners set off and returned with the prospector a few minutes later.

Greeted with hostile looks from the gathered men, Minns

licked his lips nervously when they moved aside and he saw the body of the woman lying on the ground.

'Sam's just found her floating in the shaft,' Piet said, without preamble. 'Can you explain how she got there?'

'I've no idea,' Minns declared. 'I've already told you what happened. I thought of what you'd said to me about the possibility that the attack by the Aborigines might have had something to do with her, so last night I told her to go – and she did.'

'Then how do you explain her ending up in the main shaft?' Sam demanded.

'I don't know any more than you do what happened after she left the hut. She might have fallen down the shaft in the dark . . . or she could have jumped in. Come to that, she might have been thrown there by her own people when they burned down the hut we'd been staying in.'

'If it *was* them who burned down the hut,' Piet said. '*Yuras* don't carry matches with them and they wouldn't want to hang about a mining camp going through all the paraphernalia involved in making a fire.'

'Are you saying I'm lying?' Minns demanded.

'All I'm saying is that the girl has the back of her head caved in and fire's a very handy way of getting rid of any blood that might have been around.'

'I've told you what happened. If she has a head injury it probably happened when she fell down the shaft. If it wasn't, well, it could have been done by her own people, or by anyone else in the camp once she'd left the hut. If you don't believe my story then report it to the police trooper at Blinman when we get there. I'll tell him exactly the same as I've told you – and repeat it in court, if I have to.' Minns was confident no one would be able to disprove his story. Besides, there was unlikely to be too much of a fuss about the mysterious death of an Aborigine woman.

Piet knew it too. 'It'll be reported when we get to Blinman.

What happens then is up to the police. More important right now is what we do with the body. The *yuras* are watching us and they'll have seen her brought out of the mine. If we just get rid of her like a dead dingo they'll remain a threat to us every step of the way to Blinman. On the other hand, if we show some respect and act as though we're sorry she's dead, we might just get the *yuras* off our backs.'

'What do we need to do?' Sam asked.

'We'll lay her out on a couple of blankets in the most prominent place we can find here in the mine and surround her with food and small presents. I want something from everyone – whatever you can spare – then we'll get on our way. It might work, or it might not, but if we don't do *something* we're going to lose more lives before we reach Blinman.'

The wagons set off for Blinman an hour later. As the dray on which Sam was riding lurched along the rough track from the mine, he looked back and felt a deep sense of sadness at the sight of the pitifully small body lying on blankets donated by Piet and himself, surrounded by an array of mostly cheap trinkets.

He wondered whether Charlie Minns felt any remorse for the lost life and looked along the line of wagons to see what he was doing.

The prospector was seated in one of the largest drays, surrounded by parts of the Nuccaleena mine-engine and looking straight ahead. Sam suspected that he cared nothing for the dead woman.

There were no attacks from the Aborigines on the return journey to Blinman. However, an incident occurred during the overnight stay at the Moolooloo sheep station to prove they had not gone away. And, for the first time, they indicated a clear target for their wrath.

The miners camped for the night in and around the wagons, as well as occupying a couple of the station outbuildings. None of the men heard anything untoward during the night, yet, when they woke in the morning, a spear was found thrust into the woodwork of the dray that had been occupied by Charlie Minns.

It was embedded in the very spot where he had been sitting.

Piet van Roos's peace offering had clearly been accepted by the Aborigines, but they had given a clear warning that the amnesty did not extend to Charlie Minns.

V

There was great relief in Blinman when the wagons returned from Nuccaleena. However, it was short-lived for the relatives of the men who had been either killed or wounded during the attacks by the Aborigines.

Nevertheless, it was considered the miners had been luckier than it had been feared. The presence of a large number of warring Aborigines from outside the Flinders Ranges had been confirmed and their presence had stirred up others from local tribes.

Most of their depredations had been against livestock, but there were unconfirmed reports from more remote areas of shepherds coming under attack.

Bullock drivers, for whom travelling through the outback without human company was one of the most enjoyable aspects of their work, now sought the company of as many others as was practical.

The men employed on wood cutting would also venture forth only when an armed escort was available to accompany them on their far-ranging journeys in search of fuel for the mine-engines.

Despite the current unrest, stagecoaches from the outside world still reached Blinman, although they now carried an additional armed guard.

The arrival of the weekly stagecoach from the south was always the subject of great interest. Not only did it bring in the mail, but it would occasionally carry passengers well-known to those who lived at Blinman.

A fortnight after the wagon train returned from Nuccaleena, the weekly stagecoach arrived at the Blinman hotel early in the evening. It was heralded by the strident notes of a horn, sounded by the scarlet-coated mail guard. Drinking miners spilled from the bar to watch the passengers alight from the vehicle.

There were three. One was an official of the company that owned the Blinman mine, arriving for a routine inspection. The second man was a farrier arriving to take up employment at the mine.

The third passenger was Ruth Askew.

Wearing a small round hat, perched at a jaunty angle, and a low-cut dress that revealed as much as it hid, she stepped from the dusty stagecoach and cast a bold glance at the miners standing outside the hotel.

All the men had worked in other mines before reaching Blinman, many in the triple-mining towns of Wallaroo, Moonta and Kadina. Some recognised Ruth and her appearance was greeted with cheers and ribald comments.

Only one man was so startled to see her that he immediately stepped back inside the hotel bar. As a result, Ruth did not see Charlie Minns.

'Hello, boys. Is no one going to offer a thirsty girl a drink? It's been a hot day and I've enough dust in my throat to lay a path.'

Half a dozen tankards containing various amounts of beer were immediately thrust towards her.

Taking one that was three-parts full, she downed its contents in one long, gulping draught. As she handed the empty tankard back to the grinning young miner who had offered it to her, Ruth wiped her mouth with the back of her hand, saying, 'Thanks, love. I owe you one.'

Reaching out she took a second tankard. When this had gone the same way as the first, she said, 'I think I'm going to enjoy it here, even if it is too damned hot! Now, which of you kind gentlemen knows the way to Lucy's house and will take me and my trunk there?'

Lucy was a prostitute and brothel keeper, known to all the miners standing outside the Blinman hotel. A number of younger miners, grinning self-consciously, stepped forward from the ranks of older men with offers of help.

'You . . . and you.' She pointed to two of the men. 'You're the best looking of a poor bunch and you're young enough to learn the way to treat a poor, innocent girl.'

The statement brought the raucous response Ruth had intended. As the two young men picked up the trunk, which had been off-loaded from the stagecoach, she blew a kiss to the watching miners.

'Cheerio, boys. I look forward to seeing you all at Lucy's place in the coming weeks. I want to find out whether what's said about Blinman men is true.'

As the men greeted her remark with ribald laughter, Charlie, still concealed inside the hotel, watched with mixed feelings as Ruth walked away with the two young miners.

Charlie made no attempt to contact Ruth for a week after her arrival. When they did finally meet, it was not in the shanty outside the township perimeter, where she now lived with four other girls who followed the same calling. It was outside the Blinman general store. Ruth had come to buy provisions for the household of women.

As she emerged from the store carrying a basket of provisions, Charlie stepped out from a space between the store and a stable.

'Hello, Ruth. I never expected to see you here.'

'There's no reason why you should,' Ruth retorted. 'But I knew I'd meet up with you again, one day. Bad pennies have a nasty habit of turning up where they're not wanted.'

'That's not a very nice thing to say to me, Ruth, especially in view of what we once were to each other.'

'All I ever meant to you was a means of making money without having to work for it.'

'That isn't true, Ruth. You and I could have made a go of it. I always believed that.'

'You mean I wouldn't have needed to worry myself about ending up floating in some flooded mine shaft? Is that what you're telling me?'

'You've been listening to idle gossip, Ruth. It's just not true, I swear it isn't.'

'Oh? Are you an authority on *truth* now? That's a new one for you, Charlie; you don't know the meaning of the word and never have.'

'That isn't so, Ruth. I've never lied to you—'

'No? I seem to remember you once asked me to go away with you to somewhere where neither of us was known. Said you'd be happy to marry me, as I remember.'

'I meant every word of it, Ruth. I still would, if you'd come with me. We could go to one of the gold-mining camps together.'

'Just you and me, Charlie? Or should we ask your wife to come along with us, just for laughs?'

'What are you talking about. I'm not married—'

'Cut out the lying, Charlie. Perhaps we could even consider taking your boys along too. I wonder what they'd think of life in a gold-mining camp with their ma and me and you. I don't think Tom would be very happy – and Albert certainly wouldn't. Margaret might have something to say about it too.'

Ruth watched in satisfaction as Charlie looked at her in disbelief. 'How do you . . . What have you heard?'

'It's not what I've *heard*, Charlie, but what I've *seen*. A wife and her two boys – two good boys. They've come to Australia looking for a husband and father who isn't worth a single minute of the heartache they've suffered by leaving everything they've ever known to travel halfway round the world hoping to find him. Now, if you'll excuse me, I've got food in here that's likely to go sour just talking to you.'

Ruth walked away but Charlie ran after her and caught hold of her arm. 'Wait, Ruth. Where have you seen them? When . . . ?'

She tried to walk away without replying, but Charlie pulled her to an abrupt halt. 'You've got to tell me, Ruth. Was it in Kadina? Yes, it must be, you've just come from there.'

'I've been to a lot of places and done a whole lot of things since you left, Charlie. Besides, I doubt if I'd be doing *them* any favours if I were to tell you where to find them. They're better off without you.'

'That isn't true, Ruth. Not any more. I've tried to get in touch with them in the past, honest I have. I wrote time after time but got no reply. I thought they must all be dead. There'd been a lot of fever in the village when I left. That's why I thought I was free to marry you. It's the truth, Ruth, I swear it.'

She knew he was lying. It was something that came naturally to him. She remained silent.

'Now I know they're alive I can do the right thing by them, Ruth. I've found a little gold here and there and I've changed some into hard cash and put it by.'

'Does that mean you can pay me back for what I gave you out of my earnings when you were out of work, or had you conveniently forgotten that?'

'I've forgotten nothing you did for me, Ruth. Here . . .' Reaching inside his shirt, he pulled out a leather drawstring bag, attached to a thong looped about his neck. Loosening the neck of the bag, he reached inside and pulled out some coins, saying, 'Here, take these.'

Looking at the coins he had thrust in her hand, Ruth said contemptuously, 'Five guineas! You'll need to do better than that, Charlie Minns. From what I've heard you probably made that much in an hour at Nuccaleena from what you were charging for that poor black woman. You can say what you like, Charlie, you haven't changed a bit.'

'Neither have you.' Charlie handed her another five gold coins. 'You'd take money from me that would be spent on those two young boys you said you cared so much about.'

'No, Charlie, I know you far too well. I'm taking money that would otherwise go on drink – or on women like me. If you want to find your kids and your wife, you'll find them living in Kadina, on Ewing Street – but don't say I was the one to tell you where they are. I don't want to be blamed for sending you back to them.'

4

I

'It has been a most enjoyable evening, Miss Boyce. You and your choir deserved a much larger audience.'

Stefan Mintoff was speaking at the conclusion of the first concert given by Emily's newly formed Kadina choir. She had performed the duties of accompanist on a piano donated by the man to whom she was talking.

'Had it not been for you the audience would have been very much smaller, Mr Mintoff. I am very grateful for the support you have given to me in this and many other matters.'

Emily was still not certain she fully trusted the Kadina councillor, but she could not deny he had shown enormous support for her and her various projects. At least half the concert audience was comprised of members of the council, local dignitaries and their family, all cajoled into attending by Stefan Mintoff.

She was aware her benefactor was not well liked, but he had the air of a man who was going places. Because of this, many people were careful not to offend him.

'I am happy to have been of help,' he said. 'But I do wish you would call me Stefan. Mr Mintoff is so very formal. We have met on many occasions now. Enough to be friends, at least.'

It was not the first time Stefan Mintoff had suggested they should be on first-name terms. Yet Emily still drew back from becoming too familiar with the man who, more than any other, had helped her during the time she had been in South Australia.

It stemmed from her determination to find Sam. If – no, *when* she did, she wanted there to be no complications resulting from other relationships. At least not from her side.

Emily hoped Sam would have none, but she was concerned about the part Jean Spargo might be playing in his life. She wished information about his whereabouts was forthcoming.

She had put out a great many feelers about Sam, coupling them with her efforts to locate Margaret's husband, by saying he came from the same area as Charlie Minns and might have met up with him at some time.

So far there had been no definite news of either. It was certain both had been in Blinman at some time, but she and Margaret had been advised against making the long journey on the weekly coach service to the remote mining township. Especially now, when everyone was talking about the 'Aborigine problem' in the Flinders Ranges.

It seemed a number of men had been killed there. Stefan Mintoff, in particular, had insisted it was unsafe for two women to make such a journey in the present circumstances.

'I trust you are finding Ewing Street considerably quieter now those dreadful women have left?'

There was a smugness in Stefan Mintoff's voice that Emily did not find attractive. He had made much of the fact that it was *he* who had ordered the owner of the two brothels to evict his unruly and immoral tenants or face prosecution.

The houses had been vacated a week after Ruth had left Kadina, telling no one of her destination.

'The street is much quieter, Mr Mintoff, but I wish I had been given notice of their eviction. I fear most of the women will find their way to gold-mining areas where they will have no hope whatsoever of redemption. I managed to build up a rapport with a couple of the women – one in particular. It would have given me a great deal of satisfaction had I been able to persuade either one to abandon her ways.'

'You are an idealist, Miss Boyce – that is not a criticism, I hasten to add. This country needs such women, especially those like yourself who combine action with idealism, but I fear there are some things that are beyond human endeavour.'

'When I encounter such situations I remember my late father's teachings and call on the Lord. He rarely fails me, Mr Mintoff. Now, if you will excuse me I must go and thank the choir for giving us such an enjoyable evening.'

'Before you go may I ask you something, Miss Boyce? Will you do me the great honour of acting as my hostess at a dinner party I am giving in honour of the Minister of Education, who is visiting Kadina soon? Many of the religious leaders of the area will be there and may be persuaded to support you in your work. I would also welcome your knowledge of such functions, I fear I have little experience of the protocol necessary for such an occasion.'

Emily hesitated before replying. Had it been a purely social function she would have refused. She did not want the people she was here to help looking upon her as a party-going socialite. But Stefan Mintoff was right. This was an opportunity too good for her to refuse.

'Thank you, Mr Mintoff, I will be delighted to act as a hostess at the dinner party. Perhaps you will be kind enough to let me have the details closer to the time?'

'Of course.' Stefan Mintoff was quite obviously delighted she had accepted his invitation. 'But I do wish you would call me Stefan.'

Margaret, who was a member of the choir, had seen Emily chatting to Stefan Mintoff. As they walked home together later, Margaret said, 'I saw Mr "Don't-you-think-I'm-wonderful" talking to you after the concert. He has quite a fancy for you.'

'Quite possibly,' Emily said matter of factly. 'He's asked me to act as hostess at a dinner party he's giving next week for a visiting government minister.'

'You haven't accepted?' Margaret was concerned. 'He has no wife and you have no man. Folk are bound to jump to conclusions!'

'If Mr Mintoff's guests are prepared to give their support to my work they may jump wherever they wish, Margaret. I will accept help from whatever source it is sent by the Lord.'

It should have been an excellent dinner party for Emily. Guest dignitaries from Church and Chapel all offered her their support, especially in the schemes she had for helping the families of sick and destitute miners.

Among them was a senior churchman from Adelaide who promised that the charitable organisations in the South Australian capital would turn their attention to fund-raising in support of her work.

Not to be outdone, the government minister promised that his administration would allocate monies to help alleviate the distress of miners and their families.

In this respect the party was much more successful than Emily had dreamed possible. She even gave Stefan Mintoff a genuinely warm smile of gratitude when he introduced her to a man who had grown rich from successful speculation in the copper mines of the Yorke Peninsula. Almost sober, he wrote out a cheque for a thousand pounds there and then and handed it to her.

Then Reverend Arnold Weeks triumphantly introduced her to Ezra Maddison, the minister responsible for the spiritual well-being of all who lived and worked in a vast parish that included the whole of the northern Flinders Ranges.

'Miss Boyce's father was vicar of a mining parish at the time of his sad death,' explained Arnold Weeks, speaking loudly to the outback preacher who was obliged to cup a hand to his ear in order to catch what was being said. 'She is particularly anxious to locate a couple of miners who were last known to be at the Blinman mine.'

'Blinman?' repeated the minister. 'I know it well. Indeed, I conducted my first ever triple wedding there, it must have been about two years ago.'

Trying hard to cast aside the memory of the aftermath of the wedding celebrations, he added, 'One of the bridegrooms was newly arrived from Cornwall – as indeed was his bride.'

'Did you meet either a Charles Minns or a Sam Hooper while you were there?' Emily asked, without much hope of a positive reply.

'Samuel Hooper, you say? Yes, I think that was the name of the bridegroom. In fact I'm almost certain it was. He and the young woman had journeyed from Cornwall on the same ship. They came here first of all, as I recall. I had quite a chat with the bride afterwards. She had come to South Australia hoping to find her father, but he had moved on, probably to the gold-fields. So many miners seem to rush from one mine to another in pursuit of that elusive metal. All most find are sinful and violent men and women. It is so very, very sad.'

'This bride,' Emily persisted, although she felt certain she would not want to hear the answer he was about to give her, 'was it her first marriage?'

'No . . . no, I don't think it was. I believe her husband was killed in a mine accident, back in Cornwall. She had a young daughter with a rather pretty name . . .'

'Would it be Primrose?' Emily felt as though a yawning chasm was opening beneath her feet.

'Why yes, that's it . . . Primrose. You know the young woman?'

'Yes, I know her. I know both of them. Now, you must pardon me, I see some of the guests are ready to leave and I am acting as Mr Mintoff's hostess.'

Emily hurried away before she betrayed her feelings to Reverend Weeks and his companion from the Flinders Ranges.

She felt physically sick and desperately unhappy. She had come halfway across the world in pursuit of a dream that had suddenly become a nightmare.

Coming to Australia to take up welfare work among miners and their families was an exciting adventure, but in moments of self-honesty she knew it had been the thought of a reunion with Sam that had brought her here, not a wish to serve her fellow men and women. She could have done that more effectively, perhaps, by remaining in Cornwall.

Emily somehow managed to get through the remainder of the evening. Then, declining Stefan Mintoff's entreaties that he should take her home in his light carriage, she walked home through the deserted streets of Kadina, feeling desolated, unhappy and desperately alone.

II

The morning after the party Emily was still feeling deeply unhappy about the revelations of the previous evening when there came a knock on the door of the Ewing Street cottage.

It was usual for Margaret to open the door to callers, but as Emily was passing along the passageway close to the door at the time and Margaret was working in the kitchen, she called, 'I'll answer it!'

Opening the door, she was confronted by a man in his thirties. He did not appear to have shaved for a while and his clothes had certainly known better days.

'May I help you?' Emily asked.

Belatedly, the man at the door dragged off his cap to reveal an uncombed tangle of black hair. 'I'm looking for Margaret Minns. I was told I'd find her here.'

'Yes, she is here but . . . who are you?'

Even as she asked the question Emily's intuition provided her with an answer. She thought she knew who this disreputable-looking man must be.

She hoped she was wrong. She had taken an instant but totally irrational dislike to him.

'I'm Charlie Minns, ma'am. Margaret's husband.'

'Then you had better come inside, Mr Minns.' Pointing to the living room, she said, 'Wait in there while I go and fetch Margaret. This is going to be quite a shock for her.'

Closing the door behind the errant husband, Emily hurried to the kitchen.

Margaret was making bread. It was warm work, made worse by the corrugated iron roof which considerably increased the heat inside the house. Red-cheeked and with a lock of damp hair dangling beside her face, her arms were white with flour almost to her elbows.

'Margaret, take off that apron and clean yourself up – quickly now. There's someone to see you. I have left him in the living room.'

'Someone to see me? I don't know anyone who'd come here after me. Who is it? What does he want?'

'Don't ask so many questions, Margaret. Just get tidied up as quickly as you can and go in there to see him. Here, let me do something to your hair while you wipe the flour from your hands. Hurry now, I'll clean up in here.'

As she spoke, Emily thought she might have formed a more favourable impression of Charlie Minns had he taken a little more trouble with *his* appearance before coming to the house to seek a reunion with the wife he had not seen for so long.

'You'll clean up in here while I—' Margaret's eyes opened wide suddenly. 'It's not . . . You don't mean it's Charlie? He's here?'

Margaret's hand flew up to her mouth. 'Emily, come into the room with me. I . . . I don't know what I'll say to him . . .'

'You will think of something, I'm quite certain,' Emily smiled.

'Off you go. I'll give you a couple of minutes together before I fetch the boys from the garden.'

'Oh, Emily! I'm not sure I'm ready for this after all this time. It's so sudden, like.'

Margaret was shaking and Emily put an arm about her. 'You will be all right, Margaret. Everything is going to be all right now for you and the boys.'

Watching her quaking companion depart from the kitchen, Emily wished she felt as confident as she had tried to sound. She told herself she had been unfairly influenced by the unkempt appearance of Charlie Minns. He had probably travelled a long distance for this reunion with his wife.

However, whatever she thought was of no importance. He was Margaret's husband – and the father of Albert and Tom.

Hurrying from the kitchen to the garden where the two children were playing with a ball, she called, 'Boys, come inside and clean yourselves up. I have a wonderful surprise for you . . .'

Later that day, when Charlie had gone off with the two boys to collect the few possessions he had left behind the bar at the Miners' Arms and the two women were alone, Emily said, 'Well, Margaret, you have achieved what you and the boys came to Australia to do. You have found your husband. You must be ecstatic.'

'I'm very relieved that he's alive – and delighted for the boys' sake,' said Margaret, somewhat ambiguously. 'It brought tears to my eyes to see them go off together, with little Tom holding Charlie's hand, so proud for everyone to see that he has a father. Albert is proud and happy too, of course, but I'm a little more concerned for him. He's got a strong character and has been the man of the family for so long he might well resent having someone else taking over . . . for a while, anyway.'

'That doesn't tell me how *you* feel. Has the reunion been all you hoped it would be?'

'To be perfectly honest, I'd never given very much thought to the actual moment of meeting. I was too busy thinking about trying to find him again.'

Once again Margaret had failed to give Emily a reply to her question, but she was still talking.

'He's different to how I remembered him, but I suppose we've both changed in the years we've been apart.'

Emily decided not to put her question yet again. Instead she asked, 'What do you intend doing now, Margaret?'

Uncertainly, Margaret replied, 'I . . . I just don't know. I realise I'm his wife, but we've been apart for so long we're almost like strangers. I can't go back to being a complete wife to him . . . well, not right away. I've told Charlie and he's not very happy about it, but . . . it's just the way I feel, Emily. We're going to have to get to know each other all over again. I need to learn to trust him the way I once did. It can't be any other way for me.'

'Have you given any thought to where you'll live, Margaret? Has Charlie said anything about it? No doubt you will need to live wherever he is working? Is he in work?'

'I haven't had time to think about any practical things like that, Emily. I don't think he's working right now. He said he's been prospecting and been quite lucky, so finding work isn't all that urgent at the moment. But you're right, we'll need to find somewhere to live.'

'That's no problem at all,' Emily declared. 'You'll stay right here. You, Charlie and the boys. What is more I will pay the rent for the next three months. That will be a present to you for being such a wonderful companion to me since we left Cornwall – and before that too. I'll speak to Reverend Kavanagh right away with a view to moving in with him and his wife until I find somewhere suitable.'

When Margaret began to protest, Emily said firmly, 'No, Margaret, I have made up my mind. You have found your husband. Now you both need time together with the boys in order to pick up the threads of your life. You certainly don't want me around!'

'But what will *you* do, Emily? Will you still try to find this miner friend from St Cleer – or were you only saying you wanted to find him so I'd feel better about trying to find Charlie?'

Emily had told Margaret nothing of the news she had received of Sam. She shook her head, 'I think he will have made a new life for himself here. I'll carry on with the very many projects I have started in Kadina – exciting projects which justify my presence in Australia. I would just like to say I am happy for you and the boys, Margaret. Very, very happy indeed.'

III

Emily moved out of the house on Ewing Street the following morning.

Margaret watched her departure with mixed feelings. She would miss the company of the woman to whom she had been successively maid, housekeeper and companion. They had shared each other's sorrows and enjoyed many happy moments together.

It had been Emily too who had brought about the reunion of the Minns family, but this event had left Margaret confused. There would need to be a great deal of soul-searching in the months that lay ahead.

Charlie had changed since the days of their married life in Cornwall.

Margaret had never been totally blind to her husband's shortcomings when she had married him against the wishes of her family and the doubts of her employer. She was aware he had never been the hardest working of men and always placed his own interests before those of anyone else – including his immediate family. Yet, despite such faults, he had been an easygoing man who took nothing too seriously.

Since coming to Australia a change had come about in his make-up that Margaret found disconcerting. He was harder, both mentally and physically. She suspected too that his selfishness had become ruthlessness and was no longer softened by concern for his family.

She tried to tell herself it was because he had been away from her and the boys and had been forced to adapt to the harsh environment of a new and untamed country. Nevertheless, she was rapidly realising that her husband had become a stranger to her – one with whom she felt ill at ease much of the time.

'Your friend's husband is a very interesting man,' said Stefan Mintoff, one day. 'He knows a great deal about the outback – the Flinders Ranges in particular. I hope to talk to him at some length about that area of South Australia. I believe there is great mineral wealth there and I want to learn all I can about it.'

The Kadina councillor was conveying Emily and the last of her belongings from Ewing Street to the rectory, using his pony and trap.

He had been at the rectory when Emily had gone to tell Reverend Arnold Weeks of the return of Charlie Minns and to ask the rector if she might stay at the vicarage with him and his wife until she could find new accommodation.

Stefan had immediately offered to accommodate her in one of the houses he owned in the town.

Politely but firmly Emily declined the offer. It was one thing to have him perform a neighbourly act by helping her move from Ewing Street to the rectory, quite another to provide her with a home. Although she had begun to trust Stefan more than when they had first met, she did not want to be beholden to him to any greater extent.

'. . . Yes, indeed,' the councillor continued, 'there are fortunes to be made in the Flinder Ranges. Copper is there in plenty, but there are other minerals too. It is a very rich area indeed.'

'You have been there?' Emily asked.

'Sadly, no, but I take a keen interest in all parts of South Australia. It is my firm belief that the Flinders Ranges possess vast potential to benefit the whole of the colony. If you have money to invest in our country I strongly advise you to look at what the Flinders Ranges have to offer you.'

Later that evening, over a meal in the rectory, Emily asked her hosts what they knew of Stefan Mintoff.

'Very little,' confessed Arnold Weeks. 'He arrived in Kadina some years ago and began working in Tom Bray's hardware store. Two years later the two men went into partnership. Only a year after that Tom Bray died and Stefan Mintoff took over the business. It was about that time he became involved in local politics. There has been no noticeable upsurge in the hardware business, but Stefan has gone from strength to strength. He now owns a number of properties, has interests in many ventures and his sights are set firmly on the state parliament.'

'Would you say he is a shrewd businessman?' Emily asked the question remembering Stefan's suggestion that she should invest in ventures in the Flinders Ranges.

'I suppose he must be,' Arnold Weeks replied. 'He certainly isn't earning enough from the hardware store to finance his business ventures.'

'Or his life style,' said Jennifer Weeks, tight-lipped.

'Now, now!' scolded her husband. 'You should not repeat malicious gossip, my dear. Stefan Mintoff has done a great deal for Kadina since he assumed office in local government.'

Jennifer Weeks sniffed derisively. 'He's done a great deal more to benefit Stefan Mintoff.'

'Making money is not a sin, Jennifer,' her husband chided.

'He has always been most generous to the Church and our various charities.'

'Where does he come from?' Emily put the question hastily, hoping to forestall an argument between husband and wife.

'That's as much of a mystery as everything else about him,' Jennifer replied. 'No one seems to know for certain. Some say he's Greek, others that he's of Russian descent. I've even heard it said that he's from Malta.'

'It sounds as though he might come from a wealthy family,' Emily suggested.

'It is quite possible,' Arnold Weeks agreed. 'South Australia attracts men and women from many walks of life. Once here they are judged on their merits. It makes for a healthy and well-balanced society.'

'He has certainly been very kind to me,' Emily said. 'And always shown himself to be a perfect gentleman.'

Jennifer Weeks said nothing. She surmised that Emily had probably had little experience of men. However, she did not wish to argue with her about the merits of Stefan Mintoff.

'Well, we must take people as each of us finds them,' she said. 'To be perfectly honest I have had very little to do with Stefan Mintoff. Everything I know about him is no more than hearsay, and that is no way to judge anyone.'

Her husband beamed amiably at her. 'That is very true, Jennifer. Stefan Mintoff may be a stranger to our ways but he is doing his very best to fit in – and the whole community benefits from his generosity.'

IV

Stefan Mintoff proved to be a persistent suitor. He attended most of Emily's charitable functions and ensured that they received maximum publicity in and around the three towns of the Copper Triangle.

Margaret frequently met with Emily, helping her with various projects whenever possible, although Charlie and the boys prevented her from devoting as much time to them as she had during their early days in the township.

Margaret informed Emily that Stefan Mintoff was also a regular visitor to the Minns home in Ewing Street. As a result both women had finally been persuaded to call Mintoff by his first name.

Emily, curious about Mintoff's interest in the Minns family, asked her friend about it.

Margaret shrugged. 'It's not me he comes to see, but Charlie. The pair of them talk for hours in the sitting room while I'm working. Then they'll go off to the Miners' Arms together and talk some more while they're drinking.'

'What do they talk about?' Emily asked, more curious than ever.

The two women were chatting as they washed up plates and tea cups in the small kitchen of the Kadina Institute after a meeting of the newly formed 'Township Benevolent Society'.

'Much of the talk seems to be about mining of one sort or another – that and the Flinders Ranges. Stefan seems to be very interested in the mines of that area.'

'Yes, he is. He's often telling me of the money waiting to be made in that part of South Australia and, of course, Charlie has spent some time there.'

'Yes, part of it at Blinman. That reminds me, I asked Charlie if he'd ever met up with Sam Hooper, the St Cleer miner you were asking about when we first arrived here. Charlie says he's at Blinman and he's spoken to him, but he couldn't tell me any more than that. I'm sure if you wrote to him care of the Blinman mine the letter would reach him.'

'Thank you, Margaret, but I doubt if I will bother. I was really only interested in learning whether he had settled down happily in Australia, that is all.'

The lie did not come easily to her. She still frequently thought of Sam. He held a place in her affections that no one else could fill – although Stefan Mintoff was trying hard.

'Where do you think Stefan will take us for a picnic tomorrow?' Margaret put the question to Emily. The Kadina councillor had suggested that he should take Emily and the whole of the Minns family in a carriage to a picnic the next day, which was a Saturday.

'I really have no idea,' Emily replied vaguely. 'He said it was to be a surprise.'

The picnic party set off in style. A carriage called first for the Minns family and then for Emily. It came complete with driver – and with Stefan. The boys were allowed to ride on the outside seat alongside the driver, while the four adults were accommodated comfortably inside.

Stefan kept their destination a secret, even when the sea to the south of the port of Wallaroo came into view.

When the site chosen for the picnic was reached, it became evident this was no casual choice. A large tent had been erected on the edge of the sand, a short distance from the sea, and Stefan Mintoff had sent two men ahead of the carriage, one to erect the tent and start a fire, the other to organise the cooking.

In addition, there were folding chairs, a table and other luxuries not usually associated with a casual outdoor meal. There was also wine for the adults and lemonade for the two children.

'Well! This is far superior to any picnic I have been on before,' Emily was able to say, in all honesty. 'Do you have an orchestra hiding away somewhere?'

'You think I should have arranged music for you?'

Stefan looked so dismayed that Emily put a hand on his arm in a gesture of reassurance. 'I am joking, Stefan. This is truly wonderful. The setting, the food – everything. You have put so much thought into this you might have been enter-taining royalty. I really am very impressed. Very impressed indeed.'

Relieved, Stefan beamed at her. 'Your company gives me far more pleasure than would royalty, Emily. But I am happy that it meets with your approval. Now, shall we have something to drink? I had Champagne brought here, packed in ice.'

Stefan could not have wished for a more perfect day for the picnic he had organised. While the boys happily paddled in the sea, or enjoyed playing with a ball on the beach, the adults sat outside the tent eating, drinking and talking on what was one of the most relaxed days Emily had spent since arriving in Australia.

However, Emily had a niggling feeling that Stefan had not organised the picnic as a purely social occasion and she was not entirely surprised when, halfway through the afternoon, he turned to her and said, 'Emily, shall we leave Margaret and Charlie entertaining their boys and take a walk along the shore?'

When Emily frowned, wondering what lay behind his sugges-tion, Stefan said hurriedly, 'I promise I will not take you out of sight of the others, but I would like to talk to you.'

Margaret had been unusually quiet during the day, but now Emily ignored the slight lift of her friend's eyebrows. 'I seem to have done little except eat and drink since our arrival, so a walk would be most enjoyable.'

They walked in silence for perhaps five minutes before Emily prompted her companion, 'Am I correct in assuming you asked me to walk with you for a reason, Stefan?'

'That is very perceptive of you, Emily. Yes, I do have a reason to speak to you. *Two* reasons, in fact. The first concerns Charlie – which means it will also affect Margaret, of course.'

When Emily made no reply, Stefan continued, 'You are aware, I know, of the interest I have in the Flinders Ranges. I am convinced there is a great future for mining there – once a railway links the area with the ports of South Australia – and it will be built. One of the reasons I am seeking election to the state parliament is to ensure a railway is built to serve the region's needs.'

None of what he was saying was new to Emily. Stefan Mintoff's ambitions had been the subject of local gossip for even longer than she had been in Australia.

'What has this to do with Charlie?'

'Ah, yes! Well, Charlie and I have talked long and often about the region and I am satisfied that he knows a great deal about the Flinders Ranges and its potential. I am forming a company to exploit the minerals that are to be found there. I feel so strongly about it that I am going to England in order to raise capital for my venture. Charlie intends returning to the Flinders Ranges to resume prospecting and I have asked him to act as my representative there, to keep me informed of any promising finds in order that I might register claims on them on behalf of the company.'

Emily was taken aback. 'I am ready to accept there are considerable mineral resources out there, but do you have sufficient confidence in Charlie to risk shareholders' money on his judgement?'

'I have every confidence in him,' Stefan replied. 'And he has taught me much about the region, but I will certainly check his finds against information I have already gathered over the years.'

After digesting this, Emily replied, 'Margaret has said nothing of this to me. Does she know Charlie intends going off prospecting once more?'

'That, of course, is a purely domestic matter. However, as Charlie and Margaret have only recently been reunited, she might not be terribly happy about the arrangement. I would like you to allay any fears she may have about money matters. I will ensure she has access to funds during his absence.'

'Margaret has been my friend and companion for a long time.

I will take care of her if the need arises,' Emily declared. 'But am I correct in assuming that you wish me to persuade Margaret to raise no objection to Charlie returning to the Flinders Ranges? What of the trouble they are having there with the Aborigines?'

'That's all over,' Stefan reassured her. 'These little problems arise periodically but seldom last for more than a few weeks.'

Emily was not happy that Stefan was putting the onus of disclosing Charlie's plans to Margaret upon her, but she said, 'You mentioned there were two matters you wished to discuss with me. What is the second?'

'Ah, yes! Well, this is a more personal matter – and one to which I do not expect an immediate reply . . .'

Stefan hesitated and Emily gave him a questioning look.

'You must have realised by now that I hold you in high esteem, Emily. Very high indeed. In view of this I would like you to consider becoming my wife.'

It was said in such a matter-of-fact manner that it was a moment or two before Emily realised she had just received a proposal of marriage.

When it had sunk in she looked at him in utter disbelief. 'You are asking me to marry you? It is a quite absurd suggestion, Stefan. Why . . . we hardly know each other!'

'I feel we know each other very well, Emily. Indeed, I know you better than any woman I have ever met.'

'But . . . the subject of marriage has never even been hinted at! I have a high regard for you, of course, but marriage should be based on far more than that.'

'Not necessarily, Emily. I *do* have a great affection for you, of course, but if we were younger and a marriage was being arranged by our families I have no doubt they would regard it as a highly satisfactory union. You are from a well-respected and aristocratic family in England. I am a successful businessman who hopes soon to be elected to the parliament of South Australia, with the prospects of high office and an eventual peerage. It is a union that would certainly receive the blessing of your uncle, Lord Boyce.'

Emily was taken aback that Stefan should choose to bring her uncle's name into the conversation, although she realised it was information the Kadina councillor knew about her. Nevertheless, she was not entirely happy that he should have done so.

'Arranged marriages are no longer acceptable in England, Stefan – however desirable they might be.'

'Yet they still take place, as they do in many other parts of the world, and the vast majority of such marriages are both happy and successful. I am not asking you to make such a marriage with me, Emily, only pointing out that our families, who are on the far side of the world, would consider such a marriage a *good* one. I am extremely fond of you and would not wish you to marry me if you did not have similar feelings for me. As I have said, I will soon be going to England on business. I wanted to express my feelings for you before leaving and to ask you to consider the prospect of marrying me. Will you do that, Emily?'

For a brief, irrational moment Emily wondered what form a proposal from *Sam* would have taken. She doubted very much whether it would have been as carefully considered as the one she had just received.

She tried in vain to dismiss such thoughts as being no longer relevant. 'I will certainly consider your proposal, Stefan, although I must admit it has taken me by surprise.'

This was not entirely true. Stefan Mintoff's attentions had been such in recent weeks that she had realised he had something more than a platonic friendship in mind. Nevertheless, she had not seriously contemplated what her reply would be.

She was grateful to him for giving her ample time to think about it, and she told him so.

'I am asking you to make one of the most important decisions you will ever need to make, Emily, and you have no family

here with whom to discuss it. Please, take as much time as you
wish. I will try to curb my eagerness and look forward to my
return from England and being with you again.'

Taking her hand he carried it to his lips.

As he lowered his head, Emily noticed, with slight embarrassment, that he was beginning to go bald on the crown of his head.

V

'Do you think you *will* marry Stefan?'

It was the day after the picnic. The previous evening Charlie
had broken the news to Margaret of his intended departure for
the Flinders Ranges to resume prospecting. She had taken the
news philosophically and Emily was relieved it had not been
necessary for her to become involved in the discussion between
husband and wife.

Both women were in the Kadina Institute, sorting through a
consignment of clothing that had been sent by sea from Adelaide
for distribution to the families of out-of-work miners.

They had been discussing the events of the previous day.

'I will need to give it a great deal of thought – and learn more
of Stefan's background and family than I know now. But I can
see no reason why we should *not* marry.'

'Do you love him?' Margaret asked.

'Not at the moment,' Emily confessed. 'But I find him attractive and the longer I know him, the more I like him – I think!'

'*Liking* a man isn't a good enough reason for *marrying* him,'
declared Margaret. 'Even when you *love* a man you sometimes
feel you want to send him away and live your own life again
for a while. Freedom is a very precious thing, Emily. Don't give
it up until you find a man you love so much that the thought
of life without him is unbearable.'

Picking up on a point Margaret had made, Emily said, 'You don't seem particularly upset that Charlie will be going away again.'

Margaret looked unhappy. 'Part of me doesn't want him to go, but I think it might be a good thing. For a while, anyway.'

'Why?' Emily felt sorry for her friend. Margaret had come to Australia with such high hopes of finding Charlie and resuming a happy and settled married life with him and the boys.

'Charlie and Albert aren't getting on too well with each other. It was to be expected, I suppose. I relied on Albert a bit too much while his pa was away. He got used to being the man about the house. He's happy to have Charlie back with us, I know he is, really, but I think he resents being treated as just a kid again and having the household centred around his father.' Margaret made a helpless gesture. 'It would be easier if Charlie tried to understand the way Albert feels, but he believes that children must be taught to do as they're told without question. He's taken to cuffing Albert and he's a bit heavy-handed.'

Concerned for the small boy, Emily said, 'Albert doesn't deserve such treatment after all he's been through for you, Margaret. Have you tried explaining that to Charlie?'

'He knows I don't like it, but I daren't push it too much. It will only make him hit Albert all the harder – and he's likely to turn on me, as well.'

Emily was appalled by what Margaret was telling her, but she decided to say nothing more for the moment. She had moved into a house of her own once more and would invite Margaret there once Charlie was in the Flinders Ranges. They would then be able to discuss the problem in more detail.

Charlie and Stefan left Kadina together a few days later. They travelled in Stefan's carriage which would take them to the Wallaroo docks. From here Charlie would board a boat sailing northwards to Port Augusta. He would then journey overland to the northern Flinders Ranges.

Stefan had arranged to travel by steamer to Adelaide and there board a London-bound ship.

Emily and Margaret, together with Albert and Tom, saw them off from Stefan's house, waving to the departing coach until it passed from view.

Before leaving Kadina, Stefan and Emily had discussed the company Stefan had formed to open up the mines he intended working in the Flinders Ranges. Shares in the company would initially be valued at one pound each, but Stefan assured Emily that once they had been offered to the London Market their value would soar to at least five times this sum. He persuaded her to buy a thousand shares, telling her not to discuss the deal until his return from England. When the time was right he would sell them on for her at the new price, boosted by English investors. Stefan added that she might accept it as a wedding gift from him.

'Stefan will be gone for a long time,' said Margaret as the two women walked away from Stefan's large and impressive house.

'Six months at least,' agreed Emily. 'More if he is unable to arrange passage on steamships in both directions. Has Charlie given you any indication of how long he expects to be away?'

'No. To tell you the truth we had another argument yesterday. Once again it was about his treatment of Albert. I said a few things that would have been better left unsaid. He hasn't really spoken to me since then. I did ask him how long he thought he would be away and he told me it would be "as long as it takes". I know no more than that.'

'Why don't you and the boys come to stay with me as companions at my house while Charlie is away?' Emily suggested. 'You can keep your house on for when Charlie comes back, but it would be a change for you all and I really would appreciate your company. I will pay you the wage I gave to you when you were my companion on the voyage here.'

It was a tempting offer, but Margaret hesitated before saying, 'I don't know, Emily. The boys would enjoy the huge garden you have there, I know, and the money would be very welcome – Charlie has left me a bit short – but . . .'

'No "buts", Margaret. The arrangement will suit everyone. First thing in the morning I will have someone come to the house to collect all the things you think you and the boys might need. Oh, I am pleased! It will be just like old times!'

5

I

Charlie Minns reached Blinman three weeks after setting out from Kadina. Many of the miners who witnessed his arrival recognised him, but none proffered a welcome.

However, Charlie's unpopularity did not bother him. He had no intention of remaining in the remote mining town for any longer than was absolutely necessary.

When he had passed through Port Augusta Charlie had purchased a donkey plus the provisions he would take with him to the outback, using more money than Margaret was even aware he possessed. By buying here rather than waiting until he reached Blinman, Charlie saved himself a great deal of money.

Although the Aboriginal threat was deemed to be over, Charlie chose to travel to Blinman in the company of a number of bullock drivers, all of whom were returning to Blinman with provisions for the stores and hotels dotted along the long route.

From these men Charlie was able to confirm the absence of trouble in the Flinders Ranges. It came as a considerable relief to him. When he set off again he would be travelling alone in areas visited by very few white men.

During the couple of days he was in Blinman, Charlie slept in a deserted and tumbledown shack on the edge of the town. Not only did it save him money, but it meant he could avoid the company of other miners.

When he decided he was ready to leave the mining town, Charlie called at the Blinman hotel to buy beer and brandy to take with him to the outback. As he was stowing them in the packs slung over the back of his donkey, tied outside the hotel, Ruth Askew came along the road and stopped beside him.

'Well, if it isn't the great prospector himself! Have you grown tired of family life already, Charlie – or has your wife come to her senses and thrown you out?'

'I've a living to earn, family or no family,' Charlie growled, continuing to load the donkey.

'And, of course, you don't need a family. You'll no doubt find some poor woman to keep you company in the outback.'

'Why don't you come with me and find out?' Charlie retorted.

'No thanks. Life may not be all that easy for me, but it's better than being found floating in a mine shaft.'

'You don't want to listen to what men tell you when they're in bed with you, Ruth. We're all liars then. You've told me so yourself, many times.'

The last bottle safely stowed away, Charlie unwound the reins from the post to which the donkey was tethered. 'I'm sorry I can't waste more time talking to you, but I want to be well clear of Blinman before dark. I'll call on you when I get back and you can amuse me with more of your stories.'

'If you do you'll find it doesn't come free for you any more, Charlie. I'll charge you, same as everyone else and I doubt you'll be able to afford me.'

'We'll see about that, Ruth. No doubt we'll be able to come to some arrangement, although you always did undervalue me and put too high a price on yourself.' With this, Charlie set off northward along the road, the donkey plodding, head down, behind him.

Ruth turned away and spotted Sam standing a few paces away. He had listened to the conversation between prostitute and prospector with interest.

'I hope you enjoyed what you heard,' she said, belligerently.

'I can think of nothing Charlie Minns has done that I've ever found enjoyable. I was the one who pulled the body of the Aboriginal woman from the mine shaft at Nuccaleena.'

'Oh! Well, I wasn't suggesting that Charlie killed her, if that's what you're thinking. He's a rat and not worth a minute of anyone's time, but I don't think even he would stoop to murder.'

Sam remembered Charlie entering the camp at Nuccaleena and the casual manner in which he had reported shooting an Aborigine. He remembered too how little emotion he had shown when the body of the woman had been found.

'I don't know him well enough to comment either way on that, but you and he seem to go back a long way.'

'Long enough,' Ruth agreed without elaborating. 'But I wouldn't lose any sleep if I never saw Charlie Minns again.'

As she walked past Sam and made her way to the store, Ruth told herself that what she had just said to Sam was the truth, but she was unable to convince herself. No matter what Charlie Minns did, or did not do, she still retained a totally illogical affection for him.

Charlie Minns was not setting out from Blinman on a journey of exploration on behalf of Stefan Mintoff. He knew exactly where he was heading.

Skirting the Moolooloo sheep station, he was careful to stay out of sight of the house and outbuildings. Had he been seen, outback hospitality demanded that he pay a call on the remote household to partake of a meal and pass on the latest news from the outside world. The owners would also have been interested in his prospecting plans and the area in which he intended carrying them out. This was not due entirely to their own curiosity, but also because, should anything untoward happen, they would know where to begin looking for him.

But Charlie Minns did not want to be found.

He made camp that night some distance from Moolooloo, but did not light a fire. The sheep station employed Aborigines who could smell woodsmoke at a greater distance than most men could see in these hills.

He made an evening meal of bread, cold beans and a beer. When it was over he carefully buried the bottle and scraps, so as to leave no trace of his camp. Then he went to sleep with a rifle cradled in his arms.

The following day he passed the site of the copper mine at Nuccaleena, wasting only a single glance towards the spot where the Aboriginal woman had been laid out, surrounded by the gifts donated by the Blinman miners. The blankets and cheap gifts had long since disappeared. So too had the body of the woman.

His destination was still another night and day's journey away. Stefan Mintoff had suggested that Charlie should make a brief survey of sites such as Nuccaleena, but Charlie had more urgent business to attend to.

Eventually, on the evening of the third day, Charlie reached his destination. It was a deep but narrow creek; a watercourse gouged out of the earth by torrents of water pouring from the surrounding hills during the region's brief and capricious rainy season.

There had been a few days of thundery summer rain before Charlie had set out from Blinman and this suited him very well. The water rushing in torrents along the creek had long since gone, but there were places where brackish pools remained.

Taking bearings from the surrounding hills, Charlie located a heap of innocuous-looking stones. Removing them with his bare hands, he uncovered the tools he had hidden here months before. This was where he would make his camp and commence prospecting.

He began digging on a bend of the dried-up creek the following morning, carrying the sandy earth he had removed to a nearby pool of water. When he had transferred enough to work with, Charlie squatted down by the pool. Using a mortar and pestle he crushed pieces of quartz from the soil before putting earth and quartz into a pan, dipping it in the pool and swirling the whole around, gradually reducing the contents. Finally, with a grunt of satisfaction, Charlie saw what he was seeking. It was a tell-tale tail of yellow specks around the edge of the pan.

It was gold, washed down by the rains and deposited in the place where he had found it before.

Carefully extracting the fine particles of precious metal, Charlie transferred them to a pouch suspended around his neck before continuing his work.

Charlie found more gold than ever before in the creek bed. There were even one or two smallish nuggets. By the tenth day of prospecting he had accumulated a sizeable amount – yet he was beginning to feel uneasy.

He believed he was being watched. He had seen no one, but the occasional startled bird or unexpectedly disturbed kangaroo gave him warnings he could not afford to ignore.

When a magpie suddenly took off nearby with a chatter of complaint, Charlie picked up his rifle and ran swiftly along the creek bed, stooping to remain out of sight of anyone who might be near the spot where the bird had been disturbed.

When he felt he was far enough away, Charlie climbed from the creek. Taking a circuitous route and treading lightly, he approached the spot where he thought someone was hiding.

Charlie moved very carefully now. If he made a sound that was heard by the hidden observer, it could result in his death.

Suddenly, he thought he detected a movement ahead and to one side of him. He dropped to one knee immediately – and waited.

Just as he was beginning to think he might have been mistaken, he saw another movement. A moment later an Aborigine crept into view. The man was completely naked – but he carried a spear.

His interest was concentrated upon the creek, at the spot where Charlie had been working only a few minutes before.

Seemingly puzzled by the silence, the Aborigine rose slowly to his feet, a shoulder-high bush hiding him from the view of anyone who might be ahead of him. As he did so there was a commotion from the spot where Charlie had tethered his donkey.

Charlie was alarmed to see the animal galloping off through the scrub as though pursued by the devil.

This was when the spear-carrying Aborigine turned and saw Charlie.

Before the man had time to recover from his surprise, Charlie quickly raised the rifle to his shoulder, took aim, and fired.

The Aborigine fell to the ground, but he was not dead and he began crawling away.

Reloading as he went, Charlie approached the wounded man but waited until he could have reached out and touched him before firing again, the barrel of the rifle almost touching the base of the other man's skull.

The Aborigine fell forward on his face and did not move again.

There was a sudden sound from behind Charlie and he whirled around in time to dodge a spear that had been hurled from perhaps twenty paces distant.

Charlie rammed another cartridge home in the breech of his rifle, but the man who had thrown the spear was running away, taking a zig-zag course through thick scrub.

Charlie fired again, but knew he had missed. Quickly reloading his rifle, he looked around him in case there were more Aborigines in the area, but he could neither see nor hear anyone.

With any luck there might have been only two men after him, but Charlie could not afford to take any chances. He had already collected more gold than he had expected to find, far more than he had collected on his previous trip to the outback. He would go in search of his donkey then make his way back to Blinman as fast as he could travel.

It would be a dangerous journey. He had killed only one of the two Aborigines who were after him, and the other would not give up – and Charlie knew why.

He believed the two men must be members of the same tribe as the woman who had died at Nuccaleena. He was not certain whether they were after him because of his treatment of her – or because they were out to avenge the death of her husband.

The reason did not matter. They had set out to kill him and the surviving Aborigine would not give up until either he or Charlie was dead.

Perversely, Charlie cursed the woman, blaming her for his misfortunes. Had they not met up his life would not be in danger now.

Charlie had met the woman and her husband when he was prospecting in the outback and they were mourning the death of their young daughter. In a rare moment of compassion, Charlie had shared his provisions with them.

Afterwards, they travelled together for a few days, until Charlie developed a fancy for the wife. She was not averse to his attentions, but the husband objected strongly. So strongly that Charlie decided to shoot him.

Unfortunately, other members of the tribe to which the two Aborigines belonged had come looking for the couple and found the body of the husband.

This is what had caused the unrest that resulted in the attack on the Blinman miners.

It seemed the Aborigines were out for revenge once more, but now they were after just one man – Charlie.

Charlie hoped there was now only one Aborigine left to deal

with. Any more and his chances of reaching Blinman alive were extremely slim.

II

It took Charlie two nerve-racking hours to find and catch his frightened donkey. Twice during the search he wasted shots at startled kangaroos, mistaking them for humans.

It seemed to him that every sound of the outback had been magnified tenfold and every movement by bird or animal posed a threat to his life.

Once he had recaptured his donkey Charlie was faced with a dilemma. Should he return to the site of his digging, or abandon everything he had left there and head for Blinman immediately?

The gold he had panned was secured about his body in a belt of canvas and linen that he had made himself, but there were other items at the creek – not least food and water.

He decided he would return and approached the camp cautiously – but he was already too late. Someone had been there before him.

The food had gone, as had the few items of spare clothing from his camp and the remaining brandy. Far more serious, his water had been poured away and the water carriers stabbed time and time again so as to render them useless.

Nevertheless, Charlie was able to rescue two of the containers which were capable of carrying about half their normal capacity. These he filled with the brackish, unpalatable water from the shallow pool in which he had been panning for gold.

Despite all that had happened, Charlie hoped one day to return to the spot and so set about removing all traces of his prospecting. Although mining experts had long been convinced that gold would be found in the Flinders Ranges, this was one of the few finds to yield a worthwhile return.

Charlie had not reported the find – and had no intention of doing so. Registering a claim would bring a swarm of gold-seekers to the area and quickly exhaust the alluvial gold in the creek.

When he was satisfied he had hidden all traces of his work, Charlie let the donkey drink its fill from the waterhole before mounting the animal and setting off in the direction of Blinman.

Charlie rode through the night, able to see his way by the light of a near-full moon. It was an anxious ride, full of exaggerated night noises, animal movements and shadows that in his imagination harboured a lurking assassin.

He would occasionally make unexpected changes of direction, carefully avoiding areas of deep shadow where someone might be waiting, hoping to take him by surprise.

At no time did Charlie doubt he was being stalked. There were too many unexplained night noises and movements. He was also satisfied by now that he was being pursued by only one man. Had there been any more it would have been relatively simple to ambush him, distracting his attention while armed warriors crept up on him.

He began to breathe more easily when dawn arrived, dispersing the shadows and taking away the advantage of his Aborigine adversary.

Turning the donkey off the trail, Charlie kneed the animal up the side of a hill, from where he could view the trail along which he had travelled and also see for a considerable distance ahead.

He carefully scoured the scrub on both sides of the trail. Although there was no one to be seen there were various places where a man could conceal himself. He wasted four more bullets, fired into patches of thick scrub where the Aborigine might be hiding. But all he succeeded in doing was to send a wedge-tailed eagle soaring into the air – and startle the donkey.

Had Charlie not looped the animal's reins about his arm it would have bolted, leaving him to try to catch it once more. Given his tired state that would not have been easy, and if he had had to proceed on foot he would have been far too vulnerable. He had a better view of the surrounding countryside from the back of the donkey and could remain on guard without having to watch where he was putting his feet.

After giving the donkey most of the water he was carrying, Charlie set off once again.

Like its rider, the donkey was tired and reluctant to move off with its human burden. It took persistent rib-kicking with Charlie's booted heels before the stubborn animal was persuaded to move.

Charlie felt able to relax a little now it was daylight; the situation did not seem quite as menacing as it had during the hours of darkness. Besides, in a couple of hours he should reach the safety of the sheep station at Moolooloo.

Even so Charlie did not relax his vigilance completely until the buildings of the remote sheep station came into view – and this lapse proved his undoing.

He could see the manager of the sheep station and his Aborigine employees working on the fence of a sheep pen and he put a hand to his forehead to shield his eyes from the low-lying sun. Suddenly, without warning, he was struck in the back by an object that knocked him off the slow-plodding donkey.

For one brief, unreal moment as he lay on the ground, Charlie thought he had been struck by a large stone, but when he tried to turn over to look behind him he was unable to do so. The haft of a spear protruded from his back, the blade embedded just beneath his left shoulder.

At the same time an agonising pain began to spread through his body – and he started to scream.

The sound that spilled from his mouth carried blood with it. Despite this, Charlie struggled to a sitting position, freeing the rifle he carried on a sling over his right shoulder.

Only a short distance away, a young Aborigine stood as though uncertain what to do now he had downed the man he had been tracking for so long.

Charlie fired and the shot spun the young man around, but it did not drop him.

The shot also alerted those at the sheep station. As a shout went up the Aborigine turned and ran, indicating that he had not been seriously hurt.

Charlie tried to stand up, but the effort proved too great. He slid sideways to the ground as his assailant disappeared from view in the scrub.

When Ben Carminow, the Moolooloo station manager, and two of his Aborigine helpers reached Charlie he was lying on his stomach, his face turned to one side, moaning in pain, blood trickling slowly from a corner of his mouth. The spear was still embedded in his back.

The two Aborigines reached him first, but they stood back to allow Carminow through.

His face distorted with pain, Charlie whispered painfully, 'Help me. Oh God! Help me.'

'The first thing we need to do is get this spear out – and hope we don't do too much harm in the process,' said Ben. 'You . . .' He pointed to one of his Aborigine workers. 'Hold him down while I pull out the spear.'

The Aborigine looked unhappy and held back.

'You heard what I said!' Carminow spoke angrily.

Still the worker held back and it was his companion who spoke in his own tongue to the station manager. Startled, the station manager replied in the same language and the Aborigine worker nodded.

'So you're the man who's stirred up all the trouble we've had around here,' said Carminow, looking down at Charlie. 'You probably deserve all you've got, but I suppose we can't leave you here to die.'

Without further thought, he placed a foot on Charlie's left shoulder and tugged at the spear, causing Charlie to scream out in agony. It took three attempts before the spear blade was pulled free, by which time the wounded man had lapsed into unconsciousness.

Turning to the two workers, Carminow said, 'I don't care what your friends out there might or might not do to you for helping their enemy. What's far more certain is what *I'll* do to you if you *don't*. Run and get a hurdle – and quickly. We'll put him on it and carry him to the house.'

III

When Charlie regained consciousness he was lying on a bed in the station manager's house on the Moolooloo sheep station – and he was in great pain.

It felt as though his chest and the upper part of his back were on fire. When he coughed, which was frequently, the extra pain caused him to cry out.

However, when Ben Carminow entered the room, Charlie's question had nothing to do with his wound. 'My belt . . .' he croaked, in a hoarse whisper, 'where is it?'

'It's hanging over the back of the bed – and the gold dust is still in it. But you have more things to worry about right now. That's why I'm not asking you whether the gold came from a registered claim.'

'I've carried it with me for months,' Charlie lied, feebly. 'It came from—'

What he intended saying was lost in another bout of coughing, and a stream of blood trickled from his mouth.

'I said I wasn't asking,' Carminow repeated. 'And all the gold in the world isn't going to help you if we don't get you to a doctor – and damned quick. Although why I should even bother with you, I don't know. My stockmen tell me you're behind all the trouble we had around here towards the end of last year.'

'They're lying!' croaked Charlie.

Ben Carminow shook his head. 'I've had stockmen who worked harder, but these aren't liars. It seems you had something to do with the death of the son of a pretty important *yura*. When they came looking and couldn't find you they took it out on anyone else they came across. Perhaps now they've damned near killed you they'll leave the rest of us in peace.'

Charlie remembered the man he had shot dead at his camp on the creek beyond Nuccaleena. He doubted whether honour had yet been satisfied.

'I don't know what you're talking about,' he gasped.

'It doesn't matter whether you do or you don't. The *yuras* think you *do* and while you're on this station you pose a threat to me and my family, and to Mr Rounsevell's sheep.'

William Rounsevell was Carminow's employer. A Cornishman who now lived in Adelaide, Rounsevell had made a great deal of money in South Australia by his hard work and resourcefulness.

'I'm hurt too bad to be moved,' Charlie said breathlessly. 'Can't you get a doctor to come out here?'

'I've told you, none of us are safe while you're at Moolooloo. Besides, it's not at all certain there's still a doctor in Blinman. Last I heard, there wasn't, but there's likely to be someone there who can do something for you. There's no one here.'

The last thing Charlie wanted in his present state was to make the journey from Moolooloo in an unsprung farmcart along the rough track that led to Blinman, but there was nothing he could do about it. Carminow was right, he posed a threat to the sheep station and there was no one here qualified to treat his wound.

Pessimistically, Charlie thought he would probably die anyway.

Closing his eyes, he tried unsuccessfully to avert another bout

of coughing. After it passed, he said weakly, 'Do what you like
with me – but give me my gold before you take me anywhere.'

Charlie survived the long and painful journey to Blinman. Ben
Carminow drove the cart himself, with Charlie lying upon the
station manager's own feather mattress which had been placed
upon a few dozen fleeces.

Despite the attempt to make him as comfortable as possible,
Charlie was barely conscious when the wagon, with its two
armed Aborigine outriders, entered the mining township.

As Ben Carminow had predicted, the doctor was absent from
the town and no one else was willing to accept responsibility
for the wounded prospector. Even the owner of Blinman's only
hotel would not take him in.

A solution was found when Ruth Askew pushed her way to
the front of the crowd gathered about the wagon.

Ignoring everyone else, she addressed Ben Carminow. 'How
bad is he?'

The Moolooloo station manager shrugged. 'I'm no doctor, but
I don't think he'll be a trouble to anyone for very long. He was
speared in the back. I'd say it's pierced his lung.'

Ruth winced. Peering inside the cart she saw Charlie's pale
face and the dried blood around his mouth. It took her only a
moment to make up her mind. 'Bring him up to my place, I'll
take care of him.'

There were murmurings from the women in the crowd and
one of them, speaking louder than she had intended, said, 'They
say as how like sticks with like.'

Rounding on the woman, Ruth said fiercely, 'What would
you prefer for him if he was your husband? To be left by so-
called Christians to die out in the open in a farmcart or be taken
to a bawdy house and given a roof over his head and at least
a faint chance of recovering?'

'My husband wouldn't find himself in a position where they'd
be the only two options open to him,' the woman retorted piously.

'I'm sure that's what you'd like to think, you and the rest of the women here,' Ruth said angrily. 'That's no doubt what Charlie's wife thinks – yes, and the two boys who look up to him as a father.'

Seeing the woman's change of expression, Ruth continued, 'Does it surprise you? Well, I've met his wife and their two fine boys who came over from Cornwall to be with him. Charlie Minns may not be the best husband and father in the world, but he's all they've got. I'm going to do my damnedest to see they don't lose him.'

There were more murmurings and Ruth heard such remarks as 'not worth saving', and 'deserves all that's happened to him'.

Still angry, she said, 'I suggest you keep such talk to yourself. I'll be writing to Charlie's wife. From what I know of her, when she hears how seriously he's hurt she'll come to Blinman as fast as she can. When she arrives, if she hears one word from you of what you think you know about Charlie, then me and the other girls will start telling a few tales. If we do then Margaret Minns won't be the only woman in Blinman who's disillusioned with her husband!'

Satisfied she had effectively made her point, Ruth turned her attention to Ben Carminow. He had listened to her with grudging but increasing admiration as she harangued the now-silent onlookers.

'All right, there's been enough talking. Let's get Charlie up to my cottage before he's overwhelmed by the good wishes of this kind-hearted crowd.'

IV

The letter was brought to Emily's house by the young son of the Kadina postmaster late one evening.

Following the instructions given to him by his father, the young boy said, 'I'm sorry for disturbing you, Miss Boyce, but this letter came in on the stage this evening. It's for Mrs Minns and says on the envelope that it's "urgent". Although it's addressed to Ewing Street Pa knew Mrs Minns is here with you. He said I was to bring it round here right away.'

'That is very kind of you,' said Emily. 'If you go through to the kitchen one of the boys will give you a piece of cake while I fetch my purse and find a sixpence for you.'

When the boy had left the house happily clutching his unexpected reward, Emily frowned at the letter she held in her hand. So few people in South Australia knew Margaret that the letter had to be from, or about, Charlie. She feared it would not contain good news.

Margaret was at the far end of the large garden, taking advantage of the diminished heat of late evening to water some shrubs she had planted a few days before.

She smiled when Emily approached, but the smile vanished quickly when Emily failed to respond.

'Is something wrong, Emily? It's not the boys . . . ?'

'No, the boys are in the house and they are fine, but this letter has just arrived for you. It is marked "urgent". I thought it might be better if you opened it out here, away from the house.'

'A letter for me? Is it from Cornwall?'

'No, but it's not from anyone here in Kadina either. It came in on the stagecoach. Here, open it and you'll learn what it has to say.'

Margaret took the letter and turned it over two or three times before finally tearing open the envelope and extracting a single sheet of paper.

She began reading the letter and as she progressed her eyes widened in horror. When she had come to the bottom of the page, she looked up at Emily, visibly distressed. 'It's about Charlie. He's been attacked by Aborigines. He's at Blinman and is badly hurt.'

'Who is the letter from? Here, let me have a look.'

Taking the letter from her friend, Emily said, in surprise, 'It's from Ruth Askew, the woman who lived in Ewing Street. Well, in spite of her way of life, Ruth is a very capable woman. Charlie could not be in better hands. Nevertheless, it sounds as though he is badly hurt. What will you do, Margaret?'

'I'll have to go to him, but . . . the boys?'

'You need have no worries about them. They are perfectly happy with me. I will take care of them. But when was the letter written . . . ? Tuesday the twenty-third of February. That's three days ago. You must leave for Blinman as quickly as possible, Margaret.'

Margaret left Kadina the following day, but was obliged to change coaches twice en route for Blinman. As a result, the journey took five long, weary days.

When the stagecoach pulled in to the Blinman hotel, Margaret alighted from the vehicle feeling stiff and dusty. The usual crowd of miners stood around, tankards in hand, curious about who might be arriving at the remote township.

Today Margaret was the only passenger and the landlord of the hotel stepped forward to greet her. 'Welcome to Blinman, ma'am. I'm William Barnes, the hotel keeper. Do you have somewhere to stay, or will you require a room for a while?'

'I don't know,' Margaret said uncertainly. 'Before I can decide anything I need to find Ruth Askew—'

The mention of Ruth's name provoked an outburst of raucous laughter and catcalls from the listening miners and one of them said, 'If I was you I'd take up Willie's offer of a bed – for tonight, at least. You could no doubt do with some sleep after the shaking-up you'll have had in the coach – and you'll be kept too busy up at Ruth's place to get any sleep. In fact I'll pay you in advance for your first night there. All night – and I'll guarantee you don't get any sleep.'

His offer brought more laughter and crude remarks from his companions.

Margaret had spent five days travelling on three coaches along indifferent roads. She was tired and concerned for Charlie and the boys she had left behind in Emily's care. The last thing she needed was to be the butt of the ribaldry of drunken miners – Cornish miners at that, if she had identified their accents correctly.

Close to tears, she said, 'If that's the way you would speak to a respectable woman in Cornwall, then I'm sure they're all better off without you. I'm here because I've had a letter from Ruth Askew telling me my husband has been seriously hurt and she's taking care of him. Now, is someone going to tell me the way to her house?'

Her words brought an immediate halt to the hilarity of the men and the hotel keeper said, 'You'll be Mrs Minns then, ma'am. I'm sorry you had to put up with the coarse talk of men who should know better. The only excuse I can give for them is that it was settlement day last Saturday and the miners were told no more copper would be brought up until prices improved. It's an unhappy and uncertain time for them.'

'It's not exactly a happy time for me either, Mr Barnes. Will you please find someone who will show me the way to the house of Ruth Askew?'

'Of course.'

As he spoke, William Barnes was looking about him for someone sober enough to take responsibility for Charlie Minns' wife.

It happened that at that moment Sam was walking along the street, hand in hand with Primrose.

Seeing him, William Barnes called, 'Sam, will you come here, please?'

Still holding Primrose's hand, Sam looked curiously at Margaret for a moment, then said, 'Yes, Willie, what can I do for you?'

'It's not for me, but for this lady. She's Mrs Minns, wife of Charlie

Minns. She's had a letter from Ruth, telling her that her husband's been hurt. She wants someone to show her to Ruth's house. As you're both Cornish I thought you might be happy to help her.'

Sam gave William Barnes a disapproving look. 'Yes, of course . . . but today is Primrose's birthday and I promised to buy her some sweets . . .'

Reaching into a pocket, he took out some coins and handed them to the small girl. 'Here, Primrose, take these to the shop. Tell Mr McFarlane he's to give you whatever sweets you want and then you go straight back to Mummy. Tell her I'll see her a little later.'

When Primrose ran off clutching the coins Sam had given to her, William Barnes said to Margaret, 'I'll put your things into one of my rooms, Mrs Minns. I've no doubt you'll be back later. I'll give you a quiet room at the back of the hotel and make certain you're not troubled again.'

Sam and Margaret walked in silence for a while before she said, 'You have a very pretty little girl. How old is she?'

'She's six today,' Sam replied. 'But she's not mine. She's the daughter of my best friend. He died in a mine accident in Cornwall. I travelled out here with Primrose and her mother, who's now married again. Her new husband's another Cornish miner who came out on the ship with us. He's a good man.'

There was another silence before Margaret asked, 'Do you know Charlie . . . my husband?'

'Not very well. He's a prospector and kept very much to himself. I work at the mine here.'

Sam hoped Margaret would accept what he had said and not ask any more questions about her husband. He could not tell her the truth, but lying did not come easy to him.

Much to his relief, her next question did not concern her husband. 'Do you know Ruth Askew?'

'We've met once or twice in the town and passed the time of day, but that's all.'

'I wonder why she is the one who is looking after Charlie?'

'I think I can answer that question,' Sam said. 'There's no doctor in Blinman at the moment. When Charlie was brought in Ruth was the only one around who knew anything about nursing a wounded man.' He looked at Margaret and said hesitantly, 'I don't know how much you've heard about what happened. None of us in Blinman know exactly, but Charlie's wound is serious. Very serious.'

'I gathered as much from Ruth's letter. That's why I came here straightaway.'

Margaret looked at Sam in time to catch his expression and she added, 'Ruth and . . . and some of her friends were near neighbours for a while in Kadina. She must have realised Charlie is my husband. I'm grateful to her.'

Sam believed there was much more to the relationship between Charlie and Ruth than Margaret knew about, but he would say nothing.

A few minutes later, he pointed to a rambling, rundown cottage and said, 'That's where Ruth lives.'

Margaret's pace increased and Sam let her go on ahead to the ramshackle house. As she opened the gate and hurried up the path, Ruth appeared at the door; she was in a distressed state.

'Ruth! How's Charlie? Is he any better?'

Ruth seemed to be at a loss for words for some moments and she made two attempts to reply before she finally succeeded.

'Margaret . . . I'm so sorry. So very sorry. Charlie's dead. He died only about half an hour ago . . .'

V

The news that Charlie was dead and that she had arrived too late was just too much for Margaret. She broke down and wept.

It was not that she still loved Charlie as much as she once had, but rather it was a culmination of so many things.

She and the boys had travelled to South Australia with such hopes for the future. She was coming to be with her husband and to resume the happy albeit insecure life they had once enjoyed together. The boys would have a father to support them and impart knowledge to carry them forward into adult life.

The reunion had fallen short of all their expectations, except, perhaps, for Tom, who possessed the blindness of an infant to his father's faults. Yet Margaret had nurtured a hope that things would improve when Charlie had grown used to having his family with him again.

Now he was dead and all Margaret's hopes had died with him.

Sam and Ruth helped Margaret inside the cottage to the kitchen, where two other women sat sipping tea, their attire suggesting they had not long risen from their beds. They had not applied make-up and hurriedly departed from the room after expressing perfunctory sympathy with Margaret.

'Just sit yourself down, love, while I pour you a nice sweet cup of tea,' Ruth said. 'This must be a terrible shock to you – especially coming on top of such a long journey.'

'I . . . I'd like to see Charlie first,' Margaret replied unsteadily.

'Of course. I'll take you to him and leave you for a few minutes while I make a fresh brew.'

Ruth was away from the room for only a few minutes, during which time Sam remained in the kitchen, ill at ease at being in the notorious house.

Returning to the kitchen alone, Ruth set about making tea. 'Poor Margaret,' she said. 'To come all this way only to find her husband lying dead in a bawdy house.' Looking up at Sam, she asked, 'How is it you brought her here? Do you know each other?'

'No, I happened to be close to the hotel when she arrived.

She asked to be shown the way, but it seems some of the miners gave her a hard time. Willie Barnes asked me if I'd bring her here. He's saving a room for her at the hotel.'

'I'm surprised you knew where to bring her,' Ruth commented. 'I've never seen you here.'

'No,' Sam said, without further comment. 'And, in case it's mentioned, I told Mrs Minns her husband was brought here because the doctor is away and you have a little knowledge of medicine.'

'As a matter of fact it happens to be the truth. I spent some months nursing and tended a number of injuries, but even a skilled surgeon couldn't have saved Charlie. The spear had pierced his lung and I suspect it became infected.'

'I'm sure you did your best,' Sam said. 'I'll leave you now. You can tell Mrs Minns all about it—'

'You'll stay here until she's ready to leave,' Ruth declared firmly. 'Then you can take her back to the hotel. This is no place for a respectable woman. Can I get you some tea while you're waiting?'

Sam shook his head. At that moment Margaret returned to the kitchen. She looked pale and drawn, but she was more composed than before.

'Thank you, Ruth. Charlie looks so thin and pale. There's not a scrap of colour left in his face, but he's at peace now.'

'He lost a great deal of blood,' Ruth explained. 'And he found it painful to eat – even to drink, sometimes.'

'Poor Charlie,' Margaret said, tearful now. 'He may not always have been all he should, but he didn't deserve to die in such a way.'

Sam thought otherwise, but he kept such thoughts to himself.

'I told him I'd written to you,' Ruth said, 'and before he died he asked me to give something to you if you came here. I'll fetch it for you.'

Ruth left the room briefly. When she returned she was carrying the hand-made belt that Charlie had worn about his waist. Placing it on the table in front of Margaret, she said, 'There you are. It should see you all right for a while, at least.'

'What is it?' Margaret asked, surprised by the weight of the belt and its contents.

'I'm no expert, but I'd say it's packed with gold,' Ruth said. 'It would seem that Charlie found what hundreds of men have been seeking for years in the Flinders Ranges. Unfortunately, the secret of where he got it has died with him. Charlie would have liked that.'

Margaret picked up on Ruth's unguarded remark immediately.

'Charlie didn't die in this house just because you knew something about nursing, did he, Ruth? You and he knew each other long before he was wounded. Before I came from Cornwall, even.'

'I'd met him before,' Ruth confessed, making the admission as casual as she could. 'It was a long time ago, in Kadina, or Moonta. I can't remember exactly where. But I've met so many men, in all sorts of places. Charlie needed help and I was able to give more than anyone else in Blinman. I'd have done the same for anyone who was in trouble.'

Margaret looked at the other woman uncertainly before saying, 'Yes, Ruth, I believe you would. Thank you. Thank you for looking after him and for being so honest about this . . .' She held up the heavy, home-made belt. 'I knew nothing about it and not everyone would have given it up, as you have.'

Ruth shrugged off Margaret's praise. 'I'm not short of money, but you've got two boys to bring up.' Suddenly becoming brisk, she said, 'Now, I suggest you get back to the hotel and settle in before it gets too rowdy there.'

'There's just one thing . . .' Margaret turned to Sam for advice. 'What do I do about a funeral for Charlie?'

'Leave that to me,' Sam said. 'I'll make all the arrangements. The Blinman will pay for it out of mine funds. I know Charlie wasn't employed at the mine, but that won't be any problem.'

'Thank you, thank you both.' Margaret suddenly looked weary. 'I'd like to go to the hotel now and be by myself for a while. I have a lot of thinking to do.'

'Of course,' agreed Sam. 'I'll try to arrange the funeral for the morning. Then you'll be able to catch the afternoon coach. I doubt whether you'll want to remain in Blinman any longer than is absolutely necessary.'

Turning to Ruth, Sam said, 'I'll see that Charlie is moved out of here tonight. Do you want to be told about the funeral arrangements?'

'Of course,' Ruth replied. 'All of us in the house will be at the cemetery.' She did not feel it necessary to add that it was doubtful whether anyone else from Blinman would attend.

VI

Captain Wilf Hooper raised no objection to Sam's suggestion that Charlie's funeral be financed from mine funds. Although Charlie had been disliked by all at Blinman who knew him – and a great many who did not – there was genuine sympathy for Margaret. No one wished to make life more difficult for her.

There was another reason why Captain Hooper agreed. The coach that brought Margaret to Blinman had also carried a letter from the company that owned the mine. Captain Hooper was ordered to pay off the miners at the end of the month.

If Captain Hooper agreed, he would remain at Blinman, on a reduced salary, together with just enough men to keep the pumps running and effect essential maintenance.

Such drastic measures had been brought about by the world price of copper, which had dropped to a new low, making the Blinman mine no longer viable.

There were small amounts of money left in various welfare

funds and it was the captain's task to disburse it as he felt fit.

Charlie Minns was buried on a gentle slope at the edge of
the cemetery just outside Blinman. Around him were the
graves of many fellow Cornish men, women – and even more
of their children. The hard Blinman environment had claimed
a great many lives during the few years the mine had been in
existence.

The graveside service was given by a Methodist lay preacher,
his accent that of Cornwall. There were also a few miners and
their wives who had shown grudging Christian forgiveness to
the late Charlie Minns, out of sympathy for Margaret.

They stood apart from Ruth and three fellow prostitutes, with
Sam, Margaret, Jean and Ira standing between the two parties.

Jean had gone to the hotel the previous evening, at Sam's
request, to invite Margaret to come home with her for a meal.
Margaret had pleaded extreme weariness, adding that she
wanted to try to get a good night's sleep before boarding a coach
for the return journey to Kadina soon after the funeral.

The gravedigger, called from his bed at dawn to dig the grave
that would hold the body of Charlie, was nearby, leaning on
his long-handled Cornish shovel. Impatiently, he waited for the
service to come to an end so that he might shovel earth back in
the narrow grave and hurry off to the hotel bar to spend the
money he had earned digging a grave in the rock-hard earth.

The brief and impersonal ceremony over, Margaret thanked
those who had attended before walking back to the hotel, accompanied by Sam, Jean and Ira.

Margaret was far more composed than she had been on the
previous day and Sam felt emboldened to ask her whether she
had made any plans for the future.

'I haven't thought about it in any detail,' Margaret replied. 'I
shall certainly stay in Kadina with Emily until she's married.
Then I will probably take the boys back to Cornwall.'

'Emily?' Sam asked. 'Is she a relative?'

'No, she's doing work for the Church in Kadina. I came out

from England as her companion. You might know her, she was the daughter of the vicar of a mining village – St Cleer.'

Sam stopped walking abruptly and caught hold of Margaret's arm, staring at her in disbelief. 'Emily? You're not talking of Emily Boyce? Are you telling me she's here . . . in South Australia? When did she arrive?'

Startled by his excitement, Margaret said, 'We've been in Kadina for some months . . .' Suddenly, everything fell into place '*Sam* . . . of course! You must be Sam Hooper! Whenever we went to a mine to enquire after Charlie, Emily would ask after you.'

Margaret's words gave Sam more of a lift than she would ever know, but she had mentioned something else that had disheartened him. 'You said Emily was to be married. Who is she marrying?'

'Stefan Mintoff. He's a councillor and store owner in Kadina. He's also expecting to be elected to the South Australian parliament soon. I think he and Emily will be married when he gets back from England. He's gone there to raise money for a mining company he intends setting up. He's particularly interested in the Flinders Ranges. He and Charlie would talk a lot about mining and the prospects for making money here. I think Charlie was doing some work for him in this area.'

'I wonder how much, if anything, that had to do with Charlie finding gold somewhere in the ranges,' mused Sam. 'It's very interesting indeed – but I want to know more about Emily. How is she? I mean, is she happy?'

'I think so. She's certainly a whole lot happier than when she was in St Cleer looking after her father, with that old battleaxe of a housekeeper watching everything she did.'

'This man she's going to marry . . . Mintoff. I think I met him when I passed through Kadina. Nobody seemed to like him, as I remember, but if Emily is to marry him . . . What's he really like?'

'Between you and me, I don't like him. He's far too "smarmy", but then I'm not the one who's marrying him.'

'No, Emily is,' Sam said unhappily. 'I wish I'd known she was coming out here. I'd have gone to wherever she landed, to meet her.'

'She'd have liked that,' Margaret replied. 'As I said, she tried to find out where you were when we first arrived. She was still trying, right up until the time things got serious between her and Stefan Mintoff.'

They had arrived at the Blinman hotel now and Margaret said, 'Thank you for all you've done for me, Sam. I really don't know how I could have coped without you.'

'I'm glad I was able to help.'

Sam meant it. Margaret was a very pleasant woman. However, he was deeply unhappy at the news of Emily she had divulged. If only he had known she was in South Australia!

In fact it was probably his own fault they had not met. He had taken so long to write to his parents after arriving at Blinman that by the time the letter arrived Emily had probably already left St Cleer.

Had he written sooner his father could have told her where he was and they might have met before she found the Kadina councillor.

Even as these thoughts were going through his mind, Sam had to admit to himself that he could not have hoped to compete with the man Emily was to marry. It was a deeply depressing thought.

In an attempt not to think about it right now, Sam asked, 'Are you all packed and ready to catch the stage when it arrives?'

'Yes. I'll be pleased to be back with my boys. Emily's looking after them for me and I know they're happy with her, but I miss them.' Suddenly morose, Margaret added, 'I've got a lot to discuss with them, too. With Albert, anyway. He's old enough to have a sensible opinion about the future, now there's no Charlie around.'

'I wish you well, whatever you decide,' Sam said. 'And take good care of that gold belt, it's worth a lot of money. Make sure you find an honest man to buy the gold from you; it could help you decide what you want to do.'

'Thank you again, Sam. Will I be seeing you before I leave?'

'Yes, I'll see you safely on to the stage – and there's something I'd like you to take to Emily . . .'

6

I

Margaret returned to Kadina exhausted, both mentally and physically. She dreaded the thought of having to tell Albert and Tom that their father was dead.

The ordeal was postponed for a while, at least. Arriving home, she learned the boys had been allowed to go to the Wallaroo mine with friends to watch an exhibition of Cornish wrestling.

Emily took one look at the strained face of her friend and realised something was seriously wrong.

'I wasn't expecting you back in Kadina for at least another week, Margaret. What happened?'

'I got to Blinman too late,' Margaret replied wearily. 'Charlie died half an hour before I got there. He died in a bawdy house.'

'Oh, Margaret! I am so sorry. It must have been absolutely horrible for you. Here, sit down, I will make you some tea . . . No, you need something a little stronger. I have a bottle of French brandy put away. Stefan gave it to me before he left for London. I will open that. There is also a nice hot tub prepared in the kitchen. I was about to take advantage of the boys' absence to relax in a bath for a while. But your need is far greater than my own. Take the drink in there with you, soak yourself and relax. When you have finished and put on clean clothes you'll feel very much better. If the boys come home before you are out I'll keep them entertained.'

'Thank you, Emily, it will give me time to get it clear in my head what I'm going to tell them. To be honest it's something I'm dreading. All the way back here I've been trying to think of the best way to break the news to them. Some way of lessening the blow. Albert will probably be all right, he's a stoic, but it will hit Tom hard. He thought his pa was the most wonderful person in the world.'

'I am quite sure you will not disillusion him, Margaret.' Pouring an extremely large brandy into a glass, she said, 'Collect your clean clothes and take them to the kitchen. I'll take the brandy there and make certain the back door is locked and the curtains drawn. Stay there until you feel ready to face the world.'

Margaret had been in the bath for half an hour when the boys returned, enthusing about the wrestling they had just seen. The sight of Margaret's bag in the hallway excited them even more.

'Our ma's back!' Albert exclaimed in delight.

'She is,' agreed Emily. ' And she's very tired. She is having a bath in the kitchen right now, ridding herself of the dust of the road. She'll be out to see you both in a few minutes.'

'Is our pa with her?' Tom asked eagerly.

'Don't be silly,' Albert said scornfully. 'He wouldn't be with Ma when she's having a bath.'

'I meant, is he all right and has he come home with her,' explained Tom. 'You *knew* what I meant.'

'Your mother will tell you all about it when she has freshened up,' Emily said. 'Now, I brought some cakes from the larder, in case you returned home before your mother was ready for you. They have sugar icing on them; who would like one?'

Tom accepted a cake eagerly, but Albert was aware that Emily had avoided giving a reply to his younger brother's questions. He guessed what the reason for such evasion might be.

Tears sprang to his eyes, but he said nothing. Taking a cake he made no attempt to eat it.

When Margaret came from the kitchen a few minutes later she looked much less travel weary and more in command of herself.

Tom ran to her straightaway. Flinging his arms about her, he asked, 'Where's our pa, Ma? When is he coming home?'

Albert said nothing and, with one arm about Tom, Margaret held out her other hand to her eldest son. 'Come here, Albert.'

When he came forward and grasped her hand, Margaret turned to Emily. 'I'll take them to their room and stay with them there. I'll see you in the morning. Thank you for the bath, it gave me the opportunity I needed to sort myself out.'

Desperately sorry for Margaret and aware of the heart-breaking task that lay ahead of her, Emily could only nod her head. Then she went in search of the part-time gardener who would empty the galvanised iron bath and stow it away in the shed at the end of the garden.

Margaret came into the kitchen the following morning when Emily was making herself a pre-breakfast cup of tea. She had quite obviously been crying during the night and, as a result, she was puffy-eyed and seemed drained of energy.

Emily poured an extra cup of tea without asking her friend whether she wanted one and Margaret took it from her grate-fully.

'How did the boys take the news?' Emily asked eventually.

'Much as I expected they would,' Margaret replied. 'Tom cried himself to sleep. Albert said nothing at the time, but when I put their lamp out and kissed him goodnight he clung to me and I had to cuddle him for the best part of an hour before he let go and allowed me to tuck him in.'

'He is a very sensitive boy,' Emily said. 'I am very fond of him. Indeed, I am fond of both of them. I hope that if I one day have sons they might turn out just like them.'

'That day shouldn't be too far away,' Margaret said. 'No doubt you and Stefan won't want to wait too long to be married once he returns from England.'

'I have not given him a definite "yes", just yet. I have told him only that I will give his proposal very serious consideration.'

'That reminds me,' Margaret said. 'When I was in Blinman I met someone who knew you. It's the man you were hoping to find when I was seeking Charlie, Sam Hooper. He was very, very kind to me. I told him you were getting married to Stefan and he told me to say he wished you every happiness. Oh yes, he gave me something for you. It's in an envelope in my luggage. I'll go and fetch it.'

Trying to control her emotions at the knowledge that Margaret had actually met with Sam, Emily felt a thrill of excitement when Margaret returned and handed the envelope to her. She opened it eagerly. There was a brief note inside – and something else.

Emptying the contents of the envelope into the palm of her hand, Emily looked down at the crucifix she had given to Sam as a farewell present. Ridiculously, tears sprang to her eyes and, half turning away from Margaret she took out the note. Blinking away the tears, she read:

Dear Emily,
I have thought of you often during the time I have been in Australia. I did not know you were here or I would have tried to see you. Margaret says you are to be married, so I feel you would like to have this back. I have carried it with me always and feel it has kept me safe. I trust it will always do the same for you and that you will be very happy in your new life with your husband.
Yours, Sam.

Emily felt so choked she would not trust herself to speak. She swept past the surprised Margaret and hurried off to her bedroom, leaving her friend standing staring after her open-mouthed.

It was twenty minutes before Emily returned to the kitchen, appearing composed once more. About her neck she wore the crucifix Margaret had seen drop from the envelope.

'That's a beautiful cross you're wearing,' Margaret said. 'Is it the one Sam sent to you?'

'Yes, it once belonged to my mother.'

Margaret had no need to ask how it had come into Sam's possession. As she observed Emily's reaction to having it returned a great many things fell into place, in particular the frequent innuendoes by the St Cleer vicarage housekeeper about Emily's 'fondness for Cornish miners'.

'How was Sam looking?' Emily asked suddenly. 'Was he well?'

'He looked fit and tanned,' Margaret replied. 'But things aren't going too well with the Blinman mine. The talk among the men travelling on the stage with me was of the possibility of the mine closing.'

'Yes, Stefan mentioned the troubles of the mines in the Flinders Ranges. He says it is due to the high cost of transporting ore. His first priority when he is elected to parliament – *if* he is elected, of course – will be to bring the railway to the mines.'

'Even if he does, it's not going to happen for some years.' Margaret was relieved to be talking about something other than the death of Charlie. 'It won't help Blinman though, there's not much up there apart from copper. It might be different if they found a lot of gold. Charlie found some – I have it in my room right now – but Sam said it was alluvial and didn't mean there was a rich goldfield up in the Flinders.'

'It sounds as though you talked to Sam quite a lot,' Emily said somewhat wistfully.

'I did. More than to anyone else. I found him very kind.'

'Did you meet with Jean and Primrose too?'

'Yes. Jean is expecting another baby and Primrose was with Sam when I first met him. It was her birthday and he was taking her to buy some sweets.'

'She was a small girl of about three years old when I first saw her,' Emily reminisced. 'It was at the South Caradon mine on the day her father was killed. I took care of her after Jean learned of the death of her husband. She was heavily pregnant then, but she lost the baby.'

'Poor woman,' Margaret said. 'But I think she's happy enough now.'

'I am very pleased to hear it,' Emily replied, trying hard to convince herself she really meant it. 'Things should work out well for her, she and Sam have known each other from childhood and Primrose is the daughter of the man who was Sam's best friend. He will love her as his own. The new baby will no doubt bring them even closer together.'

Margaret looked puzzled. 'Why should Jean's baby bring her and Sam closer together?'

Now it was Emily's turn to be puzzled. 'Why . . . ? Because it will be theirs, hers and Sam's, and no matter how much he might love Primrose—'

'But Jean isn't married to Sam. Her husband's name is Ira.'

'You must be mistaken, Margaret. I met Reverend Maddison soon after we arrived in Kadina. He told me he had married Sam and Jean in a triple wedding service in Blinman.'

Margaret made a derisive sound. 'I've met Ezra Maddison too! He's so confused I'm surprised he can get an ordinary wedding right. With three couples standing in front of him, they're lucky they aren't all wedded to the wrong partners.'

'But . . . he would not get something like that wrong, surely?' Emily was thoroughly dismayed. 'He told me he remembered the wedding – and Sam.'

'He might have met Sam there and remembered the wedding, but it wasn't Sam he married to Jean. Her husband's name is

Ira. He's very pleasant too. He came to Charlie's funeral – with Jean.'

'Then . . . who *is* Sam married to?'

'He's not married to anyone – and isn't likely to be while he's at Blinman. I certainly didn't see any eligible young women during the short time I was there.'

Emily felt a sudden need to sit down. The whole pattern of her life in recent months had been dictated by the belief that Sam was married to Jean. Had she *not* believed it matters might have taken a very different course. It was certain that Stefan Mintoff would not have figured so largely in her life. She would have travelled to Blinman . . . to find Sam.

Unconsciously fingering the crucifix about her neck, she said agonisingly, 'How could Reverend Maddison have told me something so untrue? How *could* he?'

'Does Sam mean so much to you, Emily?' Margaret asked gently.

Looking up at her friend in bewilderment, Emily said, 'I don't think I realised quite how much, Margaret – until now.'

II

'What shall I do, Margaret? Do I carry on with my life as though Sam went out of it for ever when he left St Cleer, or do I try to contact him and give up all I have here in Australia?' Emily voiced aloud the question that had kept her awake for much of the night. Usually a decisive and positive young woman, she was not used to such uncertainty.

It was twenty-four hours since Margaret had told her of Sam's unmarried state, but Emily was no closer to a solution to her dilemma.

'By "all" I suppose you mean Stefan Mintoff?' said Margaret.

'Well . . . yes – that and everything else I have worked for in Kadina.'

Margaret shrugged. 'I'm sorry, Emily, I would help you if I could, but this is a decision that only you can make.'

'I realise that, Margaret, but what would *you* do in my place?'

'I would never be in your place, Emily. I find Sam very attractive and someone I am comfortable talking to; Stefan Mintoff is a different man altogether.'

'That is perfectly true, they are both *very* different.'

'There is one thing you could do to help make up your mind, Emily. You could go to Blinman and see Sam again. In fact, you *must* if you're to reach the right decision.'

'No, Margaret, I go weak at the knees just thinking about the chance of meeting up with Sam once more.'

'Do you feel the same way when you think of Stefan returning to Kadina?'

'No,' Emily admitted. 'I feel apprehensive.'

'You've answered your own question about what to do, Emily. If you don't meet with Sam and go ahead with a marriage to Stefan, you'll spend the rest of your life wondering about what might have been.'

'But I feel it would not be fair to Stefan if I went off to see Sam while he is so far away.'

'It will be even more unfair to him if you don't get this settled before he gets back. As I've said, unless you see Sam quickly you'll always have a doubt in your mind about whether you married the right man. I never had any doubts about Charlie, even though I knew early on that a lot of the things folk said about him were true. If I had my time over again I would still marry him. The only thing I'd do different would be to come out here with him when he came to Australia. Charlie changed during the time we were apart from one another. He changed so much he just wasn't the same any more. I can't help blaming myself for that. I should have come out here with him . . .' Suddenly and unexpectedly, Margaret's feelings about Charlie poured out.

Emily put a consolatory arm about her. 'I am sorry, Margaret, I am so wrapped up in my own affairs that I keep forgetting you have problems of your own that far outweigh mine. You have the future of your two boys to consider. Have you reached a decision about what you might do?'

'We haven't agreed on anything definite yet. I think we might eventually go back to Cornwall, but I'll take the boys to Blinman first, to show them where their pa is buried. I'll even consider having a headstone set up on his grave. It depends how much I am able to get for the gold he's left for us.'

'Let me pay for the headstone, Margaret. It would please me greatly to be able to do it for you and the boys.'

'Thank you, Emily, that would be a very generous gesture—' A sudden idea occurred to Margaret and she said excitedly, 'Why don't we *all* go to Blinman? While the boys and I do what needs doing you could meet up with Sam again without making it a major drama and feeling guilty about it. The meeting would be a much more casual affair. Do it this way and you will get a much better idea of how you really feel about him, Emily. You know how much *I* like him, but you and he come from very different backgrounds. You might decide you just aren't suited for each other.' Giving Emily a speculative look, she added, 'At least you'll know then who it is you really want. Of course, if you *were* to decide it's Sam and not Stefan you want . . . But that's a bridge to cross if, and when, you get there. What do you say?'

Emily, Margaret and the boys set off for Blinman in late April. It had been six weeks since Margaret had returned to Kadina. Emily had been unable to get away any earlier due to her various commitments.

Emily set off not fully convinced she was doing the right thing, yet feeling more excited than at any time she could remember.

The first half of the journey was far more leisurely than it had been for Margaret when she was travelling alone. It was completed on a steamer as far as Port Augusta, where they boarded a stagecoach for a two-day journey to Blinman.

The stage halted for the night at a small hotel in Hawker. Stepping from the coach, Emily looked apprehensively towards the ranges. A heavy blanket of cloud had been building up during the day, hiding the ragged peaks.

'That looks ominous,' she commented to the coach driver as he handed her down from the vehicle.

'Don't you worry yourself about the weather up there, ma'am. It sometimes hangs around the peaks for days, then it disappears as suddenly as it arrived.'

Emily was not reassured. She was even more concerned when she caught the coach driver talking to the hotel keeper a few minutes later. Both men had their gazes firmly fixed on the cloud-capped mountain ranges.

The night that followed was not the most restful Emily had experienced. The temperature was exceptionally high for the time of year and the mosquitoes were intent upon making the most of the extended season. Unusually gregarious, they attacked every inch of exposed skin they could find.

As a result, Emily appeared for breakfast the following morning puffy-eyed and irritable. It did not help her mood when she peered from the hotel balcony and saw the storm clouds were still thick on the mountains. If anything they now extended farther down the slopes.

It seemed the hotel keeper had been keeping watch on the weather too. Appearing at the breakfast table, hands caressing each other in soapless ablution, he said, 'Ladies, boys, I trust you have enjoyed a good night's sleep?'

When confirmation was not forthcoming, he said, 'The weather to the north is somewhat uncertain . . . indeed, it causes me some concern. Should you wish to remain here until it improves you would be most welcome guests and I would be happy to offer you a substantial reduction in an already very competitive tariff.'

'Thank you, landlord,' Emily said. 'But what are the views of the coach driver?'

'Ah yes, the coach driver,' the hotel owner said unhappily. 'Well, of course, the coach carries the mail and the driver is penalised if he fails to deliver it to its destination on time. He will press on without regard for the safety of his passengers.'

'Does he believe he is able to deliver the mail on time to Blinman?'

'That is his belief, ma'am, but—'

'I will listen to no "buts", landlord. If the driver believes he can safely convey the mail to Blinman, then I have no doubt our safety is assured.'

'I hope your faith in the coachman will not prove to be misplaced, ma'am,' said the offended hotel keeper.

'So, too, do I,' Emily said. 'We have rather more to lose than you. Now, if you will prepare a bill, you may tell the coach driver we will be ready to board as soon as the coach is ready.'

III

When the stagecoach set off from Hawker, the four travellers from Kadina were its only passengers. There should have been one other, a carpet-bagger of Middle Eastern origins, who had been persuaded by the hotel keeper to spend a few days in Hawker until the weather improved in the mountains of the Flinders Ranges.

As the coach bumped and jolted along the road from Hawker and she viewed the heavily laden clouds through the windows, Emily wondered whether she should have followed her earlier instincts about the weather and not put her faith in the coach driver's forecast. She pushed aside any thought that her decision to go on might possibly have been influenced by her eagerness to meet up with Sam once more.

For a while, it seemed her misgivings were misplaced. The heavy dark clouds remained where they had been the previous day, touching only the tallest peaks of the serrated mountain range to the right of the dirt road.

Then, after they had made a final change of horses, the cloud began to lower alarmingly and the sky darkened as though night was imminent.

The wind increased too. Soon it was buffeting the coach in an uncomfortable fashion. Then a brief but fierce flurry of rain swept over the coach, beating against the windows on one side of the vehicle with the rapidity of a drummer's call to action on a man-o'-war.

When the shower had passed on, lightning began rending the dark clouds in its wake, frightening Tom. Suddenly, the coach came to an unexpected halt.

Opening a window on the more sheltered side of the coach, Emily leaned out and saw the driver donning a voluminous waterproof coat.

'Shouldn't we be seeking shelter somewhere until the storm passes over?' she called.

'I'm sorry, ma'am, but I've got mail on board. I'm subject to a stiff penalty if I get in late. Besides, there's nowhere to shelter a coach and horses between here and Blinman.'

'How long will it be before we arrive?' Emily queried.

'About an hour and a half, as long as none of the road has been washed away. Now, if you'll close the window and seat yourself, we'll get under way again.'

Moments later the coach jolted into motion and it seemed to Emily the driver was attempting to reach Blinman before the eye of the storm that was raging on the mountains swept down upon them.

If it *was* his intention to outrun the storm, his efforts were unsuccessful. They had been travelling for perhaps another half an hour, with the storm moving ever closer, when, preceded by a fierce wind, the rain returned – and suddenly the storm was raging all about them.

Tom cried out in fear as the coach driver fought to control his four terrified horses.

When the coachman had won his battle, he drove on, but they were travelling much slower now. A few minutes later the coach slowed to a crawl and began to tilt forward, as though negotiating a steep slope.

Suddenly it came to a halt and the occupants of the coach heard a new sound, this time it was of fiercely rushing water.

The coach door opened on the sheltered side of the vehicle and the driver leaned inside. He had lost his hat, his hair was plastered down against his head and face, and water poured off his sodden waterproof coat.

Shouting to make himself heard above the sounds of wind, rain and rushing water, he informed the passengers that they had just reached a creek that bisected the road on which they were travelling.

'It's usually dry,' he shouted. 'But it's carrying water from the mountains right now. It's not impossible to cross – yet, but it will be if we don't get across pretty quickly. You may have some water come inside the carriage. Just keep your feet up and you'll be all right.'

Before either woman had time to question the driver's wisdom in attempting to cross the flooded creek, the door was slammed shut.

A few minutes later the coach jerked into motion and the hazardous crossing commenced. The coach slewed sideways almost immediately and began shaking alarmingly, but it was not the wind causing the movement now, it was rushing water, the sound blending with the considerable noise of the storm raging all about them.

Suddenly the coach tilted to one side, throwing everyone off balance, before coming to an abrupt halt.

Above the noise of the elements, those inside the coach could hear the shouts of the coachman and the sharp crack of his whip.

The coach still shook alarmingly, but there was no forward movement now – then Emily became aware that water was covering the floor of the vehicle.

No sooner had she made this observation than the door was flung open. Above the noise of storm and rushing water, the driver shouted, 'Quick! Get out and make your way to the far bank! The stage is stuck and the creek is rising. A few more minutes and it's likely to be washed away.'

'We have two young boys with us—' Emily began, but the driver cut short her protest.

'Don't argue!' he bellowed. 'Get out of the creek, or you'll all drown . . . Here, give me the younger boy.'

Reaching inside the carriage, the coach driver snatched Tom from Margaret. Without waiting to see if the others were following, he set out for the far bank of the creek, fighting his way through waist-high water.

After only a momentary hesitation, Emily caught hold of Albert's hand. 'Take hold of your mother and follow me into the water.'

She stepped down from the coach, stumbled and would have been swept away had not Albert gripped her hand, holding on with all his strength. Moments later the young boy was also in the water, followed by his mother. They began fighting their way through water that threatened to carry them away with every step they took.

Twice Emily stumbled and on the second occasion was totally submerged, then the coach driver was hauling them from the raging water while they still clung tightly to each other's hands.

Water was streaming down from the road to the creek, but it no longer threatened to take them with it.

Pointing along the barely discernible road ahead, the coach driver shouted, 'Up there a little way . . . old shepherds' hut . . . falling down, but will give some shelter.'

'What about you?' Emily shouted back.

The coach driver pointed to the creek. 'My coach . . . the horses . . . the mail . . .'

Before Emily could argue that his intentions were suicidal, he had plunged back into the flooded creek and was floundering ponderously towards the stranded stagecoach. The storm had turned day into night and following his progress was difficult. In addition, the rain was falling with such force that it was painful.

Although concerned for the driver, Emily realised there were others to be considered. Margaret was holding Tom to her and, grasping Albert's hand, Emily shouted, 'We must try to find the shepherds' hut. Keep hold of me in case I get lost, Albert.'

As they were about to set off, Tom glanced back towards the creek and cried, 'Look – the coach.'

His shout was barely audible above the noise of the storm. Looking back and shielding her eyes against the force of the rain, Emily was horrified to see the coach being swept away down the creek by the ever-rising waters.

'Oh, my God! What do we do now?' Quite as wet and bedraggled as Emily, although she had not been totally immersed in the waters of the creek, Margaret put the anguished question.

Calling on all her reserves of mental and physical strength, Emily said, 'We must get well away from here, before the water rises still more and reaches us. When we find the shepherds' hut – we pray. For ourselves, and for the driver.'

The coach driver had probably been trying to boost the spirits of his four passengers when he told them the shepherds' hut was 'up there a little way'.

Buffeted by wind and rain, they were staggering through the storm for more than half an hour before Albert squeezed her hand and shouted, 'What's that – over there?'

The storm had marginally eased and visibility had improved accordingly. Had it not done so it was doubtful they would have seen the hut. Set back from the road, it was almost hidden among a small copse of gum trees.

'Well done, Albert. You are more alert than any of us.'

Upon closer inspection, the hut was not at all prepossessing. The door was missing, the window was no more than a hole in the wall and a corner of the wood-shingle roof had broken away. However, when the four travellers from Kadina staggered inside the hut they were instantly sheltered from wind and rain.

Emily felt close to exhaustion. Thankfully, she sank to the dirt floor and Margaret followed her example, Tom immediately cuddling up to his mother.

It was now possible to talk without shouting above the noise of the storm and Margaret asked, 'What do we do now, Emily?'

'We sit out the storm, then set off for Blinman,' Emily declared, hoping her words conveyed more assurance than she felt.

'How far *is* it?' Margaret asked.

'I don't know,' Emily confessed. 'But we know it's somewhere along this road. If we carry on for long enough we will find it.'

IV

The storm raged for another two hours before the rains moved on, leaving behind thunder, rumbling away in the distance, and a dark, uncertain ceiling of cloud that hid the uneven heights of the Flinders Ranges.

As the two women stood outside the derelict shepherds' hut, with heavy drops of rain dripping from the trees about them, Margaret said, 'If we try to go now it's likely to be dark before we reach Blinman.'

'If we sit it out here all night we could experience another storm tomorrow. When we tried to move on then we would be colder, hungrier and more tired than we are now. I think we should set out and trust that we reach either Blinman or some other place before nightfall.'

'What if we don't?'

'Then we walk on through the night,' Emily said firmly 'Do you agree, boys?'

'What about the coach – and the driver?' Albert asked.

'We will send men back to look for them,' Emily declared, not wishing to dwell upon the matter. 'Now, does anyone know a hymn that will set us marching along the road like soldiers? No? Then I will teach you one. It is called, "Onward, Christian Soldiers" and if you keep in step with the tune we will all be in Blinman before we know it . . .'

The four weary travellers were found by a rescue party comprised of five horsemen and a light cart – thoughtfully provided should there be corpses to be conveyed to Blinman. By this time 'Onward, Christian Soldiers' was indelibly imprinted upon the minds of the two boys and they had lost count of the number of times they had sung the chorus lines.

The light cart was immediately turned around to convey the four survivors to Blinman, preceded by a galloping horseman to alert the remote community of the fate that had befallen the mail-carrying stagecoach.

Meanwhile, the four remaining horsemen set off for the creek crossing, where the coach and horses had been swept away.

As a result of the advance warning carried by the horseman, the hotel keeper of the Blinman hotel and his staff were waiting with blankets and an assortment of clothing, donated by the sympathetic residents of the mining town.

As they were being helped down from the cart, one of the first people Emily saw was a heavily pregnant Jean, standing with Ira and Primrose.

'Jean!' Ignoring her own dishevelled state, Emily called out to the woman she had helped years before when she was in a similar state of pregnancy as today.

Jean did not recognise her immediately. Even when she did, she believed she must be mistaken. 'It's not . . . Miss Boyce?'

'Of course it is.' Suddenly aware of the state she was in, Emily added wryly, 'I am not exactly as neat and tidy as one might expect the daughter of the late vicar of St Cleer to be, Jean, but we've been at the mercy of the elements. We are all very fortunate to be alive.'

'It *is* you, Miss Boyce. You poor woman – and Margaret, you too! What are you – no, this is not the time for questions. Let me help you inside – and find you something to wear. We knew two women and two boys were on the way here and in sore need of clothing, but we had no idea what sizes you were. If there is nothing suitable here I'll find some clothes for you from home.'

'Thank you,' Emily was touched by Jean's obvious concern. 'I would apprecate a hairbrush and some soap. When I feel like a woman again I would like to meet with Sam. I believe you and he are still great friends?'

'Sam? You mean Sam Hooper? He's not here any longer. When the mines shut down, Captain Wilf – Sam's uncle – offered to keep him on, but Sam persuaded the captain to take on my Ira in his place, him being a married man and me being pregnant. Sam left Blinman about three weeks ago.'

'Left?' Emily was stunned by the news and she looked at Jean, her expression a mixture of dismay and disbelief. 'Where has he gone?'

'I don't know exactly,' Jean said. 'He told Ira he'd had enough of copper mining. He said he was going to try his luck with gold. I believe he's gone to the goldfields in the hills somewhere outside Adelaide.'

Later that night, in the privacy of her hotel room, Emily gave way to a rare bout of tears. The deep disappointment at hearing that Sam was no longer in Blinman, coming on top of the tragic and terrifying ordeal she and the others had suffered at the flooded creek, was just too much for her.

Jean had stayed with her for a while, and Emily believed she alone had realised just how upset she was that Sam had moved on from Blinman. Remembering the gift Emily had given to Sam on his departure from St Cleer, Jean had tried to cheer Emily by telling her how often Sam had spoken of home – and of Emily in particular.

Despite her unhappiness, exhaustion brought about by the events of the day meant that Emily swiftly dropped off into a deep sleep once she was in bed.

She was awakened soon after dawn the next morning by an insistent hammering on the door of her room. It took her some moments to realise where she was. Then she became aware of a voice calling her name.

'Miss Boyce! Miss Boyce – are you awake?'

'Yes . . . yes, I am awake. What is it?'

'Come outside, there's something you should see.'

'Come out? I am in bed!'

'Put something on quickly. You'll not want to miss this!'

Wondering what could be so important that it should demand her urgent attention at this time of the morning, Emily took down a man's dressing-gown from a hook behind the door. The hotel keeper had placed it there the night before, explaining it had been left at the hotel by a gentleman guest who had come to Blinman to celebrate the marriage of his daughter to the then-manager of Moolooloo sheep station. It seemed he had arived intoxicated and left Blinman in the same state, five days later.

The dressing-gown reached to the ground and Emily's hands failed to protrude from the sleeves, but it effectively hid all she wore beneath it.

Slipping on her shoes, which had not yet dried out from the soaking they had received the previous day, she went to the door and opened it to the excited hotel keeper.

'What is it?' she demanded.

'Come outside and see for yourself – quickly.'

Emily followed him outside and found Margaret and the two boys already on the porch.

Seeing her coming through the door, Margaret said, excitedly, 'Look, Emily. Look who's coming into Blinman.'

Following the direction of her pointing finger, Emily was astonished to see the stagecoach she had last seen floating away along the flooded creek. Perched on the driving seat was their coach driver, accompanied by one of the Blinman men who had gone out expecting to find his body.

Seeing the women and the boys, the driver gave them a cheery wave.

When he stopped the stage outside the hotel and climbed down from his high seat, Emily hurried forward and gave him a warm hug and Margaret followed suit.

'How did you escape from the flood?' Emily demanded as the embarrassed coach driver gave Albert and Tom a cheery smile. 'When we last saw the coach it was being swept away. There was no sign of you!'

'I was clinging to the luggage rack, at the back of the coach,' the driver explained. 'I'm not surprised you never saw me, though. I was under water more often than I was above it. We seemed to be swept down the creek for miles before the coach grounded on a shallow stretch of floodwater. I was able to get to the horses and led them and the coach clear of the creek. I found a piece of higher ground and the water gradually went down. That's all there was to it.'

'Not quite all,' said the Blinman man who had been on the seat beside the driver. 'The place where Harry here got the coach and the horses out was the only bit of high ground for miles around. The flood waters turned it into an island. We found him in the early hours, but it wasn't until first light that the waters went down far enough for us to risk bringing the coach back to the road.'

'The horses were far too tired to do anything before then,' said the coach driver. 'That reminds me, they've earned their feed this trip. I'll unload your trunks, ladies, then get the horses into the stables. I'll also need to have the coach checked for any damage before it sets off anywhere again.'

'We knew an hour or two ago that Harry and the stage had been found safe and well,' explained the hotel keeper. 'I didn't want to wake you then, but I thought you'd want to be on hand to see him drive into Blinman.'

Indicating the dressing-gown that enveloped Emily from neck to feet, he added mischievously, 'You'll no doubt be relieved to have your own clothes to wear once more, but you're quite welcome to keep the dressing-gown. It will serve as a reminder of your eventful trip to Blinman.'

V

The headstone set upon Charlie's grave proclaimed to the world at large that it was in memory of 'Charles Wesley Minns, a loved husband and father'. It satisfied the Minns family that due respect had been paid to his memory.

While she was in Blinman, Emily was able to speak at some length with Captain Wilf Hooper, who remembered her as a small child in St Cleer, before he left Cornwall for South Australia.

The mine captain told her that Sam had spoken of her often and greatly valued the crucifix she had given to him as a farewell gift, commenting that it was very similar to the one she was wearing at that time.

He was obviously not aware the gift had been returned to her. It saddened Emily that Sam had felt it necessary to give the gift back to her. At the same time she was moved that others should be aware how much he had valued it.

The mine captain confirmed that Sam had left Blinman with

the intention of trying his luck in the goldfields in the hills close to Adelaide.

'He could have stayed in Blinman and worked with me on mine maintenance,' Captain Wilf added, 'but it's not much of a life for a young man, especially when he sees everyone else leaving. It would have given him a living, but not much more. Besides, Sam became very restless during the last few weeks here, almost as though something had happened to unsettle him. Strange, really, it wasn't like Sam to let anything get to him in such a way.'

Emily did not flatter herself that Sam had changed his way of life because Margaret had told him she was to marry someone else, but it might have contributed to his feeling of restlessness. Just as news that he was *not* married had unsettled her.

Walking back from the mine, Emily decided she would pay a call on Ruth Askew at the bawdy house, which Margaret had pointed out to her on their visit to the cemetery the previous day.

Here, too, changes were in the air. Emily found Ruth and her companions packing their belongings in a somewhat lacka-daisical manner.

Ruth greeted Emily enthusiastically, introducing her to the three prostitutes with whom she shared the cottage as 'the rich lady who was my neighbour in Kadina, the one I've told you about'.

Emily was successful in hiding her distaste for the untidy state of the cottage. Instead, referring to the trunks in the passageway inside the door, she said, 'It looks as though someone is leaving.'

'We all are,' Ruth replied, adding, 'The mine has shut down. With no miners left in Blinman there'll be no business for us. Before long the only men left here will be those with families who can't afford to move on, and them in the cemetery.'

'Where will you go?' Emily asked.

'To Adelaide.' The reply came from one of the other women.

'We won't need to rely on mining to earn a living there.'

Trying hard not to dwell upon the nature of the women's means of earning a living, Emily asked, 'Are you all going to Adelaide?'

'That's right,' came the reply. 'It won't be the same as working in a mining town, but we've got to go where the business is.'

When the speaker and her companions left the room, Emily asked Ruth, 'Why not give up this life, Ruth? Come back to Kadina with Margaret and I.'

'To do what?' Ruth queried bitterly. 'I can't see anyone falling over themselves to offer me respectable work, can you?'

'I would find something for you to do, Ruth. Work that would help you regain your self-respect.'

'Self-respect and money rarely go hand in hand for a woman like me, certainly not enough to live on,' Ruth retorted.

'You could give it a try,' Emily said. 'With my help you could succeed, I am certain of it.' When her plea brought no immediate response, Emily added, 'What is the alternative for you, Ruth? What happens when you lose your looks and you can no longer attract men?'

Meeting Emily's look, Ruth said defiantly, 'Then I'll move out to the goldfields. It's the end of the road for a "working woman" and conditions are as tough as anywhere in the world, but there's money to be made there. Big money – and gold-miners are not so particular as many other men.'

At that moment one of the women returned to the room and Emily said, 'You'll find me in Kadina if ever you need me, Ruth. You can contact me there at any time. What's more, if you run into any trouble while you are in Adelaide, contact the Bishop's chaplain. I will write to him as soon as I return to Kadina and ask him to give you whatever help he can if you go to him.'

Emily stood up and began to walk from the house, but suddenly turned back. 'Do you know a miner named Sam Hooper who was in Blinman until recently?'

Surprised at the question, Ruth replied, 'Yes, he's Captain Wilf's nephew – and the one who brought Margaret to the house when she arrived in Blinman looking for Charlie. Why do you ask?'

'I knew him in Cornwall,' Emily replied. 'We lived in the same village. I was hoping to meet up with him here, but I am told he has gone to the goldfields near Adelaide. If you happen to meet him, perhaps you will tell him I was asking after him.'

Ruth gave Emily a quizzical look. 'Sam Hooper and I don't frequent the same places, Miss Boyce. To the best of my knowledge, the only time he ever came to this house it was to bring Margaret here to see her husband.'

Uncomfortably aware that she was blushing, Emily said, 'I am not suggesting—'

'I know what you're *not* suggesting,' Ruth said. More kindly, she added, 'Sam Hooper was respected in Blinman. Folk looked up to him. I hope you find him. If I hear anything of him in or around Adelaide I'll get word to him that you've been asking after him.'

VI

When Emily, Margaret and the boys arrived back in Kadina it was mid-afternoon and Emily's deep disappointment that Sam had not been at Blinman had to be put to one side immediately as she found herself caught up in a matter that was both puzzling and disturbing.

A matter that involved Stefan Mintoff.

Three years before, by a monumental feat of ingenuity and endurance, a telegraph line linking Britain and the north of Australia had been extended from Darwin to Adelaide, a distance of three thousand, two hundred kilometres, across some of the most inhospitable country in the world.

Before long, many other towns had been linked to the system, Kadina being one of them.

Emily returned to find two telegraphed messages from London awaiting her. Both were from her uncle, Lord Boyce.

The first, dated the day she had left Kadina for Blinman, congratulated Emily on her betrothal to Stefan Mintoff, but added, somewhat ominously, 'What is known of your fiancé's background?'

The second telegraph, sent only three days after the first, was longer, but less congratulatory and its tone reflected alarm.

It read:

Mintoff raising money in the City for an unknown mining company, making much of Boyce connection and investment and own political future. Nothing known here of company, or political prospects. Most urgent you confirm veracity of Mintoff's claims.
Percy Boyce.

The telegraph messages posed questions that needed to be answered as a matter of urgency. Her uncle had asked about Stefan Mintoff's background, but in truth Emily knew nothing of his life before Kadina. Neither, it seemed, did anyone else.

As Emily prepared to leave the house, Margaret came from the bedroom, where she had been putting away some of the clothes.

'You're not going out again now, Emily? I thought I would make something for us all to eat and drink as we haven't eaten since breakfast.'

'Something important has come up, Margaret . . .' After only a moment's hesitation, she showed Margaret the two telegraph messages.

Reading them, Margaret looked up at Emily in bewilderment. 'What do they mean, Emily? What is happening?'

'I wish I knew. I am going to Stefan's store, to have a word with Andrew Stewart, his manager.'

Margaret shook her head in disbelief at what the messages implied. 'I have never liked Stefan, Emily, you know that, but I have never doubted his honesty, have you?'

'I gave him a thousand pounds to invest in his company, Margaret. It sounds as though he might be using that fact to convince others to do the same – but that's pure conjecture. I shall go to the store to see how much Andrew knows about him. He has been managing things for Stefan for a long time, he probably knows more about him than anyone else.'

Margaret was unhappy. 'I hope everything is as it should be, Emily. If it isn't I shall feel I'm largely to blame. Those telegraph messages have been here for almost two weeks. If we hadn't gone to Blinman you would have been able to reply to them straightaway.'

When Emily reached the store owned by Stefan, she found it closed and there did not appear to be anyone on the premises. Even more ominous, a handwritten sign on the door informed would-be customers that the store was closed 'until further notice'.

Now Emily was very concerned indeed. She needed to speak to Andrew Stewart, but had no idea where he lived. She decided to call at the rectory and have a chat with Arnold Weeks.

Here too she was frustrated. The incumbent was not at home. His wife, Jennifer, explained that he had been called to visit a dying parishioner in nearby Wallaroo.

The two women had always got along well and Jennifer invited Emily inside for a cup of tea, adding, 'I am sure Arnold will be sorry to have missed you. Did you want to see him about anything in particular? Perhaps I might be able to help.'

'Yes, Jennifer, it is possible you can. I returned from Blinman only today, to find I had two unexpected telegraph messages from my uncle in London. He asked a number of questions about Stefan – Stefan Mintoff. They are questions to which I should already know the answers, but I don't. I called at Stefan's store a short while ago with the intention of speaking with his manager, but found the store closed. Do you know what's happening, and where I might find Andrew Stewart?'

'Of course, you have been away from Kadina for a while. Oh dear! A great deal has happened, Emily – but before I say more, is it true that you and Stefan Mintoff are to be married when he returns from England?'

'He has asked me to marry him, but I have said neither "yes" nor "no", although it seems he has told my uncle and others that we are engaged to be married. I am very angry about it – and not a little concerned.'

Jennifer Weeks had been uncertain whether she should tell Emily all that had happened, and what was being rumoured about Stefan Mintoff. Now, hearing of Emily's concern, she decided she could not keep matters to herself.

'The reason the store closed in the first place was because the suppliers are owed a great deal of money and the bank refused to honour the cheques left with Andrew Stewart by Mintoff. They wouldn't even advance enough to pay the salaries of those who worked at the store. It seems the bank is owed a great deal of money too.'

Emily was appalled by what she had heard – puzzled too. 'But Stefan has such a grand house – and his lifestyle is hardly that of a man with money problems.'

'It seems the house is heavily mortgaged. As for his lifestyle . . . Mintoff is not the first man to live beyond his means.'

'What of his companies . . . his mining interests – and his political plans?'

Jennifer Weeks shook her head. 'I know nothing of them, Emily. Perhaps Arnold can tell you something about them, but I'm not expecting him back until late tonight. Would you like me to ask him to call on you tomorrow morning?'

Emily thought about it for a moment before saying, 'No, if

you don't mind I will call here. We can talk with more privacy.'

'Of course, come as early as you like. I'll make certain Arnold doesn't go out before you call.'

'Oh, there is one more thing. Can you tell me where Andrew Stewart lives? I would like to speak to him, to see if he knows anything about Stefan's life before he came to Kadina.'

Jennifer had hoped Emily would not ask questions about Andrew Stewart. She would much rather it had been left to her husband to break the news, but she could not avoid the issue now.

'I'm afraid there is nothing to be learned from Andrew Stewart, Emily. The poor man hung himself at the back of the store the day after the bank refused to honour Stefan Mintoff's cheques. He's dead.'

VII

Emily was extremely upset to hear of the tragic death of Andrew Stewart, especially when she learned from Jennifer that the shop manager had a wife and young child.

Her distress was increased when she learned that on the strength of his employment as manager of Stefan Mintoff's store, Andrew Stewart had taken out a bank loan in order to purchase his home and some land adjacent to it. In addition, he had been persuaded by his employer to invest his life's savings in Mintoff's company, with the expectation of a high return when Mintoff returned with the money he claimed would be invested by the London bankers.

Emily wanted to call at Stewart's home to offer her condolences and more practical help to his widow, but Jennifer advised her strongly against such a course of action. She explained that feelings against Stefan Mintoff were running very high at the moment – and Emily was believed to be closely associated with him.

Reverend Arnold Weeks explained the feelings of the residents of Kadina in more detail when Emily called on him the following morning.

Speaking to her in the rectory study, across the width of a desk that brought back uncomfortable memories of the many distressing interviews she had had with her father back in the St Cleer vicarage, Arnold Weeks said, 'For some reason Stefan has never been popular with the residents of Kadina. I don't know why. Although he has always been most generous with his time and money and supported projects beneficial to the Church, he has never succeeded in winning the support of the community.'

'Yet he was elected to be a Kadina councillor,' Emily pointed out. 'People must have trusted him enough to vote him into office.'

'Regrettably, the only emotion engendered by a local election is apathy. By ensuring that votes were forthcoming from those who owed their living to him, Stefan was assured of election. Now even they are coming out against him. Indeed, since the tragic suicide of poor Andrew Stewart there is not a single man or woman in Kadina who has a good word to say for him.'

Increasingly ill at ease, the acting rector of Kadina fidgeted uncomfortably for a few moments before saying, 'Because of the present strength of feeling, everyone is anxious to distance themselves from any hint of sympathy for, or association with, Stefan Mintoff. I regret, my dear, that you are regarded as one of his closest friends.'

Emily said bitterly, 'I have lost a great deal more than most of the people here in Kadina. I entrusted Stefan with a thousand pounds of my money. I doubt very much whether I will ever see a single penny of it again.'

'I fully understand your position, Emily, and you have my

full support. I am merely pointing out the beliefs of the public at large. Your name is inextricably linked with that of Stefan Mintoff. I have already heard from a number of prominent citizens who feel unable to support our various charitable programmes if you remain involved with them.'

Emily was both hurt and confused. 'But . . . I don't understand. Why should I be held responsible for anything that Stefan has done? I have been more gullible than most of his victims. I gave him money for a company that probably does not even exist. He has made use of the name and high office of my uncle, Lord Boyce, in order to sell shares in the same bogus company. What is more, I have given serious consideration to his offer of marriage. Only the family of poor Andrew Stewart has suffered more!'

'Believe me, I am fully aware of all this, Emily. The people of Kadina will be too, in due course, but for now feelings against Stefan Mintoff are running so high that I fear some of the anger is likely to spill over and engulf you. Once started there would be no stopping it and all that has been gained for the community by your hard work would be irretrievably lost.'

Deeply unhappy, Emily asked, 'What do you suggest I should do?'

'I feel it would be better for everyone – you, me, the Church and the community – if you were to leave Kadina until this unfortunate affair runs its course and the truth becomes acceptable to all reasonable people.'

Emily shook her head unhappily. 'I came to South Australia to work among Cornish miners and their families. Men and women I understand. If I leave my work now I will have failed in my mission.'

'That is not so, Emily.' Arnold Weeks leaned forward across the desk. 'You have laid a strong foundation here for many societies and charitable organisations. Jennifer and I will ensure the work you have begun is carried on. Unfortunately, were you to remain in Kadina in the present atmosphere of anger against

Stefan Mintoff, the societies would be boycotted and much of your hard work undone.'

When Emily began to protest, Arnold Weeks added quickly, 'I realise it is most unfair, Emily, but I assure you that things will return to normal once the anger has died down.'

'What do you propose I should do until that happens?'

'I think we may have found an alternative that you will find acceptable, Emily.'

'We? Are you talking of you and Jennifer?'

'No, Emily, someone rather more exalted. When things came to a head with the suicide of poor Andrew Stewart and the anger of the Kadina community showed itself, I realised you would be subjected to a great deal of unpleasantness, if not actual physical abuse. I wrote to acquaint Bishop Short with the situation. I made it quite clear that Mintoff had taken in the whole community – myself included – but, because they feel foolish, they are seeking someone to blame for their gullibility. The mood will pass, as such things do, but until it does it would prove to be very unpleasant for you if you were to remain here.'

'I can see sense in what you are saying,' Emily conceded. 'But what can I do until the anger dies down?'

'That question has been answered by Bishop Short himself.' Arnold Weeks picked up an envelope lying on the desk in front of him and opened it. 'This is his reply to my letter. He suggests you go to work for the Church in Adelaide. Indeed, he is eager to have you there. He says the city is experiencing a problem with "fallen women". He would like to encourage them to return to respectability and, perhaps, have the Church set up a home to help them. He feels you are just the person he is looking for to put his ideas into practice. How would you feel about it, Emily?'

Emily was still smarting at the thought of being forced to leave Kadina, but the idea did appeal to her. She had regretted not being able to do more to entice Ruth away from the life she was leading. Ruth was now in Adelaide, or on her way there.

It could be another opportunity to help her – and the many others like her.

There was another consideration, which Emily tried not to allow to influence her decision.

Sam was somewhere in Adelaide . . .

'I think Bishop Short has offered me a very exciting challenge.'

7

I

Sam took a leisurely route to Adelaide, travelling first to Port Augusta with Piet van Roos. Along the way the South African reminisced about his own gold prospecting days in the hills outside Adelaide and lamented that he was not young enough to return there.

Sam left him with the advice that he should head for the Echunga goldfield and an area known as Jupiter Creek ringing in his ears. This, said the bullock driver, was where there was far more gold than had yet been dug from the ground.

From Port Augusta, Sam boarded the steamer *Pride of Wallaroo* for the journey to Adelaide, a city he had never visited.

Upon his arrival, Sam was immediately impressed by the sheer size and incredible bustle of South Australia's capital. It was like nothing he had seen before, even in Plymouth, the only place of comparable size he had ever visited.

Yet, despite the activity, there was a remarkable sense of order about Adelaide, the streets being laid out in a regular and orderly pattern.

Sam took lodgings at a small hotel in Flinders Street, an establishment recommended by Piet van Roos.

Quite apart from the name of the street – which would have appealed to anyone from Blinman – the hotel was frequented by miners and prospectors. According to Piet it was a suitable setting-off point for anyone wishing to mine in the hills around Adelaide.

Sam was made to feel at home as soon as he entered the hotel and was greeted by the desk clerk. The clerk had emigrated to Adelaide from Redruth in Cornwall. He booked Sam into a room with a balcony, from where he said it was possible to 'watch the whole of Adelaide pass by'.

Having ascertained that this was Sam's first visit to the capital city, the clerk suggested he take a walk along Hindley and Rundle Streets in order to see the shops and experience the busy streets illuminated by gaslight.

His clothes stowed safely in his room, Sam enjoyed an evening meal that made up in substance for what it lacked in presentation. By the time he had finished the meal, darkness had fallen over the city and Sam decided to act upon the clerk's suggestion that he view Adelaide's shopping area by night.

Obtaining simple directions from the clerk, he set off from the hotel, heading for Rundle Street. Arriving there he found himself in a new and fascinating world. There were more shops than he had ever seen before, stocked with everything that man, woman or child could conceivably desire, and it seemed to Sam that the entire population of Adelaide must be here in the thronged streets.

He was impressed too by the gaslights, their hissing blue flames adding greatly to the magic of the scene.

Sam spent well over an hour walking along the busy thoroughfare and gazing in awe at the amazing array of goods offered for sale.

Eventually, the effects of the long journey he had completed only that day began to tell on him, and he decided to return to his hotel.

He had almost arrived at his destination when he heard what

sounded like a violent scuffle in a narrow alleyway alongside the building.

Stopping, Sam called out, 'What's going on? Are you all right?'

There was a momentary lull in the sound from the alleyway, then a man's voice called, 'Mind your own business and go on your way—'

He was interrupted by another voice, this time that of an older man. 'They're trying to rob me—'

The scuffling began again and, without further hesitation, Sam dived into the alleyway. The only light here came from the curtained windows of the hotel, but it was sufficient for him to see two men struggling with an ageing, grey-bearded man, who was desperately fighting to retain possession of a heavy bag.

As Sam reached the scene one of the younger men knocked the older man to the ground and snatched the bag.

'Stop him!' cried the old man. 'Get my swag!'

The young man carrying the bag tried to rush past Sam, who stuck out an arm, catching the thief across the throat. Thrown off balance, the thief crashed heavily to the ground.

The bag dropped from his hands and the old man promptly fell upon it, covering it with his body. Fists flew for a few more moments, but Sam's blows were landing with more effect than his opponents'. When he knocked down one of the assailants, the man scrambled to his feet and ran from the alleyway, closely followed by his companion.

'Are you all right?' Sam put the question as he helped the older man to his feet.

'I am, thanks to you. And do I detect a Cornish accent?'

'You do,' Sam said. 'Sam Hooper, from St Cleer. And you?'

'Abraham Gundry, originally from Redruth. My friends call me Abe.'

Suddenly the old man chuckled. 'We certainly showed them two larrikins what Cornishmen are made of.'

Sam did not argue the accuracy of the other man's account

of the incident. Instead, he asked, 'Are you staying near here?'

Pointing to the hotel where Sam had a room, Abe said, 'I'll be staying right here. And you?'

'I've got a room here too. I arrived today from Blinman.'

'I'm on my way in from the Lofty Ranges to the east of Adelaide,' said Abe Gundry. 'I suspect these two have been following me for much of the day.'

'Why?' Sam asked. 'Why were they following you?'

'They thought an old man would be an easy target for 'em, but they picked on the wrong man. Long before I'd reached their age I'd reckon it to be a poor day if I hadn't shot half a dozen better men than them before breakfast.' The old man caught the look Sam gave him and he added, 'No, I'm not mad, boy. I'm talking of the days in Texas when I was fighting for Sam Houston against old Santa Anna.'

'Sam Houston . . . ? Santa Anna . . . ?'

'In America . . . but it was before your time, boy. I went mining to Mexico when I was fifteen. But where are my manners? Come in to the hotel with me.'

Raising the bag to his shoulder, Abe said, 'When I've booked in and had what's in here put away in the hotel safe I'll buy you a drink or two. I reckon I owe you that.'

Once inside the hotel reception area, Sam was able to see that Abe Gundry was hardly dressed for the city. He looked as though he had come straight off a mining shift, having hand-brushed away any excess mud that might have been on his clothing.

The hotel was small and informal, but Sam doubted whether the desk clerk would give the old man a room.

To his surprise, the clerk greeted Abe effusively. 'Mr Gundry! Good to see you again, sir. Your usual room is free at the rear of the hotel. Do you have something for the safe? You have? I am pleased to know things are still going well for you.'

Abe Gundry produced a small but heavy sack that had been carefully stitched up in order to efficiently seal its contents. 'Weigh it before you put it away,' he said.

'Of course.'

Placing the sack on a set of scales sitting on the desk counter, the clerk added and subtracted weights until he was satisfied. 'There you are, thirty-three ounces. You *have* done well, sir.'

The clerk's admiration was genuine. Moments later he put the bag in the safe behind the desk and wrote out a receipt, which he handed to Abe Gundry.

Slinging his bag on to the counter, Abe said, 'Look after this for me, Clarence. I'm taking this young man for a drink. He stepped in when two young larrikins bundled me into the alleyway beside the hotel and tried to rob me.'

'What a *dreadful* thing to happen – and so close to the hotel! I should think you *do* owe Mr Hooper a couple of drinks. I shall report the matter to the manager. I have no doubt he will send a bottle of something special to Mr Hooper's room. We don't expect this sort of thing to happen to our guests – especially to our regulars like yourself, Mr Gundry.'

On the way to the hotel bar, Sam said to his companion, 'I take it that was gold you had put in the safe?'

'That's right. Gold enough to kill for – and I've seen men die for a whole lot less.'

When they reached the bar Abe ordered two cold beers. As the two men carried them to an empty table, he asked, 'Are you a mining man, Sam?'

When Sam confirmed that he was, Abe asked, 'Gold mining?'

'Just copper, so far – both here and in Cornwall. I've left Blinman because the mine there has stopped working.'

'Why come to Adelaide? There's no copper mining around here to speak of right now.'

'I've been bringing copper to grass since I was eleven and don't have a whole lot to show for it. I thought it was time I had a change. To see if I could make myself rich and not someone else.'

'You mean you want to go looking for gold? I'd have thought you'd be heading for Victoria. That's where most go who want to get rich quick.'

'I might go on there one day,' Sam said. 'But I was friendly with a bullock driver up at Blinman, a man named Piet van Roos. He said he'd made his money in the hills near here, so I thought I'd give it a try.'

'You know Piet van Roos? I thought he must have died years ago. Him and me were partners for a while and did a bit of prospecting together. He should have stayed with me. He wouldn't need to be tramping halfway across Australia beside a bullock cart if he had.'

'He enjoys the life,' Sam replied. 'He once told me that if he died in the outback on his own he'd leave this life a happy man.'

'I don't doubt he would,' said Abe. 'Hey, your pot's empty, I'll get another couple of beers.'

'No, I'll get these in,' Sam said. 'You've said "Thank you", now we'll drink together because we're two Cornishmen who have met on the far side of the world.'

While Sam was at the bar, waiting to be served, Abe watched him speculatively. When he returned to the table and both men had taken a swig from their newly replenished tankards, Abe asked, 'If you were to find enough gold to give you a decent stake, what would you do with it?'

'I've been thinking about that a lot just lately,' Sam replied. 'I suppose it would depend on how much I made. I'd like to send something to my family in St Cleer. My pa's a farmer and things are no better for Cornish farmers than they are for Cornish miners. It would be good to think he could take things a bit easier.'

'That's taken care of your family. What about yourself? Isn't there something you want to do? Someone you'd like to impress?'

Sam grimaced. 'There was a time when I had ideas way above my station in life, but that's behind me now. I used to enjoy working on the farm, back home. I quite like the idea of farming here – if ever I find land anything like that in Cornwall.'

'Have you been up in the Adelaide Hills yet and seen the country out towards Scott's Creek?'

'I've never been this way before. Why do you ask?'

'Some years ago I bought a piece of land out that way. A few hundred acres. I'm no farmer, but there *are* farms around there and they seem to be doing well. I'll be going back through there in a few days' time on my way to my claim. Come with me for a while. You can see at first hand what gold mining's all about and on the way I'll show you land that's like nothing you'll have seen around Blinman.'

II

'This is beautiful! It's wonderful!' Sam said excitedly. 'I haven't seen anything to match this since I left Cornwall – and there weren't too many places there that had better soil. A man could grow anything he wanted here.'

Abe had stayed in the Adelaide hotel for a full week. When he left, heading for the Lofty Ranges, he took Sam with him.

While Sam was extolling the breathtaking beauty of the hill country, Abe's fingers had been linked together on the top of a gatepost. Now he rested his bearded chin upon them briefly before saying, 'Your father would be proud of you, Sam. You're a farmer at heart.' Pausing to look along the valley, from left to right, he added, 'Perhaps all Cornishmen are. I knew as soon as I saw this place that I wanted to own it.'

'You own this land? This is the place you brought me out to see?'

'The whole valley is mine, Sam, from the trees at the far end, to the creek below us – and up the hills on either side to beyond both ridges. Just about everything you can see belongs to me – and I paid cash for it.'

'You have an eye for scenery, as well as good land, Abe, but why are you still grubbing for gold when you could build yourself a grand house and live here in style, enjoying what you've earned?'

Scratching his grey, unkempt beard, Abe said, 'You know, I sometimes ask myself the very same question, but I haven't yet come up with an answer I can believe. I guess the truth is that I'm a bit like a mole. I've been prospecting for so long that I'd probably shrivel up and die if I had to spend all my life above ground. Now, we'll cook ourselves something to eat, spend the night here, then tomorrow go on to Jupiter Creek and I'll let you help me dig out some more gold.'

Jupiter Creek had been the scene of a gold rush some years before. When gold was discovered hundreds of men had descended upon the area and the slopes of the denuded hills all around were pitted with the results of their inexpert and largely fruitless labours.

The successful finds had been of alluvial gold, washed down to the creek by countless centuries of rain. In a bid to find the source of the riches, men with little or no knowledge of gold-mining had spread over a vast area, scratching out shallow holes in a frenzy of activity, in the vain hope of discovering the source of the elusive mineral and making themselves an instant fortune.

Very few succeeded in finding anything worthwhile, but each minuscule success would send the hopeful prospectors scurrying to a new area to repeat the largely futile process all over again.

Gold *had* been found in workable quantities, but usually only by men with knowledge and patience. Eventually, as the finds became smaller and less frequent, the disappointed prospectors moved on, in pursuit of an elusive dream. When they had gone, nature took over once more, gradually hiding the scars they had left behind.

It was now that Abe Gundry appeared on the scene, but first

he spent a great deal of time in the mining and assaying offices in Adelaide. After carefully checking their records he set out for Jupiter Creek, armed with a detailed map.

Studying the land and his map with great care, he began fossicking for the gold he was certain others had missed.

Within a week he had found what he was seeking. This was alluvial gold too, but it had been deposited many years before that found by others. It was deeper than the other prospectors had gone, richer too – much richer.

It was from this find that Abe had been making his money, quietly and unobtrusively, for more than a year.

Yet the prospector was still not fully satisfied. He believed the main source of the alluvial gold was not too far away. He was already making a great deal of money from his present workings, but it had become a matter of pride with him to find a lode that might profitably be mined on a grand scale.

Sam and Abe toiled through the scrub, following the course of what was once a deep creek but was now barely discernible. Suddenly they both heard the sound of spades striking rock.

'I thought you said you were the only one working here,' Sam said.

'That's right,' Abe replied. 'And I will be again very soon. Unless I'm mistaken that's *my* claim that's being worked – and without my say so.'

Abe turned off along another shallow depression until they came to an area where recent excavation had gone far deeper than most of the workings they had passed.

This was where the sound was coming from. Three men were digging with long-handled spades, while a fourth was operating a gold 'cradle', using water from a pool dug out of the creek bed with which to wash the gold-bearing gravel through a primitive separation system.

'What the hell do you think you're doing?' Confronting the diggers, Abe put the question to them angrily as he dumped his heavy bag on the ground.

The four men stopped work and looked at each other before one replied. 'We're digging for gold. What's it to you, old man?'

'You're working on my claim, that's what it is to me. If you want to dig for gold around here, that's fine, but you can do it somewhere else And before you go you can hand over any gold you've already taken out.'

Again there was an exchange of glances and the same spokesmen said, 'No, old man, it's you who can find somewhere else to dig for gold. We're here and we're staying.'

'Then we'll make it a case for the police trooper over at Echunga,' Abe said. 'I'm sure he'll be interested in you. You'll no doubt be from one of the prison colonies. Did you serve out your time – or are you escapees?'

The odds were four to two, with one of the two being an old man, and Sam believed the four men were probably quite as tough as they appeared to be. 'Come on, Abe, let's go and find a trooper. We'll let him sort this out.'

'Wait! If you have a licence to work this claim, show it to me.' It was more of a command than a request from the spokesman for the illegal prospectors.

'Do you think I'm foolish enough to let you get your thieving hands on it? I'll show it to the trooper and to no one else.'

'First you have to get to Echunga. That might not be so easy, old man. It's a very long way. I think you should find the licence for me – and quickly.'

The spokesman gave his companions a brief nod. Downing their spades two of the men closed in on Abe, the others, led by the man who had been operating the cradle, moved towards Sam.

'Now, just wait a minute . . .' Sam made a half-hearted attempt to reason with the two men advancing on him, knowing full well it would be fruitless. He was ready when the first of them rushed at him. Slipping easily beneath the man's outstretched arm, Sam dived towards a long-handled shovel that had been resting against the cradle.

He straightened up with the shovel in his hand in time to strike the second man a resounding blow across the face with the flat of the spade blade, knocking him backwards into the creek.

Swinging the spade back again in a pendulum motion, he struck his first assailant on the head as he was about to rise to his feet.

The other two men temporarily turned their attention from Abe. Picking up the spades they had dropped before taking on the old man, they rushed at Sam.

He succeeded in parrying the blow from the first assailant and almost did the same with the second, but the spade bounced up and caught him on the side of his face.

It was fortunate it was the flat of the spade that hit Sam, or it would have sliced his face open. As it was, it caused an explosion of light in his head. He dropped to one knee, the spade he was holding falling from his grasp.

The man raised his spade to strike what would undoubtedly have been a mortal blow when the loud sound of a shot caused Sam's assailant to stop in his tracks.

Gathering his senses, Sam saw Abe sitting beside his open swag, smoke gently trickling from the barrel of a handgun in his hand.

'Hit him!' The self-appointed spokesman for the illegal prospectors shouted at his colleague. 'The gun's been fired now—'

Before he could say any more Abe fired again and the speaker was knocked backwards. The smoking barrel of the revolver now pointed towards the man with the raised spade and Abe said, 'Throw it to the ground. Now!'

The frightened man immediately did as he was told. Abe then used the gun he was holding to motion the man towards the other two prospectors, who stood with their hands held shoulder-high.

Abe patted the gun and said to Sam, 'It's a six-shot Army

Colt. I fought in the American civil war, as well as in Texas. First time I've needed to use it since then, but I don't seem to have lost my touch. Are you all right?'

Sam worked his jaw from side to side. It hurt, but he doubted whether anything was broken. 'I'll live.' Nodding towards the wounded man, who lay in the mud of the creek bottom, moaning, he added, 'I'm not so sure about him.'

Abe climbed to his feet and walked over to the man he had shot, keeping the revolver pointed in the direction of the other three men.

Looking down at his victim, he said, 'He's lost a bit of blood, but he'll probably be all right. I aimed to shoot him in the shoulder. It's a bit lower than I intended, but I've seen men pull through when they've been hurt a whole lot more.'

To the three men who still stood with their hands held in the air, he said, 'Take him away. Well away. If I ever see any of you near Jupiter Creek again I'll shoot you dead, is that understood?'

'What do we do with him?' One of the men lowered a hand long enough to point towards their wounded companion. 'He needs a doctor.'

'Then find one for him,' Abe said callously. 'But make it a long way from here. When you've gone we'll be heading to Echunga to tell the troopers what's happened. No doubt they'll come looking for you. Whether or not you want them to find you is up to you. Now, take him away – but leave everything else.'

One of the men seemed inclined to argue, but a slight shift in the aim of the revolver effectively silenced him. Making for their wounded companion, the three men lifted him to his feet. Ignoring his screams of pain they dragged him away, along the creek.

When they had passed out of sight, Abe said to Sam, 'You're a sight quicker than me. Climb to the top of the hill there. Make sure they keep going without stopping. Don't let 'em see you but don't come down until you're certain they're not likely to turn back.'

'Will we go to Echunga and tell the police then?'

Abe shook his head. 'No need. We've sorted out our troubles in our own way. That's the way things are done out here. It's easier for everyone concerned, including those four. They're no doubt all wanted men. Hurry up now, go and make sure they're not likely to come back.'

When Sam returned from the hilltop to report that the four would-be claim-jumpers had seemed in an almighty hurry to get as far from the Jupiter Creek gold diggings as they could, he found Abe calmly brewing tea on a wood fire as though nothing untoward had taken place.

'How's that face?' Abe asked. 'You're going to have a nasty bruise. Sit yourself down and I'll pour you a mug of tea.' Nodding towards the few belongings the four men had left behind, he said, 'There's a few ounces of gold among that lot that should help ease the pain a little.'

'Are we going to share it?' Sam asked. They had not discussed how any gold they found would be apportioned. They had not even talked of Sam helping Abe work his claim.

'Of course we are, that's the way partners usually work.'

When Sam stared at him, wondering if he had heard him correctly, Abe said matter of factly, 'Oh, didn't I tell you? It must have slipped my mind. When I was in Adelaide I called in to the Gold Commissioner's office. Had your name added to the licences I took out on the claim. We're legal partners now.'

III

Sam had very little sleep that night.

It was not entirely due to the possibility that the three able claim-jumpers might return and try to retrieve the gold Abe had forced them to leave behind. His mind was also filled with the implications of what becoming the partner of a successful gold prospector would mean to him.

It had already made him considerably richer. The work of the claim-jumpers had yielded at least four ounces of gold. Abe believed they had hit upon a rich pocket, with more gold to be taken out.

Abe also told him that in addition to having him made an official partner on the claim licence he had taken out licences on a whole section of the creek they would be working.

The reason for this was that one of the assayers in Adelaide had warned him that a large mining company had been to the Assay Office to carry out a similar search to the one Abe had made prior to taking out a licence on the successful Jupiter Creek claim.

'We don't want no big company coming in and benefiting from the work we've already done,' declared Abe. 'I thought we'd best get in ahead of 'em and stake a claim for ourselves, just to keep 'em out.'

Sam was already aware that Abe was not only a very successful prospector, but a shrewd businessman as well. If they were able to enjoy a few trouble-free months working on their claim, Sam's dream of owning land in the Adelaide Hills could become a reality.

He marvelled at how much his life had changed in little more than a week – and all because two young men had tried to rob an old man in an Adelaide alleyway.

'What's the matter, boy, you having trouble sleeping?'

Sam had not thought he was being particularly restless, but it seemed he had succeeded in disturbing Abe, who was wrapped up in a blanket on the far side of the dying campfire.

'What is it? You worried them claim-jumpers might come back? Would you rather my revolver was tucked in your belt instead of mine?'

Sam grinned in the darkness. 'No, Abe, you can handle it a

sight better than me. Anyway, I don't think they'll be back. They've learned it's not a good idea to try to rob helpless old prospectors like you.'

'Then if it's not them, what *is* coming between you and sleep?'

'I started thinking how well I was doing out of the misdeeds of others. The two in the alley in Adelaide got me a partner, now the four we've met up with today have given me enough to buy the first few acres of a piece of land like yours.'

'Is that what you're going to do with the money you make from the claim?' Abe asked.

'That's right – and send enough home so that my pa can come out here if he wants to and see what really good land looks like. Perhaps by then I might have a house built there, one large enough for the whole family. Do you have any idea what sort of house you'll build on your land one day, Abe?'

'I've known from the first time I set eyes on the land,' Abe replied, speaking more quietly than was usual for him. 'It'll be just like the house once owned by my wife's family in California.'

In the darkness, Sam sat up, intuitively aware that Abe's revelation was not one he was in the habit of sharing with others.

'You're married, Abe?'

'I was, for all too short a time. I had a child too. A daughter.'

'What happened to them?'

'It's a long story, boy, and I don't intend spending the night telling all the details, but when I was a whole lot younger than you are now, I went out from Cornwall with some others to work in the silver mines in Mexico. I was quick to learn the language and grew to like the people, although I wasn't very taken with the men who governed them. Things eventually became so bad I left the mines and made my way to Texas.

'I arrived there just as Santa Anna, the Mexican president, and Sam Houston met head on. Seeing as I was there, I felt I should join in, so I became part of Houston's army.

'We won the war, but one government's as bad as another,

so I headed out west and ended up in California. That's where I first started prospecting. I met a girl there too.'

Once started it seemed that Abe *wanted* to speak of his earlier days. It was more than Sam had ever heard him say at one time.

'California belonged to Mexico in those days and she was the daughter of a Mexican landowner,' Abe continued. 'He didn't think much of me at first, but Rosalia and me were married anyway. Little over a year later we had a daughter and life was pretty good.

'Then another war came along. I didn't get too involved in this one, but Rosalia's pa did and by the time the war was over he'd lost everything. We hung on to a small piece of his land for a couple of years, then there was a gold find not too far away and I was one of the first to join in the rush to have a share of it.'

Quieter now, he said, 'I found gold all right – but I lost just about everything else.'

Abe was silent for so long that Sam had to prompt him. 'What happened?'

'I got back home and found that Rosalia and the little 'un had died. An epidemic that took off more than half the Mexicans in that part of California. Funny, though, it didn't touch any of the Americans who'd moved into the area.

'I didn't care very much about things after that. I went back up in the hills prospecting for a while, found more gold – and managed to lose it all again, one way or another. Then, as there weren't enough Mexicans left for them to fight in the United States, the Americans decided to fight each other.

'I met up with a general who'd fought alongside me in Houston's army and before I knew it I was an officer in the army of the North. Because I'd been a miner and knew something of explosives and shoring up tunnels, I spent most of the war either blowing things up or putting them together again – although I did get involved in a bit of shooting now and then.

'When the war ended I thought I'd head back to Cornwall,

but I found one of us had changed too much during the time I'd been away. We didn't suit each other any more so, like you, I came out here to South Australia, first to Wallaroo, then to the Flinders Ranges. The trouble was I'd got out of the habit of working for others, so I turned to prospecting again – and here I am.'

Sam had listened, enthralled, to the abbreviated story of Abe's life. However, he was aware the older man had left out far more than he had revealed.

'You've led a very adventurous life, Abe – and had more than your share of bad luck.'

'I wouldn't argue with that, boy, but I've known good times too. More than most men I've met with. Because of that I take issue with something you said to me in the bar of the hotel back in Adelaide when we'd just met. You said there'd been a time in your life when you'd had ideas "above your station". There's no such thing as having a "station" in life. I've worked with men who've been thought of as being so low that folk would cross the street rather than have to walk close to 'em, yet they've been men as fine as any I've ever met. Then there've been presidents like the Mexican Santa Anna. I was with him for nigh on a month when we took him prisoner and I wouldn't trust him any more than I would those four we saw off today. A good man is a good man, and a bad man is – just bad.'

Part of the fire collapsed inwards and for a few seconds a flame rose high enough for Sam to see Abe's bearded face above the blanket he had wrapped around himself. Then the old man was talking once more.

'When a man talks about having "ideas above his station", it usually means there's a woman involved in his thinking. Well, I had designs on a woman whose family had high-faluting titles in Spain going back hundreds of years. We got married and our years together were the happiest of my life – of both our lives. If there's someone you feel strongly enough about then you should go ahead and tell her. Let *her* make up her mind about it. Most women with anything about 'em can tell the worth of a man – whatever his so-called station in life.'

The flame had died now and in the darkness Sam heard Abe turn over. With his face turned away now, the old prospector said, 'There, I've finished telling you a bedtime story now, so just get off to sleep. We've got work to do tomorrow if you want to dig out enough gold to buy your land and build a house and a future on it.'

IV

The promise of Sam's first few days on the Jupiter Creek diggings with Abe were not entirely fulfilled. Nevertheless, by the end of three weeks they had gathered sufficient gold to make a trip to Adelaide advisable and this was a routine they maintained for four months. They would work for three weeks, then take the gold they had unearthed to Adelaide, remaining there for about a week.

Sam was delighted with the amount of money accumulating for him in the Adelaide Bank. It was more than he had ever dreamed of possessing.

He was happy to be working with Abe as his partner and learned a great deal from the older man about the art of prospecting. Sam had also grown very fond of the old man. He was tough without being aggressive and the toughness belied a streak of gentleness that occasionally showed in his dealings with the various animals that found their way to the remote camp.

The two men had one brief worrying occasion when prospectors from the Southern Goldmining Company arrived at the diggings. This was the company Abe had been warned about by the assayor in Adelaide.

Fortunately, it turned out to be a reputable company. Although extremely interested in what Abe and Sam were doing, the visitors acknowledged the men's prior claim to the area around their diggings and did not interfere with their work. Instead, they invited the two men to share a meal with them at their camp and left them with some welcome provisions when they moved on.

Nevertheless, Abe was unsettled by the visit. 'The fact that they were here at all means word has got around that we're doing well. The company will try to keep it quiet, of course. They won't want men swarming all over the place taking out licences for land they hope to work, but sooner or later we're going to be overrun with folk hoping to make their fortunes in just a few days – and many of 'em won't be fussy about the way they do it.'

'But we've got a legal claim to this whole stretch of the creek. Surely it won't affect us that much?'

'You haven't seen men – hundreds, perhaps *thousands* of men – when gold fever's got into 'em. I've seen fights to the death over whether a strip of earth no wider than a young girl's ribbon belongs to this claim or that one. Although this is our claim, we can't guard it twenty-four hours a day, every day of the week. They'll all know we're taking out gold – and gold is what they want.'

'What are you saying, that we should pack up and go if they move in?'

'No, boy, I've never been a quitter, but I think we should make our plans. I suggest we work ourselves fit to bust for as long as we can, then offer to sell out to this Southern Goldmining Company. The more gold we can take out between now and then, the more we can ask from them.'

'Then what will we do, Abe, you and me?'

Abe did not allow Sam to see how pleased he was that the younger man had not suggested they would go their separate ways if they were forced to leave the Jupiter Creek diggings.

'Let's cross that bridge when we come to it. In the meantime, let's see what we find if we extend our digging out to the north a little. I have a hunch it'll be a move in the right direction.'

On their next trip to Adelaide, Sam and Abe were carrying almost double the amount of gold they usually took to the city, as a result of working even longer hours than before.

On the way they called at Abe's landholding, adjoining Scott's Creek. It was not the best of days to view land, although Sam still thought it incredibly beautiful.

There was an impressive build-up of storm clouds over the whole area and they had decided they would not remain in the valley for too long.

As they stood looking at Abe's property, Sam asked, 'Where will you build your house when the time comes, Abe?'

Without hesitation, the older man replied, 'Over there, to the right of those blue-gums, halfway up the slope. There's a natural level platform that's an ideal site for a house. It's protected from the winds, yet makes the most of the view. Where would you put a house, if you was me?'

'In exactly the same place,' Sam said honestly. 'The spot has everything. But I think we should be moving on now. Judging by the look of those clouds there's a whole lot of rain up there and it's not going to be long in coming.'

'I reckon you're right, boy. It'll be on us long before we reach Adelaide.'

Abe's forecast was uncomfortably accurate. The two men had been walking from Abe's valley for no more than twenty minutes when the deluge began. It was accompanied by thunder and lightning, making it too dangerous to take shelter beneath a tree.

For perhaps fifteen minutes they battled on through the downpour, buffeted by rain and wind and unable to see more than a few paces ahead. Then, fortuitously, Sam made out the outline of a building ahead of them. It was a smithy, standing beside a flooded crossroads.

Pulling open the door, both men stumbled inside and found at least fifteen men already in there, also sheltering from the storm.

Most had sought shelter before the storm broke and there were murmurs of sympathy for the two sodden newcomers.

'Here, there's room by the forge for the pair of you,' said the blacksmith. 'But keep away from my tools. There's enough water coming off you to turn them rusty.'

Space was made for the two newcomers beside the forge and as their clothes began to steam, Sam said, 'Shouldn't you change out of those wet things, Abe? It can't be healthy having them dry on you like they are.'

Abe grinned at him. 'The clothes in my swag are just as wet as these I'm wearing. What do you suggest I do, stand here with nothing on while they dry?'

Pipe in mouth, Abe was contentedly breathing out smoke to mingle with the steam. 'I've been as wet as this before, boy, and had nowhere warm like this to dry me off. There have been times when I stayed wet for days on end. By the time we set off again today I'll be near enough dry right through.'

'Wouldn't it be just as well to stay here for the night?' Sam suggested.

Abe took the pipe from his mouth and shook his head. 'I've got my heart set on a whisky or two, followed by a night in a comfortable bed. Besides, if we waited until morning it would most probably be raining again.'

Knocking out his pipe in the forge, he added, 'As a matter of fact it looks as though the storm is moving on. A few more minutes and we'll make a move.'

Soon most of the men inside the smithy began leaving. Darkness was falling and they wanted to reach their destinations while it was still light enough to negotiate flooded creeks. It was not long before Sam and Abe followed their example.

* * *

It took them three and a half hours to reach the Adelaide hotel. By the time they arrived the temperature had plummeted to depths Sam had not experienced before in South Australia.

Although his outer clothing had dried off to a great extent, that against his skin was still wet. When they stood in the hotel entrance hall he was so cold he could barely return the reception clerk's friendly greeting.

Sam saw that, despite his earlier bravado, Abe was shivering too, and he was concerned for him. He was relieved when Abe declared his intention of taking a bottle of whisky to his room, getting out of his damp clothes and enjoying a drink in the warmth of the hotel bed.

By the following morning Sam felt better, especially when a maid came to his room with his clothes, which had been dried for him overnight. However, he became concerned for his friend when Abe did not appear for breakfast.

As soon as he had eaten, Sam made his way to the room occupied by his partner. He found Abe sitting in a chair, still not fully dressed. The old prospector appeared older and more frail than Sam had ever seen him.

Thoroughly alarmed, Sam asked, 'Are you not feeling well, Abe? Is there something I can get for you?'

'No, I'm all right, boy,' Abe lied. 'A bit stiff after all the walking we did yesterday, that's all.'

He had hardly finished talking when he began coughing, giving the lie to his statement. It was a cough that had him fighting for breath for a few minutes.

Sam was extremely anxious, but Abe waved his fears aside. 'Don't fuss over me, boy. Go off and take our gold down to the Assay Office. By the time you get back I'll be as right as rain.'

The Assay Office was only a short distance away and Sam was waiting for the staff when they arrived to open up. His business completed, Sam stopped off on his way back to the hotel to buy some of Abe's favourite tobacco for the old man.

However, when he went to Abe's room, Sam was concerned

to find that his partner had not improved and was coughing more than before. His breathing too was increasingly laboured and Sam insisted, 'I'm not happy with the way you are, Abe. I'm going to get a doctor to come and take a look at you.'

'I don't want no doctor touching me!' Abe's outburst brought on another bout of painful coughing. When it had passed, he said, with less vehemence, 'The only time in my life I've ever seen a doctor was in Texas. He'd have taken off my arm if I'd let him, just because it had a bullet lodged in it. I had a horse-doctor dig it out for me and a week or two later I'd forgotten all about it.'

'Well, if I can't find the right man for you I'll fetch a horse-doctor instead,' Sam said. 'But I'm going to get one or the other in to listen to that chest.'

Wheezing painfully, Abe conceded defeat. 'All right, boy, I'll go along with you because I know you mean well, but if I don't like what he says I'll likely throw him right out of the room. You make sure he understands that.'

The doctor's surgery was close to the hotel, but by the time a doctor arrived to examine Abe, the old man was in no condition to throw anyone from his room. The pain in his chest was worse and his breathing was increasingly laboured.

Only a cursory examination was necessary in order for the doctor to make a rapid diagnosis.

'He's got pneumonia,' he told Sam, removing the stethoscope from his ears. 'And he's got it bad. I'd say it's certainly as a result of the soaking you said he got yesterday. He needs to go into hospital immediately.'

'I don't want to go into no hospital,' Abe protested breathlessly.

Sam looked at the doctor questioningly and the medical man shrugged. The doctor walked to the door, followed closely by Sam, and confided in a low voice, 'I don't guarantee that we can save him, even if he goes to hospital, but *unless* he does there is no hope for him at all.'

Sam needed to consider the doctor's words for only a moment. 'All right, doctor, you make arrangements to have him taken in right away. I'll make sure he's ready.'

Abe was on his way to hospital less than half an hour later. Sam accompanied him in the ambulance carriage and realised by the swift manner in which the sick man was dealt with once they arrived that he *was* seriously ill.

Despite his protestations, Abe realised it too. When Sam made a return visit to the hospital that afternoon, Abe handed him an envelope.

'What's this?' Sam asked.

'It's my will, boy, all signed up and witnessed by two of the doctors. It's not that I intend dying, because I don't, but as I told them, I thought I'd better get it done because I don't trust them not to make mistakes.'

Because of the will he carried, unopened, in his pocket and the poor condition of his friend and partner, Sam was feeling very depressed when he left the hospital; he was lost in thought and not looking at anyone he passed along the way. It therefore came as a great surprise to him when a voice suddenly called his name.

'Sam! Sam Hooper! It is you, isn't it?'

Coming to a halt, Sam turned to face the speaker.

It was Margaret Minns.

8

I

When Emily was obliged to leave Kadina, Margaret decided she and the boys would go with her.

Emily protested that it was not necessary for the small family to disrupt their lives because of her problems, but Margaret reminded Emily that they had already decided they would most probably return to Cornwall and the passage home would be easier to arrange from Adelaide. The family was finding it difficult to settle in Kadina because of the uncertainty in the copper-mining industry, and it would be even more difficult now Charlie was dead.

In addition, although Margaret would never say so to Emily, because of their close relationship with her, the boys were already being targeted by malicious neighbours.

The party arrived at Port Adelaide by steamship, then travelled to South Australia's capital city on a train that was more sophisticated than the one that connected Wallaroo with Kadina.

Once in Adelaide, Emily and her companions went first to the bishop's office. It was here Emily received the first intimation that she could no longer expect the welcome previously extended to her as the niece of a minister of the Crown.

Because of the possibility that she might become involved in a scandal, all those who held a position of authority were most anxious not to be considered closely associated with her. The bishop himself was 'not available', and it seemed most of the senior cathedral clergy had pressing engagements they were unable to break. It was left to a comparatively junior clergyman to welcome her to Adelaide and escort her to a house that had been rented on her behalf.

Although the house was in an area somewhat superior to that where Emily had first lived in Kadina, it was a considerable distance from the bishop's palace and the homes occupied by the scions of Adelaide society.

If Emily was aware of the downgrading of her social status, she certainly did not allow it to show.

'What a delightful house!' she exclaimed to the distinctly embarrassed clergyman. 'We will be very comfortable here, will we not, Margaret?'

The house was small and because it had only two bedrooms, one of the living rooms would need to be adapted to accommodate the two boys.

Aware of the house's shortcomings, the young clergyman said, 'I don't think His Grace expected you to be accompanied by a companion . . . and two children.'

'Had His Grace enquired about my requirements, I would have been happy to acquaint him with them,' Emily replied, smiling sweetly at the young churchman. 'Now, where are Adelaide's bawdy houses?'

Her question was so unexpected it left the young clergyman speechless for some moments. When he had recovered sufficiently to reply, he stammered, 'I . . . I am sure I don't know, Miss Boyce.'

'Come now,' said Emily, 'I was asked here to take on the task of saving "fallen women". Surely His Grace is not the only man in the Church who knows the whereabouts of Adelaide's bawdy houses? I would hate to cause him embarrassment by having to put such a question to him.'

'I think . . . I have heard that Knox Street has a certain reputation – as have the taverns in Hindley Street,' said the red-faced clergyman. 'But I wouldn't know for certain. Our duties rarely take us there.'

'Then they should,' Emily said firmly. 'The women – and the men too – in such areas are those most in need of the Church's help and guidance. You must accompany me there some time.'

When he felt the two women and Albert and Tom were sufficiently settled, the young clergyman said a relieved farewell and hurried away.

'You gave him a hard time,' Margaret chided Emily. 'I don't suppose he has ever met a woman quite like you before.'

'That matters very little,' Emily declared. 'What is so sad is that he has apparently never met any women of the sort I am here to help. It isn't the type of priest I expected to find in a young, vibrant country like this.'

'Well, *you're* here now,' declared Margaret. 'I have no doubt you'll soon sort things out.'

Emily set about 'sorting things out' the very next day. Her first call was to the police headquarters to inform a slightly bemused police commissioner that she would be working among the prostitutes of the city in a bid to save their souls – and their bodies too, if these were not beyond redemption.

Over the next weeks Emily found the prostitutes to be almost as bemused as the police chief by her presence among them.

Initially Emily faced resentment from some of the older women when they realised she was trying to persuade them to give up their way of life. Consequently they went out of their way to shock her. However, they soon discovered that Emily did not shock easily.

Gradually they learned to accept her and soon discovered she was someone they were able to talk to, someone outside of their immediate and necessarily narrow circle of friends with whom they could discuss their problems in the knowledge that whatever was said would remain confidential.

Emily was soon able to claim that the rapport she had built up with the prostitutes had borne fruit. One of the older women actually came to Emily's home to tell her about a young girl who had arrived in Knox Street only the previous day.

'I spoke to her last night,' said the woman. 'She's run away from home with an older man. He wants her to go on the streets to earn money for them both. I doubt if she's more than sixteen. She's so confused about what's happening in her life that before she knows it she'll be one of us except that she'll be keeping a ponce as well as herself.'

'The only way I can do anything for this girl is to have her and her "ponce", as you call him, arrested,' said Emily, after giving the matter some thought. 'She's probably so infatuated with him that if I try to persuade her to leave him and go home they'll both run off somewhere else. I'll have a word with the police first and after the arrest do my best to persuade this girl to go home. Do you think she might?'

Now it was the prostitute's turn to be thoughtful. Eventually, she said, 'I think she will, once you've got her away from his influence.'

'Good.' Emily was grateful for her information, but she wondered what had prompted this woman, whom she recognised as one of the oldest and most hardened of the prostitutes, to come to her.

When she asked the question, the woman was at first reluctant to explain. When Emily persisted, she said, 'I have a daughter of my own. I had her before I took to the streets. I wasn't married and it brought such shame on my family that I ran away, leaving my baby behind. I know she will have been properly looked after, but I often think of her. She'd be about the same age as that young girl.'

* * *

After a meeting with a senior policeman at the main Adelaide police station, a raid was carried out on the house where the girl and the man were staying.

The man remained in custody while the girl stayed with Emily and Margaret for two nights, during which time both women had many talks with her.

Emily then accompanied the girl to her farmhouse home, a few hours' journey from Adelaide. Here she met the girl's parents, who were so relieved to have their daughter back that they would have forgiven her anything.

It was possible that Emily had other successes too. At least three of the younger women with whom she spoke at length left the Knox Street area without telling anyone where they were going and Emily liked to think her talk with them had persuaded them to leave Adelaide and return to a respectable life.

Some of the prostitutes had children and Emily claimed another small victory when she persuaded the women to allow their offspring to attend Sunday school classes. She realised it was too much to ask that they attend a church for the lessons, so they took place in an empty house in the street.

Some of her other efforts were less successful. Her attempts to organise various social events to interest the women were well intentioned but failed dismally.

Nevertheless, Emily persisted with her efforts to help the city's 'fallen women' in any way she could and gradually their confidence in and respect for her grew. She still had the support of Margaret, who was not yet certain that she really wanted to return to Cornwall.

One Sunday, after Emily had been in Adelaide for some months, she had dismissed the children from the afternoon school and was locking the front door of the empty house, when she was approached by a young woman whom she recognised but she could not remember from where.

The woman was the first to speak and it was immediately apparent that she knew Emily.

'Hello, Miss Boyce, may I speak to you?'

'Of course, but do I not know you from somewhere?'

'We met at Blinman where I shared a house with Ruth. You called in to see her when we were getting ready to move.'

'I knew we had met before. Are you still with Ruth? How is she? I was rather surprised not to have found her here when I arrived in Adelaide.'

'We decided we would go to Port Adelaide, close to the docks. Ruth is there right now, but she's very sick, that's why I've come here to find you, to see if you can help her.'

'What is wrong with her?' Emily's tone was urgent.

The prostitute hesitated for a few moments before saying, 'Most of the men we meet at Port Adelaide are seamen, from all over the world. Some of them can be a bit rough after they've been drinking. Ruth, me and some of the other girls were in one of the beerhouses close to the docks a couple of nights ago when we picked up with a few of the seamen off a foreign ship. The blokes me and the other girls were with were happy enough to drink half the night away, but Ruth's man went back with her to our house early on. By the time I got back there it must have been after midnight. The house was in darkness, but as I went to my room with my man I thought I heard someone groaning. I didn't take any notice then, but I wish I had.'

The woman showed signs of distress, but she continued. 'The next day – that's yesterday morning – I got up a bit earlier than usual and went to the kitchen to make myself a cup of tea. That's when I heard this groaning again, coming from Ruth's room. I knocked at her door but got no reply, so I went in. Poor Ruth was lying on the floor and there was a lot of blood around. She'd been badly knocked about.'

Aghast, Emily demanded, 'Is she seriously hurt? Did you call in a doctor?'

'I got one to come round to the house, but he wasn't a lot of help. He kept saying, "If you live this sort of life then you've got to expect to have violence like this occur." He wouldn't even examine her properly. He made me pay him right away and promised to come back later in the day, but he didn't. Last night I tried to get her to take some soup, but she didn't want anything. This morning she was in a whole lot of pain and I didn't know what to do. Then I thought of you. We'd heard you were in Adelaide and had been told of what you were doing. Ruth always said that if any of us were in trouble we couldn't do better than to come to you for help.' Looking at Emily, she finished lamely, 'So here I am.'

Emily was touched that Ruth should have such faith in her, but she felt Ruth probably needed more help than she could give to her.

'How far is it to the house where you live?'

'If we were lucky enough to catch a train right away we could be there in half an hour or so.'

'Then we'll set off right away. I will tell Margaret where we are going.'

When the two women arrived at Ruth's home, Emily realised the prostitute had not been exaggerating about Ruth's condition. She was in great pain and kept drifting off into delirium. One moment she was expressing gratitude to Emily for coming to see her, the next she was babbling incoherently.

'She needs to be seen by a doctor – a *good* doctor – immediately.' Emily was extremely concerned by Ruth's condition. 'Are there any doctors other than the one who has already seen her in Port Adelaide?'

'I don't think so – but there's a big immigrant ship alongside in the port. There's bound to be a doctor on board.'

'Come along and show me where it is. We must go there right away.'

At the busy Port Adelaide docks, Emily had a great stroke of luck. Not only was there a doctor on board the immigrant ship,

but he was being visited by his brother, who was th
surgeon at the Adelaide hospital.

At first the two doctors were reluctant to involve themselves
with the problems of a dockland prostitute. However, they
realised Emily was a woman of some education and breeding
and when she told them of the work she was carrying out on
behalf of the Bishop of Adelaide, they agreed to accompany her
and Ruth's friend to the prostitutes' house.

Their examination of the injured woman was swift but thorough. After a brief consultation with his brother, the Adelaide
surgeon agreed with Emily that there was cause for concern.

'That she has been the victim of a vicious attack is quite
apparent from the number of cuts and bruises that are to be
seen,' he said, 'but I am far more concerned with the injuries
that *cannot* be seen. She has a possible fracture of the skull, but
– and I believe this to be far more serious – I fear she has
sustained damage to one of her kidneys, possibly as the result
of a kick. She needs to be taken into hospital. I suggest my own
hospital in Adelaide is best equipped to carry out the necessary
tests and give her the care she needs at present.' Looking at
Emily from beneath bushy eyebrows, he added, 'Unfortunately,
such treatment is not free, nor is it cheap.'

'I will pay for all the costs incurred,' Emily declared. 'Now,
how do we get her to the hospital in Adelaide?'

'The harbour authorities have an ambulance,' said the ship's
doctor. 'We used it for two of the immigrants who were ill upon
arrival. I'll hurry to the docks and make arrangements for it to
be sent here immediately.'

'Good!' said his brother. 'Come here with the ambulance,
Charles. We will both travel to Adelaide with the patient and
you can spend a few days with me there.' Smiling reassuringly
at Emily, he said, 'You can be certain this unfortunate young
woman will be well cared for on the journey to Adelaide and
will be given my personal attention once she is there.'

'Thank you. Thank you both for your kindness,' Emily said

gratefully 'I will return to Adelaide by train and come to the hospital tomorrow to visit Ruth and discover what is likely to happen to her.'

II

'What are you doing here?'

Sam and Margaret both asked the question in unison and Margaret laughed, explaining, 'You remember Ruth – Ruth Askew from Blinman? She left there some time ago to come to Port Adelaide. Unfortunately, she hasn't changed her ways and has been badly beaten by a foreign seaman. She's here in the hospital and we've just been to see her. But why are you here?'

'My prospecting partner is in here seriously ill. We were caught out in a storm a couple of days ago. He has pneumonia. But you said "we"?'

'That's right, me and Emily.'

It was a deliberately blunt statement on Margaret's part, in order to gauge Sam's reaction.

Sam jumped as if a firecracker had exploded behind him. His mouth opened and closed several times, as though he would speak, but no sound came.

Acting as if she had noticed nothing out of the ordinary in his reaction, Margaret said, 'We were on our way out when Emily remembered she hadn't asked the nurses what she could bring in for Ruth to eat or drink. The doctors suspect she's got a damaged kidney and they're being careful what she is given. Emily will be out in a minute, she'll be absolutely delighted to see you—'

'No – I won't stop. Wish her well for me.' Sam turned with the intention of hurrying away, but Margaret grabbed his arm and brought him to a halt.

'Don't go, Sam. Emily will be very upset if she misses you again—'

Sam tried to free his arm, but Margaret said hurriedly, 'She travelled all the way to Blinman hoping to find you there, but you had left a couple of weeks earlier.'

He stopped pulling against her. 'She went to Blinman to see *me*? Why? What did the man she is to marry think about that? Or is she married already?'

'She's not married and there will be no wedding.' Suitably contrite, Margaret added, 'I had my facts wrong, Sam. Stefan Mintoff *had* asked Emily to marry him, but she had neither accepted nor turned him down. Since then a whole lot has happened. Mintoff went to England to raise money for a bogus mining company. I think he's made a great deal of money by telling everyone he was to marry into Emily's family. He even persuaded her to put a thousand pounds into the company. She's lost that money and there's no question of her marrying him now. Besides, long before he came on the scene she was trying to find you. Indeed – and I may be telling you far more than she would wish me to – I believe that the real reason she came to Australia was because she hoped to meet up with you again.'

Sam was more in control of himself now, but he found it impossible to fully take in the implications of all that Margaret had told him.

'I . . . I'm not sure I'm ready to meet her right now.'

'Of course you are,' Margaret said confidently. 'Look, you go and sit down over there, by the window. You'll see Emily when she returns. I'll break the news that you're here and you gauge her reaction for yourself. Go on, Sam – and remember, she'll be just as nervous as you when she knows you're here.'

It was all too much for Sam to take in immediately. Emily was close at hand. He would soon see her – and she was *not* about to be married to someone else!

He sat down heavily upon a chair on the far side of the hospital reception area and began looking apprehensively at every woman who emerged from the wards, wondering with an increasing degree of panic whether she was a much-changed Emily.

Suddenly Sam's attention was distracted by a woman leaving the wards hand in hand with a seriously disturbed child of about twelve. Sam watched as the woman showed great patience in coaxing the child to the exit door.

When the pair had passed out of the building, Sam returned his gaze to the corridor that led from the wards – and there he saw Emily.

Seeing her made him wonder how he might ever have imagined that any of the other women could possibly have been her. She was perhaps thinner than before and she had matured since their last meeting, but she was everything he remembered – and he realised immediately that his feelings for her had not changed. He still experienced the same thrill at seeing her that he recalled from his church days at St Cleer.

He wanted to jump up and call out her name, but he dared not. He had promised Margaret he would let her speak to Emily first.

Getting to his feet, he waited quietly.

'It seems there is very little we are permitted to bring in for poor Ruth . . .'

Emily continued talking as she walked towards the hospital exit, expecting Margaret to fall in beside her. When her friend did not move, Emily stopped and turned back, clearly puzzled.

'Is something wrong, Margaret? I thought you were in a hurry to get home and prepare tea for the boys?'

'I am, but something unexpected has happened, Emily. I've just seen someone I think you've been anxious to find.'

Startled, Emily said, 'You are not trying to tell me that Stefan Mintoff has had the gall to return to South Australia?'

Margaret smiled at Emily's indignation. 'No, I think this will be a far more pleasant surprise for you.'

Emily was momentarily puzzled. Then, aware that Margaret was more than ordinarily pleased with herself, her eyes widened and she reached out to grasp the arm of her friend. 'You don't mean . . . ? Not *Sam*? Where, Margaret? Where was he?'

'He was standing right here and we talked about you. Now he's over there, by the window, waiting to meet you again.'

Emily spun around and looked towards the window. The hotel reception area was extremely busy, but she saw Sam immediately. Tall and suntanned, he was nervously screwing up the brim of the soft hat he held in his hands.

As blood rushed to Emily's face, she thought she might faint. Margaret thought so too and she held out a hand to support her friend.

It was doubtful whether Emily felt it. Leaving Margaret behind, she hurried across the hospital foyer with eyes for only one person.

'Sam! How wonderful to see you again . . . and you are looking so well!' She wanted to hug him, but contented herself with kissing him warmly on the cheek.

Now it was his turn to blush as he murmured, 'It's good to see you too, Emily. You haven't changed a bit . . . well, not much.'

Aware of the crucifix dangling on a chain about her neck and the reason he had returned it to her, he added feebly, 'I . . . I thought you were to be married.'

'No, Sam . . . but it is a very long story and we have so many much more pleasant things to talk about. How is your family – do you hear from them regularly? And what are you doing in Adelaide – and here, at the hospital?' Suddenly, overcome by emotion, she reached out and touched his arm. 'Oh, it really *is* wonderful to meet up with you again, Sam, truly it is.'

Sam felt at a complete loss for words, but fortunately his expression spoke for him.

Watching them from across the reception area, Margaret felt a pang of envy. Turning away, she left the hospital to make her

way home. She realised that Emily and Sam had a great deal
to talk about and would prefer to be alone.

III

Margaret's departure did not go unnoticed, but neither Emily
nor Sam made any attempt to stop her. Leaving the hospital
soon afterwards they walked slowly to a small park situated
nearby, talking all the while.

In the park they found a seat and sat down and talked some
more.

Sam gave an outline of all that had happened to him since
leaving St Cleer and Emily related the story of her own life and
why she was now in Adelaide.

'So you're still a very important person, even here in
Australia,' Sam said despondently. He realised he had allowed
the euphoria of their reunion to obscure the differences in their
backgrounds and ways of life.

Aware of what he was thinking, Emily said firmly, 'No, Sam,
I am what I have always been, deep down. My *own* person. It's
what no one would ever allow me to be back in Cornwall. I
was told how I must behave, how I should talk, who I was
allowed to talk to. I always had to live up to someone else's
expectations: my father's, sister's, titled uncle's – even Maude,
the housekeeper's. I came out to South Australia because I
intended being myself at last. To live my life the way I choose
– and that is what I intend doing. As for being important, thanks
to Stefan Mintoff I have become an *embarrassment* to anyone
who considers themselves to be in any way "important". He
has turned out to be thoroughly dishonest. As a result people
look at me and wonder how much I was involved in his
schemes.'

'Surely no one thinks you had anything to do with his dishonest dealings. It's quite ridiculous!'

Resting a hand on his arm, Emily said, 'Thank you, Sam. No one has actually *said* they believe me to be involved in any way, but they are all keeping me at arm's length, just in case. It doesn't worry me because it means I can get on with my work with no social distractions, but it sometimes hurts when I see churchmen turning their backs on those they believe to be sinners. It is contrary to fundamental Christian principles.'

'No one can accuse you of doing that,' Sam said. 'How *is* Ruth?'

'Hopefully she will recover. But what of your partner?'

Sam shook his head unhappily. 'The doctor says there is very little hope for him. They say his heart is affected. I've promised to go in and see him again this evening.'

'I am so sorry,' Emily expressed genuine sympathy. 'I can tell by the way you've spoken of him that you are very fond of him.'

'He's a very special friend who's lived through a great many adventures during his lifetime. It's ironic that he should die as a result of getting wet in a rainstorm.'

'Do you think he would mind if I came with you when you visit him this evening?' Emily asked.

'It would give him a great deal of pleasure,' Sam said delightedly. 'I'd like it too.'

'Good! I was about to ask what we should do until it's time to visit, but I just heard a clock strike six o'clock. Would you like to go and visit him now?'

'That sounds a good idea, I don't want to leave it too late.'

On the way back to the hospital, Emily asked, 'Where are you staying while you are in Adelaide?'

'At a small hotel on Flinders Street. Abe and I always stay there. They've known him for a long time and he trusts them to look after our gold when they have it in their safe.'

'You mean you have actually *found* gold? Enough to make your prospecting worthwhile?'

'Very much so. I probably have enough right now to buy a nice piece of land, up in the hills. That's what Abe has done. It's really beautiful up there.'

'Perhaps you will take me to see it some time,' Emily suggested. 'I haven't been outside the city since I arrived in Adelaide.'

They chattered on happily until they arrived at the hospital. Here, their mood became more sombre.

Abe was in a ward with more than a dozen men, occupying the first bed inside the door, close to the ward sister's desk. He appeared to be asleep, but as the young couple stood by the bedside, uncertainly, he opened his eyes and managed a weak smile for Sam before his glance shifted to Emily, who had been brought a chair by a ward orderly.

'Abe, I'd like you to meet Emily. We knew each other in Cornwall. Her pa was vicar of St Cleer. I knew she was in South Australia, but didn't know she was in Adelaide until we met up this afternoon, just after I left you. She said she'd like to meet you, so here we are.'

'Sam has been telling me so much about you I felt I just had to meet you. Abe . . . is that short for Abraham, the father of the Hebrew nation?'

'It is, miss.' Abe's voice was little more than a weak whisper. 'I think Sam has told me of you too, but he never put a name to you.'

Emily looked up at Sam questioningly, but realised an explanation would need to await the right occasion.

'Sam was telling me of the land you own in the hills outside the city. He says it is really beautiful.'

Showing an unexpected knowledge of biblical history, Abe said, 'Like my namesake, the Lord showed me the promised land and gave it to me . . . but I'm afraid I've left it too late to reap any benefit from it.'

'Nonsense!' Emily lied. 'Sam is convinced you can overcome *anything*. You certainly won't allow a setback like this get the better of you. He says you never acknowledge defeat. You will win this battle too.'

Glancing towards Sam, Abe whispered wearily, 'He's a good boy, but he needs someone to take care of him and teach him the things that are important in life.'

'I will see what I can do,' Emily promised. Suddenly and unexpectedly, she leaned over and kissed him on the forehead. 'God bless you, Abe.'

Her gesture delighted the old man and he said, 'He's never been mean with his blessings to me, Emily. Mind you, the devil's been in there running against him at times, but I reckon the Lord left him far behind.'

Abe was looking very tired now. Sam said, 'We'll leave you in peace now, partner. I'll be here to see you first thing in the morning. I hope you'll be feeling a whole lot stronger then.'

As Sam moved forward to clasp his hand in farewell, Abe pulled him down towards him and whispered, 'She's a fine girl, Sam. Don't let her get away from you again. Remember what I told you, you're as fine a man as any she's ever likely to meet, and you'll be able to give her more than most – whatever their station in life.'

IV

Sam walked Emily from the hospital to her modest home and accepted her offer to have his evening meal with the household. Margaret made a big fuss of him and when she told the boys that he was a 'gold prospector' his acceptance was assured.

'Our pa was a prospector,' said Tom. 'He found gold too.'

'I know he did,' Sam agreed. 'And he found it near Blinman, where no one else had.'

'Did you know our pa?' asked Albert.

'Not very well,' Sam replied guardedly. He did not want to be drawn into a conversation where he might be questioned on his views of the character of Charlie Minns. 'But I did meet him at the Nuccaleena mine on one occasion, and travelled back to Blinman with him and a whole lot of other miners.'

Emily changed the subject at that moment, telling the boys that Sam came from St Cleer. After this much of the conversation was of Cornwall, people and places they all knew.

They spoke of what Margaret and the boys were likely to find different when, or if, they went back. Margaret would not consider returning until she had seen Emily settled and out of the shadow that Stefan Mintoff had cast over her life.

The evening passed all too quickly for Sam, even though he did not leave the house until long after the boys had gone to bed.

Emily came out to the front verandah to see him off. As they stood in the shadows, she said softly, 'I really am glad to have found you, Sam. I never gave up hope that I would, one day.'

'I'm glad too, Emily. I thought of you often after I arrived in South Australia, but I couldn't see how we could possibly meet again. It would have been a lot easier had I been able to write direct to you. As it was I could only send messages through the family. I was never sure whether they would reach you.'

'They did not, I'm afraid, but I think that was due largely to the influence of my father.'

'Probably,' Sam agreed. 'Then, when I learned you'd been out here some time and were due to be married to this Mintoff man, I despaired of us ever meeting.'

'That was when you sent back my crucifix?'

'Yes, and left Blinman shortly afterwards. I thought that if you were to be married it might embarrass you to remember you'd given such a valuable and treasured present to . . . to a miner.'

'I gave it to you because I wanted you to have it, Sam. I still want you to have it.'

'Thank you, but I believe the proper place for it is around your neck.'

At that moment a crowd of some seven or eight young men came around the corner and walked along the street towards the house, talking loudly. As they neared, Sam and Emily edged farther back into the shadows close to the door.

When the young men made their way past, Sam became aware that he and Emily were standing very close.

'Do you remember that last night, in the church porch, when we heard someone coming?' she asked.

'There have been very few days when I *haven't* remembered it,' he replied. 'I sometimes wonder what might have happened had those miners not passed by, going on shift.'

'I suppose you could always find out by kissing me good-night now, Sam Hooper. That is if you want to, of course.'

If he wanted to! There were many replies he might have made, but he tried not to allow his desire to run away with him.

'I'm not going away this time, Emily.'

'And I don't have to hurry home for fear of what a spiteful housekeeper might tell my father.'

When he still hesitated, she said quietly, 'Don't you *want* to kiss me, Sam?'

He stepped forward then and, taking hold of her, kissed her with a pent-up passion that left them both breathless.

Then the voice of Albert, in the room alongside them, called, 'Ma! Ma! I feel sick. Can I have a drink of water?'

Pulling back from Sam, Emily was confused and not a little frightened by the emotions that Sam had stirred up. She had never felt like this before. 'I think I had better go inside now, Sam.'

'Yes . . . I think you should.' Sam, too, was shaken by the sheer intensity of their embrace. 'But . . . can I see you again?'

'Of course, Sam. Shall we go to the hospital together

tomorrow afternoon? I have to see the cathedral treasurer in the morning about a scheme I wish the Church to finance. Shall we say two o'clock? I should be free by then.'

'That will be fine,'

Sam was greatly relieved. He had half believed Emily to be joking when she suggested he might want to kiss her, that she was perhaps teasing him about that night in the St Cleer church porch when he had been slow to take up her shamelessly bold offer. He had feared she might have taken offence at what he had just done.

'I will probably call in to see Abe early in the morning though,' he said. 'I was very worried about him today.'

'Of course. Tell him I shall come with you again in the afternoon and hope to see him looking much better.'

They remained standing close without saying anything for a few minutes before he said, 'I really am glad we've found each other.'

'And so am I, Sam. Until tomorrow then . . .'

She kissed him again. A kiss as perfunctory as the last kiss she had bestowed upon him in the St Cleer church porch but this time they parted with a feeling not of despair but of anticipation.

V

Sam arrived at the hospital early the next morning. Making his way to the ward where Abe was being treated, he walked through the door – and came to an abrupt halt.

Abe's bed was empty.

As he stood there, thoroughly confused, a nurse came hurrying towards him from farther along the ward. He had not met with her on the ward before and she said, 'May I help you?'

'I'm here to see Abe . . . Mr Gundry, but his bed is empty . . .'

'Are you a relative?'

'I'm his partner and the closest thing to a relative that Abe has.'

The nurse hesitated, but for only a moment. 'I am very sorry, but I am afraid Mr Gundry passed away during the night.'

Observing the shock and disbelief on Sam's face, she added gently, 'He died very peacefully at about three o'clock this morning and his body has been taken to the chapel. Will you wait here while I go and find the sister in charge of the ward? I believe there are some formalities to be completed and one or two items of personal property to be handed over . . .'

Sam left the hospital in a very upset state later that morning, having made the necessary arrangements for Abe's funeral.

He wished Emily had not been at a meeting; he would have liked to talk with her. She would understand how he was feeling.

Returning to the hotel, he was thankful the desk clerk was busy and so did not ask after Abe.

Once in his room, Sam sat down heavily and considered for the first time what Abe's death would mean. He was not at all certain he was capable of working the Jupiter Creek claim on his own. Indeed, he was not at all sure he *wanted* to work it without Abe.

Suddenly, he remembered the envelope Abe had given to him, saying it contained his will. Sam had told the hospital authorities that the old prospector had no living relations; it was possible the will might prove him wrong.

He opened the drawer where he had thrown the envelope the previous evening, after returning to the hotel from Emily's house. He had a moment of panic when he thought it was no longer there, but then he discovered it had slid to the back of the drawer.

Tearing open the envelope, Sam unfolded the two sheets of

paper it contained and read the last will and testament of
Abraham Wesley Gundry.

When Sam called upon Emily that afternoon, she was saddened
at the news of Abe's death, yet she was as supportive as Sam
had known she would be.

'I'm so sorry, Sam,' she said. 'But at least he did not die a
lonely old man, with no one to care about him. He cherished
your friendship and I am convinced both your lives were
enriched by knowing each other. What would you like to do
now? You probably won't want to accompany me to the hospital.
I could ask Margaret to go in my place, she'll understand.'

'No, you go to see Ruth. I won't come with you, there are a
great many of Charlie's affairs that will need to be sorted out
– but I would like to see you later in the day, if I may?'

'Of course. Come to the house for dinner.'

The funeral of Abe took place on a wet and dreary day in the
cemetery to the south-west of the city. The only mourners were
Sam, Emily, Margaret and a desk clerk from the hotel where he
had always stayed.

There was no gathering of mourners afterwards, but Sam
declared all was much as Abe would have wished it to be.

That evening, Sam arrived at Emily's house carrying a cylin-
drical leather case which, at first glance, appeared to be a
container for a telescope. Inside were plans for the house Abe
had hoped one day to build on his land, as a reminder of his
young wife's family home in California.

On the dining-room table, Sam laid out the plan for the main
house, using two candleholders, a vase and a heavy, leather-
bound dictionary to weigh down the corners of the document
and prevent it from curling up.

'What do you make of it?' Sam put the question to Emily as
she studied the detailed plan.

'It's magnificent!' Emily enthused. 'Who would imagine that

a prospector would carry a dream like this around with him for so long?'

'Abe was no ordinary prospector,' Sam said sadly.

'I must agree,' Emily said. 'I do wish I had been able to know him better . . . Look at these.'

She held up a number of excellent sketches, apparently drawn by Abe, and which had been used by the architect to produce a professional sketch of how the house would appear from front, side and rear aspects.

'It is sad to think he died with his dream unfulfilled. I wonder what will happen to his land now?'

Aware of the impact his words were going to have, Sam was unable to make them sound as casual as he would have wished. 'I haven't made up my mind yet. You see, Abe has left it to me. I thought we might all go out to look at it tomorrow.'

There was a squeak of delighted surprise from Margaret, and Emily looked at Sam accusingly. 'Sam! How could you keep something like this a secret from us until now. How large is this piece of land?'

'*Very* large,' Sam replied. 'You'll be able to see for yourselves tomorrow. The boys must come along too. With any luck they'll see a koala or two. Abe and I have seen them there.'

Margaret looked slightly puzzled and Sam explained, 'The koala looks like a small, cuddly bear. They live in the trees up in the hills.'

The following morning Sam arrived at Emily's house with a one-horse buggy he had hired for the day.

The boys were very excited to be riding in the vehicle and along the way Sam allowed each of them to clamber into the front seat beside him and take the reins for short distances. Then, as they reached the winding road that led into the hills, he took the reins once more.

It was not long before they topped a rise and, as they rounded a bend, a valley opened up, extending away to their left.

'This is quite breathtaking!' Emily exclaimed. 'Just look at that marvellous view along the valley.'

'You wait until you see it from the far slope,' Sam said. 'You can see even farther, with views of higher peaks in the distance.'

The pride in his voice caused Emily to look at him quickly. 'Is this the valley, Sam? It is! How much of it belongs to you?'

'It's marked on the map I brought with me,' Sam replied. 'Roughly speaking, it's everything you can see.'

Emily was incredulous. 'Truly, Sam? All this valley is yours?'

'That's right. My reaction was the same as yours when I first saw it. Abe's must have been, too. He saw it, fell in love with it – and bought it.'

'What a wonderful thing to do. But tell me, where did he intend building his house?'

'We'll drive into the valley so you can see it properly, then you can say where *you'd* put it and I'll tell you how close you are. It's a game we can all play.'

'What's the prize for the winner?' Tom asked cheekily.

'Whoever wins can have first choice from the picnic basket Emily has brought along for us,' Sam declared.

When they arrived at a suitable spot in what Sam still thought of as 'Abe's valley', he set the brake on the buggy, gave the horse a nosebag and they all set off to choose the spot where they thought a house should be built.

After half an hour they all met back at the buggy and told Sam where they would like their own home to be.

Emily was the undisputed winner, choosing the exact spot where Abe and Sam had both agreed a house should be built.

Margaret and Albert preferred a spot a short distance away, hidden in the fold of a hill from the winning site.

Tom said he would prefer to live on the valley floor, so that he would not need to tire himself out coming back to the house when he was out playing and his mother called him in.

They all enjoyed a wonderful day in Abe's Valley. The crowning pleasure came when Albert spotted not one koala but *two*, perched in a eucalyptus tree, close to the water-filled creek which encroached on a section of the valley floor.

It was a very happy group that drove back to Adelaide, although Emily seemed unusually silent.

Later that evening when the boys had gone to bed, Margaret, Emily and Sam sat out on the front verandah of the small house discussing Abe's Valley.

'You are from a farming family, Sam,' Emily said, after a while. 'What do you think might be grown there?'

'The soil is so rich that I can't think of anything that *wouldn't* grow. What I'd really like to do is have a huge apple orchard. Apples for cooking and eating. There could even be cider apples. With a press on the farm I could make cider and sell it. I'd also run cattle and, while I was waiting for the trees to establish themselves, I'd probably grow wheat. From what I've heard it's been grown very successfully elsewhere in the area.'

'Is that what you *will* do, Sam, or what you would *like* to do?'

'I haven't quite made up my mind yet,' Sam said cautiously. 'I still haven't got used to the idea that the valley now belongs to me.'

At that moment, Margaret decided she would go into the house and make drinks for them all. When she had gone, Emily said, 'This farming venture, Sam . . . if it's a question of money, I would be very happy to let you have an interest-free loan. You would not need to begin paying me back until you started making a profit.'

Deeply touched by her generous offer, Sam reached across the space between their chairs and found her hand. Squeezing it affectionately, he said, 'Thank you, Emily, I appreciate the offer. But I have one or two decisions to make before I start planning my future in earnest. Not least of them is what to do with the mining leases Abe took out on the land around our claims. I need to go along to the Mines Department tomorrow and sort out just what we have.'

Retaining a hold on his hand, Emily hoped Sam might decide

to give up mining, accept her offer and begin farming in his newly acquired valley. That way she was certain of seeing far more of him.

It might even be that he would not need to repay the loan at all . . .

It was as well that she could not look into the very near future.

VI

A week after her visit to the Adelaide Hills with Sam, Emily received an unexpected visit from the Reverend Gordon Glover, chaplain to the Bishop of Adelaide.

She had been in Adelaide for more than three months, during which time she had spoken no more than a few words to the chaplain – and none at all to the bishop.

She was therefore taken aback when the chaplain greeted her with a warm smile and said, 'How are you, Miss Boyce? His Grace asked me to call on you to make certain you are receiving all the co-operation you need from the Church and other official bodies in Adelaide. We have received a number of reports on the success of your mission. He regrets he has been remiss in not acknowledging your progress before now. But he is, of course, a very busy man. This is a fast-growing colony and the Church must keep pace with its growth.'

'Of course,' Emily said, smiling sweetly at her visitor. 'We must try to regain some of the ground we have lost to the non-conformist faiths. I fear it will not be easy.'

For a few moments the chaplain's smile appeared somewhat forced.

While they were speaking, Emily had been leading him through the house. She now invited him to sit down in the kitchen, explaining that this was the only room in the house that was not in use as a bedroom.

Looking about him, he said, 'Dear me, I had no idea you were living in such cramped conditions, Miss Boyce. Something will need to be done about it right away.'

He had still not given her a hint of why she had seemingly been re-admitted to the fold of the Established Church and Emily was curious.

At that moment Ruth entered the kitchen, wearing night attire, over which she was wearing an unfastened and somewhat shabby dressing-gown, which Margaret had somehow managed to acquire for her.

The chaplain stood up hurriedly and Ruth said, 'Oh! I'm sorry, Miss Boyce, I didn't realise you had company. I see the kettle is boiling, I'll make myself a quick cup of coffee and get out of your way.'

The chaplain was looking at Ruth's bruised and battered face with great concern and Emily explained, 'We are looking after Ruth for a while. She only left hospital yesterday after being brutally attacked.'

When the chaplain murmured a few meaningless words of sympathy, Ruth said cheerfully, 'The doctor at the hospital told me that if Miss Boyce hadn't got me to him when she did I'd have died for sure. I've very good reason to be grateful to her.'

When Ruth had wandered out of the kitchen with her cup of coffee, the chaplain asked, in a strangled voice, 'Is that . . . is she one of the women you are trying to redeem?'

'That's right. I first met her when she was in a bawdy house in Kadina. We met again in Blinman. A few days ago a friend of Ruth's came to ask for my help when Ruth was attacked by one of the seamen she took to her home in Port Adelaide.'

'But you . . . you should not have such a woman wandering about your home!' The chaplain was aghast.

'It was either that or send her back to the bawdy house in Port Adelaide,' Emily said bluntly. 'Had I done that she would have been back to her bad old ways within days. As it is, I feel there is a very good chance that Ruth will change and, hope-fully, be able to persuade others to do the same.'

'But . . . to have her living in your home, in such close prox-imity. My dear Miss Boyce, we must take immediate steps to move you to more suitable premises. To a house where you can have your own private quarters – and servants to help with such women!'

'When I first came to Adelaide I sent a number of letters to the bishop suggesting that if we were to wean some of these unfortunate women from their ways we would need properly supervised accommodation for them. My letters were not answered.'

The chaplain appeared uncomfortable. 'His Grace *has* been extremely busy, but I feel certain he would have acted upon your request had he seen the letters. Unfortunately, his secretary was replaced very recently, for inefficiency. Your letters must have been mislaid during the period of uncertainty we have suffered. However, things are running more smoothly now – as I believe they are for you. You are no doubt relieved that your unfortu-nate problems with Mr Mintoff are at an end, Miss Boyce.'

'At an end? I am afraid I don't know what you are talking about, Reverend Glover.'

'Really? I thought you would have been informed by your uncle, Lord Boyce. He is widely quoted in the London news-papers that have recently arrived from England. It seems his lordship was able to prevent a great many influential men in the City from investing in Mintoff's fraudulent companies and so losing large sums of money. His lordship gives credit to you for telegraphing him in time to thwart Mintoff's schemes. Well done, Miss Boyce. Well done indeed.'

Rising to his feet, the chaplain said, 'I feel it is time I returned to my office. Be assured I will treat the question of more suit-able accommodation for you with the utmost urgency.'

*   *   *

The Reverend Glover was as good as his word, and only four days later Emily was invited to look over a house in the prosperous and growing suburb of Walkerville, to the north-east of Adelaide.

A solidly built two-storey house, it had been erected by one of the township's earliest residents, who had recently died and bequeathed the property to the Church.

Emily was told she could live in the house, rent free, and continue the work she had begun so successfully. The chaplain felt it was ideal for her purposes. Surrounded by large and attractive gardens, it enjoyed considerable privacy.

The messenger also brought her an invitation to a reception being held at the bishop's palace in a few weeks' time.

Emily despatched a note to the chaplain confirming her acceptance of the house and expressing a wish to take immediate possession. As a result, Emily, Margaret, the two boys – and Ruth – moved to the rather grand new house only two days later, assisted by Sam.

Albert and Tom thought it a marvellous new home. Not only did they share an upstairs room but it possessed a balcony. Once they had settled who would occupy which bed, they set off together to explore the extensive gardens.

Margaret would occupy a room next to the boys, while Ruth was allocated one of the four spare bedrooms in which Emily intended housing any other women she could tempt away from a similar lifestyle.

With Sam present to help and share with her each idea she had for utilising the facilities offered by the vastly superior accommodation, it was a very happy day.

Unfortunately, the happiness lasted only until late that evening when the bishop's chaplain arrived to see how they were settling in. With him he brought some mail for Emily that had arrived from England the day before and been delivered to her former address.

When the chaplain had left, Emily opened the first of the

letters while she chatted to Sam in the lounge. Meanwhile, Ruth and Margaret were in the kitchen preparing an evening meal.

Emily glanced down at the letter, then she looked again and suddenly stopped talking in order to concentrate on the contents of the letter, her expression one of increasing consternation.

'Is something wrong?' Sam asked.

Continuing to read without replying for a few more moments, Emily eventually looked up, more shaken than Sam had ever seen her. 'It's from my uncle Percy. It seems that Stefan Mintoff has been forging my signature on banker's drafts and cheques. My uncle says he has been able to draw a great deal of my money. Because of his standing in the City, Uncle Percy has been able to persuade the banks not to honour any further demands for money bearing my signature, but I need to return to England in order to sort out the mess. Oh! Why did I ever get involved with a man like Stefan Mintoff?'

'It sounds extremely serious,' Sam said. 'But is there no way to deal with it other than going to England?' He was deeply concerned that once there she might never return. 'Can't you at least leave making a decision until you have had time to think about it?'

'No, Sam. I have probably already lost a great deal of money. More than I can afford. I wish I did *not* have to go, but Uncle Percy would not have said I was needed if he could possibly deal with it himself. I will go into town tomorrow, find out when the next steamship is due to leave, then telegraph my uncle.'

She looked at Sam and, suddenly and unexpectedly, tears welled up in her eyes and she said, 'It would have to happen now, just when everything seemed to be working out.'

Sam was not sure whether she was referring to *their* relationship or to the fact that she had just moved into a new house and was once more in favour with the Church.

He moved to comfort her, but at that moment the two boys

burst into the house, shouting that they had just seen an uniden-
tified animal run up one of the garden trees.

Ruth and Margaret were both upset that Emily was going to
have to return to England. Margaret wondered whether it might
be a good time to return with her, but she did not need a great
deal of persuading to stay in Adelaide and continue the work
Emily had begun.

Later that night when the boys were in bed and Sam and
Emily had been left alone on the spacious verandah of the new
house, Sam asked, 'You *will* come back to Australia, Emily?'

'Of course. Everything I want is here, Sam. *Everything.*'

'Then it will all still be here for you when you return. But if
you decided you didn't want to travel all that way I'm sure we
could work something out here.'

'If you mean what I think you do, I would rather it remained
unsaid until my return, Sam. Unless . . .' She looked at him
excitedly as an idea took shape in her mind. 'Unless you come
to England with me! I would pay your fare.'

Sam thought of what she was offering him. It was tempting,
but . . . He shook his head. 'No, Emily.'

'Why not?' she asked eagerly. 'It would be a wonderful opportunity for us to really get to know each other. To make up for
all the time we have lost.'

He dared not allow her to realise how much the idea appealed
to him. 'I have a great many things to attend to here, Emily.
There's my land . . . and I must make plans for the future.
Besides . . .' He faltered and fell silent.

'Besides?' she prompted.

Sam knew that what he was about to say to her might change
things between them for ever, but it had to be said and there
would never be a better opportunity than now.

'Emily . . . before I left St Cleer I had grown far fonder of
you than I should have. Your father saw it. That's why he had
me sent out here – and I don't think there's any doubt that he

did. While I was here and you were back in Cornwall I thought of you constantly and I had your crucifix to remind me I had meant something to you too. Then, when I learned you were here and was told you were getting married to someone important, I felt I'd been fooling myself all along, that our backgrounds are so far apart that I was reaching for the moon. I told myself I had to forget you, though I knew it wasn't going to be easy. Then we met again and somehow I seem to have moved towards you, and you to me. Our ways of life are not quite so far apart now. Even if they were, it doesn't seem to matter quite so much here, in Australia. I've come to feel I'm as good as anyone else. I like things this way, Emily. I believe that if we both stay here, we . . . well, things could be different to the way they were in St Cleer. But if I came back with you to England, once we arrived there you'd be mixing with your uncle and his friends. Peers and government ministers. I don't think I'd show up very well in their company . . .'

For a moment it looked as though Emily would protest, but Sam had more to say.

'I don't think I'd show up well in their company, any more than they would be at their best tramping through the outback or working a claim. I could offer you a good life here, Emily. I have my land and it's good land, but I don't think we could be happy together in England.'

Very quietly, Emily said, 'You know, Sam Hooper, if I was an impressionable young girl I might think you *almost* proposed to me then.'

'I couldn't do that, Emily, not when I know you're returning to England and will be going back to the life you used to lead before coming out here. I'd rather you thought of what I've said as an explanation of the way I feel. The way I've always felt, and always will. I don't *want* to hold you to anything until you've been back to England and had a chance to make up your mind about the life you want, so you won't ever regret whatever you decide is right for you.'

Embarrassed at having made a longer speech than he could ever remember, he shrugged awkwardly. 'I suppose that, really, the decision is whether you want Australia and a different way of life here – or whether you want England and all that means.'

Emily remained silent for some time before saying, 'No, Sam, the choice is far more important to me than that. It's a choice of whether I want you or whether I don't – and you are a very special man to me, Sam Hooper.'

VII

Emily left Adelaide three days after receiving the letter from her uncle. She travelled first to Melbourne, from where she would take passage in one of the fast steamships that now made the voyage between Australia and England in slightly less than two months. Even so, it meant she would most probably be away for at least five months.

Sam travelled with Emily to Melbourne and saw her safely on board the ship. As they were about to part at the top of the ship's gangway, Sam self-consciously pulled a small, velvet-covered box from his pocket.

Handing it to her, he said, 'I'd like you to have this to take with you, Emily.'

Surprised, Emily took the box from him. Opening it, she gasped with delight. Inside was a gold ring, mounted with a large, expertly cut precious opal that captured light and set it free again in a myriad colours.

Speechless, Emily looked to Sam for an explanation.

'The gold is from the claim,' he said. 'I dug it myself and had a jeweller make it into a ring. The opal was dug out by Abe, years before he met me. It was among his things when he died. I know he would have liked you to have it.'

'It's an absolutely wonderful gift, Sam. It will be my most treasured possession for as long as I live – but won't you put it on my finger for me?'

She handed the ring back to him, then held out her left hand. Sam hesitated, uncertainly, 'Where . . . ?'

By way of reply, Emily folded back three fingers, leaving only the third finger of the hand she had extended.

It was a somewhat tight fit, but eventually the ring slipped over the knuckle joint and Emily held it up, delighted. 'There! You may be keeping your proposal until I return, Sam, but you have just staked your claim.'

The call went up for all visitors to go ashore and for a moment Emily looked alone and very vulnerable. Then she said, 'I love you, Sam. I love you very much.'

'I love you too, Emily.'

They had time for only the briefest of embraces before a crew member said, 'Time for you to go ashore if you're not travelling, sir.'

'Take care, Emily – and hurry back.' Sam released her reluctantly.

'You take care too, Sam. I will let you know by telegraph as soon as I know when I will be leaving England. And the name of the ship.'

Sam made his way down the ship's gangway, past sailors who were impatient to have the gangway lifted ashore in order that they might begin their long voyage home to England.

He stood on the quayside, waving, until the vessel moved off and was lost in the gathering dusk.

For five months, Margaret carried on the work that had been started by Emily. For all this time she was ably assisted by Ruth, who seemed determined to put the life she had been living behind her.

Early in November, Sam received a telegraph message from Emily telling him she was taking passage on the SS *Great Britain*, on what would probably be the great liner's farewell voyage to Australia.

Emily made no mention of whether or not her stay in England had been successful, but as the telegraph charge was a pound for each word sent, Sam had not expected a long message. She would tell him all when she arrived. It was sufficient for now that she had decided to return to Australia – and to him.

He contacted the harbourmaster in Melbourne and made arrangements to be informed by telegraph when the *Great Britain* docked.

Meanwhile, Ruth would take on an ever-increasing role in the day-to-day running of the Walkerville house. She was having some success among her former colleagues, having enticed two young prostitutes away from the city's bawdy houses. Even Chaplain Gordon Glover was forced to concede that she was fully justifying Emily's faith in her. He was finding it far less embarrassing to hold conversations with Ruth now and had even developed a sneaking regard for her.

Sam had hoped, somewhat optimistically, that Emily might manage to return to the colony for Christmas. However, her telegraph stated that her ship was departing from Liverpool on the 17th November. It meant she would not arrive in Australia until mid-January of 1876, at the earliest.

Sam, too, was away from Adelaide for long periods of time. But in January he let Margaret into the secret of his activities, and took her and the boys away from the house for a few days, leaving a curious Ruth behind in sole charge of the home for 'fallen women'.

On 19th January, Sam received the message for which he had been waiting. The SS *Great Britain* had docked at Melbourne. Emily could be expected home within the next couple of days.

Anxious to learn what she had achieved in London and, of even more importance to him, how she viewed her future in

Australia, Sam called at the Walkerville house three times a day, hoping to find her there.

On the afternoon of the third day, when he was considering telegraphing his misgivings to the Melbourne harbourmaster, Sam knocked at the door of the house – and it was opened to him by Emily herself.

For a moment they looked at each other uncertainly, then Emily flung herself at him and amidst a mixture of laughter and tears he was able to ascertain that she had missed him, was deliriously happy to be back in Adelaide, and that she never intended leaving him again.

Later that evening, after a scorchingly hot day, Ruth and Margaret discreetly retired to the kitchen, leaving Emily and Sam sitting close to each other on the verandah, in the shadows cast by a full, midsummer moon and taking advantage of a slight breeze.

'I'm glad your trip proved successful,' Sam said. 'But it's galling that Mintoff should have got away with so much of your money. Does anyone know where he's gone?'

'Opinion has it that he is probably in hiding somewhere in eastern Europe. Unfortunately, although Uncle Percy ensured that City financiers did not lose their money, he was unable to help a great many smaller investors. Even so, I believe I lost more than anyone else. Perhaps that is as it should be. I was certainly the most gullible.'

'I prefer to see you as the most trusting,' Sam said gallantly. 'But I doubt whether Mintoff will enjoy his ill-gotten gains. He'll be forever looking over his shoulder, expecting someone to catch up with him.'

'Well, he may have defrauded me of a great deal of my money,' Emily said philosophically, 'but, thanks to Uncle Percy, he was stopped before my losses became disastrous. There is enough left to finance your farming venture, if that is what you still want to do?'

'Shall we talk about that tomorrow?' Sam suggested. 'You've

had a very tiring time. You should have an early night and a good rest. I know! Why don't we ride out to Abe's Valley tomorrow? You have riding clothes?'

When Emily affirmed that she had, he said, 'Good! I've been doing quite a bit of riding myself recently. I'll hire two horses and pick you up here at about nine o'clock. We'll ride out to the valley and you can tell me more about your visit to England and who you met there.'

When Sam had gone, Emily was left with a sense of frustration and deep disappointment. She still wore Sam's ring on her engagement finger. Indeed, she had worn it throughout her time in England. Although it had aroused a great deal of curiosity among friends and family, she had said nothing to anyone about its significance.

On the voyage back to Australia she had felt a growing excitement at the thought of meeting with Sam once more, wondering whether he would propose to her immediately, or wait until they were alone – as they had been for almost an hour on the verandah.

Instead, he had made no mention of his intentions towards her. Indeed, when Emily had tried to guide the conversation in that direction he had carefully side-stepped the issue.

It had been the same when she asked about his future and what he intended doing now. He had also ignored her offer of money to finance a farming venture on the land he now owned.

Emily went to bed bitterly disappointed with Sam's apparent lack of enthusiasm. She wondered whether there might be something on his mind. Perhaps some difficulties he had not been willing to disclose to her.

Such thoughts kept sleep at bay for much of the night.

VIII

Emily rose from bed the next morning determined to voice her fears to Sam as soon as they met. However, he seemed so happy at the prospect of riding to Abe's Valley with her that she decided she would put it off until a suitable opportunity arose, possibly later in the day.

It was a very pleasant ride out to the valley. On the way Sam pointed out a couple of cottages that had been built since they last made the journey together.

Soon, the beauty of the countryside through which they were passing mellowed Emily's mood, especially as Sam was being as attentive to her as she could have wished.

Then, when they were almost at the brow of the hill that marked a boundary of Sam's land, he pulled his horse to a halt. Uncertainly, she did the same.

'I am going to blindfold you now,' he said unexpectedly.

'You are going to do *what*?' she said, taken aback.

'Blindfold you,' he repeated, as though such a thing should have been commonplace in her life. 'When you last came here it was winter. Now it's summer and everything has changed. I want all the summer colours and flowers to come as a surprise to you.'

'Can't I simply close my eyes?'

'No, I couldn't trust you to keep them closed.'

She made no further protest, but Sam could sense her deep indignation as he secured a folded neckerchief about her eyes.

'Don't worry, I'll lead your horse and make sure we stay on level ground.' He was glad she could not see his smile.

'This is *silly!*' Emily declared as they moved off and she grabbed at the pommel of her saddle in order to retain her balance. 'I have already seen the different colours of the trees and bushes as we rode along – the flowers too.'

'Ah, but this is special. When I take off your blindfold you'll gasp in admiration, I promise you.'

Despite his reassuring words, Emily grumbled in a good-natured manner as the horse left the dirt road and trod the soft grass of the valley floor.

When Sam brought the two horses to a stop, Emily said quickly, 'Can I remove my blindfold now?'

'Not for a minute. Let me lift you down from your horse first.'

He helped her down, then guided her a few paces from the animals before saying, 'Right, now you may remove it.'

Untying the neckerchief, she squinted against the strong sunlight. As her eyes became used to the light, she frowned. 'I can't see anything different in the trees and bushes here. They are all very much the same as those we have seen along the way.'

'That's because you're facing the wrong way. Why don't you turn around?'

Emily did so and gasped in utter disbelief. 'Sam! You've tricked me! You've built a house . . . Abe's house. The one he had drawn up plans for. But . . . how? How have you managed it so quickly? It's quite impossible!'

'No, Emily, I found a wonderful builder who told me that nothing is impossible – if the money is there. We must have had every skilled man in Adelaide working on the house.'

'But where did the money come from?' she asked anxiously. 'You haven't put yourself in serious debt with a bank? I can help you with money, but not as much as I would have wished.'

Sam shook his head. Taking her hand he said, 'Let's go up to the house. I'll tell you all about it on the way.'

Once they began walking, he said, 'Abe didn't only leave me the land, Emily. Because he had no living relatives he left me everything he owned – and I discovered he was a very wealthy man. So wealthy that I doubt whether *he* knew just how much money he had. What's more, I don't think he cared. He enjoyed what he was doing too much. It's taken me a long time to sort out his affairs, but it's done now. There's money in the bank – a great deal of money – and I don't owe a penny to anyone. What's more, the day before you arrived back I sold the leases Abe and I had on Jupiter Creek to a mining company. They paid me six thousand pounds, together with enough company shares to ensure a good income for the foreseeable future.'

'Sam! You have done wonderfully well! I am so proud of you I could cry!'

Tears had sprung to her eyes as she was speaking but she brushed them away with an embarrassed laugh.

'There are still one or two important matters to be cleared up,' Sam said. 'But let me show you around the house before we talk about them.'

The interior fulfilled all the promise of the exterior, even though there were very few furnishings just yet. Standing on a balcony with breathtaking views over the valley and the surrounding country, Emily said honestly, 'I don't think I have ever seen a lovelier house, Sam. Certainly not one with a view like this. When do you plan to move in?'

'Well now, that depends entirely upon you. When you left for England we left a lot of things unspoken between us. I wanted you to experience the life you had led before – and could lead again – in order to make up your mind. I wouldn't want you to regret giving up your society friends without thinking seriously about it. I can give you a good life here in Abe's Valley, in this house, and I promise you will never want for anything, but I can't give you the prestige you could enjoy, if that's what you want.'

'I have never wanted any of that, Sam. *Never*. I always hated being told how I must behave; how I must talk – and to whom – and all because my uncle is a peer of the realm and my father was a vicar. All I have ever wanted is the chance to live my life in my own way, doing the things I want to do, with those I want to be with.'

'Do you really mean that, Emily? Are you absolutely sure?'

Close to tears, Emily said, 'I have never been more certain of anything in my life, Sam.'

'That's the way I feel about you, Emily. I am absolutely certain too. So . . . will you marry me?'

'I was beginning to think you would never ask! Of course I will – and it's not just because you'll be bringing me to the most wonderful house in the whole world. I would marry you if all you had to offer was a cave at some remote diggings. I love you, Sam – and I think I always have. I believe you know that . . .'

They clung to each other for a very long time before Emily suddenly said, 'But what of Margaret . . . and the boys . . . and Ruth?'

Sam smiled. 'Just around the corner from here, in the place where Margaret and Albert said they would live if they had a chance, the builders are putting the finishing touches to their new home. Margaret has agreed to stay in Australia and run this house for you, in whatever way suits you best. The boys will work on the farm as soon as Margaret thinks they're ready. As for Ruth . . . I had a word with the bishop's chaplain a couple of weeks ago. He's extremely impressed with her – in spite of his earlier misgivings. He's quite happy for her to continue the work you started, remaining in the house where you all live now. I think he feels you've stolen a march on the other churches. He wants to keep it that way.'

'Well!' Emily looked at Sam with a new respect. 'You *have* been busy, Sam Hooper. But you took a great deal for granted!'

'Was I wrong, Emily?'

'No, Sam. You have made me even more proud of you than I was already . . . but you don't seem to have left anything for me to do.'

Hugging her happily, Sam said, 'I can't imagine you ever being idle, Emily – and there's plenty to do here. First there's the house to be furnished and a wedding to organise. There'll be a whole estate to plan too, because I have ideas about expanding into the next valley. That will need workers. Then there are my mining interests and I'll need your help to manage the money Abe has left me . . .'

Sam's voice trailed away but he had said enough to excite Emily. She gazed towards the valley where he intended expanding and in her mind's eye envisaged a whole new community of those who, like herself and Sam, had come to a new land, seeking a fresh beginning.

There would be houses . . . a school . . . a church too, perhaps.

Turning to Sam she said, 'Yes, Sam. I know we're going to be very happy here . . .'